# Another One Bites The Dust

The creature circled me, looking a lot less intimidated by Great-Great Grandpa's knife than I would've liked.

*Well, screw it.* I ran straight at him, yelling like a pissed-off soccer mom, waving my blade like a samurai warrior. I faked left, right, left, watching as his shield opened wider and wider. It could not keep up with his bobbing head as he tried to avoid getting his throat cut. One more feint and I jumped forward, burying my blade in the shield gap his movements had caused.

He died instantly.

I pulled my weapon free and cleaned it on his stolen uniform. Glad the bolo had saved me. Sorry the same family had subjected it to nearly one hundred years of blood and guts. We seem to spawn killers, no doubt about that. I found myself hoping hard that E.J. could break that chain. Maybe when I got a free second I'd give her a call and make that suggestion. Never mind that she was less than a month old and would spend the entire time trying to eat the receiver. It's never too early to start brainwashing your young.

BY JENNIFER RARDIN

Once Bitten, Twice Shy
Another One Bites the Dust

# Another One Bites the Dust

## A JAZ PARKS NOVEL

## Jennifer Rardin

www.orbitbooks.net

ORBIT

First published in Great Britain in 2007 by Orbit

A CIP catalogue record for this book
is available from the British Library.

ISBN 978–1–84149–639–9

Papers used by Orbit are natural, recyclable products made from
wood grown in sustainable forests and certified in accordance with
the rules of the Forest Stewardship Council.

Typeset in Granjon
Printed and bound in Great Britain by
Mackays of Chatham plc, Chatham, Kent
Paper supplied by Hellefoss AS, Norway

Orbit
An imprint of
Little, Brown Book Group
100 Victoria Embankment
London EC4Y 0DY

An Hachette Livre UK Company

www.orbitbooks.net

*For Katie . . . When you look in a mirror,*
*see the miracle. I love you.*

# ACKNOWLEDGMENTS

Thanks to everyone who helped make this work the best it could possibly be: My editor, Devi Pillai; my agent, Laurie McLean; Bob Castillo; Alex Lencicki; Penina Lopez; Katherine Molina; Gabriella Nemeth; and all the folks at Orbit whose kindness, creativity, and professionalism I appreciate and admire. I'd also like to thank my readers Laurie McLean, Hank Graves, Hope Dennis, Erin Pringle, Jeremy Toungate, and Katie Rardin for taking the time to review the manuscript. Your feedback is pure gold. As for you, Reader, thanks for coming. Whether it was a return trip or a first outing, I hope you enjoyed the ride!

# Chapter One

Y ou are what you drive. My personal ride is a fully recondi-
tioned 1965 Corvette Sting Ray 327 convertible, inherited
from my Granny May after Pops Lew passed away. He taught me
everything I know about fast, powerful cars. How to drive them,
keep them running, love them with unrelenting passion.

So maybe it was understandable that, despite wearing a helmet
that currently hid my entire face from view, if a pit had suddenly
yawned open before me, I would've happily leaped into it and hur-
tled to my untimely death rather than spent another second with
my ass pinned to the seat of a 1993 moped.

Sometimes my job just sucks.

Nobody would've agreed with me less than my mo-buddy,
Cole Bemont, who chugged along the Bay Trail beside me at a
stately rate of speed, humming a little ditty into his helmet mike as
he avoided crashing into yet another stray Texan. On this mild,
sunny afternoon it seemed like half of Corpus Christi had read our
adventure-seeking minds and said, "Cool. Let's go get in their
way."

Skaters, bikers, and fishermen vied for space along the wide
stretch of asphalt we shared with parents guarding strollers and
scampering kids. To our left a bright white seawall punctuated by
an inviting little gazebo divided land from water, a sparkling blue

inlet to the Gulf of Mexico. To our right, a broad strip of grass led up a gentle slope, past a deserted bandstand to rows of hotels, restaurants, and the occasional dance club. Ahead of us a palm-lined parking lot and boat-happy marina marked the end of everyday recreation and the beginning of extra-special fun. Which was where we came in.

We'd taken upon ourselves the task of scoping out the Corpus Christi Winter Festival, which was even now rising from the trampled grass just beyond our vision. Afterward we planned to report our findings to our boss, Vayl. Once he rose. As in, from the dead. He's a vamp, one of the growing minority who've cast their lot with society for better or, as has commonly been the case, for worse.

At any rate, Cole and I, having already been given most of the necessary details regarding our target, figured it might be fun, and indeed professional, to locate the spot where said target was digging in. It wouldn't hurt to become familiar with the overall plan of the festival, either, considering the fact that we were going to become attractions ourselves all too soon.

Within minutes we reached the site. Hundreds of scurrying roadies and home business owners infused the place with an atmosphere of anticipation as they set up game booths, food trailers, and shops where you could drop a load of cash on potions, pendants, or candles whose scent made you dream of lost loved ones. As we wound our way past craft tables and warding booths Cole said, "Jasmine, promise we'll stop there before we leave this place!"

He pointed to a stall whose four-foot-high hand-painted sign announced its name in neon orange letters as Boogie Chickens. According to the smaller print, you only had to invest a dollar to watch four Brahma hens groove to classic hits by the Bee Gees.

"We should hire them to open for us," I said.

"It won't work," Cole replied. "I've seen that look in Vayl's eyes before. You're not talking him out of the belly-dancing gig."

*Ouch.*

Vayl hadn't even tried to soften the blow. He'd smacked me with it two days before, while we were still motoring through Indiana. When I'd asked him what our crew would be doing at the Corpus Christi Winter Festival he'd replied, "Our target, whose name is Chien-Lung, is taking a troupe of Chinese acrobats to divert copious crowds of Texans throughout the last week of February. Because his security is unparalleled, the best way for us to lure him into the open is to become entertainment ourselves. As a Seer and Reader of Tarot, Cassandra will be our main draw. Lung is obsessed with psychics and will not be able to resist attending her show. Before she arrives onstage we will whet his appetite with our own unique talents. Cole will juggle, I will sing, you will belly dance, and Bergman will attend to all electronic apparatus including lights, sound, and surveillance."

I held up my hands as if they could actually stop this rocket. "Whoa! Now, wait a minute. I'm not belly dancing."

"Yes, you are. It is a beautiful, ancient art. One you should be proud to share."

"I can't belly dance."

"Yes, you can. It is in your fi—"

"Will you stop reading my goddamn file!"

Nobody had said a word. It reminded me of a classroom right after the teacher has gone ballistic and thrown a textbook out the window. I'd briefly considered making my own exit that way, but since we'd been traveling down I-70 in a gigantic RV at the time, that option had seemed a little extreme.

The whole show-must-go-on concept explained the presence of Cassandra, who'd helped us tame the last monster we'd faced, though the Tor-al-Degan had nearly chowed down on my soul before our black-braided beauty had finally sent the beast back to Kyronland where it belonged. It didn't clarify Bergman's presence, however. A mom-and-pop show like the one Vayl meant for us to stage didn't require a brilliant, neurotic inventor to babysit the spotlight and the CD player. However, I was willing to leave that mystery until later. My integrity was at stake here!

"Surely there's another, better way to get close to this Chien-Lung," I said, very reasonably I thought, considering the fact that I wanted to rip off Vayl's eyebrows and Super Glue them to his upper lip.

He didn't reply. Just sat back on his beige couch. It exactly matched the one on which I perched directly across from him. But he ignored me, looked instead at Cassandra, who sat beside me, and said, "Chien-Lung is an ancient vampire with a dragon fixation. It is said that soon after he turned, he was caught draining the chieftain's daughter. For this crime he was boiled alive." Cassandra made a sound that landed somewhere between compassion and disgust, and smoothed an imaginary wrinkle from her bright red skirt. "He claims a dragon saved him, though not soon enough. He lost his sanity but not his brilliance. In him it has become an explosive combination."

Vayl went on. "During at least three previous presidential administrations Chien-Lung enjoyed diplomatic immunity while he stole nuclear technology and influenced foreign policy toward China. Then he disappeared. Our sources tell us he was trying to complete his transformation from vampire to dragon."

Without taking his eyes off the road (good thing, since he was driving) Cole said, "Hang on a second. Transformation? To dragon? What's that all about?"

"He believes his vampirism is a larval state from which he can, when stimulated correctly, emerge as a dragon."

Bergman, sitting beside Cole in the passenger seat, spun completely around at that comment. "You can't be serious."

"I did say he was insane."

*Yeah, but that's no cause to call in the assassins,* I thought. So I asked, "What's he done this time?"

Vayl raised his left eyebrow just enough to let me know he was about to say something momentous. "He has been conspiring with Edward Samos."

Moment of silence while we all digested. During our last mission we'd averted a national disaster planned by Samos and a few of his newest allies. Only we'd been calling him the Raptor then, for want of a true identity. Unfortunately, only the partners had paid for their crimes. Samos had slipped our net entirely.

"What have they been plotting?" I asked, managing a casual tone despite the fact that I badly wanted to punch something.

"We were able to intercept a cell phone call during which they discussed exactly how Samos would arrange for Chien-Lung to get in and out of White Sands undetected."

Bergman perked up like a dog that's just smelled a T-bone. "I know that base," he said. "I've sent a few things to be tested there."

I was still so distracted by the belly-dancing news combined with this new bombshell I almost didn't catch Vayl's nod or the tightening of his lips. Sure signs of trouble on the horizon. I said, "Are you telling me the same son of a bitch who nearly released a plague on our country gained access to one of our military installations?"

Vayl clenched his jaw so hard I could see the muscles spasm in his cheeks. "The prospect horrifies me as well," he admitted. "But we know Chien-Lung traveled to Las Cruces last week with his Chinese acrobats. He took the show to the base, and while he was there we believe he used the Raptor's inside knowledge to steal a vital piece of technology."

He looked at Bergman, who shifted uneasily at being the focus of the vampire's gaze. "Miles, I am sorry. The item is your invention."

"But the only thing I have at White Sands right now is . . ." Bergman's eyes lost focus. He turned red, paled, then slumped so far forward in his seat I thought he'd passed out. "Oh my God," he moaned, clenching tufts of his limp brown hair between his fingers. "Not M55. Not that. Not that."

"What is that?" asked Cole.

"The researchers I was working with called it dragon armor. It's a type of personal protection for soldiers in the field that actually binds to its wearer at the cellular level. It took me eight years to develop it and now you're telling me it's gone?" Bergman put his hand over his mouth as if to keep himself from gagging.

"We will get the armor back, Miles," Vayl said, in a tone so reassuring even I felt better. "That is part of our mission. Though during the conversation we overheard, Chien-Lung and the Raptor did not reveal why they were working together, we can assume Samos feels his nefarious schemes will be furthered once he controls the armor. That we cannot allow."

Despite the gravity of the situation I took a second to delight in Vayl's continued connection to his eighteenth-century roots. Oh, he tried to fit in. Back at the home office (we work out of Cleveland, I think because the CIA's tired of paying DC rental prices), Vayl and our boss, Pete, could trade football stories like they'd both played for Ohio State and hoped to God the Browns needed a fifth-string quarterback the year they graduated. True for Pete. For Vayl, well, as soon as he fumbled a word like "nefarious" you knew he'd never touched a pigskin in his life. Unless it was attached to an actual pig.

He met my eyes. "The second part of our mission is directly related to the first. In order to retrieve the armor, we must terminate its wearer. When Bergman feels better, he will help explain why."

I couldn't stand it any longer. I went to Bergman, knelt beside his chair, and took his trembling, chapped hands in my own.

He peered down at me through blasted eyes. "Oh, God, Jasmine, please. Please get it back." He looked like he'd lost his only child. And in a way he had. That's how much he invested in his creations.

"We will," I said. "I promise."

Bergman had barely spoken a word since. When we'd finally parked our colossus at a gas station/convenience store called Moe's, I'd been relieved when Cole had suggested our present mission. It would finally give me a chance to escape the gloom that had permeated our ride so thoroughly I'd begun to feel like I was breathing thunderclouds.

"There's a booth with an actual phone book inside," I'd said as we'd exited the RV, pointing to the plastic-encased stall at the north corner of Moe's lot. I'd headed toward it.

"Who're we calling?" asked Cole.

"A cab. I assume the festival is too far from here for hiking."

"Oh, we don't need to walk," he said. I stopped, turned, and followed him back to the trailer we'd towed all the way from Ohio. Though small, it still looked like it could hold everything I owned. Since he'd been the last one to drive, Cole had a set of keys in his pocket. He unlocked the doors and threw them open. I looked inside, and every one of my ribs knocked against its neighbor in a domino drop straight to my feet. No doubt they heard the *rattle, rattle, clunk* all the way to Amarillo.

"Oh my God, this can't be happening!" I cried.

7

"What?"

"Mopeds? Those are the wheels Pete gives us? I *knew* he was pissed off at me! It was all that time I spent in the hospital, wasn't it? Or was it the wrecks? But I only tore up one car last time! And that wasn't my fault!" I wailed.

"Jaz, calm down!" Cole pleaded. "They don't allow anything more powerful on the festival site. He thought it would give us the best mobility for what the rules permit."

"Oh." I watched mournfully as Cole backed the mopeds out of the trailer and relocked it. The manufacturer's pallid color choice, white with pale blue gas tanks and tan seats, defeated even my Sensitivity-enhanced vision. These vehicles blew. Worst of all, their top speed would probably only finish middle of the pack in the Boston Marathon.

But they did get us to the festival, where we put-putted past the mass of tents housing a national flower show, the future site of a hamburger-eating contest, the rides. *Seedy*, I thought when I caught a good look at the old equipment, peeling paint, and dripping oil, looking as sorely used as the people forcing it all back into action.

"Get a load of that," I told Cole, nodding at the multiarmed monster that would soon be twirling people around like plates at the top of a circus performer's pole. "Next time we need to interrogate somebody, what do you say we stick them on that puppy for about twenty minutes first?"

"Think how much money we'd save on truth serum."

"Pete would probably promote us."

"Is it just me or is this crowd thicker than burnt oatmeal?"

"It is getting kinda tough to avoid the rug rats. Let's park these wagons and walk."

We headed north of the crush to a Four Seasons parking lot,

ditched the mopeds, and took the helmets with us. Hopefully someone would steal the ridiculous little bikes while our backs were turned. If not, I would seriously consider dropping my keys into some wild-eyed teenager's lap.

For the next half hour we strolled the wide, mulched walkway that ran the length of the festival site. It wound around and between attractions like a long piece of dark red licorice. Besides all the sales booths and rides, we passed eight separate stages where singers, dancers, comedians, mediums, and magicians would enthrall the masses for the next seven days. But not us. Cole told me we had our own tent, the better to control those random happenings that can, if left unchecked, slam an operation right against the wall.

We found Chien-Lung's Chinese acrobats setting up their performance space in an enormous clearing toward the northwest corner of the festival site. At the moment a seemingly infinite series of air pumps the size of Cassandra's makeup case lined up next to neat tunnels of plastic. Eventually these would inflate the mass of red, yellow, and purple material the acrobats were still unfolding into an actual building. Since Vayl and I had tailed a guy through a similar structure in France four months earlier, I knew it could be done. But from this point of view, it seemed unlikely.

"Wow," said Cole. "They look so organized."

"And clean-cut," I added. "Apparently you're only allowed to let yourself go if you're a U.S. citizen."

A squeal and a giggle followed my comment. I looked around to see who found me so amusing, so naturally it had nothing to do with me. A young Chinese woman wearing red capris and a plain green T-shirt had set up a checkered picnic blanket where she sat with her legs folded underneath her hips while she threw her baby up in the air and caught him. And when I say up, I don't mean up like a preservice tennis ball. I mean like an NFL kickoff. And he *loved* it. Every time he flew he laughed uproariously, and every time his mom caught him he wiggled madly, clearly encouraging her to toss him even higher the next time around.

I nudged Cole, whose grin told me he also thought Flying Baby rocked. "You know," I said, "if I tried to do that with my niece she'd puke in my face."

"Sensitive stomach, huh?"

"Let's put it this way. I helped take care of the kid for three weeks, and every day by noon I had so much spit-up on my shirt I could've squeezed it into a trough for the neighborhood cats."

Not that I was complaining. After spending a month in the hospital recovering from the punctured side, broken ribs, and collapsed lung I'd suffered during our final showdown with the Tor-al-Degan on our last mission, I couldn't wait to fly to Evie's and help out after the birth of her daughter, E.J. It should've been fun. The new parents were like kids at Christmas when I talked to them the day E.J. was born. But when I arrived she was five days old. They hadn't slept more than four hours a night total, and she'd been howling like a coyote pretty much ever since they'd brought her home.

"Colic," the pediatrician had said at her first checkup, when Evie asked frantically why E.J. cried so much. "She'll outgrow it," he told us absently, as I struggled not to charge him and shake him until his stethoscope fell off and, if there was a God, whacked him right in the cojones. I'm sure Tim would've done the same, but he'd taken his chance to catch forty winks in the rocking chair in the corner of the room.

That was the day I discovered a new way to vent my frustrations.

After driving the exhausted family home and leaving Evie to tuck Tim into bed and then watch E.J. go another round in the living room with her swing, I grabbed a six-pack of Pepsi and re-treated to the backyard.

It had snowed the night before, covering the frozen ground with a fine white powder that sparkled with vivid, spirit-boosting colors. Tim's maul leaned against the redwood deck where he'd left it after splitting some logs. I straightened the handle and twirled it absently. Then I got an idea.

"You know what?" I murmured, releasing a can from the pack and setting it on the ground. "This could be a good thing." I took a moment to measure the distance, swung the maul high over my head, and brought it down hard. The can crushed with a lovely, metallic *crack* and pop flew everywhere. I couldn't help it. I had to smile.

Eventually I introduced my little sanity saver to Evie and Tim. But I didn't think Chinese Mom would have need for it. Not with such a cooperative boy in hand. She finally got tired and grounded her little astronaut, tucking him into a sit-and-stroll contraption whose wheels she seemed to have locked. With his own personal joyride closing without warning, and his new one temporarily on blocks, I expected him to throw a massive tantrum. But he just grinned, his four teeth twinkling like little pearls in the dying light. I caught his mom's eye as she gave him a handful of hot dog wedges and a sippy cup full of milk.

"He's adorable," I said, smiling.

She smiled back. "Thank you." From her accent I suspected she didn't know a heck of a lot of English. Still, I had to ask. "Is he always this happy?"

She nodded proudly. "He only cry when he hungry or tired."

"Wow, that's great. So, you're with the acrobat troupe?"

"Yes, my husband and I both perform. But I am having slight injury"—she pointed to her ankle, which was wrapped and taped in the classic "badly sprained" style—"so I sitting out this week."

Suddenly Cole lunged forward, startling us both. "Something's wrong with the baby," he explained as he knelt in front of the new-age walker, his face very close to the boy's. "He's not getting any air."

Chinese Mom and I exchanged horrified looks as we both realized the baby's lips had begun to turn blue.

Cole tried to clear his throat. "It's not coming out." He pulled the boy out of his seat and laid him on his back. Then, gently but firmly, he performed the Heimlich maneuver on him, using just two fingers from each hand to force air out his lungs and back up his throat. After four fruitless tries it worked. The baby spit out a chunk of hot dog that looked big enough to choke an elephant.

He took a deep breath. Looked at his mother in surprise. And burst into tears. That worked for her. Within seconds she was crying too, holding out her arms so Cole could transfer him for some dual boohooing and a comforting rock while we watched.

"Should we leave?" Cole finally asked.

"I'm not really sure about Heimlich etiquette," I replied. "But it is getting kind of late." I patted Chinese Mom on the arm. "We're so glad he's okay," I said. "You're okay too, right?" She nodded. "Great. Well, we have to go."

"Oh, no, but I must thank you properly! And my husband! He will want to thank you also!" She looked so horrified at the thought of us leaving that Cole quickly reassured her.

"We're not leaving for good. We're performers too. Tell you what, why don't you come by our tent tomorrow? We'll give you tickets to our show and we'll have a chance to meet your husband then."

"Oh, yes, that will be fine. And then you will come to our show as well. Yes?"

"Of course," Cole agreed, before I could throw an elbow to remind him we'd come to kill a vampire, not make friends with his employees. We all smiled and bobbed our heads at each other. Then Cole and I said our goodbyes to Flying Baby, who'd already dried his tears and moved on to more interesting diversions, like trying to snag his mom's earrings while she thanked us about three dozen more times.

As we moved on I said, "Wow. I think you get gold stars in heaven for stuff like that."

Cole shrugged. "I dated a nurse for a while. And an EMT." When I glanced at him he gave me a wink. "I went through this whole women-in-uniform phase."

"Which is my cue to change the subject. That kid is amazing. Don't tell my sister some babies hardly ever cry. As freaked as she is about motherhood right now she'll probably leap to some bizarre conclusion about the colic being her fault, and next thing you know she'll be in a convent somewhere, reciting her sins into some poor priest's ear between her hourly lashings."

"I didn't know you were Catholic."

"We're not."

It didn't take long to cruise the rest of the site. Past the Chinese acrobats' building, a cheap orange fence manned by two security guards cordoned off the northwest border. The guards, big-bellied men with self-important attitudes, stood with their backs to the building and the scattering of booths here at the end of the path, watching a group of nine picketers who'd commandeered the last twenty-five yards of a narrow access road for their demonstration.

Four women and five men circled a group of kids who sat in lawn chairs, pretending to be homeschooled when, in fact, they were carefully studying the festival setup. I picked out two teenage boys in particular who could probably be counted on to sneak off and hop a ride or two later in the week. But for now they continued the charade as their parents lugged gigantic billboards around their perimeter. These signs had apparently ground the grown-ups down so far all they could manage was a weary staggered chant: "*Others* are *not* our brothers." The sign slogans delivered their messages with a lot more punch. SUPERNATURAL IS UNNATURAL. TO BE HUMAN IS DIVINE! GOD HATES OTHERS. UP WITH HUMANS! And, oddly, VOTE FOR PURE WATER!

"Who *are* these people?" murmured Cole.

"Well, I'm ninety percent sure this is about half the congregation of the Church Sanctified in Christ the Crucified."

Cole laughed.

"That is not a name I could make up that fast."

"How do you even know about them?"

"One of their members sent a letter to the president threatening to kill him if he agreed to give *others* the right to vote, so Pete sent out a memo."

"The president doesn't even have that power."

"I don't think that question came up during the sermon." I looked for the group's van. According to Pete, its slogans were so offensive that even *others* trying to blend might be tempted to roll it over a cliff. Yup, there it was, parked just up the road. I couldn't see much from this angle, just a cracked front window, two American flags flying off the corners of the front bumper and a white banner someone had tied across the grill that screamed, GOD IS ON OUR SIDE!

Cole said, "Do you think they ever stop and walk the other direction?"

"I imagine that's a sin."

Cole threw me a look I couldn't interpret. "What?" I asked.

"Don't these idiots make you mad?"

"Why?"

He shrugged. "Vayl's an *other*. Plus, considering what happened in Miami, technically *you* may be one. Dude, they're putting your peeps down."

"You worry too much about what other people think of you. Plus, they have a right to their opinions. For that matter, so do I. The problem isn't that we disagree."

"No?"

"The problem is that they can't disagree without getting so mad they want to kill somebody. Like the president, for instance. And if it really does go that far, somebody calls me and then I have to go kill one of them. And the first rule you learn in this business is . . ." I waited for him to finish my sentence.

"Never kill when you're mad," he complied, "because that's when it might be murder." I didn't tell him how often I'd broken that rule. He'd figure that out on his own soon enough.

Eventually I felt about as bored as the guards looked. I was just getting ready to suggest Cole and I hike back to our (hopefully missing) mopeds when one of the guards turned to speak to his companion.

"Did you see that?" I asked.

"See what?"

Some instinct made me pull Cole into the shelter of a white party tent, the sides of which had been rolled down to keep the wind from blowing away several boxes full of cone-shaped cups that would eventually contain a ton of ice and a teaspoon of syrup. I peeked through the crack between the material and the pole it had been tied to. A second later I saw it again. "The guard on the right. Watch his face when he moves."

Cole stared hard, squinching his eyes until he kind of resembled Chinese Baby. "I don't see anything."

*Weird.* I'd been counting on confirmation from him. A childhood accident had changed him, made him a Sensitive like me. It allowed him to pick up on the presence of vamps and other things that go bump in the night. But then, since I had donated blood to a vampire—my boss, in fact—I sort of had an advanced degree.

"What did you see, Jaz?"

"Every time he moved, his face sort of blurred, like it was catching up to the rest of him."

Cole blew out a breath. "Bizarre."

"Yeah. And I get the feeling he's not the type we should just stroll up and introduce ourselves to."

"What do you think? You want to stick around, see what he's up to?"

I took another peek. "He's not going anywhere. Let's get the rest of the posse. Maybe they'll know something."

I realized Fate, which had often punched me so hard I couldn't see for the swelling, may have dealt me a pair of aces in Cassandra and Bergman. Though I always had reservations about using consultants, those suddenly disappeared. I had a feeling this new wrinkle was going to need all our resources if we ever meant to lay it flat again.

# CHAPTER TWO

I'll say this, RVs have developed panache since the bang-your-chin-on-the-sink-while-using-the-toilet days of my youth. The one Vayl had reserved for our use was tricked out. A plasma TV took up headspace behind the cab. Cassandra's couch had a small reading table. Beside Bergman's there was enough room for a light brown leather banquette to wrap around a glass dining table. Behind it a black granite counter that could be used as a standing breakfast bar rounded back toward the wall, which held a mirrored wine case, a black refrigerator, and maple cabinets. On the opposite wall, more cabinets framed the stove, microwave, and black porcelain sink. The designer had even left room for another, smaller TV.

Down the carpeted hallway, the bathroom looked like it had been lifted straight out of the Ritz. And the bedroom had its own TV plus a big old queen-sized bed and plenty of drawer space. Oh, we still had that RV thing going on, where the couches and banquette all made into beds and you could store stuff in every conceivable nook and cranny. But, baby, we were stylin'.

I'd just entered the RV when I heard Vayl come to life. The gulp he took reminded me of a kid who tries to hold his breath past too many rows of tombstones. I nodded to Cassandra, who'd looked up from her book when I came in. "Cole's securing the trailer," I whispered, since Bergman was snoozing, his face buried in a red tasseled pillow, his right arm and leg dragging the gold carpeted floor.

Cassandra nodded and went back to her reading.

I went to Vayl's room and knocked on the door.

"Jasmine?" His voice sounded gruff and slightly pained.

"Yeah."

"Come in."

The light-impermeable tent he slept (died?) in every morning engulfed the top of the bed. He came around from behind it, closing the top button of his tailored black slacks, his navy blue shirt hanging open, revealing a broad, muscular chest covered with black curls and an empty gold chain that had once carried the ring I now wore on my right hand.

I forced my eyes to the ring, swallowing a spurt of highly inappropriate *wowsa*. The rubies that marched around their gold settings glittered in the soft lights Vayl had turned on when he woke. I concentrated on the craftsmanship Vayl's grandfather had put into the ring, the love and artistry and power that had been required to turn gold and gems into a relic that protected, and connected, us both.

"What are you thinking?" he asked. He stood so close I could feel his cool breath against my heated face.

"Your grandpa must've been an amazing man to have made such a beautiful ring for you."

I peered into Vayl's eyes. At the moment they were the soft brown that characterized his most relaxed, real self. They squeezed at the corners, as they often did when I forced him into his distant, painful past.

"He was . . . devoted to his family, but also very set in his way of thinking." His lips drew back at some memory.

"Vayl?"

He began forcing the buttons of his shirt through their holes so abruptly I was surprised they didn't pop off. "Do you know how the Roma regard vampires?" he demanded.

"No, not really." Though I should. Why didn't I delve more into Vayl's roots? *Because to know him is to love him, and you're so not ready to go there.*

"To the Roma we are dead. And therefore unclean. But that impurity is spread also to our family." When I didn't seem suitably impressed Vayl said, "When my grandfather found out about Liliana and I, he led the mob that came to kill us."

"But . . . he made the ring for you. He knew your soul would be in danger—"

"Yes, but he expected me to be attacked by demons. He did not think I would become one myself."

"And, what, infect your family somehow?"

"No, not infect them. Kill them, turn them, destroy their very souls."

"Well, that's just stupid."

Vayl's finger brushed against the ring he'd given me. He called it Cirilai, which meant "Guardian." The barest hint of a smile lifted his lips. "I appreciate your support. But you must remember the age. It was 1751. Long before computers, cars, penicillin, or anything approaching civil rights. Even now the Roma are a tortured people. But then, it was magnified a thousand times. All they had was one another."

"So what, they had to cut you out of the flock in order to save the rest?"

"I suppose you could look at it that way."

"But you're here. How did you survive?"

"My father arrived first. He could not bear to lose me. He said I was all he had left of my mother. He moved us to a safe place as we slept. And then, that night, for our own safety he returned and banished us."

"You can do that? Banish vampires?"

He fixed me with his most piercing glare. "You can, if you have the power and the means. But it is not common knowledge. I tell you this strictly as *sverhamin* to *avhar*, which means you may not share this information with anyone else."

"There you go again, invoking our special bond, like I know all the rules or something. Is there a book I can read somewhere? Because I'm getting a little tired of being in the dark on the parameters of this relationship."

Twitch of the lip. In any other man, it would've been a full-face smile. Maybe even an outright laugh. But I guess when somebody murders your sons, and your closest relations all try to kill or kick you out before you turn forty, you learn fast how to nail those emotions in the coffin you refuse to sleep in when the sun rises.

Vayl said, "You do not strike me as the type of person who enjoys being lectured. In fact, I sense that if I began to list all of the intricacies of the *sverhamin/avhar* connection and the related rules, the moment I turned around you would fish out your tape recorder, set it on the nearest flat surface, and sneak off to the closest all-night monster truck rally."

"Okay, although my taste runs more to auto racing, I get your point. Just don't get all pissy when I break a rule I'm not even aware of."

"Fair enough." Vayl collapsed his tent with a couple of quick moves, and suddenly there was a nice big bed at our backs. Vayl's eyes strayed to my neck and I knew we were both remembering the time I'd bared it to him.

His eyes lightened to green and my heartbeat must have tripled at the thought that we could so easily ignite those feelings again.

"So, banishment," I blurted, so loudly they probably heard me three blocks away. Vayl dropped his hand. I didn't even know he'd reached for me. He turned away.

"Yes."

"What exactly does that mean for you?"

"Liliana and I were forced to distance ourselves from all members of our family for ten generations."

"What happened if you didn't?"

Vayl whipped me a look over his shoulder that told me he'd had about enough. You can only scratch a scar so long before it becomes a wound again. "Magical banishment is not like a restraining order, Jasmine. It is quite effective. Well, it was."

"You mean, it's over now?"

Vayl nodded. "The banishment expired three years ago." *Fat lot of good that does me,* said the bleak look in his eyes. *The family I knew is all dead now. Dead and gone.* Or, as he so desperately hoped in the case of his boys, dead and reincarnated.

I felt like such an ass. I'd made Vayl dig up some bad old memories just so I wouldn't have to face down my own growing desire to toss that tape recorder he'd mentioned off the nearest flat surface and throw Vayl down there instead. Thing was, when I looked in those remarkable eyes and thought of sharing that ultimate moment of ecstasy with him, the image that came to mind was not me and Vayl. It was me and Matt. My fiancé had been dead nearly sixteen months, but parts of my brain still couldn't seem to believe it.

Vayl had fished some socks out of a drawer and sat on the bed to put them on. "Are you all right?" he asked.

Great, I'd hurt him and he was asking after my welfare. Typical. "Yeah, look, I'm sorry I made you talk about that stuff. It's none of my business—"

"Actually, it is. As my *avhar* you should be privy to all my secrets, past and present." His lips twisted. "It is just that, there are so many to tell. And very few of them are pleasant."

"Well, by all means, take your time. I know, maybe every couple of weeks we can have a slumber party. You can come over to my apartment and we'll play Truth or Dare. You can let a couple juicy ones slip while we gossip about how Cassandra wears too much jewelry and Cole always smells like grape bubble gum." An image came to mind of Vayl wearing SpongeBob SquarePants pajamas and pink fuzzy slippers and I started to giggle. When I got a load of the confused look on his face I laughed even louder. The sharp rap on the door didn't stop me, but the look on Cole's face when he stepped in did. He looked pissed. When he saw that Vayl and I were practically on opposite sides of the room his shoulders dropped and his fists opened.

*Oh man, he can't still be carrying a torch for me, can he? I mean, we had it all out already, right? Yeah right,* drawled my cynical self, a chain-smoking echo of my mother, who wore hair curlers like diamond tiaras and was a master at keeping her kids out of the house.

"Yes, Cole?" Vayl's tone could've frozen a pitcher of lemonade.

"I just wanted to know what you thought about the security guards." When Vayl gave him a blank look Cole's shoulders bunched right back up. "What've you been doing in here all this time?" he asked me.

Before I could reply Vayl said, "The conversations that occur between *sverhamin* and *avhar* are private. If information arises that concerns you, we will let you know."

"That's enough," I told them both, holding out my hands, which immediately seemed kind of stupid. Did I really want to be the one standing in the middle of a pissing match? Ick. "If you boys can't play nice I'm sending you to your rooms."

Vayl raised an eyebrow as if to say, *But I am already here.*

I went on. "Cole makes a good point. I should've told you straight off that we went to scout out the festival, and while we were there I saw something funky." I described the guard. Luckily that made Vayl forget all about how much he didn't care for Cole. Which made his presence on our current mission something of a minor miracle. Enter the flaming ball of guilt who is me.

I'd met Cole on New Year's Eve during a reconnaissance mission. His connection to our target's wife had piqued Vayl's interest. That attention had not gone unnoticed by our enemies. It had resulted in the burning of Cole's office, his kidnapping and severe beating. At the end of that mission he'd held my hand in the dungeon below Club Undead, tears flowing unchecked down his battered face. "I'm so sorry," he kept saying.

The pain of my injuries had nearly overwhelmed me. I badly wanted a paramedic with a needleful of morphine. But it helped to concentrate on the men, Cole on my left and Vayl, running soothing fingers through my hair, at my right.

"Why?" I asked, my voice raspy with barely checked agony.

"I should be in your spot. If you hadn't pulled me off that bomb and taken my place—"

"She would have been fired," Vayl told him.

I squeezed Cole's hand. "And that really would've killed me."

"But—"

I squeezed harder, making him wince. "You saved me just now. We're even."

But I hadn't really felt that way. I still had a job, after all, while Cole's was little more than a pile of ash. So when he visited me in the hospital a week later to ask for a recommendation, I called my boss, Pete, that afternoon.

"Does he know what he's talking about?" Pete had asked.

"He was there for the big showdown. I can tell you he has no illusions," I assured him. Then I listed all the reasons Cole would make an excellent agent. It took me quite a while. I finished with the two items I knew Pete couldn't resist. "He currently knows seven languages and can pick up new ones in a snap because of his Sensitivity. Plus he's an ace shooter. He started competing in high school. Still does when he can. And he rarely loses."

"I thought you told me he was a private investigator. Isn't there enough supernatural crime in Miami to keep him busy?"

"He doesn't want to be a PI anymore. I tried to talk him out of this decision and realized he's made it for all the right reasons. You know, Amanda Abn-Assan was a childhood friend of his. He said after losing her, he just can't sit on the sidelines while somebody else chases down scumbags like her husband."

Cole had just completed his first course of training when this mission came up. Since he spoke Chinese—and we didn't—Pete figured he could help us out while we gave him some on-the-job experience. Vayl hadn't seen it that way. I'd made some very intelligent, convincing arguments, none of which he'd bought. In the end I'd promised to personally drop off and pick up his dry-cleaning for a month, since he suspected the new delivery boy was rifling through his mail, and we had a deal.

I wondered idly if the shirt Vayl currently wore was a dry-clean-only model as he said, "I am not sure what kind of *other* you detected, Jasmine. Maybe Cassandra will have a record."

We all moved into the living area to check with her. But with so little data to give the *Enkyklios*, her portable library, we came up dry.

"My books may have something," Cassandra said. "I'll check them."

"Thank you," Vayl said graciously. He pulled a bag of blood out of the refrigerator and poured it into a mug. In our time together I'd learned that he liked to let it slowly warm to room temperature. He said nuking it burned away most of the flavor. And while I thought my skin should've crawled at learning those kinds of details, it didn't, because it implied a trust I felt honored to have earned.

Our noise had awakened Bergman, who sat rubbing his eyes on the couch I had decided to dub Mary-Kate. Cassandra sat across from him on its twin, Ashley, already leafing through a heavy old tome whose pages were thick as postal paper. Cole grabbed a piece of gum from a green bowl on the table beside her couch (um, Ashley) and dropped down beside her.

"I'm researching," she told him sternly. "No funny comments about the pictures."

"But look at that guy! He's clearly constipated."

"He eats people's brains!"

"Exactly!"

I took a seat beside Bergman and gave him the once-over. His nap hadn't done him much good. Though he shouldn't, he reminded me of a bereaved parent. He dreamed, incubated, birthed his inventions, and was very choosy about where he let them go to work. Knowing some lunatic currently wore his baby, and that the Raptor was circling overhead, waiting to swoop in and hook it, probably made him feel desperately helpless.

Vayl, still standing in the kitchen, leaned his elbows on the counter that backed the banquette. He didn't even clear his throat and suddenly we all snapped to attention. He said, "Before we leave for the festival site, I want to complete your briefing on Bergman's armor. I will ask him to explain the details of its workings in a moment. As he said, it is an incredibly advanced piece of biotechnology that physically binds with its carrier. Once they are united, the only ways you can separate the suit from its wearer are to kill him, or administer a chemical bath that fools the suit into thinking he is dead."

"I take it Mr. Bubble isn't manufacturing that particular brand of bath additive just yet?" asked Cole.

Bergman sat up, then laid his head against the back of Mary-Kate despondently. "That's what the experiments at White Sands were about. They were trying to target which chemicals administered in which way would throw the suit into death response."

"But they haven't had any luck yet?" I asked.

Bergman shook his head.

"Is it that big of a deal?" Cole inquired. "We're going to kill the guy anyway."

"You can try," moaned Bergman.

Vayl nodded. "Go on," he urged as he took a sip from his mug.

Bergman looked at each of us in turn, shook his head, and ran a hand across the reddish brown grizzle that had appeared on his jaw sometime in the past twenty-two hours. As he spoke, he gazed out the window at the glaring lights of Moe's gas station and the city beyond. "The armor will repel every kind of projectile in existence. It's impervious to fire, can't be shredded, and can withstand pressures equal to those found in the deepest parts of the ocean."

"What about cold?" I asked, feeling a rush of pleasure as Vayl looked at me proudly. Maybe his greatest power was the ability to leech heat from an area so fast people had frozen to death inside his circle of influence.

But Bergman shook his head again. "Cold will slow it down, but not destroy it."

"Water?" Cole ventured.

"When the hood is closed, the armor becomes self-contained. It has its own internal breathing system that functions just fine when it's immersed."

"Tell us more about this hood," I said.

"It activates automatically when it perceives the wearer's in danger. It's the only part of the armor that can be deactivated at will. The rest is permanent."

Cassandra stirred. "You've begun at the end when the most important details may be at the beginning. What does this armor look like?"

Bergman shrugged. "We've had it on all kinds of animals, including fish, cats, and monkeys. It's looked different on each one, probably because it binds differently to each depending on body chemistry, physical size, species type—"

Cassandra waved her hand impatiently, making Bergman crook his eyebrows with frustration. "A general overview, if you please," she said.

"Scales," said Bergman. "The material is made up of thousands of individual units that are physically and chemically bonded together. The colors vary as widely as the texture. On the fish it was rough, almost like steel wool. On the chimp it was softer, more elastic."

"Is it just a defensive thing?" asked Cole. Another excellent question. My, weren't we just operating on all cylinders this evening?

"No." Bergman's eyes filled with passion as he described offensive capabilities that only made me shudder because I had to find a way around them. "When the hood is activated, the wearer can ignite volatile chemicals that are contained in the nostril cavities."

"What does that mean?" I asked. "Are you telling us the guy can breathe fire?"

"Exactly."

"What else?" Vayl demanded.

"Contact poison in the claws that paralyzes the victim. Detachable spikes carried along the back that are so well balanced they can be launched to hit targets accurately at forty feet."

"And when they hit?" I asked.

"They explode."

I felt my shoulders droop. *Holy crap! This one is definitely Mission Sucks-Out-the—*

Vayl interrupted my thought, which was probably just as well. No sense in depressing myself any more than necessary. "We knew it would be difficult," he said. "But that is why this task has been assigned to us. We *can* do this. And we will."

Somehow that little pep talk allowed us to move to other issues. As Cole drove us to the site, we discussed the stage setup. It would take place tonight while Vayl could help. We talked about the show, realizing we'd probably have to spend the entire day tomorrow practicing in order to present anything remotely entertaining. And I privately wondered how a 291-year-old vampire and a thousand-year-old Seer didn't seem at all familiar with the creature I'd seen pretending to be human today.

# Chapter Three

As we pulled into our space, Cole and I noticed the Winter Festival setup had chugged ahead, making steady progress since our recent visit. We all agreed our parking spot seemed ideal, situated as it was where the mulched walkway almost met the seawall before it turned back north toward a series of craft and game booths that led to Chien-Lung's Chinese acrobats' half-inflated building.

Cole parked the RV south of the walk, parallel to the seawall, and we began to unload the trailer. A barbecue cook-off site stood so close to our performance location that if we stretched we'd hit a grill. But that meant we could let them take care of outdoor lighting for our customers. Several gray-headed gentlemen wearing ball caps and stained aprons had already strung yards of pink-shaded patio lights across the area. Now they were moving in several green-painted picnic tables.

Still, as we carried poles, canvas (probably something Pete had ripped off an old tent revival preacher), more poles, tons of wooden slats, and absolutely no directions whatsoever from the trailer to the tent-erection site, it was apparent we'd have enough room for our purposes. As long as one of us could figure out how to put the damn thing together.

Already the bickering had begun. Cole picked up two poles and connected them.

"Cole!" snapped Bergman. "You need to put them all in piles first. That way you know what you have!"

"We have poles and canvas, dude. You stick the little end in the big end." He demonstrated on another pair. "It's like magic how they go together."

Bergman looked at Vayl. "You tell him."

Cole gave his imagined rival a smirk. "I'm thinking you know how a tent goes up by now, Vayl."

Cassandra decided to bail first. "I need to do some research. Weird-faced man, you know," she murmured, and disappeared into the RV.

*That woman is brilliant.* I turned to follow her.

"Where are you going?" demanded Vayl.

*Quick, think of a marvelous excuse he'll totally swallow. Aha!* "To practice. Unlike you guys, I haven't tried my particular talent since Granny May signed me up for belly-dancing classes when I was fifteen." *And, by the way, why the hell did I consent to that? Or decide I loved it? Never mind, he's buying it. In fact, he seems to be hot on the idea. Are his eyes glowing? And is Cole's tongue hanging out? This is why I didn't want to dance in the first place!* "Anyway," I rushed on. "I'm going to find a private place where nobody can see to laugh at me while you beat this tent" —*or, more likely, these two idiots*— "into submission."

"Aah," said Vayl. He took a couple of steps toward me, got hopelessly entangled in a mound of canvas, and stalled. But that didn't stop his eyes from roaming. "Believe me, Jasmine, no one who sees you dance would ever dream of laughing."

"I could come with you," Cole offered. "You know, give you some tips. Run the camera. Maybe oil your hips for you when they get rusty."

I couldn't help it: I started to laugh. It was a combination of

Vayl bristling like a threatened porcupine while Cole wiggled his eyebrows suggestively and Bergman stealthily organized the poles just like he wanted them.

"I'll be over there," I said, pointing west, where you could just make out a strip of white sand where the seawall stopped and a series of abandoned piers began. "By myself."

And I was alone for about an hour. Then this couple came strolling by, making enough noise that I didn't totally humiliate myself in front of them. I couldn't see them well. Didn't need to. They were holding hands. Kissing every fifth step or so. Smitten. And suddenly my brain cut the power to my knees.

I plopped down, watching like a starstruck fan as the lovers strode across the sand in front of me. It was the laughter that did it, transforming me from watcher into participant. Suddenly I was part of the couple, reliving a moment I hadn't dared to remember until now.

Matt and I had taken our first real vacation together, a trip to Hawaii, to celebrate his twenty-ninth birthday. The night after we landed on the island we'd walked the beach, arm in arm, the boom of the surf echoing the music from a distant luau. Lights from hotels, bars, and all-night parties gave the evening an effervescent sort of glow. We passed other couples, whole families even, but it was as if we moved within our own love-lit world. If a giant marlin had swept out of the ocean and offered us three wishes I wouldn't have been surprised. It was that kind of evening. Magical.

We'd walked the length of a pier lit by tiki torches. At the very end, a table dressed in china and crystal awaited us. We ate like royalty under the shelter of a thatch-roofed gazebo. And after dessert we danced to the music of a four-man reggae band called the B-tones.

"This is amazing," I breathed as Matt held me close, moving me to the sultry rhythms of a song whose name I never learned.

He pulled back far enough to look into my eyes. "*You're* amazing." He smiled, his teeth extra white against the natural deep tan of his skin. "But not so observant."

"No?"

He shook his head, pulled his hand out of my clasp, took a ring off his pinky, and held it in front of my face. "I really thought at some point you'd ask me why I was wearing a girl's engagement ring."

"Have you had that on all night?"

He grinned. "Only since dessert."

Then I realized what he'd just said. "Are you — are we —"

"Say yes, Jaz."

I'd screamed, and jumped up and down, and jumped on him, and made him jump up and down with me, which turned out to be pretty funny. At which point he put the ring on my finger. It was a full-carat pear-shaped emerald. "For my green-eyed vixen," Matt had said before he kissed me breathless.

I still had that ring. Carried it with me everywhere, in fact. I slipped my hand into the left pocket of my jeans. My seamstress had sewn a silver key ring into these, and indeed, every pair of pants I owned. A similar key ring attached the band of my emerald to the one in my pocket so I never had to go anywhere without it.

"Thank you, ma'am. Enjoy your stay." I blinked. *What ... happened? Where am I?*

Across a wide, shiny counter stood a smiling young clerk wearing a blue blazer and a name tag that said, THE FOUR SEASONS AND JUNIE TAYLOR WELCOME YOU. In my hand I held a receipt for room 219 and the key card.

# CHAPTER FOUR

*H*oly crap, I've had another blackout! But as soon as the suspicion hit me I knew otherwise. I hadn't experienced the usual warning signs, and I'd never before left my mind in a daydream while the rest of me got busy. This was something new. Something scary. Because after the knock-down drag-out with the Tor-al-Degan, I thought I'd kicked those nutty little habits that made me seem, well, nuts. Okay, the card shuffling kept up without much of a break. And sometimes words still ran loops around my brain until I forced them back on the road. But those moments were rarer now. And the blackouts really had stopped, along with the dread that someone I knew would find reason to recommend an asylum and a heavy dose of Zoloft.

Familiar laughter caught my attention. The couple from the beach. They were here, just entering an elevator. Without conscious thought I'd followed them to their hotel and booked a room. I checked the receipt. At least I'd used my personal credit card. If I'd had to explain this to Pete, well, maybe I could've come up with something. But I probably would've just resigned.

I shoved the stuff the clerk had handed me into my back pocket and strode outside. I needed to do something concrete. Something to bring me back to myself. So I phoned my sister.

"Evie?"

"Oh, Jaz, I'm so glad you called."

"You sound tired."

"I am. E.J. has hardly stopped crying all day. This doesn't seem right, does it?"

*Hell no! But then I'm the least qualified to say.* "Did you call the pediatrician?"

"No. I know he'll just say it's that colic." Her voice started to shake. "I just feel like such a terrible mother that I can't make her stop crying!"

Now here was something I could deal with. "Evie, you are an awesome mother. This I can tell you from experience. I've seen you in action. Plus, I have had a crappy mother. So I know what I'm saying here. You rock. It's tough on you guys having a baby who cries all the time. The lack of sleep alone is probably making you a little crazy. I'm still kinda grouchy and I've only been gone, what, a couple of days? But listen, you will figure this out, okay?"

Big pause. "O-kay."

"Did I say something wrong?"

"It's just . . . usually you tell me what to do. Then I do it, and things get better."

"That was before you started playing out of my league," I said, smiling when I heard her soft laughter. "Just . . . trust yourself, okay? You and Tim know E.J. better than anybody, including the pediatrician. And get some sleep, would you? You're going to have bags under your eyes that you'll be able to store your winter clothes in."

"Okay. How are things going with you?"

*Well, let's see. I think my vampire boss should pose for his own calendar and I'm having a crazy-daisy relapse. Otherwise —* "I'm doing okay. Call me when you can, okay?"

"Okay. Love you."

"Love you too."

Feeling somewhat rebalanced now that I'd touched base with the most stable person I knew, I walked around to the back of the building, which faced the festival site. As I wound my way through the first tier of cars in the parking lot, a green glow near some fencing that disguised a large garbage bin distracted me from my inner teeth gnashing. It didn't mesh with the white of the lot lights. I drew Grief and chambered a round. The glow brightened, changing color from pine needles to ripe limes.

I closed my eyes tight for a couple of seconds, activating the night-vision contacts Bergman had designed for me. They combined with my Sensitivity-upgraded sight to show me a greenish gold figure standing beside the fence. It faced me, but leaned over every few seconds, fully engrossed in whatever lay at its feet. Oddly, a black frame surrounded it, as if someone had outlined it with a Sharpie.

I moved closer, sliding past the dark hulks of parked vehicles, taking quick glances every few steps, trying to identify the thing on the ground that acted as both the source of the green glow and the subject of the outlined figure's interest. When I finally caught a glance, I bit my lip to keep from gasping. It was the body of the security guard, the one who'd been hanging out with the two-faced man. *His* face, a twisted photo of his last tortured moments, warned me not to look any further. But I had to. One of the suckier parts of my job.

*Okay, enough with the procrastinating. You're at a possible murder scene with a potential suspect. Look at the body already.*

Blood, everywhere, as if someone had tapped a geyser. Exposed ribs. Dark, glistening organs. Someone had ripped this guy's chest open from neck to navel! The smell, damn, you just never get used to it. And thank God we were outside; otherwise I'd be puking like a bulimic after an Oreo cookie binge. Above it all hovered a jeweled cloud I could only think of as his soul. I wanted to regard it as untouched. The one part of the man his murderer couldn't soil. But I could not. Because this is what had his killer's attention.

No doubt, the one who'd taken his life stood right next to him still, and had been all day, posing as a man with only one face. "Man" was the wrong descriptor though. That outline—nobody I'd ever met had that. And when he leaned over, the frame split at his head and his fingers, allowing some of the greenish gold of his inner aura to seep through.

His mouth opened wide and from it unrolled a huge pink tongue covered with spikelike appendages. He ran it along the length of the dead man's soul. It shivered, frantically trying to fly apart, to meld with his family, his friends, his Maker. But the spikes released some sort of glue that forced the jewels into immobility. At the same time the soul cloud bleached to pastel.

The two-faced man looked up, his eyes closed, ecstasy lifting the corners of his flabby lips. And then a third eye opened on his forehead—a large, emerald-green eye that darkened at the same rate at which the dead man's soul lightened. *Coincidence? I don't think so.*

I'd had enough.

I stepped forward, skirted the bumper of an Eldorado Coupe, and trained my gun on the monster's face.

"Dinner's over, pissant."

The two-faced man opened his regular eyes, which were blue, took one long look at me, and growled.

"Give me a break," I drawled, sounding oh-so-bored though my stomach spun like a roulette wheel. "I know special-effects guys who can produce scarier roars than that." Okay, I don't really *know* any, but I've watched *Resident Evil*, haven't I?

This time he bellowed, and I admit, it gave me something of a chill. But it didn't freeze me like it was intended to. I was ready when he charged, leaping over the body like some meat-hoarding gorilla, his hands stretched wide, a full set of lethal-looking claws appearing and disappearing as he moved. If he raked those vein-poppers across my throat while they were just fingernails, would they still leave stitch-worthy gashes?

Not something I wanted to find out. I fired five shots in quick succession. They staggered him, though I could see the black outline had worked as a shield, preventing them from delivering any fatal wounds. Five more shots backed him up, almost to the body. Thanks to Bergman's modifications I still had five left. And I intended to make them count.

As he moved on me again, I concentrated on the breaks in his shield. They came and went in rapid succession, but I noticed a pattern based on his movements. It helped that he approached more warily this time. Apparently it still hurt to be shot. I should be thankful, but small favors sometimes suck.

I watched his face, waiting for the blur and the accompanying break in his shield. There!

I fired once, but the shield had already closed. I would have to anticipate the breaks, rather than wait for them to reveal themselves. Four rounds left. I took careful aim and fired. One. Two. Three. Four. Damn! The timing just missed with every shot. And now I'd used the last of my ammunition. If Grief didn't work in gun mode I didn't anticipate much success from it as a crossbow. I holstered my weapon.

But I was still armed.

Unlike Vayl, I don't use blades as a rule. Generally if I have to get that close to a target, something's gone terribly wrong. Same deal defensively speaking. Still, I keep one on me. My nod to the wisdom of weapons redundancy.

My backup plan started life as a bolo. It had been issued to the first of my military ancestors, Samuel Parks, before he marched off to war in 1917. Handed down father to son since that time, the ugly old knife had lost its appeal for David after Mom threw it at Dad upon finding him on top of her best pal. Since it had sailed clear through the bedroom window on that occasion, I'd discovered it on the lawn the next morning. Thus, it came to me.

I carry the knife, sheath and all, in a special pocket designed for near invisibility by my seamstress, Mistress Kiss My Ass. I call her this because it's the response she gives me every time I call and say, "Sherry Lynn, guess what. I just got a new pair of pants!"

Reaching into my pocket, I grabbed the artfully disguised hilt and pulled. A blade the length of my shin slid out. Originally meant more as an all-purpose tool, the bolo had been refined to my needs thanks to Bergman. Now it was sharp enough to cut metal or, better yet, defend my life.

The creature circled me, looking a lot less intimidated by Great-Great-Grandpa's knife than I would've liked. *Well, screw it.* I ran straight at him, yelling like a pissed-off soccer mom, waving my blade like a samurai warrior. I faked left, right, left, watching as his shield opened wider and wider. It couldn't keep up with his bobbing head as he tried to avoid getting his throat cut. One more feint and I jumped forward, burying my blade in the shield gap his movements had caused.

He died instantly.

I pulled my weapon free and cleaned it on his stolen uniform. Glad the bolo had saved me. Sorry the same family had subjected it to nearly one hundred years of blood and guts. We seem to spawn killers, no doubt about that. I found myself hoping hard that E.J. could break that chain. Maybe when I got a free second I'd give her a call and make that suggestion. Never mind that she was less than a month old and would spend the entire time trying to eat the receiver. It's never too early to start brainwashing your young.

# Chapter Five

As I leaned over the body, trying to figure out what I'd just killed, Vayl stepped from the shadows, our crew dogging his heels. I looked up, surprised to see them. "I had a feeling you might need some assistance," Vayl said.

"You did?" *Oh.* "Of course you did." Ever since he'd taken my blood, Vayl could sense strong feelings in me, apparently at some distance. I thought he was referring to that until he nodded at the ring on my finger.

"Cirilai gave me the impression you were fighting."

"He rushed us all over here; then he wouldn't let us help," Cole told me apologetically. "Said we might distract you at the wrong time. But we had your back!"

I nodded my gratitude.

Bergman crouched beside me, prodded the two-faced corpse's third eye open with the clicky end of one of the pens he usually kept stuck in the pocket of his shirt. "What the heck is this?" he wondered aloud.

"I don't know, but keep that eye open," I told him. The color leeched out of it even as the murdered guard's soul brightened. Soon it was the forest green that had caught my attention to start with. It shivered for another tense moment, then split into hundreds of tiny pieces that whizzed off into the night.

"Cool," I whispered.

"I don't know," said Cassandra. "I'm thinking more along the lines of stomach churning." She stared at Bergman, who'd dug out another pen and used it to roll the spiked tongue out of the monster's mouth.

"What does the *Enkyklios* say about that?" he asked, his eyes shifting to the multileveled collection of bluish gold orbs in Cassandra's hand.

"Nothing yet," she answered defensively, "but it will. *Propheneum*," she said sharply. A single orb rolled to the top of the marble plateau. She began reciting the battle as she'd witnessed it, asking me for details here and there. When she'd finished, Cassandra said, *"Daya ango le che le, Enkyklios occsallio terat."* The marbles rearranged themselves, always touching, never falling, until a new globe sat on top of the plateau with the one we'd just recorded my story into.

"What did you just do?" Bergman asked, his eyes darting from the *Enkyklios* to Cassandra as if one or both of them might suddenly explode.

"Cross-referencing," she said shortly. "Now we will see what is already on record." She touched the new orb, pressing hard enough to make a temporary indent, and said, *"Dayavatem."* Then she held the magical library at arm's length while the home movies began.

At first, all we saw was a blinking light, as if the orb's eyelids were just fluttering open. Then, *voila*, full color and sound poured from it, the images so detailed it didn't seem like she should be able to hold them in her hands.

Dark gray clouds scudded across the sky. A wild wind tossed the green-leafed trees, making them look as grim as the elderly couple who bumped along the rutted road in their fancy carriage. Had they just come from a funeral? Their black clothing led me to think so, though for all I knew they'd dressed for the opera. Suddenly the gentleman reigned in the horses and both he and the wife looked to their left, a dawning horror stretching their faces.

As if sensing my frustration, the cause of their consternation came into view. A mounted bandit wearing a black tricorn. His dirty brown jacket covered a stained white shirt and even more blemished brown breeches, and his battered riding boots were falling apart at the seams. He brandished a rusted gun that seemed more likely to blow his own hand off than injure the person it threatened. A dirty red kerchief hid the lower third of his face.

"Gimme yer valuables!" he snarled. The couple snapped to, laying a load of jewelry and cash into the hat he held out to them. He had to lean over to collect his loot, and when he sat back up in the saddle the kerchief slipped off his face.

"Randy," gasped the woman, "how *could* you?"

"Goddammit!" swore the bandit. "Now I have ter kill ye!"

The old man stood up. "No, wait!"

Randy leveled his gun, but before he could fire, another rider came into view, pulling up so hard that clods of dirt flew and a cloud of dust lifted at his arrival. He'd run his horse so fast its sweat-soaked flanks heaved as it panted for air.

The man himself looked harmless enough. If you had to pick him out of a lineup you'd say, "No, he couldn't have beaten that poor woman over the head with a tire iron. He must be the desk sergeant you slipped in there to fool the witness." He did have the broad-shouldered, straight-faced, lean-on-me look of the dependable cop. But when he turned his head to wink at the old folks, it blurred, as if another face hid behind the one he showed the world.

"Who er you?" Randy demanded.

The man grinned, exposing crooked yellow teeth and a hint of something horrid lurking behind them. "My name is Frederick

Wyatt, and I am a great admirer of yours. Ah, Randy"—he rolled the R around his mouth as if it tasted like chocolate—"someday you will provide me with such pleasures. But just now, I have a job to do. So off with you. Shoo!" He smiled as a third eye opened in the middle of his forehead, making Randy scream like a kid in a haunted house. The bandit wheeled his horse around and galloped away.

When Wyatt turned to the couple, that extra sphere rolling gleefully in its socket as it beheld their terrified faces, I thought the old guy was going to have a heart attack. He slapped his right hand to his chest and fell back in his seat, his hat flying out the rear of the carriage as his wife screamed and screamed.

"Shut up, you old bat!" Wyatt kicked his horse forward so he could slap her across the face, leaving a thin line of blood on her cheekbone.

It didn't work. She just shrieked louder. "Run, Joshua, run! It is Satan made flesh!" They rolled out of their seats onto the floor of the carriage. From there they dropped to the ground. But Wyatt hemmed them in with his horse, edging those sharpened steel hooves close enough to keep them pinned beside the back wheel.

"I feel I must correct you," he said. "I am, in fact, only a servant of the Great Taker. Though we reavers are his favorites." He chuckled fondly as he dismounted. I expected the horse to wander off, but it stayed close, dripping globs of sweat and stringy bits of spit all over Joshua's bald head. The reaver went to the old gal and lifted her by the scruff of the neck.

"Now, you stop flailing and shut it tight, or I'll rip your lungs out and call it self-defense," he said, throwing her back into the carriage and returning for her husband.

The picture froze just as Wyatt sunk his hands/claws into Joshua's chest.

"I fainted then," said the tired, hopeless voice of Joshua's widow. "The next thing I knew . . ."

Wyatt had remounted. Joshua's body lay across his legs, his chest torn open, his soul struggling for freedom as the reaver bent to run his spiked tongue over it. As I'd just witnessed, the soul slowly drained of color even as the reaver's third eye filled. In the end, the husk of Joshua's soul disintegrated, falling back into his body, which jerked eerily at the impact.

Another fade to black, this time with no accompanying narration. *Poor woman.* My mind would supply no other thought. *Poor, poor woman.*

When she came to again, the woman had been moved, along with her carriage, to the site of an old, abandoned cemetery. Tombstones peered through long tufts of grass. Most of them leaned hard to the left, as if a gigantic pissed-off chess player had tried to clear the board before stomping off into the hills beyond.

Wyatt spurred his horse to the middle of the stones, reached into the corpse's chest, yanked out the heart, and fastballed it at a vine-covered tree stump. When the vines blackened and crumbled, I realized the stump was actually a tall, spire-shaped monument.

The woman hadn't made a sound since the reaver's threat to her life. In fact, I figured she was nearly catatonic by now.

But when the heart hit that stone and shattered, and the etchings began to ooze thick gobbets of blood down the white marble, she moaned like a dying animal. I reluctantly acknowledged a growing feeling of we're-so-screwed as my hands itched for my playing cards. I'd left them in the RV. *For the last time,* I vowed. *This is some sick shit we've stepped into.*

As soon as the blood touched the ground it solidified, growing, building into a fence, a wall, an arched doorway that pulsed like a gigantic aorta. The reaver rode up to it, tossing Joshua's body aside as he went. A smaller, fist-sized door within the door appeared in the middle about three-quarters of the way up. Wyatt leaned toward it, his saddle creaking eerily as he moved. The small door flew open with a *bang*! Out of it shot a thick, sinewy, red tentacle covered with tiny suction cups. It latched on to the reaver's third eye and yanked, making the reaver scream and pound his fists on the door.

Eventually the eye gave and the tentacle retreated with it, slamming the small door behind it. Wyatt leaned his bleeding forehead against the big door for several minutes while the stunned old woman looked on. Then it turned to her. "I cannot take your life," it said in a fearfully joyous voice, "but I find I have need of your eye."

The picture faded as he advanced on her, grinning malevolently.

But we weren't done. Next came a slide show narrated by a woman whose delivery reminded me of all the times I'd slept through Environmental Biology.

"This is the only visual record we have of a reaver," the professor said blandly as a still shot of Frederick Wyatt appeared. "Our research tells us they are parasitic fiends, which must find host bodies in order to move among humans. The reaver's sole purpose is to rip souls from hapless victims and transfer them to the netherworld. This is not a random occurrence, but one governed by rules wherein the murder must either be commissioned by an enemy of the victim, or perpetrated by one human against another. In the latter case, the reaver acts as a scavenger, snagging the soul before it can release.

"Reavers are known to run singly and in packs and can often be found traveling on the shirttails of human evildoers. The reaver is extremely difficult to vanquish. In fact, all sources recommend the wisest tactic when encountering such is to retreat. Quickly. Please note: True Believers are somewhat immune to their powers. See also, Holy Dagger of Anan. See also, Reaver Pack Tactics."

The picture faded to black this time. Bergman watched the *Enkyklios* nervously, as if at any moment some new horror flick might leap out of it. He scanned the parking lot, looked over each shoulder repeatedly. "I don't *see* a pack."

"I do not think there is one," said Vayl.

"Why?" demanded Bergman.

"Because if there were, we would have been attacked by now."

"Oh. Well, if you don't mind, I'm still going to set up the security system I brought for the RV. Just in case the pack is back at the watering hole." On a snide scale of one to ten, I'd say Bergman had just hit a 7.5, which meant he was one scared puppy. I held my breath, waiting to see if Vayl understood Bergman would chill as soon he'd put the system into place, or if he'd take offense, in which case I'd be spending the rest of the night soothing ruffled feathers. Not my strong suit, which was why it would take so long.

"I approve your plan," said Vayl, watching with one eyebrow slightly cocked as Bergman threw the pens in the Dumpster and headed back to the RV. Luckily he had no idea Vayl was broadcasting his I'd-love-to-knock-your-block-off expression. Cassandra seemed to have more of a clue. After a moment during which she considered Vayl with a look of mounting alarm, Cassandra followed Bergman. She caught up to him within fifteen seconds and moments later they were deep in conversation.

The rest of us stared down at the two bodies. Finally Vayl said, "Cole, call the office. I believe it would be best if our people disposed of these. There is no need for it to become common knowledge that Jasmine knows how to kill reavers."

*Capital idea, Sherlock. Let's not make them think they have to terminate me before I have time to organize a How-to-Stab-a-Reaver Workshop.*

Cole nodded and took out his cell phone.

"Hang on," I said. I bent down and slipped the two-faced man's watch off his wrist. At the guys' puzzled and somewhat grossed-out glances I said, "I wouldn't ask Cassandra to touch the body, or even this, if I could help it." Psychics had been known to lose their minds when they came into contact with the belongings of known murderers. "But if we get desperate, we may ask her to touch this. See what it can tell her about this monster, where it came from and why."

Vayl said, "All right, but only if we must."

# Chapter Six

I'd gotten into a bad habit while staying with Evie, Tim, and E.J. I blamed it on the baby. If she'd slept through the night even once I wouldn't have needed multiple naps to make up for the 2:00 a.m. feedings. (Tim and Evie had taken all the other shifts, so I shouldn't complain. But I did anyway.) During the three weeks I stayed with them, I'd developed the ability to fall asleep anytime, anywhere. Waiting in line at the DMV. On the floor while Evie and I played with E.J.'s toys and pretended it was all for the baby's benefit. Once on the toilet.

I hadn't quite shaken the habit by the time we'd reached Corpus Christi. As soon as we entered the RV and I felt this immense exhaustion creep over me, I figured I'd better grab forty winks before somebody caught me snoozing on the crapper.

"Do you want to discuss tonight's plan?" asked Vayl.

"Yeah, absolutely, but you know what? I need to freshen up first. Give me five minutes?"

"Take all the time you need," Vayl said gently. "We will finish the tent while you recoup." *He's not really being nice. He just wants me fresh for later on. It's going to be a demanding couple of hours.* That's what I told myself. But I still felt warmed as I went to the back of the RV, stretched out on the queen-size, and almost totally avoided thinking about how big and empty it felt.

"No more beds for me," I murmured into the pillow. "I'm switching to hammocks when I get home. Who could be lonely and depressed sleeping in a hammock?"

Jasmine, wake up!"

The hammock I snoozed in jiggled and swung so drastically I was either going to fall out or puke. Or both. I opened my eyes. Oh wait, never mind the hammock. I was still in bed. I checked my watch. I'd only been asleep for eight minutes.

"What the hell —?" I demanded irritably.

"Shush," David hissed. "We don't have much time. They're coming." Weird. I'd thought he was thousands of miles away, kicking terrorist ass somewhere in the Middle East. But here he stood, his urgency catching more easily than the chicken pox.

I jumped out of bed, knowing he was absolutely right. And I knew who "they" were too. A nest of newbie vamps and their surviving human guardians, all severely pissed that we'd killed their leaders, the ones we called vultures.

I followed him out of the RV, my eyes searching the empty beach and the swarming festival site. I couldn't see them, but they were out there. Their *other*ness combined with their evil intent to send waves of psychic stench ahead of them, making my stomach churn.

We conferred in front of the RV. "We have to lure them away from here," he said. "Otherwise Jesse and Matt are goners."

The thought sent a shaft of alarm through me. If either of them was hurt, I'd never forgive myself. Moving in concert, we ran west, across the last strip of grassy slope nobody had covered with some commercial venture. We jumped a low concrete wall and dove onto an undeveloped section of beach. Here the grass grew almost as high as our heads. We plowed through it, dodging mounds of trash, jumping the pilings from a crumbling pier that had been built for higher water. Soon we heard them behind us, stumbling, cursing, moving like a herd of buffalo. I actually thought we could outrun them. Then we emerged from the grass to find a swampy inlet blocking our forward progress.

We looked at each other grimly. Out of choices, we turned south, wading into the moonlit water of the Gulf, counting on it to slow the attack, give us more time to load and fire. Dave raised his crossbow. I looked at it with a pang. It had been Matt's favorite, one he'd only recently abandoned. I pulled Grief from its holster and thumbed off the safety. True to form, the humans appeared first, sprinting into the clearing between the grass and water as if they too had expected a more protracted chase.

I mowed them down like ducks at a carnival.

The vamps came more warily, spreading out in the grass, surveying the battlefield, yelling directions to each other. I pushed Grief's magic button and—presto change-o—my gun transformed into a miniature crossbow.

David and I stood shoulder to shoulder, expecting a rush, trying to keep our minds empty so our training would kick in when the time came. What we didn't expect were the two vamps who came strolling toward the edge of the water, holding hands like creepy Hansel and Gretel. They seemed familiar, though I couldn't make out their faces at first. I could, however, smell the blood. They'd been freshly turned, which was why they'd been unleashed on us. Nothing fights harder or dirtier than a newborn vamp.

"Oh my God," Dave moaned, dropping his crossbow.

"David, don't—" I followed his eyes to the approaching vampires. His wife, Jesse, and my Matt stood gazing at us, their faces set in that flat, otherworldly look that signals the loss of a soul.

"Matt," I whispered.

He heard me. Of course, he could hear ice cubes melting too. "Jasmine." The way he said my name, as if it was a foreign language to him, broke my heart.

"We shouldn't have left them." Tears coated David's words.

"They should've come with us," I said, my voice curiously harsh and unforgiving in my own ears.

"It's your fault!" David turned on me. He grabbed Grief from my hand. Pointed it right at my forehead.

Inside, a part of me broke. And I knew nothing he did or said could ever fix it.

Another part of me thought how remarkable it was that, after all those who'd tried to kill me so far, my twin would be the one to finally get it done.

"JASMINE!" Startled, I looked back toward the beach. Bergman, Cassandra, and Cole huddled together there, like they needed each other's body heat to keep from freezing to death. Vayl waded into the water. The whites of his eyes made a shocking counterpoint to the blacks of his irises. I'd never seen him so shaken. He held out a hand that trembled ever so slightly as he said, "Please, Jasmine, please, give me the gun."

And that's when I realized I'd been dreaming. David hadn't set foot in the States in over a year. Matt and Jesse were dead. And I was holding my own gun to my head.

# Chapter Seven

I lowered my arm, thumbed the safety, and set Grief in Vayl's outstretched hand. As soon as I let it go he pulled me into his arms. It didn't feel so much like a hug as it did a straitjacket. *Don't move, you crazy fool.*

"Jasmine, I never knew you felt so desperate. You should have spoken to me. I would have helped you. I am your *sverhamin*." As if that explained everything. After a few moments of escalating struggles, I disengaged from Vayl's embrace. I didn't like his tone. It was too . . . freaked. And Vayl never freaked. Never.

I said, "I know what it looked like, but I wasn't trying to kill myself. It was a dream."

"You mean, you were sleepwalking?"

"Looks like it." *Be calm. Pretend that wasn't the most insane thing you've done so far. And, for God's sake, shut off that Pink Floyd soundtrack in your sick, twisted brain.* But no matter how hard I tried, I kept hearing the song "Brain Damage" and Roger Waters crooning, "*The lunatic is in my head.*"

We'd made shore. Cole, Bergman, and Cassandra turned to lead Vayl and me back to the RV.

"I've heard of sleepwalkers acting out their dreams like that. There's a name for it," Bergman offered.

"There's a name for everything," I said dryly. I sounded calm, but inside my psyche had drawn up with a *snap!* The normal order had, once again, gotten all mangled in Jazland. Only this time I couldn't hide it from my coworkers and pretend all was right with the world. *Damn, damn, damn . . .* I bit my lip. *Okay, Jaz, you are now in damage-control mode. That means you may not flip out all the way. No word looping. No blackouts. And no card shuffling—until you're alone. At which time if you want to swing from the chandelier and bark like a German shepherd, go right ahead. Until then—play sane.*

Inside the RV, several cups sat on the table, but someone had dropped a pile of paper plates on the floor. I retrieved them, set them on the counter beside the sink, and headed toward the shower.

"Jasmine," Vayl said softly. I turned around. He remained on the entry steps, trying not to drip onto the carpet. He'd let the others come in before him, and they huddled together between Mary-Kate and Ashley, staring at me with varying expressions of concern. The kids looked achingly normal. A multicolored hair band held Cassandra's braids away from her face. She wore at least five pairs of gold earrings, the biggest of which reached the shoulders of her teal-blue knit blouse. Her black peasant skirt touched her ankles and she wore matching black pumps edged with blue ribbon. Bergman's gray sweater with its stretched sleeves topped old blue jeans and the same snow boots he'd worn when they'd picked me up at Evie's house. Cole wore his red high-tops, khakis, and a black T-shirt with a pile of lumber on it. The caption underneath read *Hey Lady, Need A Stud?*

"What is it, Vayl?" I asked.

"What just happened was not mere sleepwalking. Your finger was pressed against the trigger of a cocked crossbow. We cannot simply disregard this problem and hope it goes away."

So, okay, I did want to say, *We can so ignore this!* But I knew he was right. What if I'd come awake with that gun pointed at

Cassandra's head? Or one of the guys'? I nodded. "What do you suggest?"

That's where speech failed him. Cassandra waited a moment, and when it was clear he didn't have an immediate plan, she stepped up. "I know someone who might be able to help."

"Okay, when this mission is over—"

"Actually, he lives in New Mexico. He could probably meet you tomorrow."

"Is he a doctor?"

"Of a sort."

*Alternative medicine. Okay, I can deal with that.* "Fine, set it up."

"And . . ." Cole began.

I swallowed the urge to snap. They just wanted to help. It wasn't their fault the idea of getting to the root of this bizarre behavior terrified me. In my point of view, any explanation of what causes a person to point a gun to her own head is not going to start with "Good news, Jaz—" But considering the current potential for a bolt to my brain, pretending it never happened wasn't the smartest tactic I could choose. "Yes?"

"Until we're sure how to deal with this, someone should guard you while you sleep."

"Naturally. You can all draw straws or something. And stop with the war orphan faces, will you? I'll deal."

"Of course you will," said Bergman. "You're Jaz."

I nodded, appreciating his vote of confidence. Unlike Bergman, however, I knew my limits. Sometimes I could see that line in my mind, a stark black wall at the horizon reminding me that sanity, unlike the earth, is flat. And there is a point at which you can fall off. I just hoped this dream didn't mean I already stood on the wrong side of the gate.

# CHAPTER EIGHT

E vie had bought me the outfit I changed into after my shower, a white scoop-neck peasant top with lace and crochet accents and a pair of jeans somebody had beaten soundly with a jackhammer before forwarding to the retailer. So I knew I looked good. My girl's got an eye for these things. Plus—übercomfy. And not just because she knows my size. There's something about stuff from your family. For instance, when I'm home, I sleep under a comforter Granny May made for me. Ugliest damn blanket I have ever seen. But it makes me feel better to snuggle under fabric and thread she put together to warm me. Evie's outfit, Granny's blanket—they're part of the basic core of my life that assures me I matter.

For the same reasons, Bergman handpicked where his inventions traveled and who put them to bed at night. And the more I learned about the freak who'd stolen his baby, the less I blamed Miles for totally losing it when he'd found out the baby had been kidnapped. Because after spending Vayl's shower time with my face in my laptop, reading the file some intrepid agent had gathered on this guy Chien-Lung, I had come to a single conclusion. The guy was a total whack-job.

Frankly it made me feel better about my own peculiarities. But there was a method to Lung's madness. For instance, dragons are deeply revered by the Chinese. According to legend they have megapowers that include weather control and life creation. And they're seen as kind, benevolent creatures. Funny. Every fairy tale *I'd* ever heard involving dragons starred daring knights trotting off to kill said dragons. Probably the real reason every time East meets West they get pissed off and throw tea in our faces.

Vayl came out of the shower wearing jeans and a hunter green T-shirt. "Where is everyone?" he asked.

"The guys went back to the tent raising and Cassandra decided to supervise so Cole wouldn't be tempted to clonk Bergman over the head with a stray pole." Which was when I realized we were all alone.

"I was just researching Chien-Lung," I said quickly, motioning to the laptop on the table in front of me. "I guess when he didn't actually turn into a dragon he decided to settle for second best and go for the armor."

Vayl raised an eyebrow. "From the sound of it, I would hardly describe the armor as second best."

"No, that's not really how Bergman operates, is it?"

Vayl sank onto the banquette beside me and sighed. "We are not going to talk about this sleepwalking issue, are we?"

"Nothing to discuss. I'm seeing Cassandra's guy tomorrow. He's going to slap me with a cure. *Bam*. I'm ready to roll."

"Do you understand how few things actually get accomplished with a *bam*?"

"You've never watched *The Flintstones*, have you?"

Twitch of the lip. For him it was practically a giggle. "Fair enough. Let us talk about work then."

"Okay. Just how were you planning to take out an ancient vampire wearing invincible armor?"

"The simplest approach would be to find his resting place.

When dawn breaks, he dies, so the armor automatically detaches. We pull it free and then smoke him like a Cuban cigar." He said it with such zest I could imagine him sitting on the balcony of some Caribbean villa, sharing a hand-rolled cancer-carrot with Hemingway while they mused over the aroma of vaporized vampire and discussed which shoes to wear for the next running of the bulls.

I snorted. "Sometimes you are about as PC as Peter Griffin."

"Who?"

"This cartoon guy . . . Never mind. I am curious, though. You did notice that the majority of people are against smoking these days, yes?"

"Yes. And a good thing too. We used to lose houses and barns left and right to careless smokers. Now it is usually just faulty wiring or children with fire fetishes. I imagine the rate of fire loss has dropped drastically since smoking became so unpopular."

I crossed my arms, pursed my lips, and nodded through his entire statement. As hard as I stared I could not unearth a single twitch of the lip. Vayl seemed absolutely sincere. But really, what did a guy who could live forever under the right circumstances care about malignancy?

"You know what," I said. "Your get-him-while-he's-zonked idea seems solid. And yet I'm thinking if it had a chance, somebody would've made it work a long time ago."

Vayl held up a finger. "Ah, but you see, this somebody you speak of never had you." He pointed the finger at me and I still had to fight the urge to look over my shoulder. *Who, me?*

"Vayl—"

"Tonight we will scout out the most likely locations. And then tomorrow you and Cole will revisit those locations as well as any others you can think of. If you sense any vampires—what is that word? — Ah, yes: *bam*."

# Chapter Nine

Vayl and I left the RV thinking we'd check out the Chinese acrobats' camp. Lung housed his employees in RVs like ours. Okay, not like ours. Like regular-people versions of ours. They stood in neat rows behind the inflatable stadium. Maybe Lung had his own little pop-up tent set up in one of their bedrooms. Okay, highly unlikely. But it was a place to start.

We were distracted almost immediately by loud talk and even louder laughter coming from the site of our soon-to-be Psychics-R-Us extravaganza. Upon further investigation, we discovered our crew had made friends with three of the barbecue cook-off chefs, who'd brought over a cooler full of beer, some lawn chairs, and quite a bit of friendly advice.

"I'll tell you what," said one big-bellied gentleman as he leaned over a pile of poles, his tooled leather belt waging a heroic struggle to keep his butt crack at a PG rating. "I believe they used this very same tent as headquarters for the 82nd Airborne during World War II."

"I get it: it's old," said Cole with his good-natured grin. "Now, I told you my three-breasted tennis star joke, which fulfills my end of the bargain. So it's your turn, Steve." He grabbed a section of canvas and held it to his chest. "Is she gonna live?"

"Oh yeah, we'll get her up. But I think we're gonna need help." He turned to his buddies. "Hube! Is Larry still awake?" One of the seated gentlemen took a swig of beer and turned toward his companion, a red-faced guy whose goatee worked mainly to divide his puffy cheeks from his bloated neck.

"Didn't he have to go somewhere?" Hube asked him.

"Yeah," replied Goatee Guy, "his sister called. She had some weird, last-minute catering job right around here. I guess this Chinese fella, you know, the one in charge of the acrobat show? He's having a big party and his cook's stuck in Chicago. But get this: The party doesn't start until one a.m. So Larry's gotta help her get the food done, set it all up, and then get out before the guests arrive."

"That doesn't sound so bad," said Hube. "At least she doesn't have to serve it."

"Nope, but she's gotta get it there."

"Where's there?"

Goatee Guy twisted in his chair, making it creak so loudly I was pretty sure it had just reached its maximum-weight capacity. He pointed to a large white yacht floating serenely on the water. "Should be a helluva party," he commented. "They ordered escargot."

Vayl and I nosed-to-nosed next to the RV like a couple of gossips at the beauty parlor. "Did you hear what he said?" I hissed.

"Of course I heard what he said. I am a vampire!"

"Are you getting snippy with me?"

"Maybe, but if I am it is because I dislike obvious questions."

*Oh really?* "Are you thinking what I'm thinking?"

"I have no idea."

"We need to get hold of this caterer. Get onto the yacht with her. See if Lung's got himself a daytime hidey-hole somewhere aboard. And then plant some cameras."

"It looks as if I was thinking what you were thinking."

"Actually, you weren't. I was really thinking I needed to ask you a question."

"What was that?"

"Do you think we should ask Goatee Guy how to find the caterer?" I smiled at him innocently as his eyebrows practically met above his nose.

"I am never going to share my pet peeves with you again."

"Should we ask Bergman to get a few cameras ready for us?"

"Jasmine!"

"Maybe break out those nifty communications devices so you and I can talk even if we end up in different rooms?"

It happened so suddenly I didn't even have a chance to react. One second Vayl was glowering at me, practically speechless with annoyance, and I was feeling all righteous and superior. The next moment his lips were on mine. As kisses went, it barely qualified. Just a quick brush of the lips and a swift withdrawal. But the gesture left me gasping.

"That will teach you for pushing a vampire over his limit," Vayl said, the huskiness of his voice a stark counterpoint to the sternness in his eyes. The words combined with that look to transport me back to our fourth mission together.

We'd been assigned to eliminate a vampire named Leonard Potts, who'd made himself a small fortune smuggling his own kind into the States. It's so tough for *others* to legally immigrate that creature smuggling is quite the booming trade. However it's not a killable offense. Unless you're providing your clients with innocent civilians to snack on as soon as they make landfall. To be honest, it probably still would've remained a local issue if Potts had just grabbed homeless people and the occasional stray tourist. But when he hooked a cabinet member's daughter, he wrote himself a one-way ticket to Smokesville.

As we prepared to confront Potts in his Connecticut Colonial, Vayl warned me to keep it low-key. "I do not understand why you like to enrage our targets before we eliminate them, but in this case I would appreciate a little self-control. Potts is a known coward. He will probably go down easily as long as you do not goad him."

I went in with good intentions. But when I saw him lounging on his chaise, watching David Letterman while a couple of his clients slurped at the girl like she was a strawberry shake, I forgot myself.

"He's mine," I growled, leaving Vayl to deal with the hungry vamps while I zeroed in on Potts, who was just now rising from the lounge, the first vamp I'd ever confronted who actually looked scared to see me.

"So what is it with you?" I asked him, coming in close enough to shove him back down to his seat. "Like messing with defenseless women, do you?" I shoved him again. His feet came up and he flew backward, tumbling off the chaise. When he got up he looked pissed. I didn't really care. I could hear fighting behind me. I figured Vayl was winning, but I wasn't worried about that either.

"Who are you?" Potts demanded. "What are you doing in my house?"

"We're just a couple of drifters looking for some action," I told him.

"Look"—I held up my hands—"no weapons. So come on, ya big brave vampire. Show me what a badass you really are."

He leaped over the chaise. I wished for a second I had vamp strength so I could meet him head-on. Bash that complacent look right off his face. I dodged at the last second, not soon enough to escape a blow from his right fist, which sent me staggering into the wall. But I'd landed one myself, a kick to the shoulder that left it sagging.

"Jasmine!" Vayl yelled. "This is not a boxing match! Smoke him!"

The girl moaned from where they'd dropped her on the floor. She was so covered in bites it looked like she'd been dog-mauled. No way would she survive the night. It didn't seem enough to just kill the son of a bitch who'd engineered that damage. I wanted to hurt him first. Make him feel a piece of her pain.

I whirled into him, attacking with every move in my arsenal. Kicks designed to shatter bone. Punches meant to induce unconsciousness, coma, even death. I put so little effort into defense that any other vamp would've kicked my ass into the next century. But after the first couple of seconds this guy wanted nothing to do with me. Coward that he was, he covered his face and backed away, screaming, "Get out of my house, you witch!"

Thing was, once he hit the corner, realized there was nowhere left to run, he remembered I was human.

"Jasmine!" snapped Vayl. I heard the warning too late. Potts ducked inside my attack as if I was standing still. He grabbed my chin, forced my eyes to his, and started talking.

I felt the power in his words, knew his special Gift was reaching into people's minds and picking out their deepest, darkest secrets. And yet I believed everything he told me. "The government's blessing changes naught, Jaz. You are nothing more than a murderess. The bloodstains on your hands will never come clean. Because even if you could justify the villains, you will never be able to sidestep responsibility for your Helsinger crew, your sister-in-law, your fiancé. Their deaths scar your soul and you will pay and pay and pay until the end of time."

My hands dropped. I stood as helpless before him as any of his victims ever had, and the feeling chilled me to the marrow. No, wait, it was Vayl, sending a wave of his own cold power through the room, hoping maybe it would clear my mind. It worked.

I jerked my right wrist upward and the syringe of holy water I kept sheathed inside my sleeve slid smoothly to hand. A second later I'd plunged the needle deep into Potts's gut. He died writhing in pain, huge blisters rising and popping on his steaming skin before he finally exploded like he'd swallowed a grenade.

Vayl finally dispatched his last vamp and joined me where I'd collapsed on the chaise, watching dully as the cabinet member's daughter died. When he touched my leg I jerked away as if I'd been shocked.

"You are bleeding," he said.

"It's nothing."

And that's when he'd given me the look and the words he'd repeated just now, followed by round after round of missions in which I wasn't allowed to say a single thing.

*Just take out the target, Jaz,* I reminded myself again. *It's not your job to decide who needs to be punished how much. And yeah, experience has taught you that when you push a vampire past his limit* — I looked at Vayl, standing still as a painter's model, his leather coat billowing behind him, a mouthwatering mix of power, strength, and sexuality — *you're bound to get hurt.*

"What do you want to do now?" asked Vayl.

I licked my lips. He tensed, his eyes flaming to green in the mellow festival light. I turned to Goatee Guy. "Actually we're going to need a caterer pretty soon. Do you know how we can get hold of Larry and his cousin?"

# CHAPTER TEN

W e stood at the end of the pier, looking out at the yacht we'd learned Lung had bought the previous week. "If this was a James Bond movie," I said, "we'd just change into our skimpiest suits, snorkel out to the *Dragon*—"

"Because that's obviously what the boat's name would be," put in Cole.

I nodded. "We'd clamber up the side without alerting the one, sleepy guard, sneak into Chien-Lung's room—"

"And then get caught and fed to the sharks," said Bergman.

"Are there sharks in Texas?" asked Cassandra.

"There are sharks everywhere," said Vayl.

We watched the yacht's twinkling lights awhile longer. "Well, this party is never going to start without the caterers," I said, turning to eye my crew's outfits critically.

Larry's cousin, Yetta Simms, had provided them. In fact, she'd turned out to be quite the patriot. She couldn't wait to cooperate. Said she felt we'd accomplish our task much better without her folks getting in our way. So she'd handed her entire catering gig over to us. "Just remember," she'd said as she'd handed me the map she'd drawn of the bar and food tables with detailed descriptions of what went where. "Chien-Lung left strict instructions for us to be off the yacht before he and his guests arrived."

Which probably meant Lung spent his daylight hours in an entirely different location. It made sense. Even a floating palace wouldn't be able to provide a vamp with much protection against a raging fire. Underground, that's where we'd find him — if we were due a miracle anytime soon.

Though we didn't expect to make direct contact, we'd made some major changes to our looks just in case. We all wore prosthetics on our faces, which altered the shapes of our noses and chins. In addition, Bergman had chosen a cap that gave him the look of a Hair Club for Men candidate. Cassandra, Cole, and I had gone for wigs; mine was black, hers red, his sandy brown. We all wore red bandanas and pirate outfits. Not our idea. Yetta called her company Seven Seas Succulents, thus the leather vests, poofy white shirts, and tight black pants tucked into tall black boots.

Speaking of which: "I like these boots," I told Vayl. "Do you think they'd sell them to me cheap? I keep ruining mine."

"Since when do you fret over money?" he asked with amusement. "I was not even sure you knew what to do with it."

I shrugged. "A woman has needs."

"Still?" said Cole. "Gosh, Jaz, why didn't you say something to me? I'd never let you suffer."

"Be quiet and get in the boat," Vayl barked, giving Cole such a pointed look I was surprised he didn't burst a couple of vessels right then and there. We did as we were told, piling into an ancient vessel covered in flaking green paint that looked as if it would sink if one of us tapped our feet just a little too hard. The metal seats were topped by life jacket/cushions that probably came over on the *Mayflower*. Coolers, boxes, and trays filled every spare bit of space, so we squeezed in where we could, Cassandra in the middle with me, Bergman and Cole on each end. Vayl cast us off, jumping lightly into the rear of the boat as it floated away from the dock. To my relief, he didn't fall through.

The engine roared to life, sounding so powerful I was afraid it would rip the back of the vessel completely off and, like the characters in a Bugs Bunny cartoon, Vayl would ride that Evinrude clear to Brazil while the rest of us sank to the bottom of the bay, looking glum and yet somehow resigned as the last of our air seeped from our lips in perfect round bubbles. *Glug. Glug, glug.*

On second thought, if this sucker broke up I intended to leap onto Vayl's shoulders. If he had to travel all the way to South America with only his eyebrows above water, so be it. I gauged my distance, got ready to jump, and in the meantime, grabbed hold of the edge of the boat and held on tight.

Bergman said, "Vayl? Can we do one more test of the equipment?"

"We just did one on the dock," Cassandra protested.

He gave her a dirty look. "It might function differently when we're surrounded by water."

*It* was a dandy little system wherein wires, kindly sewn into our collars by our resident psychic/needlewoman, bounced some sort of wave off surrounding objects. A machine Bergman had wired to the boat then translated those signals. Ideally it would keep us from getting caught by wandering guards while we installed the surveillance cameras. We each had five of the little gadgets in our pockets, none bigger than a Tic Tac. Is it a bad thing when you need a magnifying glass to examine your examining equipment? I'm thinking maybe.

Vayl's job, besides keeping our getaway boat buoyant enough to ferry us back to shore, was to monitor the monitor. If someone was coming, he would contact us via mouth-mint, or as Bergman liked to call it, wireless oral transmitter. We each wore minute hearing aides that allowed us to receive the communication in barbershop quartet bass, while preventing us from looking like we'd spent way too much time dancing by the speakers at a KISS concert in our intrepid youths. Vayl could also receive our messages, though we'd been cautioned against blabbing any old time we felt like it. Enhanced hearing is a common vampire trait and Vayl thought maybe we should leave any stray bad guys who might be listening out of the loop.

"You know, I could probably get us all talismans that would do the same job," Cassandra said casually, glancing at Bergman out of the corner of her eye. My God, she was baiting him! Didn't she know better? Especially with him wired to blow any moment, now that his invention was in the hands of a psycho? The potential for disaster suddenly spiked to orange, the same level you get when you tell a group of prom queen candidates their shoes don't match their dresses.

Bergman's face looked like he'd just stuck it in a vacuum-pack machine. His cheekbones may have actually touched. Concerned that if he lunged for her he would either fall out of the boat or knock a hole in the bottom, I leaned forward and patted his knee. Hard.

"She's kidding, Bergman. Your inventions are essential to us."

"I was not kidding," Cassandra mumbled.

*Holy crap, what has gotten into her tonight? It's the pirate outfit; I just know it.* "Cassandra," I mumbled back, "I know you're, like, a millennia older than me. But trust me, this is not the time for a magic versus machine debate. Bergman is not a cat you want to poke with a stick right now."

"Not even a little?"

With my lips still burning from my recent vamp teasing I said earnestly, "Not even."

"Jaz, look." Cole pointed to Chien-Lung's yacht as we pulled up beside her. Big black letters spelled out the name *"Constance Malloy."* "I didn't expect that, did you?"

"Hmm. A Chinese vampire on an Irish yacht. Nope, I wouldn't have thought it."

Vayl maneuvered us to the back of the yacht, which opened nearly at the water's level. Cole tied us on and the three of us unloaded right there on the mini deck. Straight through a set of glass doors we saw metal tables and benches, the crew's mess, no doubt. It looked about as comfortable as the cafeteria at St. Mary's Medical Center in Cleveland. At least it had a view.

Two ladders on either side of the doors led up to the main deck. I was just considering the wisdom of running up one and taking a peek when I caught a scent that made me wrinkle my nose.

"Company coming," I whispered as I took the last cooler from Vayl.

Moments later a Hollywood-thin Asian vamp wearing a purple suit, ruffled white shirt, and shiny black shoes emerged from the glass doors as if walking onstage. Cassandra, Bergman, Cole, and I exchanged glances. Were we supposed to applaud?

"*You* are late," he fussed, running his pinky across his forehead, where his thin black hair traversed it on its way to the opposite ear. He spoke to Cole, which pissed me off. Why is it that the jerks always assume the good-looking guy is in charge?

"Sorry about that," I told him. I stuck out my hand, which meant I released the handle of the cooler. As expected, he caught it instantly, but he was not happy to be touching the menial's equipment. I shook his limp fist hard enough to make him wince. And he could've broken my back without breaking a sweat. Theoretically at least.

I went on. "The oven caught fire while we were baking the cheese puffs and it took us forever to put it out. You know how cheese likes to burn." I smiled, letting go of the other handle to adjust my bandana. Oops! Now he held the entire cooler. He put it down and wiped his hands on his violet slacks.

He looked down his nose at me, not an easy feat considering I had him by a good five inches. "I know nothing about cheese," he said. As I began to speak again he held up a hand. "Moreover, I wish to know nothing about cheese."

*Moreover? Who says that?* "What a lovely outfit," I said, pouring every ounce of sarcasm I could muster into the statement. "Where did you find such a stellar suit?"

He totally missed my undercurrent as he began to preen. "Oh, this old rag? I just picked it up at a little men's store called Frierman's. The tailor there is a genius. But then, you don't look as if you could afford his wares."

*Okay, this guy is obviously color blind* and *a social leper. I may have to kill him now.* "If you would just point us to the kitchen?"

"You mean the galley?" he asked with a superior little sniff.

Cassandra slid in front of me before I could act on my brilliant plan to tie an anchor around the twit's neck and toss him overboard. She shoved a box in his hands and picked up the cooler. "If you would be so kind," she said.

He swished toward the doors, followed by my crew, with me lagging behind. Vayl cleared his throat. I glanced over my shoulder. He made three short gestures that clearly meant *Get in. Get out. Don't screw up.* I made a gesture of my own that was also quite clear. Unfortunately he took me literally and I think I left him in a state of rising excitement.

The twit led us through the doors into the crew's mess. Beyond the tables a stainless-steel counter separated the dining area from the *galley.* "What a lovely kitchen," I said as the twit scowled at me and Cassandra hid a smile. I opened the fridge, checked out the cabinets. "Very . . . organized."

The twit set his box down on the counter. "Chien-Lung is quite particular about cleanliness," he told me sternly. "Please see that you straighten up after yourselves before you leave."

"Why certainly. We are here but to serve." I gave him a bow with just enough angle on it to let him know if he ever hit the Midwest, nine of ten farmers would agree he had a cob up his ass. He sniffed and tossed his head, perhaps wishing he had long curls that would allow him to emphasize the huffy. He left through a large arched doorway at the other end of the galley. Having studied the plans of this particular vessel before we left, I knew he was taking a twisting ramp up to the main deck.

Together we unloaded the goodies. Vamps may not require delicious layouts of shrimp cocktail, bite-sized crackers topped with funky green veggies, and gallons of margaritas to survive, but they sure do relish them. (Hah! Pun intended!) By the time we finished, the galley resembled a behind-the-scenes Food Network show. I half expected an abnormally thin TV chef to step out of the broom closet and start breaking down the recipe for the mini kebobs.

"I'm starving," Cole said, his hands full of small square brownies. "And since there's no room on the tray for these . . ." He popped them all into his mouth.

"Cole!" Cassandra smacked him on the shoulder.

"Wha—?" When he opened his mouth all you could see was half-chewed goo.

"How old *are* you?" I demanded. I threw a shrimp at him and it got stuck in his tangle of wig hair. Bergman fished it out, wiped it off, and put it back on the serving dish.

"Now, *that* is disgusting," said Cassandra.

"Children!" Vayl's voice boomed in our ears, loud and sudden enough to make us all jump guiltily. "I trust you are performing actual work right now."

"Chill out, Vayl," I replied. "Bergman is just conducting an experiment to see how vampires respond to ingesting brown hair dye."

"That makes me curious, Vayl," said Cole in a sticky, goodie-between-the-gums voice that reminded me of Winnie the Pooh after a major honey binge. "Have you ever colored your hair? You know blonds have more fun."

"Not when they are in the hospital."

Cole suddenly struck a pose that bore a remarkable resemblance to the twit. "What a meanie bo-beanie. God."

We all spent the next three minutes swallowing huge peals of laughter, and when one did escape, disguising it as a cough. Before we were done our eyes were streaming and we were hacking like a bunch of cigarette hounds. Some people play video games when they stress. Some people kick their dogs, beat their spouses, have heart attacks. I laugh. Usually at exactly the wrong moment. Apparently my crew had caught the bug. But it worked. It was, in fact, just what we needed to help us relax into our assigned roles.

Having consulted Yetta's map and figured out where to situate all the goodies, we grabbed the boxes marked "table coverings," threw the booze, a few trays, and the tableware on a cart, and hoofed it upstairs.

We emerged in a huge open space divided into a formal dining room at the back, an entertainment area complete with baby grand in the front quarter, and a conversation corner in which someone had arranged two overstuffed couches and six chairs around a fake fireplace. The decor combined gleaming maple with rich blues and just a touch of ivory. Uh-huh, fancy.

We headed toward a set of open glass doors that led to the main deck. Cole stopped at the serve-yourself bar just outside the doors to stock up and attach a couple of cameras. A built-in awning provided protection from the weather, but it stood at least ten feet above the deck, so no cameras there. Gold silk had been wound around the railing, which meant anything we attached there could be covered by the blowing material, discovered by whoever cleaned up in the morning, or butt rubbed right into the bay. Everything else was portable. Straight-backed chairs lined up to starboard, waiting-room style. To port, two bare and embarrassed-looking buffet tables waited for our touch.

"Time to explore," I murmured. Cassandra nodded, and while she and Bergman began wind proofing the tablecloths I went back to the galley. Grabbing a tray full of dime-sized sandwiches, I headed through the arch once again. But instead of taking the ramp, I went down the adjoining hall. Passing several closed doors that led to crew quarters, I walked to the very end, where metal steps led me up two levels to the pilothouse.

What a sight. Recessed lighting combined with maple cabinetry and state-of-the-art navigational equipment to make the place resemble a cruise ship. At the very least I expected to find some bored young sailor babysitting a bank of inactive dials while the captain spent his evening on land. But the room practically echoed.

"Huh." We'd seen no staff while we were in the galley and I'd encountered nobody while I was on their turf. Had Lung sent them all ashore?

Well, hey, if the wind was blowing my way, I sure wasn't going to turn my head and spit. I planted a camera and took a different set of stairs to the guest level, where a long hall carpeted in blue Berber offered up all kinds of options in shiny arched doors with glowing gold latches. After knocking lightly on the first one to my right, I inched it open and looked inside. Empty. I left a camera near the porthole and moved across the hall. I'd just opened the door when Vayl said urgently, "Jaz, someone is coming."

*Crap!* I slipped into the room, closed the door behind me, and scoped the place out. Bed against the wall wearing black sheets and matching pillows, topped by a red velvet throw. Black bedside table with built-in lamp. Mirrored closet to the left. I checked inside. Definitely no room for me unless I found another place for the shiny silk suits and neat lines of shoes. Look at all those loafers! The guy was definitely gay.

I reached for Grief, realized I held a tray full of party food in my shooting hand, and by then it was too late. I turned to face the door as it swung open and the twit walked in.

"What are you doing here?" he demanded.

"We were told to bring a tray of sandwiches to this room," I said, smiling politely as I switched it to my left hand.

"I did not order anything," he snapped.

"Well, she definitely told us to bring it here." I could see him mentally thumbing through the list of possible women to whom I could be referring. It must've been pretty short, because within seconds he was considering me with less irritation and more interest.

"Pengfei must know I like chicken salad with my brunettes."

He moved toward me and I backed up, wishing for more room to maneuver. "Now, wait a minute," I said, my heart beating so hard I was surprised my bra straps didn't snap. "The caterers *provide* the food. We aren't food ourselves." I didn't want to smoke the creep. It would so compromise the mission, and I'd done enough of that last time around.

I'd run out of floor space, so I stepped up onto the bed. The twit continued to stalk me, enjoying his abbreviated hunt, sure of the outcome.

"Listen," I said, trying not to sound desperate. He'd take it as a signal to charge. Grief weighed heavy on my shoulder as I tried to talk him out of his own demise. "Chien-Lung's your master, right? Surely he won't be happy knowing you've eaten the caterer. After all, he's here to entertain, not mop up."

"Chien-Lung is no master of mine," the twit snarled, wrinkling his lips as if he'd just bitten into something rotten.

"Pengfei then," I said, latching on to the name he'd dropped earlier.

He drew himself up to his full height, threw his thin shoulders back. "Those two are barely fit to lick the soles of my *sverhamin*'s boots. It is a wonder to me that Edward even bothers with them sometimes. I have never met a more unbalanced pair."

I did a quick expression check. Mouth shut? Eyes focused? Inner turmoil completely masked? I sure as hell hoped so, because given the circumstances, the twit could only be referring to Edward the 'Raptor' Samos. Samos must not have been able to attend to this affair directly, so he'd sent his *avhar* to take care of it in his place. Weird to have the *avhar* thing in common with Mr. Thin-and-Pasty. I'd assumed it was only a human thing. Apparently vamps could form that kind of bond too.

"If you're planning on eating me, could you at least tell me your name?"

He appeared to consider my request. Finally he nodded. "My name is Shunyuan Fa." He didn't ask for mine in return. Which brought us right back to our cat-and-mouse game. I was just moving into the acceptance phase, where Grief would come into play and this whole job might explode in my face, when Vayl blew into the room. He slammed the door hard enough to make the bed shake. Both the twit and I froze, looking at him in shock.

"*There* you are!" he said, waving his hands expansively, reminding me of my uncle Barney, a man who does everything on the Big and Loud. "I am so sorry"—he bowed to Shunyuan Fa—"she is always flirting with clients when she should be overseeing operations."

He turned to me. "There seems to have been some sort of accident with the shrimp and the punch. Miles insists he has just invented a new hors d'oeuvre, however the guests may not agree. Also the cheese puffs have exploded. And I cannot be certain, but I believe I saw Cole sneeze all over the bar glasses."

The twit gave a horrified little scream that nearly made me laugh out loud. However, since my knees were still shaking from my close call with mission-screwed, I managed to maintain an air of calm as Vayl took my arm and escorted me out the door. I purposely turned the wrong way, managed to plant two cameras on two separate doorframes before Shunyuan Fa joined us in the hallway and set us on the correct path. We parted ways at the deck.

Vayl and I found the rest of our team in the galley. After some hurried conferring during which we all agreed our cameras had been planted, the buffet set up, and the empty coolers packed back on the boat, we decided to blow on outta that joint before our luck completely deserted us.

# Chapter Eleven

We made it back to shore without sinking, which, I decided, was the second-best thing that had happened to me that night. We lingered just long enough to tie the boat to the dock, although it might have been kinder to let it drift. Then the kids moved the party to the RV while the grown-ups stood side by side, surrounded by sailboats and speedboats and fishing boats. The moonlight reflected off the soft waves of the bay, combining with the gentle breeze to create an ideal atmosphere for conversation.

"Close call," I said.

"Yes."

"Sounds like Shunyuan Fa is linked to the Raptor."

"I agree."

"I wish you'd stop to take a breath once in a while. I can hardly get a word in edgewise."

Tightening of the lips. Corner-of-the-eye look. At last he spoke. "You would tell me if I had offended you in some way, yes?"

"Of course."

"You know I did not think you needed to be rescued just now. I just supposed it would be nice to leave Shunyuan Fa alive so that, perhaps, we could trace him back to Samos."

"Yeah."

"And, before"—he let out a huge breath—"when our lips touched—"

"I know you were just trying to teach me a lesson," I rushed in, glad of the night so he couldn't see me blush. It had been a very pleasurable lesson.

Weird the way his eyes narrowed slightly like that. Usually that only happened when he was hurt. "Of course." He nodded. "Exactly. I am glad we have that settled then. Shall we go?"

"Okay." Nothing had changed. The breeze still wafted across the bay. The moonlight still provided a lovely backdrop for a walk along the pier. But I shivered anyway. I glanced at Vayl. Why did I suddenly feel so cold?

As I stepped inside the RV, I said, "Good God, our mobile home has swallowed a Radio Shack!"

Bergman had wired a bank of electronic whatsits to our plasma TV, making it look like it had sprouted a blocky beard. The screen itself was divided into multiple quadrants, showing views of the common area and the deck of the *Constance Malloy*. We settled down to watch, Vayl and Cassandra on Mary-Kate, Cole and I on Ashley, with me pretending I didn't mind a bit that my *sverhamin* had forsaken my company for the psychic's.

*No big deal. Stop feeling like the kid who gets picked last in PE class.* In these times I looked to my old friend and roommate for comfort. Bergman sent me a wry smile from his position at the banquette where he'd set up a couple of laptops, one of which I recognized as Agency equipment. He said, "I've fixed it so we'll only see views from the party area cameras. The rest will record straight to the computer. We can review that footage later."

"What's that?" Cole pointed to a black box about half the size of a DVD player sitting on top of Ashley's table. It was fronted by eight dials and a red button.

"Brains of the RV's security system," Bergman said, as he tapped at his keyboard and tried to keep his eyes on all the screens at once. "Since I couldn't hardwire anything I had to get creative. We've got cameras in the Chinese lanterns we strung along the edge of the front and back awnings. The dials control them, and they'll only activate when they detect movement, in which case the bedroom TV will automatically switch on and begin feeding us video. That way nobody can sneak up on us."

Okay, that explained the thin black cord snaking from the black box all the way back to the bedroom. Another ran from the box up the wall and out a vent in the ceiling. I assumed it ended up outside where it connected to the cameras. Old Miles had been a busy little bee.

"Vayl said I couldn't play with the door lock, but it's a good one. Everybody just make sure you memorize the key code. I've set a welcome mat I just designed outside the front door. Any visitors we're not happy about get a punch of the red button there on the side of the black box. The mat will deliver a jolt that'll knock them flat."

"Impressive," said Vayl.

"Thanks." Bergman shifted in his seat, darting a glance out the window at the padlocked trailer, which still held a couple of boxes full of equipment he thought he might need but didn't want us to see. He was just one of those guys who'd much rather be working from an underground bunker somewhere deep in the heart of Montana. One with its own special vault just for him.

"Don't sorcerers have some sort of contract they make their apprentices sign?" I asked. "You know, where they promise not to give away any secrets upon pain of death?" I directed the question to the room in general, but my eyes were on Cassandra. As the eldest she should know damn near everything by now. But she deferred to Vayl.

"I suppose."

"Write something up, Bergman."

He went from resembling a parakeet, darting glances from trailer to monitor to TV screen, as if somewhere something was going to leap out and eat him, to watching me with the still sharpness of an owl. "What are you saying?" His voice broke on the last word, making him sound like a seventh grader at the Valentine's Day dance. He cleared his throat.

"It's close quarters. None of us can help seeing whatever you're forced to trot out of that trailer during this mission. So we'll all sign a paper guaranteeing that we will never utter a word of what we have seen to anyone anywhere ever, or else, well, you figure out the or else."

Bergman immediately ducked behind his laptop screen so none of us could see his face. Off went the glasses. Left arm crossed the face to blot the tears. We heard a couple of sniffs. And then, "Thanks, Jaz. I'll get right on that."

Satisfied, I sat back to view Chien-Lung TV. Cole popped popcorn, handed out sodas, and for the next half hour we watched guests arrive from the mainland. At first it looked like any other party where the guests wear uncomfortable clothes and pretend to like each other. Vamps mingled with humans throughout, all of them Chinese. Shunyuan Fa was there, but acting a lot more like a guest than a host.

"Recognize anybody besides the Raptor's boy?" I asked Vayl.

"No."

Bergman said, "If you want, I can capture the video of every face on that yacht and send it through your database."

"Fine," said Vayl. His plethora of terse replies finally hammered the message through my thick skull. I'd brushed that kiss off like it was nothing. And he'd meant it as more. Maybe a lot more.

*But it's not like you can even tell he has feelings*, I reasoned. *Most of the time he walks around wearing the same frozen expression he woke up with.*

*What, so that means he can't be hurt?* demanded Granny May from her perennial spot at a card table near the front of my brain. Currently she seemed to be playing bridge with Spider-Man, Bob Hope, and Abraham Lincoln. She plunked down her glass of iced tea, fed Bob an Ace of Hearts, and said, *Have you ever stopped to think how hard a man has to work to show that kind of face to the world? It's like the Hoover Dam, that mug. Can you even imagine the depth of pain that must be pooled behind it?*

I peeked at Vayl from under my lashes. Actually, I could.

As Bergman tried to identify the people in the crowd, they remained quiet, polite, expectant. They didn't have long to wait. First a petite, willowy woman wearing a red satin dress walked out of the living area. She'd put her hair in that funky Chinese up do that always looks like it's about to leap off the lady's head and wrap itself around some poor schmuck's throat. Traditional makeup whitened her face, blackened her eyes, and reddened her lips. She carried a pair of shiny black rods at her side.

One quick flip of her wrist and the rods transformed into huge fans, one painted with the image of a warrior wearing a long golden robe and a sword belt. The other depicted a golden dragon lounging at the bottom of a river. She began to dance with slow graceful movements, manipulating the fans so it looked like the warrior first fought with the dragon, and then as if the dragon emerged from the warrior.

"She's good," Cole breathed.

"Now, how am I supposed to compete with that?" I asked.

Vayl fixed me with the icy-blue gaze that I inwardly referred to as his "intellectual" look. And then, because I knew him so well, I could see him imagining me in my costume, undulating to ancient rhythms while he watched. His eyes darkened. "For some, there will be no comparison," he said.

My throat went dry. As my eyes dropped to his lips I wondered what would have happened if either of us had been bold enough when we'd kinda kissed to just let go. Would our worlds have exploded with new colors, wonders, miracles? Or would we have already destroyed each other?

Our eyes locked. By his count he hadn't known me long. But he knew me well enough that I could often tell him things without speaking. Usually it was job related. *There's a guy hiding behind that bush. Give me thirty seconds to get into position before you move. I'll take out the one that's pissing me off.*

This time I had something else to say. *That kiss caught me off guard. Scared the hell out of me. Let me know how bad you could rock my world. I loved it. Now give me some time to deal, okay?*

He sat back, a smile slowly lifting one side of his mouth. When his eyes softened to brown and he gave me a brief nod I knew we were all right.

The sound of clapping brought my attention back to the TV. The dancer had finished. She waited for the applause to fade, then turned toward the dining/entertainment area and bowed so low she could've gnawed her knees if the urge had hit her. The rest of the crowd bowed as well as Chien-Lung emerged from the shadows and stepped into camera range.

I'd seen pictures of Lung taken on his previous trips to the States. They'd showed a robust man of average height with an elegant mustache and beard, fierce brown eyes, and an expression of haughtiness that told you right away he totally bought the concept of racial supremacy. This shot of Lung showed a radically changed man. He'd lost so much weight his skin seemed to adhere directly to his skull, with no layers of fat or muscle to soften it. No hair covered his head. He didn't even have eyebrows to soften the harsh lines of his face.

"Does he have cancer?" asked Cole.

Nobody knew how to answer that.

The dancer held out her arm. Lung rested his hand on it. At first I thought he wore gloves. Then I realized dark material covered both of his hands. Something about the shape of them bothered me, but before I could get a better view the dancer turned and led him toward a cushioned chair that had been set up for him at a point exactly opposite that of the doors he'd just exited. Two flags that hadn't been there before hung from the edge of the awning. They flanked the chair, and though they flapped steadily in the breeze, I could tell they depicted gold dragons on a lush green background.

Lung swept past his guests at a stately rate of speed, his golden neck-to-ankle robes swishing with each step. When he reached the chair, the dancer stood in front of him, blocking the view while he rearranged his clothes. When she stepped back he was sitting. On his knees.

"Okay, that's just weird," I said.

Eating, drinking, and polite conversation followed, during which the dancer played an instrument she'd retrieved from inside. Though it wasn't the kind of music you could rock to, it worked for drinks and appetizers. Then she started to sing.

"Holy crap!" I exclaimed. "It sounds like somebody's seesawing dental floss inside her nose!"

Cole stuck his fingers in his ears. "Are you sure she's not our target? Because I think a strong case can be made for that racket being a threat to national security."

"Bergman," said Vayl, ignoring our juvenile outbursts, "do you have any idea why Lung is sitting on his knees?"

"None at all. Every part of him but his head is covered, so I can't tell how the armor is interacting with his body." Very professional wordage, but underneath it all Bergman's voice shook with a rage that said, "If I had the son of a bitch alone in a lawless universe I'd rip his head off and parade it through town on a pike."

Responding to those unspoken feelings, I said, "Vayl, I wonder if you and I should go back out there." *In a seaworthy boat this time.* "Lung's a perfect target right now."

Vayl nodded. "It looks that way. But he has not lived this long through carelessness." He thought awhile. "We will wait," he decided. "Let him believe his current security measures suffice."

"They probably will," said Bergman, managing to sound depressed and proud at the same time. "As soon as the armor detects danger, the hood will automatically cover his head. This vamp is not going to die by conventional weaponry."

"He's got to have some vulnerability," I said, getting the urge to throw something. Like Bergman. "You do want to get your invention back, don't you?" I asked him.

"Of course!"

"Then you're going to have to find a way to beat it!"

Bergman tapped a few keys and said, "Do you think there's any way I can get a piece of it? I could do some tests."

"Why can't you just make some more and test that?" asked Cole.

"Because it physically changes once it's been put on according to who, or what, is wearing it. We had that, at least, figured out before it was stolen."

"How much do you need?" I asked.

"A fingernail. A scale—"

I looked at Cassandra. "We're the ones most likely to get close to him. Do you think, between the two of us ... ?"

She suddenly had a hard time meeting my eyes. "Maybe. I would like to consult the cards first."

Bergman snorted. "Like *that'll* help."

I grabbed a pillow and winged it at his head.

"Hey! What was that for?"

"Just jogging your brain out of asshole mode."

"Something is happening," Vayl said, the urgency in his voice calling everyone's attention back to the plasma screen.

At first we could only see quick movements at the limits of the cameras' range. Then the woman with the criminal singing voice screamed. A group of maybe ten masked intruders raced into view, still dripping from their recent swim. They headed straight toward Lung, accompanied by several men and a couple of women from the crowd. The rest of the guests scattered, clearing out so fast you'd have thought they participated in duck-the-violence drills on a regular basis. Only Shunyuan Fa and the singer remained.

The singer grabbed a passing guest and ripped his throat out with her delicate little fangs before moving deeper into the fray.

Shunyuan Fa struck a straggler of the attackers, jerking the man's head sideways and burying his fangs in his jugular. The man died flailing, his last word an anguished gurgle.

The man's companion was better prepared. He pulled a short, straight sword and cut off Shunyuan Fa's head as he leaned over his victim's body. Vayl and I shared a silent moment of dejection as our best clue to the Raptor's location went up in smoke. Then we turned our attention back to the screen. We still had Lung, and our original connection to Samos was faring quite a bit better.

Lung's headgear had activated instantly, moving up from his neck so fast it was a blur. Later, when Bergman slowed the footage down, we witnessed how the scales erupted from his skin like immense golden blisters, growing up and outward at his eyebrows and mouth, so by the time the scales stopped moving two pairs of barbed horns jutted from his forehead and his long, square snout bristled with fangs.

Lung shed his robe in a single, quick motion. Scales covered his entire body, flashing gold and red as he moved, which brought my attention to his legs. He hadn't been sitting on his knees after all. They seemed to have become fused in a permanently bent position. He'd actually been crouching on his feet, which had grown at least another twelve inches. His toes had lengthened to the point that he could walk on them like an ostrich. It looked awkward, but he moved just as fast as his would-be killers.

The first wave was almost on him when he stopped it with a single burst of blue flame that caught two of the attackers in the face. It burned so fast and hot that seconds later nothing remained of their skulls but smoking craters. Despite the fact that their clothes were soaking wet, the three men standing nearest those unfortunates also caught fire. They immediately stripped off their jackets and threw them overboard.

"Remarkable," Vayl murmured.

Watching through clenched fingers, Bergman muttered angrily, "Just wait."

Lung dropped off his perch, held his hands in the air, and flexed. The wrapping material shredded as they swelled to twice their bandaged size. In fact, *he* was growing, filling out in height and breadth until he at least doubled the size of his largest attacker. My gaze went back to his hands. As Bergman had described earlier, they were gnarled claws now, massive weapons tipped with poison that he used with deadly efficiency, raking deep furrows in faces, necks, and chests. He left his victims writhing on the ground as he met the next wave.

This group carried a variety of machine guns — Uzis, MAC-10s, MP40s, likely bought out of the back of some thug's van — which they trained on Lung's face. Made sense to me. The eyes, nostrils, mouth, any one of them should admit a round, especially one traveling nearly three hundred feet per second. But, as Bergman had said, the armor deflected the ammunition, closing over the vulnerable areas with lightning speed. And while the assassins concentrated on Lung's head, his tail swept into action.

He'd kept it tucked behind him all this time. Now it whipped through the gunmen like a snapped guy wire, leaving a wake of severed and broken bones.

"That's new," said Bergman. His hands were in his hair now, pulling it in two directions, just like his heart. The scientist in him was fascinated. The creator in him had never been so violated.

Lung's cohort had kicked ass too, though she much preferred the hand-to-hand method highlighted by the occasional terminal bite. I watched her work with grudging admiration. She spun to deliver a head kick and her opponent chose the same block and counter I would have used. Neither worked.

"Look at that speed," I murmured, my eyes unable to keep her movement from blurring as the man went down, leaving his neck open to her final attack. I felt a sudden need to work out old-school, accompanied by some stirring music from, say, *Rocky IV*. Just in case she and I squared off, I did not want to find myself flat on my butt with the heel of her foot as my last living visual.

Within three minutes it was over. Lung and his partner stood triumphant in a spreading pool of blood while the chicken-shit party guests slowly made their way back to the deck. For the first time, Lung spoke. Holding out his massive arms he challenged the crowd. In Chinese.

"What's he saying?" I asked Cole.

He'd sat absolutely still through the action, a toddler at his first pay-for-your-ticket movie. Had he done any better than a three-year-old at connecting the pictures on the screen with actual reality? I studied him. Relaxed face and shoulders, hands crossed quietly on his lap. But his heel jumped up and down like it needed to telegraph a battleship, and his hand inched toward the bowl on the table where he'd dumped his bubble gum. Somewhat relieved to see our rookie wasn't as green as the bowl, I waited to hear his translation.

"See me. Hear me. I. Am. DRAGON!" Lung looked slowly around the crowd. "You have witnessed my enemies. Though they try to destroy me, they are powerless against my strength. I *will* be your next emperor!" Nobody said a word. One by one, they began to bow.

# Chapter Twelve

We sat in the RV, watching Lung's cocktail bash become a mop-up. Nobody felt like talking. Not on the yacht. Not in our bus.

Cassandra sat hugging her knees, her luxuriant braids hiding her face.

Cole slumped beside me, warming up a new piece of Dubble Bubble, looking away from the TV every few seconds to check on the rest of us.

I couldn't read Vayl, but if I had to guess, I'd say he looked the way you'd expect a Roman warrior to appear right before being impaled by an enemy lance.

And there was Bergman, immersed in the technology, calling out the names of the guests as the software matched their pictures.

"General Sang Lee and wife."

"General Ton Sun and wife."

"General Wing Don."

Clearly Lung had designs on the People's Liberation Army. No doubt he'd convinced the surviving generals to ally with him. And if he could figure out how to replicate the armor, his military, already the largest in the world, would be unstoppable.

It felt like someone had sucked all the hope from the room along with most of the air.

"This whole deal pisses me off," I said. Rising from the couch took effort, made me realize the battle had already begun. Our foe had made the first sortie. And dragon fear was no myth. But now that I'd hit my feet, I felt better.

Cassandra swept her hair back from her face. Nodding at her I went on. "This guy is nothing but a duded-up version of Tammy Shobeson."

Cole straightened and turned to listen.

"Who is Tammy Shobeson?" Vayl asked.

"My childhood nemesis. If God is just, she is now a fat, pimply divorcée with a chronic yeast infection." I even had Bergman's attention now. This had been our first point of commonality as college students. His bully had been a redheaded jerk named Clell Danburton, and I thought sometimes he still had nightmares about their showdowns.

"So what's your point?" he asked, sounding less like a robot and more like my old jogging partner.

I looked him in the eye. "Bottom line, Lung is just a spoiled brat who gets his way by scaring people. He may have found an effective way to do that, but it is not assassin-proof. We" — my gesture took in everybody in the room — "are being paid to kick this bully's ass. And that's exactly what we're going to do."


Almost dawn in the Body of Christ. As gross as that sounds, Corpus Christi glowed like a promise from our vantage point on Bay Trail. The breeze felt great, invigorating. Or maybe it was the renewed hope that our plans could work, that we might all make it to the other side of this mission without being roasted alive by Iron Chef Lung.

The five of us watched the lights of the *Constance Malloy* wink out one by one. We'd emerged from the RV by silent agreement.

Even Bergman stepped out for a breath of fresh air, as if the massacre we'd watched had somehow poisoned the RV's ventilation system. He didn't stay long.

"Gotta get some sleep if I'm going to come up with anything workable in the morning," he said. By "anything workable" he meant a new invention. One that, after several hours of brainstorming, we agreed could actually destroy Lung if we could get him to ingest it.

"Okay, that puts me at the monitors," said Cole. He'd stay up while the rest of us slept. And if I dreamed again, my safety would be his responsibility. Maybe Cole could tell how much the whole deal bothered me, because he patted me on the shoulder and grinned. "Don't worry, Jaz. If you try anything funny I'll wrestle you to the ground and tickle you until you pee yourself."

"Oh great, that gives me something to look forward to," I drawled. "Killer nightmares *and* incontinence. Thanks a lot."

He spread his arms and gave me a disarming grin. "I am here but to serve." With a parting chuckle he followed Bergman back into the RV.

Cassandra remained with us, arms crossed over her chest, staring into the dark water.

"You are troubled," Vayl said.

She didn't roll her eyes at him, but it struck me as a close thing. "Naturally."

"A vision?" he asked hopefully.

She shook her head. "Nothing that specific. Just a feeling." She stood a little straighter, and you could almost see her slamming all the doors and windows. "Never mind," she said.

"But—"

"Believe me, Vayl, if I knew anything that would help, I'd tell you." She stared at him. I got the feeling she was talking about two things at once. She left at a regal, controlled pace although I suspected she would've enjoyed it more if she could've stomped on his foot and run off, cackling madly as she receded into the Texas dawn.

Vayl and I stood quietly for a couple of seconds while I tried to decide how much I was about to upset him. In the end, it didn't matter. We were on the job, which meant the team came before everything. Even our personal feelings.

I decided to be blunt. "What did you do to piss her off?"

"Nothing I know of." I felt a surge in his power and the temperature dropped a couple of degrees.

"Don't you pull that vamp crap on me," I told him. "If you don't feel like talking about something, just say so."

"I do not feel like discussing it." He gave me that raised eyebrow that I'd come to learn was a challenge. *Go ahead,* it said, *just try and go there. We'll just see who's more stubborn.*

"Fine," I said. "But you and I both know that allowing your search for your boys to come between you and the people who are helping you complete this mission is not only wrong, it's stupid. And I am not losing another team to one member's idiocy." Vayl believed Cassandra might be able to connect him with the men who had, in another life, been his sons. A long succession of Seers had led him to believe they were Americans. But he'd had no luck finding them.

"I am not some amateur slayer who is going to call doom upon the heads of another group of your companions," Vayl said, his voice deepening, as it usually did when he was seriously disturbed. "I simply want what is mine."

*Here we go again, tromping into no-reasoning-with-the-man territory.* If his boys had lived out their natural lives they'd have still died over two hundred years ago. But he couldn't, wouldn't let them go. And who was I to judge, when the pain of my own losses still had the power to bring me to my knees? I wouldn't have said another word if the job had only involved the two of us. But we'd attracted a crowd that I felt a deep need to protect, the way I hadn't been able to protect my first crew.

"You're just going to have to be patient—"

"I am tired of being patient!" Vayl blasted the words toward the water, as if to challenge some unseen god who'd been playing hide-and-seek with his boys all these years. He looked down at me. "I want to know where they are. I want to see them. Speak to them. Tell them everything I have been holding in my heart since the day they died. Cassandra can do that for me. She can connect me to them if she would just try! So stop coddling her and let her do her job!" Desperate tone in his voice now. Raw and angry. Patently unfair.

"Cassandra's not going to pull a vision out of her ass just to appease you. But she is going to tell you where to shove it if you keep pushing her. And we need her if we're going to do this job right. So knock it off!"

I tried to make a graceful exit, but apparently Cassandra had the market cornered on that one. I tripped over a bunch of electric cords Bergman had run from the RV to the closest outlet and nearly fell on my face.

"*Fuck!*" Funny how sometimes that one word says it all. And how, having said it all, I felt much better. Maybe I'd even sleep right through the next eight hours.

I didn't. Awake and restless after only forty-five minutes on a couch that felt more like a pile of rocks covered by a thin layer of batting, I wandered around the empty RV. Figuring everybody had gone outside to investigate the mouthwatering aromas coming from our neighbors' grills, I followed suit.

Bergman, Cole, and Cassandra had made themselves scarce, but I found my brother sitting at a picnic table, stirring a bowl of glop that might have once been ice cream. It broke my heart to see him so sad. And it didn't help that we were surrounded by families who were having a blast eating greasy food and riding in various spinning, rolling, teeter-tottering contraptions that looked like they could fly apart at any moment.

"I can't believe she's gone," Dave said as I sat down beside him. I waited for him to jump down my throat, accuse me of destroying the only woman he'd ever loved. In some twisted way I wanted his rage, knowing it would make me feel better if he couldn't stand me. I could hardly bear the look in his eyes as they met mine.

"Is there a way to bring her back?"

"I don't . . . no, Dave, there's no way."

"Why did she go?"

"I don't think she had a choice." But we both knew better. Unwilling people cannot be turned. I looked down at my hands as they rested on the table, watched them curl into fists. I felt a strange sense of detachment as I realized I had never hated Jesse more than I did at this moment.

When I looked up it was dark. Dave was gone and Matt sat in his place. He looked hungry. And not for ice cream.

"Wanna tango?" he asked, giving me his lazy, come-get-me smile. But the fangs ruined the effect.

"You're not a vampire," I said, digging my fingernails into my palms to keep myself from punching that look off his face. It mocked everything we'd been, everything we might have become. "Aidyn Strait killed you. I saw your soul . . . fly away. Remember?"

"Can I help it if this is how you dream of me?"

"Yes!" I yelled, though I knew I was lying. "You have all kinds of choices, you son of a bitch, and they all affect me! Did you think of that even once before you turned?" *What?* Now I was confusing myself. Was he a vampire or not?

I looked at him and felt something inside me shatter. "I hate you."

He grinned. "You love me."

"You left me."

He held out his arms, looked down at himself as if to say, "What the hell am I doing here then?"

"You know what I mean! This isn't really you!"

"Come on, baby. If I'd needed a transfusion you'd have given it to me, no question. This way we can be together forever."

I started to shudder from the effort it took to hold back a torrent of sobs. "My Matt would never ask that of me."

He lunged over the table, but I'd known he was coming. I was already up and running, threading through the jostling crowd, which now ran heavily toward gangs of loudly laughing teenagers and young couples in the sizzling stage of romance. Bad place for a showdown.

I darted off the main walk, between food booths, through the parking lot of a Christi's Crab Shack, deeper into the city. Matt's vampiric scent dogged me, reminding me that I could only outrun him as long as he allowed me to. And then what?

*You know what I want,* his voice whispered in my head.

I stopped. I stood on the sidewalk of a busy street, surrounded by office buildings whose windows glared at me between evenly spaced streetlights as if through the reflective sunglasses of a hard-ass cop. *Of course. I get it now. Matt wants to drive me crazy.* It was the price he'd set for allowing him, Jesse, and the rest of our crew to die. Because he knew me so well, he understood that for me, insanity equaled hell.

*Burn, baby, burn,* came his voice, laughing uproariously inside my pounding head.

"No. Not like that." I looked down the street. Vehicles sped past, probably fifteen miles over the forty-mile-per-hour speed limit. I stepped forward.

"Jasmine!" I looked back. Cole was three steps behind me, reaching desperately for my arm. Oh God, was Matt after him too?

I teetered on the curb, one foot floating in the roadway, the other leg shaking with the effort of holding my unbalanced body weight. I reached back and Cole grabbed my hand, yanking me toward him so hard I stumbled and fell. When my knees hit the concrete I came fully awake.

Cole lifted me to my feet. Traffic roared behind me. The sun beat down on my head, which I promptly dropped to Cole's shoulder. *Oh please, no, not again.*

"I'm so sorry, Jasmine," Cole said, stroking my hair. "I just left the RV for a second. Chinese Mom came by to exchange tickets, our show for theirs — remember the deal? And I got distracted by the baby."

I would too. He was almost as cute as E.J. "What time is it?" I asked. Though I still wore the watch Bergman had made for me, my arm felt heavier than a cannon.

"It's almost two o'clock."

"So tired."

"Come on." He put his arm around me and began leading me back to the bay. "I'll find you something criminally caffeinated."

My head ached. And my heart . . . wiser not to go there. "I think I'm going to need something stronger than coffee."

"Yeah? What would that be?"

"Chocolate."

Cole gave me a brotherly kiss on the cheek that nearly did me in. "You got it, chief."

*Chief. He called me chief. Oh, Jesus, how am I going to keep this crew safe when they can barely prevent me from killing myself?* No answer. Not from Jesus, anyway. I had another open line, of course.

Raoul.

But when I thought of him, I experienced a sort of full-spirit cringe. Raoul dwelt among my most inapproachable memories. He'd brought me back from death. Twice. His guidance, while it had been vital, nearly overwhelmed the senses. I wasn't sure what kind of being he was. Only that he'd been a warrior in life, and his ability to command had followed him into the afterlife, where he conducted his activities from a place that looked a lot like a suite at the Mirage. But I couldn't go there. Because I suspected that whatever I discovered would be more devastating than anything I'd experienced so far.

# CHAPTER THIRTEEN

Cole stepped into the RV first. As soon as he turned to me with that aw-crap look on his face, I knew all was not right in Castle Kick-Ass. Then I heard the sobbing, not quite muffled by a pillow we would all want dry-cleaned very, very, very — I bit the inside of my cheek to stop the inner chant — soon.

I walked all the way in and closed the door. Cassandra sat on Ashley, swiftly drying her eyes, refusing to meet mine.

"I'm fine," I ventured. "No need to worry. Cole caught me in time."

"Oh, it isn't that," she replied. As soon as she heard herself she looked at me apologetically. "I didn't mean — of course I was worried —"

"Don't sweat it." I faked a smile, sinking into Mary-Kate. "I know you don't cry that easily."

"No, I can't remember the last time . . ." She wiped more tears off her clear, dark skin, then wiped her damp fingers on her lacy orange skirt. She wore matching orange suede boots and had topped it all off with a fluffy white short-sleeved sweater that would've made anyone else resemble a poodle. Not Cassandra. Even in the midst of emotional turmoil she maintained this incredible grace of motion, this self-assured *I am*, that let you know she would never waste your time or steer you wrong.

Cole had headed straight for the fridge, rummaged around inside, and come back with a Hershey bar the size of my forearm. He brought it to me with such a look of triumph I had to laugh. I motioned for him to sit beside me, then shared it out among the three of us. Bergman still slept on the converted banquette, so we saved a square for him.

After a moment of munching that bordered near to holy, I said to Cassandra, "Can you talk about this?"

She shrugged. "It would do no good."

"How do you figure?"

"It never does."

"You know what my Granny May used to tell me?" I asked, taking another luscious bite.

"What?"

" 'Never' is a dirty word."

"No wonder you swear so much," said Cole. He spun on his butt, flopping his jeans-clad legs into my lap, laying his head back on the arm of the couch. His army surplus jacket fell open to reveal a white T-shirt peppered with realistic red spatters, I'd guess from a .22, along with the slogan PAINTBALL IS FOR SISSIES. "You're obviously very confused about the English language."

I did a number on the sides of his knee that made him yelp and he settled right down. "Come on," I said, waving my hand at Cassandra as if I was moving her through a construction zone. "You know I'm going to weasel this information out of you sooner or later, so you might as well cough it up right now."

She sighed, her shoulders slumping as she surrendered to my well-developed powers of persistence. Laying her hands on her legs so all twelve of her rings showed clearly, she worried at her skirt as she spoke. "I have had a vision" — she swallowed — "of my own death."

*Wow. No matter how you look at it, that just sucks.*

"Are, uh" — Cole rose to his elbows — "are your visions always right?"

"Very nearly."

"What did you see?" I asked.

Cassandra began chipping away at the red polish on her fingernails. "I was in the show tent, alone, with the dragon."

"With Lung?" I clarified.

Her shrug said, *either way.* "I had just given him a reading that put him into a murderous rage. He . . ." She shook her head, trying to dispel the vision, but it wouldn't go. "I could feel the fire of his breath shriveling my skin." The tears welled up and spilled over. The pillow went back to her face, muffling her next words. "I can feel it even now."

*Aw, man, Jaz, you gotta fix this. And I mean now!* Poor Cassandra was just about to go out of her mind. Without even thinking, I said, "Not gonna happen."

"Wh-what?"

"I won't allow it. It's that simple. I will not let Lung kill you."

"How are you going to prevent it?" she cried.

She would have to ask. I decided to take it slow. If I talked it out logically, maybe it would make sense to both of us. "Well . . . I'm going to start off by keeping two things clearly in mind. Number one, your visions are sometimes off. And number two, if he does try to kill you, he'll be in for a nasty surprise. Because, having been forewarned, I am already forearmed." *So there.*

The tears picked up. Soon Cassandra was sobbing big-time. Cole and I shared an anxious look. "I'm sorry," I told her. "Did you misunderstand me? I'm not going to let him kill you."

Cole rustled up a box of tissues, sat down beside her, and put them in her flailing hands. After a while she slowed down, blew her nose a few times, and squeegeed the tears from her face. "I am so sorry. I just didn't expect you to believe me."

"Why not?"

"So many people don't. Vayl, for instance . . ." She trailed off, aware he probably didn't want her to share. Despite the hot water it had already thrown me into, I made a mental note to prod him on the issue of his sons again. He must really be hounding her to pinpoint their present locations for him, like she was some sort of human GPS. And instead of telling him to quit obsessing, she'd clumped that worry with her current stress, with the result that she was positioned to keep Kleenex in business well into the next century.

"I am an old woman, you know," she said pitifully.

I leaned over and patted her hand. "Don't be so hard on yourself. Even now you don't look a day over seven hundred."

Her smile trembled, but it held. "I spent the first years of my life in Seffrenem."

"Never heard of it."

"It's a lost city, buried deep beneath the desert now. But once it was a center for art, trade, and religion. All the gods lived there, each within his or her own temple. And I was the oracle for the greatest of them all, Seffor. People would travel for months to kneel at my feet, hear my prophecies. They brought me gifts of rare jewels, foods, and furs. They treated me like a goddess. And with such visions as I had, is it any wonder I began to think of myself as divine?"

I had no answer to that. I knew what I'd thought of myself after hearing the immense, booming voice of Raoul, and it wasn't anything nearly that elevated.

"How the gods must have laughed," Cassandra said bitterly. "They knew what lay in store for me. Perhaps they had orchestrated the entire tragedy." She paused, mulling over her past while Cole and I tried not to bounce up and down in our seats and yell, "What tragedy? What tragedy?"

Finally she continued. "One morning I woke to a vision of such horror I was nearly struck dumb. I saw my husband thrown from his horse, Faida, and killed under her hooves. I told him what I'd seen, but he just laughed. He had trained Faida from a filly. She was a fine, obedient animal, not at all skittish. He told me my pregnancy had me on edge. It was my third, and had lasted into the fourth month, twice as long as the first two."

She swallowed painfully, as if she had a knife at her throat. "He died that afternoon. They never saw the snake that bit Faida, causing her to rear in panic, to throw him, to crush his skull with her flying hooves. All the men who were with him could tell me was that Faida had died shortly afterward. I lost the baby the next day."

She looked at us with pain-drenched eyes. "It's been the same for me ever since. I can't save the people closest to me, because they never believe my visions."

Cole and I shared a moment of stunned silence. There was no way to grasp the scope of a life that long. But the love. And the pain. I could connect to that. And I was always awed by the survivors.

"People only hear what they want to hear," I said finally. "One of the more idiotic traits of humans, but one that has its perks. For instance, when someone says, 'Don't be stupid, there's no way you can come up with a cure for AIDS.' That's an excellent time to develop situational deafness."

"So what do *you* want to hear?" she asked.

"That you're relieved because we believe you," I said, glancing to Cole for confirmation. He nodded quickly.

"You know what I think this means?" he asked us both. We shook our heads. He took Cassandra's hands, smoothing over the flaked polish, the chipped nails. "I think the gods have stopped laughing."

# Chapter Fourteen

Having already eaten dessert, we decided a healthy lunch was in order. While Cole opened three cans of ravioli and Cassandra made orange Kool-Aid, I called Evie.

"Jaz, the best thing happened!"

*Thank God. I am so ready for some good news.* "What's that?"

"E.J. cried all night last night."

"Awesome!"

"Okay, I can see how you don't get that's a good thing. But you've got to understand. There we are, just me and her, rocking in the chair beside her crib at four a.m., both of us crying buckets. And suddenly it hits me. This is complete and utter bullshit!"

I held the phone away from my ear and stared at it. Evie does not swear. And I mean never. I finally realized the extremity of her situation. "So what happened?"

"I woke Tim up and I said, 'Tim, you can only cry so long before it doesn't do you any more good.' I don't think he really knew what I meant by that, but he did think it was a good idea to take E.J. to the emergency room. We met this amazing pediatrician there who said E.J. had an awful ear infection. She said E.J. had to have been in utter misery. Plus she said there's medicine we can give her for the colic, which is actually reflux. She doesn't have to suffer, Jaz. Isn't that incredible? And we are sticking with this new pediatrician. She's amazing!"

"That is such a relief! I can't tell you how happy I am to hear that! Hey, are you listening really closely to me right now?"

"Of course."

"Because I want to make sure there's no interference on your end when I say I told you so."

Evie's laugh, finally stress free and full of the same joy I'd heard the day her daughter was born, lifted my spirits like nothing else could. "Yeah, I guess you did."

"Okay, you keep on being an excellent mom and I'll get back to work. And, hey, next time she takes a nap, you take one too." I, on the other hand, would be avoiding sleep like a bad concussion victim until further notice.

"Yes, ma'am!" Evie sang.

"That's what I like to hear."

I took ten minutes to shower and change. By then lunch was ready. After I'd related my good news we ate in relative silence, which might've been why Cole's eyes quickly lowered to half-mast and, if not for Cassandra's rapid reflexes, his entire face would've been masked with pasta sauce when he fell asleep a minute later. I woke Bergman and he willingly changed places with Cole once he learned we'd saved a can of ravioli and a handful of chocolate for him.

"Are you women going to stay in here all day?" he asked as he sat down to his meal. One glance at the monitor had shown him what Cole had reported seeing all morning. A whole lot of nothing. "Since the *Constance Malloy* seems to be in a temporary coma, I thought I'd do some experiments."

"Are these tests so painfully shy they can't stand an audience?" I asked.

"Something like that." Despite the fact that we'd all signed

Bergman's lip-zip oath the night before, it looked like old habits would be dying real hard, or possibly not at all, on this trip.

"No problem," said Cassandra. "It's time for Jaz to meet my friend anyway."

"What, did he send you a message by courier fairy?" Bergman asked, his lip curling.

*That is it.* "Bergman—" Cassandra cleared her throat, shook her head, and mouthed, "Later."

We each grabbed ID and money and I holstered up, covering Grief with my leather jacket. I also wore the outfit Vayl had bought me to replace the one that had been ruined on our last mission, a soft red silk blouse with an ornate, scooped neckline and black jeans. I'd stuck with my boots, since Cole said a guy from Seven Seas Succulents had come for theirs, plus all the other stuff we'd borrowed, earlier in the day.

We left Bergman to pull a couple of boxes of electronics from the trailer and start playing in them like a kid with his LEGOs. As the door slammed behind us I told Cassandra, "I want to say, 'Don't mind him,' but you should. He's acting like such a jerk."

"He's afraid," she replied.

"Fear is the locus of his entire existence. But that doesn't make it okay for him to demean you and your work every time he opens his mouth. If he wasn't so damned brilliant I'd have given him an earful weeks ago. It's just, he's very thin-skinned, so you always run an excellent chance of mortally offending him. And then we can kiss our dandy gadgets goodbye."

"I can deal with him," she said. "I have just been so distracted ever since . . ." She looked at me with good-humored accusation. "Ever since I met you, in fact."

"What can I say? I just have a way with people. Now, where is this buddy of yours?"

"At a sidewalk café called Sustenance. We'll have to take a taxi." Though I would've preferred to arrive in my corvette, I found that as long as she didn't suggest mopeds I'd be fine with whatever mode of transport she chose.

We took the twenty-block trip from the festival to Sustenance in a cab that looked like it had been the site of a major WWE showdown. If it wasn't dented, it was torn and if it wasn't broken, it was stained.

"Is that blood?" Cassandra whispered, pointing to a spot on the floor near her feet.

"That or amniotic fluid," I joked.

She looked at me in horror. "Tell me no one has ever given birth inside of this car."

"Why not? The seats still have plenty of spring and when a contraction hits, all you have to do is grab this grimy strap here." I acted as if I was going to slip my hand through it. Cassandra let out a little shriek and clutched my wrist. *Shit!*

"Don't you dare get that faraway look!" I snapped. Too late, she'd pulled a vision out of our brief contact.

"You must take me and Bergman on your next mission," she whispered.

"What?"

"We'll fight about it later."

"Everything all right back there?" asked the driver, his accent placing his parents squarely south of the border.

"No problem, thanks," I replied. "My friend here is just a little germaphobic." Okay, maybe I was hunting a little stop-touching-me revenge when I advised her, "Watch out for the back window. I think that smear could be vomit."

Cassandra flinched. "Do you know I spent an entire year cleaning out a rich man's stables and I never once felt like bacteria were skittering up my dress like a herd of mindless insects? It's not me. It is this *car*!"

"Do you need a shower?" I asked.

"Yes!"

"Too bad, we're here." She leaped from the cab and, as I paid the driver, ran into the café and demanded to be shown the bathroom. Funny how a good gross out will take your mind off scary dreams and visions. I know I felt better.

I eyed the tables outside of Sustenance, all round four-seaters with large yellow umbrellas sticking out of their centers. Yellow and white striped tie-on pillows cushioned the black metal chairs. Only three were in use at the moment. Two moms with toddlers in strollers lingered over a cup of coffee while their kids shared a power nap. At the other end of the narrow veranda sat a man who would make me believe in aliens, if I were so inclined.

His thick white hair grew straight up from his head, as if he'd just spent the past fifteen minutes hanging upside down from a trapeze. His eyes were such a light blue they bordered on silver. Deep wrinkles crisscrossed the bits of skin showing beneath his bushy white eyebrows, handlebar mustache, and collar-length beard. He wore a poet's shirt, complete with poofy sleeves and a V-neck presently closed with leather ties. His corduroy pants were dark brown and matched his intricately tooled cowboy boots.

"I like your boots," I told him as I closed the distance between us. I noticed he wore a single diamond in his left ear.

"Thank you. I had them made special in Reno. I found a store there called Frierman's that I would highly recommend to any of the gentlemen in your life." His soft, Southwestern accent invited you to be comfortable, even sit a spell if the spirit moved you.

I stuck my hands in the pockets of my jeans, mostly because it would've been polite to shake his hand. Polite, and stupid.

His gesture invited me to join him. I sat in the chair opposite his, thinking I'd heard that name—Frierman's—somewhere before. But this was no time for mental inventory. The old gentleman was looking at me expectantly.

"Cassandra will be out in a second. She just had the most harrowing cab ride."

He smiled. "It is so difficult to put your life in another's hands."

"Yeah."

"My name is Desmond Yale." The waitress cut him off, asking for my drink preference. I ordered iced tea.

"I'm Lucille Robinson. Cassandra tells me you're from New Mexico," I said after the waitress left.

"Born and raised," he agreed.

"She didn't really tell me any more than that."

"What would you like to know?"

I considered him for a moment. "How did you come by your Gift?"

He thought awhile. "After my wife died I became something of a hermit. I spent a lot of time in the desert . So I would have to say the loneliness did it." He took a sip of his coffee and smiled. "I spent so much time in my own head that I finally found a way beyond the grief and the loss. After years of study I learned to do the same for others."

I nodded, but a kernel of doubt popped in my stomach. Yale didn't come off like the wise old dream interpreter Cassandra had described. What the hell did this guy have in mind?

"Can you give me some idea of what to expect? Cassandra made it sound so easy."

"It is," he assured me. "We simply clasp hands and away we go."

"Away where?" Was this kook going to make me literally revisit my nightmares? And where was Cassandra? She had some explaining to do!

The waitress came back with my drink, a refill for Desmond, and three sets of napkin-wrapped silverware. "Are you ready to order?" she asked.

"Still waiting on my friend," I told her. "Actually, maybe I'll go check on her, make sure she hasn't fallen in." The waitress smiled at my pathetic joke as she left, for which she would be tipped at least 15 percent.

I tried to stand, didn't get the chair pushed back far enough, and knocked the table with my thigh. Biting back a curse as my tea wobbled, I put both hands on the table to steady it. But Desmond's coffee cup tipped precariously. He caught it before it could crash, however, saving himself from a lap full of hot caffeine.

*His hands.* I looked at the waitress, hoping she'd confirm what I'd seen, but she was looking over her shoulder at the babies, who'd awakened at the same time, howling. I knew that cry. It expressed something-spooked-me hysteria, the kind E.J. experienced every time she heard a siren. Tim now had to watch *COPS* in his bedroom with the door shut and the volume as low as he could stand it.

At the same time the toddlers were inspiring their moms to quick action, I saw Cassandra through the window. She rushed toward me, pointing at Desmond, shaking her head so hard her braids whipped across her face.

I looked at him again, almost sure now that I'd seen his hands blur as they'd moved to grab the coffee cup. That underneath those long, pinkish white fingers I'd caught the hint of claws.

"Don't let him touch you!" screamed Cassandra as she burst through the café door.

I pulled my hands back, but too late. He caught them, pinned them to the table by sinking his fingernails (*claws*, my mind whispered frantically) deep into the soft areas between knuckles and wrist. It hurt so much I screamed. Blood welled up instantly, much more than such an injury should release. It flowed onto the table, dripped to the floor.

The babies wound it up a notch, and as soon as their moms saw my situation they joined right in. We were making a regular ruckus in the heart of the city. I'd heard so much about Texas SWAT, all of it good. Where were they in my time of need?

"What are you doing to me?" I yelled. I tried to pull my hands free. They might as well have been nailed to the table. Hell, maybe they were.

Desmond fixed me with those gleeful alien eyes and said, "You killed my best student, you little bitch. He had a real gift for reaving. Now I have only one left." He cocked his head to one side, as if tuning to his own personal radio station. "Stop whining, all right? I'm getting to that."

I fought panic as the schizoid reaver held me down, and one of the moms yelled into her cell phone, "Police! Woman being attacked! Sustenance on East Leopard!" I was glad to know the cavalry was on its way. But at the rate blood flowed from my hands, I'd be dead long before then. I was positioned so awkwardly I couldn't have delivered an effective kick if I'd strapped on six-inch heels. So I went with my last resort.

Gathering all my breath, all my power, every last iota of energy in my aching body, I focused it all on that wrinkled piece of parchment between Desmond's eyebrows. I imagined that spot highlighted with a big, black X, and slammed my head right into it.

The old reaver staggered backward, looking as stunned as if he'd been shot. Cassandra used that lull to drag the moms and their kids off the street and into the relative safety of the café. I used it to bind my bleeding mitts with two of the brown linen napkins that had been wrapped around silverware moments before.

The thought of pulling Grief never entered my mind. And I didn't care if Desmond looked like somebody's kindly Martian grandpa. I'd forgotten every lesson Vayl had tried to teach me about keeping a reasonable distance and decided to kick this reaver's ass up close and personal.

I started with his torso. *Bam, bam, bam.* Three kicks to the diaphragm. Damn, it felt like hammering concrete blocks! Still, if he could breathe through his ears, now would be the time to start. The force of the blows backed him hard into a table. It caught him just under the ass and the momentum took him off his feet.

I hadn't seen his shield, not once, until now. Maybe my attack had distracted Yale enough that he'd allowed it to show. Maybe I'd hurt him. But if so, no gaps appeared in the thick black outline that danced around him like a live wire, so I doubted I'd done much damage. However, I figured if I beat on him long enough a weak spot would eventually appear. Then I'd finish him. For now I kicked him again. Twice to the shoulder and once to the head to make sure he hit the ground.

But he hadn't come to the game without a few tricks of his own. As he fell, he swept one leg around and caught me behind the knees, bringing me down. I rolled with the fall, taking the brunt of the impact on my butt.

Something came flying at me as I began to rise and I hit the deck again. Metal clattered against metal as it hit. Knife? Throwing star? Whatever, I figured it for lethal, and part of a set.

I rolled to my feet and lunged to my right as another missile flew past my head, the high-pitched whir of its spin making my ears throb. I watched it whirl into the street. It was a knife. An ancient one by the look of the black rune-covered hilt, with a curved blade that punctured the first minivan tire that hit it.

I upended a table and dove behind it just as Desmond pitched another close one. It sliced right through the metal and stopped just inches from my eye. *Holy crap!* Apparently they had access to Ginsu technology in Reaverland.

I wrestled Grief out of its holster, not an easy task with mummy hands. I nearly dropped it, and accidentally pushed the magic button as I recovered, which meant I suddenly held a crossbow rather than a pistol. At this point I didn't even care. Anything that could fly through the air and hit the son of a bitch worked for me.

Sirens wailed somewhere close at hand. *Yes! Come on, boys! There may just be a big fat kiss in it for you if you get here before I pass out!*

Another knife thudded into the table, ripping sleeve but missing skin. I bobbed up and took a quick shot. It hit Desmond's shield, knocking him backward. But it didn't even penetrate to his body. In full defensive mode now, he spun three more knives at me as he backed out of the seating area. When I rose to return the volley, all I could see was his back receding into the distance. The professor in Cassandra's *Enkyklios* had neglected to mention the reavers' vampirelike speed.

I considered chasing him. Okay, not really. The cops sounded interested, at least that's how I interpreted those sirens. Which meant they'd want to get in on the fun. Plus I felt like hell.

I holstered Grief, took a couple of steps, and decided sitting sounded more appealing. My hands began to throb so loud they drowned out Cassandra's first words to me.

"What'd you say?" I asked as she righted the chair that had been lying beside mine and took a seat.

"You look morbidly pale," she told me.

"I lost a lot of blood." I nodded to the small pool I'd made beneath my original table.

"Can I get you anything?"

"Orange juice and some chocolate-chip cookies." *And somebody to pat me on the back and tell me I didn't just screw something up here. I mean, I was the victim, right? Plus, nobody died, and our mission is still viable. So I feel like crying right now because . . . adrenaline and blood loss,* I decided. *It's all chemistry, baby, and don't you think any different.*

Cassandra went back into Sustenance. When I saw her rise to her full height, I realized the manager preferred that we leave as soon as possible. But it was hard to deny that regal command in her slashing hands (*How 'bout I just cut off your head, you uncooperative peasant?*) and her tone of voice. The snacks turned up just before the cops.

I wolfed down my first cookie, watching with interest as five squad cars pulled up, forming the spokes of half a wheel with Sustenance at the hub. A couple of nice officers began interviewing the hysterical moms, shortly after which two cars pulled away and headed off in the direction Desmond had taken.

A ruckus behind me distracted my attention. A small man with a pointy nose and enormous ears waving from behind his straight black sideburns came rushing out of the café followed closely by the manager.

"I have been banging on that door for a solid fifteen minutes! Don't tell me you didn't hear me!"

"I am so sorry, sir," said the manager. He had a please-don't-sue-us tone in his voice as he said, "Could I offer you a gift certificate for two complimentary dinners before you leave?"

Cassandra rose from the chair beside me. "Gregory?"

He came to her and grabbed her outstretched hands. "Cassandra! You wouldn't believe what I've been through!"

Her eyes went wide as he touched her. "Actually, I would." She looked sharply at me. "The reaver locked him in their storeroom."

I studied Gregory thoughtfully.

"What happened to her?" asked Gregory.

Cassandra filled him in. Even though she skipped a lot it still came out sounding überscary. He started backing toward his car before she was halfway through. "Where are you going?" she asked.

"I . . . I'm sorry, Cassandra. I can't become involved in this."

"But . . . her dreams. They could kill her, Gregory."

I held up my hand before Cassandra felt like she had to beg the guy. "Let him go. He's safer away from me. It's what I've been trying to get you, Bergman, and Cole to do practically since the day we met."

Gregory nodded his thanks and took off, not even waiting for his gift certificate.

"Very interesting." We turned our attention to the handsome, bald black man from SWAT. The van had pulled up shortly after Gregory had charged out the door and though the five guys who'd dismounted seemed pretty disappointed to have missed the fun, one had strolled over to listen in. He'd also used Cassandra's distraction to his advantage, openly admiring her while I wondered if there was any way on earth I could hook them up.

I stood. "Cassandra, my ID is in my left front pocket. Would you show it to Sergeant . . . ?"

"Preston," he said, his voice a silky bass that made Cassandra stand a little straighter.

Cassandra retrieved my CIA identification, allowing me to sink back into my chair before the street could spin any faster. *More juice,* I decided, taking a couple of generous swigs before I inhaled another cookie.

Preston took some time examining the plastic he held. When he gave it back to Cassandra, their hands brushed and she gave him a long, sad look before turning away. Was she truly shrugging off this gorgeous young ass-kicker? *But . . . Cassandra . . . he's SWAT!*

"What can you tell me?" he asked. I knew it. Quick to pick up on my unspoken message but no doubt patient enough to lie still in the hot sun for hours until he got the order to pull the trigger. If these guys resembled Cleveland SWAT at all, they worked the paranormal cases. If not, oh well. I still felt I could trust them.

"Are you familiar with reavers?" I asked. He shook his head. Unsurprised, I said, "They're killable, but just barely. I got one last night near the festival. He'd already murdered a man, but I nailed him before he could rip the guy's soul off the good and narrow. You getting me?"

"You're talking some high-level demon shit, right?" he asked. I nodded. "We don't get much of that here. Mostly run-of-the-mill stuff. Coven wars. Revenge cursings. Domestic disputes over questionable potion use. That kind of stuff."

"Well, here's what I can tell you. I was just attacked by another reaver, apparently the first one's floor boss. I seem to be the only one around who's able to see these monsters' weak spots, but I wasn't finding one on this creep." I gave him a full description. "You find Yale, I suggest you use the big guns. Flatten him with a steamroller. Drop a bomb on him. Do not underestimate him, okay?"

"Should I expect some weird shit to go down at the festival this week?"

"If it does, and we need backup, I'll give you a call."

He reached into his pocket and pulled out his card. Handing it to Cassandra, he said, "See that you do."

Sergeant Preston made sure nobody else came to bother us, except an EMT who smelled of stale cigarette smoke and looked like she'd been up for the past forty-eight hours. I was the only one who didn't wince when the makeshift bandages came off.

Desmond had marked me permanently. Four deep wounds in the back of each hand still oozed blood, but at a much less life-threatening rate. "You're going to need stitches," said the EMT.

For some reason a picture came to mind that I couldn't shake. Granny May bent over her quilting, moving that needle steadily up and down as she hummed "Rock of Ages," looking up every once in a while to smile at me as I lay on the floor playing solitaire, trying to get her cat, Snookums, to move its butt off my cards. Unexpected tears filled my eyes.

"I am?" I said. *What the hell?* Counting grade school, I'd probably had more stitches than a Victorian ball gown.

"She may be feeling a little shocky," the EMT told Cassandra.

Cassandra pointed to the puddle under the table. "All that blood is hers."

The EMT nodded. "Better bring the cookies and juice then." I let the ladies help me into the ambulance and didn't even protest when the EMT covered me with a blanket. Sometimes it's nice to be comforted.

# Chapter Fifteen

Thirty-two stitches, twelve cookies, and five cups of juice later, Cassandra and I arrived back at the RV. Bergman's irritation abated somewhat when he saw my war wounds, but he still didn't want us there, watching him do his top-secret, need-to-know-level engineering. So we dumped our gear and went back outside. Someone, probably Cole, had set five neon-green lawn chairs out front under the awning. I supposed we were now TV stars, having set off the cameras inside the Chinese lanterns, but it didn't matter. Nobody was awake in the bedroom to watch us.

"I am beat," said Cassandra, slouching down so she could rest her head against the back of her chair. "How am I supposed to do any readings tonight when I feel like burnt toast?"

"Fake it," I suggested.

She looked at me with the kind of horror Granny May might've experienced upon hearing me utter a dirty word. "Are you kidding me?"

"Cassandra, you have to do an hour-long show plus one 'prize' reading afterward, and if you're lucky it'll be for dragon-breath. Where's the harm in telling people they'll find true love or get a lucky break?"

Her face pinched like she'd just bitten into a lemon. "It's just not done by genuine psychics. It's unethical."

"Okay, chill. I was just trying to help you out."

She rolled her head toward me and smiled tiredly. "It's just been such a long day . . ." Yeah, I guess I had put her through the ringer. The fight had been bad enough, but in its own way, the hospital visit had been worse.

I'd ended up enjoying the ambulance ride in a pathetic I-haven't-driven-this-fast-in-weeks kind of way. On the way I'd developed a strange sort of sugar rush. At the hospital I'd been transferred to a wheelchair and almost immediately freaked Cassandra out by popping a wheelie. Hey, I might as well celebrate my recent triumph, since clearly no one else would. We'd been waiting in an interim room (the hallway) for several minutes when I noted her swiping at an escaping tear. Now that bothered me.

"Are you still upset about your vision? Or was the fight too much for you?" I knew she'd seen plenty of violence in her time, but I still hated to expose her and Miles to the seamy side of my work. A thought hit me. Was I truly about protecting them? Or did I just fear the way they'd look at me when they finally figured out what I was capable of? Ouch, definitely too hot to handle until later.

She'd thought about it awhile, her lips pressed tight, then she'd shrugged. "As much as I complain about my lot, I do enjoy living. When I think of all the places I've been, all the people I've met, all the wonderful curiosities I've explored and how, after all this time, there is still so much to see, so much to know"—she shrugged—"I'm afraid it's finally slipping through my fingers."

"Your visions, I know they come true a lot, but I really believe they're just possibilities. I think what you see is more likely to occur. But in a world where anything can happen, you have to believe we can choose things. And we can change things."

"I want to . . ."

"What about that guy, Sergeant Preston? How come you brushed him off?"

More tears welled in Cassandra's eyes. "When I touched him, I *saw* . . ."

"What?"

"He has a little boy from his first marriage. His widowed mother depends on him and his three brothers adore him. And he is going to die trying to save me."

"Wow, that does kind of put a big old stinky blanket on the budding romance."

"Jasmine, I'm serious!"

"Oh for chrissake, Cassandra, why do you have to be all gloom and doom lately?" I had an inspiration. "Why can't you just jump in the sack with the guy, do the happy hoppy, and wallow in regret later like the rest of us lowlifes?"

"The happy hoppy?" She smirked.

"Hey, I'm a quart low here. You want clever, you better get me some replacement blood."

"You are such a hypocrite. I know you have never just 'hopped in the sack' with anyone. It's not in you."

"Hey, if I want a lecture on my faults I'll call my dad. Oh, that reminds me, I should call my dad." I pulled out my phone.

"Jasmine," Cassandra hissed, "we are not done here."

"Yes. We are," I said. "We have clearly established that your recent visions suck so bad we're going to have to take drastic steps to break them. Also that you really need to get laid." I bulldozed over Cassandra's shocked intake of breath by greeting my father. "Hey, Albert." I pointed to the phone, mouthed, "It's my dad," and turned my back to her before she managed to reach past her civilized veneer and smack me a good one.

"Jaz? Did you try to call earlier?"

"Nope."

"Huh. Somebody keeps calling and hanging up."

"Probably a telemarketer. Um, could you call me right back?" As in, on his scrambled line.

"All right."

We hung up. Seconds later we'd reconnected in a way that was safer, at least from his end. "Look, Albert, I've encountered a creature nobody seems to know much about. It's called a reaver. Third eye in the middle of the forehead. Badass shield that repels bullets and blades unless you can find the sweet spot. Takes souls but only under certain circumstances. I've been able to get some background on them but not much. I was hoping you could call some people. Maybe see if anybody's ever dealt with one of these things before." I really didn't expect Albert to be able to help me on this one. But he'd rediscovered quite a bit of his pride assisting on my last case, so I was hoping we could continue the process on this one.

"Absolutely."

"Thanks. Talk to you soon."

"Will do." Funny, in our thirty-second conversation he seemed to have shed ten years. Had he really felt that useless in his retirement? If so, maybe I should talk to Evie. No way could I keep him busy enough to maintain this new outlook. Maybe she could think of something.

"Lucille Robinson?"

Cassandra wheeled me toward the white-jacketed forty-something holding my file folder in her hand. She was studying me with an air of disbelief. "How in the world does a person get eight nearly identical wounds in her hands?"

"I've been hanging with the wrong crowd. My mother always told me it would come to this. I guess I should've listened to her, huh?"

She eyed my gauze-covered fists. "What did you do?"

"Would you believe I wiped out while trying to surf the hand-rail at the telephone building?"

She shook her head, her ponytail waving a double negative behind her.

"Would you believe I punched a skateboarder who was surfing the handrail at the telephone building?"

"That I'll buy."

"Sounds like we've got a winner," I said just as young black guy with the name "Dr. Darryl" stitched on his lab coat entered the picture. For a minute there he couldn't seem to decide which one needed more attention, me or my file.

"Ms. Robinson."

"Hi, Doc. Would you believe I punched a skateboarder —"

"No."

*Clunk.* All at once my adrenaline rush from the fight fizzled, my goofy survival high vanished, and the don't-worry-be-happy bubbles in my poor blood-deprived brain burst. "I think I need to lie down."

Cassandra helped me to the table and laid her hand under my cheek because some sadistic nurse had stuffed the pillow with concrete blocks. As I rested my head in her palm, I had my own vision. My blood-soaked corpse lay on the glowing wooden deck of the *Constance Malloy*. Desmond stood over it, tonguing my quivering soul while his third eye glowed brighter and brighter blue.

Dr. Darryl stuck a needle in my left hand so he could numb it, at which point I decided the entire medical profession was an oxymoron. My brain wanted to rant further, but the vision expanded.

Now the Tor-al-Degan arrived on the yacht. Not vanquished after all, just transplanted from Miami so she could finish the job she'd started. She shambled toward my failing soul, licking her chops, her pincers waving with delight at the prospective meal before her.

"Do you feel this, Ms. Robinson?" Dr. Darryl asked, pinching the skin of my numbed hand.

*Do I feel it? Are you kidding me? I am in the middle of something absolutely epic. Me, Jasmine Parks, the girl who's barely equipped to run her own microwave. I'm telling you, this guy I know, Raoul, has made a huge mistake recruiting me to fight these freaks. I can't deal with them anymore. It's not like they want to steal my credit card or sell me a bag of weed. Ramos wants to be emperor of the damn world, and Chien-Lung's dragon suit could just get him there. And as if that isn't scary enough, Creepy Reaver Dude is after the source, the stuff that makes me Jaz. And he could get it. He could do me till I'm done, and then what? Then what? THEN WHAT?*

I started to shake. It wasn't making the sewing any easier, therefore the doc did not approve. He frowned at me.

"She's afraid of needles," said Cassandra, shrugging when he gave her a perplexed look, as if to say, "Who can explain the human mind?"

*I can. It's a bat cave. A warren. A maze. And I'm about to get lost in mine.*

Cassandra leaned over and whispered into my ear, "I saw that vision too, Jaz. It's what they want you to see. They want the fear to mold to you, like a body cast. Because if you can't move, you can't fight. You were right before. We have a choice. We can change the vision. You were right."

*Was I?* Big blank moment when I hoped somebody with the Big Answers (*Yo, Raoul?*) would jump in and give me a big yuh-huh.

*Raoul's busy, Jaz. So pick one. Are you right? Or are you crazy?*

I had to be right. Had to. If not, I'd be spending the rest of eternity lying on rock-hard hospital beds, peeing into metal bowls and yelling for the nurse to pump up the volume on *Wheel of Fortune*.

I watched the thread pull the pieces of my broken skin together, one tiny stitch at a time, and thought it strange to be able to see yourself mended.

"Do you get torn up like this a lot?" asked Dr. Darryl.

"Yeah."

"Well, as long as you're in Texas, I guess I don't have to worry about job security."

*Ha. Ha-ha. Hey, Doc, while you're at it, can you stitch my soul back on nice and tight? I'm afraid it's coming loose at the edges.*

"Jaz?" I looked up, so immersed in the memory of our hospital jaunt that I was surprised to find myself sitting under the RV's awning with Cassandra while kids yelled in the background and the smells of pulled-pork barbecue made my mouth water. She stood. "I think I'll take a walk. Maybe it will clear my mind."

"Okay." I watched her go. When I looked back out at the bay, nothing had changed. The *Constance Malloy* sat there like a sore on the water, and nobody knew. "Bitch needs to burn," I murmured. Checking my watch, I saw it was nearly setup time. Though we'd put the basics in place and practiced until we didn't actively suck, we still needed some audio stuff and a couple of lights. Clearly Bergman's area, but maybe he could use a hand. I hauled myself out of the chair, various aches and pains reminding me it was time for another dose of painkillers, and went inside to see if he needed a roadie.

He sat on the floor, his back supported by Mary-Kate. He'd returned all his gadgets and gizmos to their respective boxes. At present he clutched a small plastic cup in his hand the same way you might expect King Arthur to grasp the Holy Grail.

"I got it!" he gushed.

"Got what?"

"Our weapon! Here, let me show you." He took a red capsule the size of an Advil out of the cup and handed it to me.

"What's this?"

"A time-release neural jolt that will make Lung's brain tell his body it's had severe ultraviolet exposure. It's hard to explain—"

"Even if you wanted to—"

"Which I don't. The cool thing is, it's mostly fueled by his biochemistry!"

"So . . . the energy his body generates is what will set it off?"

"Not just set it off, magnify it several hundred times. He should be dead within two hours of ingesting it."

"So now we just need to make sure he gets a colossal headache?"

Bergman shrugged. "Or the munchies. However you can get him to swallow the pill."

I shook my head, viewing Bergman with renewed respect. "Can I ask you something, Miles?"

I could tell by the set of his shoulders he wanted to say no. But he surprised me.

"Okay."

"Why do you do this?" My gesture took in the monitor, showing the empty decks and hallways of the *Constance Malloy*, the laptops currently snoozing on the floor beside sleeping Cole, the lethal pill in Bergman's hand.

He adjusted his glasses, tried to meet my eyes and failed. "Because I have to," he mumbled. Was he embarrassed? At the moment, I didn't care.

"No, you don't," I said.

"Yes, I do," he insisted.

"What if you didn't?"

He thought about that a second as he drummed his fingers on his leg and studied the TV over my shoulder. Now he met my eyes. "I'd probably be dead."

"Really? How do you figure?"

"Boredom. You know, I'm not much good with people."

"You could be."

He shook his head. "I've tried. The wrong things keep coming out of my mouth. And honestly, most people annoy the hell out of me. I'd rather be alone than put up with their idiocy. I mean, all I have to do is watch two minutes of any reality-TV show and I'm reminded why I never go out. Anyway, I've come to accept that I'll be spending the majority of my life with machines. And that's okay, because I love them. I love everything about them. All the tiny parts that have to work together in perfect order so the whole will operate exactly as planned. I love the entire process, from concept to actuality. I even love the setbacks."

"In other words, you're hooked."

"Yeah."

"Are you happy?"

He gave a kind of sideways nod. "Most of the time."

Wow. Another first. I never thought, of the two of us, that I'd end up being the one envying Bergman.

# CHAPTER SIXTEEN

As Miles and I finished the prep work for our show, the tent flap opened and in walked the Chinese woman Cole and I had befriended, carrying Smiling Baby on her hip.

"Well, hi there," I said as I hopped down from the stage.

She bowed a couple of times, smiling widely as she said, "Hello. Hello."

"You know, I don't think we ever exchanged names. I'm Lucille Robinson," I said, pointing to myself because I still wasn't sure how much English she understood. Then I bowed.

"My name Xia Ge," she said sweetly. She pointed to the baby. "This Xia Lai."

"Pleased to meet you."

"Is Cole there?"

I looked over my shoulder. Oh, she meant—

"Did someone call for me?" asked Cole as he strutted through the tent's back opening and grinned at Ge and her little boy. He'd showered and changed into his costume—tight black dress pants, matching shirt, and a glittering red vest with enormous black buttons. Lai immediately reached for him, so Cole obliged, grabbing him firmly under the arms and swinging him in circles until he giggled and squealed.

"You are perform tonight?" Xia Ge asked him shyly. I could tell she approved of the outfit.

"Yeah. Are you still coming? If I have time, maybe I can fit Lai, here, into my juggling act."

She nodded happily. "Yes, we will be there." She touched his hand briefly as she added, "Then you come see acrobats show end of week. Yes? You still have tickets?"

Cole nodded. "Yeah. You know, unless something prevents us, we'll definitely be there." He handed Baby Lai back to his mom, she bowed some more, and they left.

*Hmm, should I lecture or let it go?* "Do you always have this effect on women and small children?" I asked.

Cole stuck his hands in his pockets and looked down bashfully at the toes of his high-tops. "Pretty much."

"You're a regular flirting fiend, you know that?"

"I don't flirt with married women," he said with an absolutely straight face. *Really?* I wasn't sure I bought it and he must have been able to tell. "Did that look like flirting to you?" he demanded.

I considered his expressions, his body language, not much different than usual. But then he was usually flirting. "Maybe."

He was in my face in moments, grinning like a lunatic. "Then I haven't been flirting with you enough lately." He grabbed my arm, kissed down the length of it as he made French lover noises. "Hwah, hwah, hwah, my *ravissant mademoiselle.*"

"Oh my God, you are such a dork!" It kind of tickled so, despite my best intentions, I was laughing by the time he got to my hand, where he stopped with genuine horror.

"What the hell?" So much for funsies. My giggles dried up like a desert stream.

"Ambushed by a reaver," I said shortly.

"I hope he looks worse than you do."

"Um, probably not. He ran before I could do any real damage."

"Woman, you need a keeper."

"It's probably my fault. He was pissed about the reaver I killed last night," I said. "You know what they say, look before you shoot."

"They say that?"

"Yes. And it pertains to making friends while on the job too. Did you realize you've arranged for your new pals to possibly be sitting in the same audience with Chien-Lung?"

"Actually, yeah, I have. The way I figure it, the dad's one of his acrobats, so they've been under his thumb for a while. Which also means they might know something that would help us."

"You don't seem to have much confidence in Bergman's inventions."

"Just planning for just in case."

I considered him, a twenty-six-year-old stud who loved women and children but wasn't married, who'd lost his business but had found a way to progress, who popped bubbles like a sixth grader but made sensible, thoughtful, professional decisions. "No wonder you fit right in. You're just as warped as the rest of us!"

He wiggled his eyebrows suggestively. "It took you long enough to figure that one out. Speaking of which, it's almost dark, beautiful lady. Aren't you supposed to be getting into something a lot less difficult to see through?"

The costume. My dive into belly-dancing denial had gone so deep I hadn't even seen it yet. Oh man, if I was going to make any sort of adjustments to what promised to be a too-sexy outfit, I'd better get busy. I ran out of the tent, half wishing my newly found awkwardness would allow me to break an ankle before I reached the closet and, as I saw it, my impending doom.

When I got back to the RV, Vayl had already risen. Grumpy. His first words to me as I entered the kitchen were "I want to talk to you. Outside."

I felt like punching something because, despite my hurt feelings, I still responded warmly (okay, hotly) to his getup. He'd dressed for the show in clothes so retro he'd have looked at home on the set of *A Christmas Carol*. But the pants were just tight enough, the jacket just the right length, the shirt showed just enough chest hair that all I wanted was to slide down the wall and stare.

I followed him out the door to the water's edge, trying not to slink guiltily, fighting the feeling that the dean had caught me smoking in the girls' room.

"What happened today?" he demanded. "Neither Cassandra nor Bergman would give me any details."

"I'm not surprised. You look ready to pounce."

"I am!" He realized he'd been close to shouting and lowered his voice. "Consider this a formal debriefing. Leave nothing out. Go."

*Go? What am I, a sprinter? And what the hell with the* I Spy *talk?* With a mounting sensation of *you suck* feeding my attitude, I gave him his damn debriefing: dream, reaver, hospital, killer pill, Xia Lai, and all.

After I'd finished he stood staring at me, one hand in the pocket of his gray slacks, the other clutching his cane so hard I expected the jewel on top to pop off at any second.

"And why do you smell like Cole?"

"Oh, we were just goofing around." Vayl's eyes blazed dark green with gold flecks exploding like depth charges at random intervals. "Not like *that*. Like, joking."

He started to pace, his cane making an irritating *clack!* as he hit it against the seawall every other step. Also there was muttering and some very sharp gestures stopping just short of punching the air. When he whirled on me I actually jumped, which didn't help my frame of mind. One. Bit.

"You are driving me mad!" he thundered. "Do you have no sense of restraint whatsoever?"

"You're the one who volunteered me to strut my stuff in front of mobs of weirdos!"

"This has nothing to do with belly dancing!"

"This has everything to do with belly dancing!" *In a round-about way, but still.*

"If you had not killed that reaver last night—"

"That poor man he murdered would have lost his soul!"

Vayl jabbed his cane into the concrete so hard it shivered. "You could have *died* today! And how would I have learned? Perhaps the barbecue chefs would have had another fortuitous gossip session? Or maybe Cole would have mentioned it between play dates with Chinese Mother and Baby Charms-Them-All."

"What's your point?"

He struggled to bring his voice to maybe-they-won't-hear-us-in-Mexico level. "I would like to wake up one evening without wondering whether or not you will be alive to greet me!"

"I am what I am, Vayl! I take risks. Sometimes that means I get hurt. Someday that means I'll die. And I won't come back. You're going to have to deal with that."

"Why should I, when you could be like me?" The words ripped out of him as if yanked by an invisible hand. He jerked, as if I'd slapped him. I'd never have had the energy. His last pronouncement had left me completely zapped. Vayl wanted to turn me? So I could hang out with him forever? I didn't know whether to cry or puke.

"I apologize," he said. "I had no right—"

"No. You didn't."

More silence. He heaved a big sigh, and I suddenly wondered if it felt extra good to him, taking a deep, sweet breath of air after not breathing the entire day before. Judging from his present stance, not so much. He'd turned his side to me so that he faced the bay and his feet were placed just right to knock one out of the park if I had one to pitch.

"The dreams."

"Yes."

"Without Gregory's help . . . do you have any idea what to do next?"

"Yes."

He turned, fully facing me in his surprise. "You do?"

"I think I need to talk to David."

"Not over the phone, I take it."

"Nope."

"I want . . ." He ground his teeth together. "Would you mind doing that while I am awake? I would appreciate the chance to watch over you."

"No problem."

Vayl came to me, lifted a curl from my face, brushing my cheek with his fingertips as he did so. I didn't understand why, with his powers so closely related to cold, his touch couldn't leave me numb. No such luck. Just that slight graze of skin on skin had sent little spikes of flame rushing through my bloodstream. It took an effort not to pant. *This is your boss. Who has mentally taken you through the whole human-to-vamp scenario. Where is your pride, woman?* "Please believe," he said, "no matter how much I wish it, I would never ask you to become a vampire. I do know better."

"I should hope so!" *There it is! You go, girl! At least until he touches you again!*

He nodded. "But I wish you would try somewhat harder to lengthen your life."

"Now you sound like Pete." *Oh, hey, somebody sound a gong.* I'd just spotted a hint of dimple. "Look, I am good at this job, Vayl. You of all people should know that."

"I do. I just—ever since Miami, I have been haunted by the vision of you lying limp within the Tor-al-Degan's jaws. It has forcefully reminded me how vulnerable you are."

Wow, how often do you really get to step outside your own selfish view? And here I thought I was the only one who still had nightmares starring that monster's putrid scent and her bright red tentacles.

"Jaz!" Bergman yelled out the RV door. "Half an hour till show time."

"Gotta get into my costume," I told Vayl. I smiled brightly, pretending my stomach hadn't just tied itself into a noose. *You can do this, Jaz. No problem. Just pretend you're back on the beach, not in a tent full of strangers.*

"Are you nervous?" asked Vayl.

"No, who me? Of course not! Why would I be? Ha, ha, ha!" I skipped off to the RV, ignoring the undeniable sound of Vayl's low chuckle behind me.

# Chapter Seventeen

Bergman had estimated our fifteen double rows of benches could comfortably hold about one hundred fifty people. Since nobody looked that relaxed, I guessed our crowd tipped the scale around two hundred.

*No doubt about it,* I thought as I stood waiting in the wings. *My skirt's going to fall right off. Oh God, did I remember to put on underwear?* I checked. *Whew! Plus the skirt's tied on pretty tight. Oh geez. What about the top? There's nothing to this damn thing! What if I fall out? What if I just plain fall?*

Vayl had forced me into this, the lout. I began to plot my revenge. The next time he slept I would sneak into his tent and draw a mustache on his face in red marker. I'd insist he go shopping with me and then make him stand next to a bin of panties while I tried on clothes. I'd take him to Evie's first PTA meeting and volunteer him to serve cookies and punch.

*Hey, Cole's not a bad juggler. Bowling pins, rings, a couple of cans of tennis balls. Didn't know he had it in him. What? Is he done already? Holy crap, it's my turn!*

Bergman switched from general lighting to a single spot and pumped up the music. I swishy swished onto the stage. The crowd greeted me with loud, prolonged applause. Now that I could no longer hide behind the curtain and obsess, I felt better. After all, I wore three tons of makeup, most of Cassandra's traveling jewelry, and six layers of skirting, under which I'd strapped my leg holster and a sweet little .38 I usually reserved for pants-free occasions. My gold sequined top erred on the skimpy side, but rows of flat golden discs had been sewn to it so it looked less like a sports bra and more like a lets-play-banker costume. Long, sheer black sleeves covered my arms, and black lace fingerless gloves disguised the bandages on my hands.

And those posed the real challenge. The hands are an integral part of the belly dance and do a lot to make you look graceful. Despite being under the influence of painkillers, they hurt like hell to hold correctly. But concentrating on that really helped me ignore the fact that Chien-Lung had indeed shown up and sat front and center, where he smiled and bobbed his head in time with the music. He wore another traditional Chinese robe, this one black embroidered with red dragons. I caught his eye once, and immediately felt grateful he had to keep his hands stuffed in those oversized sleeves. Otherwise he probably would've been waving dollar bills around like the best man at a bachelor party.

Lung's lady sidekick, who sat to his right, didn't seem too thrilled with his interest in the belly dancer either. She kept nudging him with her elbow, until finally he leaned over and said something to the vamp to his left and they both shared a quiet laugh. I thought I recognized the new vamp as one who'd waited out the fight the night before to see who'd win.

On the other side of the aisle, the Xia clan seemed to be enjoying their night out together. Mom sat straight and proper, hands in her lap, but her eyes had shone extra bright when Cole took the stage. Xia Lai stood on his dad's muscular legs, bouncing in time with the music.

Before I knew it the first song had ended. The next one was much faster. Harder, yes, but more fun too. About halfway through the crowd started to clap in time, which inspired me to try moves I hadn't attempted in years despite the very real possibility that I might be too sore to move in the morning. I must've pulled it off, because they cheered at the end.

Now I remembered why I'd always been the first one to arrive at my dance lessons and the last to leave. Forget tattoos. Done correctly and received with an open heart, belly dancing is true body art. And my audience was ideal. Besides Lung and his pal, who I pointedly ignored, it was mostly families. No wolf whistles. No whooping and hollering. Just lots of clapping in time as I moved them through the music, telling them a story they understood at the gut, where rhythm speaks its universal language. *Okay*, I admitted, as I bowed to yet another round of avid applause, *this is a freaking blast.*

The last song had barely begun before Vayl began to sing along from the back of the tent. I didn't even know the thing had words, and I sure hadn't expected him to turn it into a group performance. But there he was, walking toward me down the center of the aisle, singing Romanian in his husky baritone.

*Definitely a love song,* I decided as I turned and swung my hips at him. I looked over my shoulder. His smile was definitely predatory. I gave him a little torso roll and he rewarded me with a look of such piercing hunger I nearly jumped on him. How we maintained a PG rating through the rest of that song I will never know. But the thunderous applause at the end told me it was big fun.

I strutted off the stage, waving and blowing kisses to my new fans. Which was undoubtedly why, as soon as I made it past the backstage curtain, I ran straight into a support pole. I damn near brought the whole house down. Literally. I held the pole very still and tried not to think of what would happen if we couldn't lure

Lung into a one-on-one because the Assistant Assassin ran her head into a steel rod.

A sound to my right caught my attention. It was very subtle, landing somewhere between a quiet snort and a faint gurgle. I took a short hike outside the tent and found Cole rolling on the ground.

"Are you all right?" I rushed to him, trying to hold him still so I could see the site of his injury. Then I got a look at his face. "Are you *laughing*?"

"Oh my God, you should've seen your face!" He was trying to hold it in so the audience wouldn't be distracted from Vayl's singing. But the laughter kept slipping out the edges of his mouth.

"Don't you have anything better to do?" I demanded.

"Than to watch a gorgeous woman belly dance? We are talking about *me*, right?"

"So it was good?"

"I sure couldn't figure out why you were freaking out about the whole thing. Until the pole incident, of course. Good thing nobody saw you but me."

"I saw her." Cassandra came up beside us, laughing so hard her shoulders were shaking.

"Oh for—isn't it your turn?" I glared at her.

"Yes, and I was dreading it so badly I threw up three times. But now I feel better." Her smile was as warm as a hug. "Thank you."

"Hey, anytime I can entertain you with my humiliation, I feel I've done my job. What the hell is it with me lately?" I wondered aloud. "I can't seem to make it through a single day without running into or falling over something. And I was a college athlete!"

Cassandra regarded me soberly. "The universe requires balance, Jasmine. Your powers as a Sensitive have increased, have they not?"

"Well, yeah."

"Perhaps your recent spate of awkward incidents is the price you are required to pay for that boost."

"Well, if it's true, that sucks."

She nodded, clearly distracted by other, more important considerations. "Will you"—Cassandra licked her lips as her eyes darted toward the tent, as if she could see Lung through two layers of canvas and a black curtain—"when the time comes, you will stay close by, won't you?"

"Is in the room close enough?"

"Oh, really? I can't tell you how relieved I am to hear that."

"It was Vayl's idea. When we give away the free reading, we toss in a private belly dance too. That puts me right beside you the whole time he's there." There was a moment of silence from inside the tent, followed by a healthy round of applause. Then Vayl began his final song. "We know from talking to Yetta Simms that Lung loves the escargot. So we'll offer him a tray of delicacies and hope he's in the mood to indulge himself." Cassandra already knew this stuff, but I needed to keep her thinking, thus the review. If her analytical mind let go, she was going to freeze like a math whiz at a spelling bee.

"And if he won't eat it?" she asked.

"We'll figure some other way to get him to swallow the pill. Maybe stuff it in his vitamins or something. That comes later—maybe. For now, encourage him to eat. Eat with him even, but stay away from the snails."

She nodded, looking fairly calm until your eyes dropped to her hands. Her long slender fingers kept twining in and around one another like newborn snakes.

"Hey, Cassandra," said Cole, "I meant to tell you. Your boyfriend's in the audience." He said it as if we'd teleported back to junior high, and he suspected she'd just contracted a terminal case of the cooties.

"My . . . what?"

Cole went into his superhero pose, legs spread, hands on hips, chin directed squarely at the sky, and sang, "Na-na-na-na, na-na-na-na, SWAT man!"

"Oh, God!" Cassandra clutched at me, her fingernails digging into my arms. *Ow!* "Jasmine! The vision!"

I hid the dread that twisted my insides at the realization that everybody in her divination had now reached his or her appointed place. "Don't worry, Cassandra. When I see the snake, I promise I'll shoot it before it strikes."

"I'll be there too," Cole assured her.

I watched Cassandra, wondering how she'd manage to keep it together with her head full of death and her future depending on a rookie assassin, a woman with more stitches than sense, a distracted vampire, and a paranoid engineer. But I guess I already knew. She would because she had to. That's always how people like us end up getting through hells like this.

The applause built to a crescendo and then faded as Vayl began to introduce our main event. Cole held the back tent flap aside for Cassandra and she stepped into the staging area, gracefully avoiding the pole that had nearly concussed me minutes earlier. She took a couple of deep breaths. "How do I look?" she asked.

She'd pulled her braids back and tied them with a vivid-blue scarf. Her matching skirt was embroidered with black sequined flowers. Her black sleeveless top provided the perfect backdrop for one of the pieces of jewelry she hadn't lent me—a gold choker that started just under her ears and ended slightly above her collarbones. "Very Egyptian queen," I said.

She nodded and smiled, but the pleasure never reached her eyes.

Vayl swept the backdrop curtain aside. The applause pulled her forward.

Cole asked, "Is she going to be okay?"

"I think so. But SWAT man's presence is not a good sign. He dies in her vision too."

"It must suck to be psychic." Under his breath, Cole added, "We have company."

I heard it then, a soft step accompanied by the squeal of a pumped-up baby. Xia Ge's husband stepped around the corner of the tent. He carried Lai, whose resemblance to his dad was remarkable considering the difference in their ages and emotional states. Lai obviously thought walking with Dad was the be all, end all of great times. He bounced his butt against his dad's forearm and patted him repeatedly on his broad chest and shoulders, as if Lai was a one baby band and Dad his instrument.

Dad, on the other hand, looked like he wanted to cry. It wasn't the face he'd worn inside the tent, but then his family and manager had been around. I felt an instant connection to him. It sucked having to hide intense fears from the world. I gave him a warm smile and bowed.

"Hi. I'm Lucille, and this is Cole."

He bowed too, which Lai thought they should do twenty more times. He communicated this by lunging forward so Dad had to catch him and pull him upright again. He kept it up the whole time we talked.

"I am Xia Shao," said Dad. "My wife, Ge, tell me you save Lai's life. I thank you." He bowed deeply.

"It's our pleasure," Cole said.

When he straightened, Shao said, "Ge telling me you very nice people. *Good* people." He stared hard at us, as if his eyes alone had the power to reveal any evil tendencies we might be hiding. In the end he shrugged helplessly. "She *know* people. I trust her. She say I should talk to you."

"She's very sweet," I replied. "A good mother." I shook my head in amazement. "So patient."

He cracked a smile. "Usually." We watched Lai do some more waist bends before Shao continued. "I work —" he jerked his head toward the amazing acrobat arena. "Many friends there." He shrugged. "You travel together, work together, you become close."

Cole and I nodded.

"I have friends . . ." Shao looked away, his eyes scrunching at the edges as he struggled to hold back tears. "They disappear. Their clothes, equipment, all still in trailers, but no friends. They not coming to show tonight." Now he looked at us, trying to communicate how bizarre he regarded this behavior to be. "Something is terrible wrong."

In my mind I saw the men who had attacked Lung, still dripping from their swim from shore, and agreed with Shao that something was terrible wrong.

Now that Shao had said the hard part, the words came much faster and tougher to understand as his accent also increased. "I believe Chien-Lung have something to do with this. You know?" He pointed a thumb toward the tent. "Front row?"

We nodded. Boy, did we ever know.

"Lung own that boat." He pointed to the *Constance Malloy*. "He bringing all Chinese crew to run it, but they stuck in Chicago." He tried to find the word, couldn't, and showed us instead, his free hand starting above his head, lowering slowly as he wiggled his fingers.

"Snowstorm?" guessed Cole. Shao pointed at him and nodded.

*Aha!* Now I understood how we'd lucked into the catering gig. I'd thought it out of character for Lung to allow strangers aboard his yacht. But with his staff snowbound in Chicago and a big shindig in the works, he'd had no other choice.

Shao went on. "My brother, Xia Wu, is part of crew. I fear what will happen when he arrive. I fear he disappear too."

"What makes you think he'll be in particular danger?" asked Cole.

Shao looked over both his shoulders and behind us. He leaned forward, giving Lai access to the huge buttons on Cole's vest. He grabbed one and tried to put it in his mouth as Shao whispered, "Wu in army. So was my friends. Very shhh." He held a finger to his lips to emphasize the secrecy.

*Huh. So the People's Liberation Army wants Chien-Lung dead. Well, I don't suppose you can plan a coup without rumors flying into the wrong ears.* Wu, undoubtedly, was supposed to help overthrow Lung last night, but his flight delay had kept him out of the fighting.

"What if Chien-Lung find out about my brother?" Shao asked. "Maybe he disappear too." I thought that a definite possibility. "I cannot talk to Chinese authorities. I do not know who is faithful to Chien-Lung. But you. You from America," he told us, as if we needed to be reminded. "You know who can help?"

Uhhh, well . . . Cole and I looked at each other. He gave me an it's-your-call shrug.

"What exactly do you want us to do?" I asked Shao.

"I think my friends on that boat." He pointed to the *Constance Malloy*. I thought them more likely under that boat, since I'd seen the generals weight the bodies before throwing them overboard. But I let him go on. "Maybe your police go on there, find them. Maybe arrest Lung?"

Maybe Lung would die tonight and we wouldn't have to worry about it. "I know a policeman here," I said, thinking of Cassandra's SWAT man, Preston, and of how badly she and I both wanted to keep him alive. "I'll talk to him tomorrow," I said, knowing I wouldn't. Unless I absolutely had to.

# Chapter Eighteen

With a promise to report to Shao in the morning, I convinced him to go back into the tent. Hopefully Lung would just think Lai had tired of sitting still and nothing would come of their absence. Lai might even help perpetuate the illusion, because the constant bowing and foiled attempts to eat Cole's button had evidently worn him out. As we said goodbye, he turned in his dad's arms and rested his head on his shoulder. I figured he'd be asleep before they made it back to the entrance.

"Okay, you were right," said Cole. "I never should have brought the Xias within a hundred feet of this mess, because now I'm not going to sleep for worrying about them." He fished a piece of gum out of his pocket and popped it into his mouth.

So the gum had graduated from a kicking-smoking habit to a hindering-stress routine. Like shuffling cards only saner. I linked arms with Cole, liking him even better now that we had something else in common. "They were already in this mess, or weren't you listening? And hey, if everything goes okay tonight, they'll be fine. Speaking of which, did you get the food?"

"Yeah. Yetta brought it over just after you went on."

He took me back into the tent, into the staging area behind the black backdrop, and showed me a round, lace-covered table I hadn't seen before because it sat in the corner, hidden by shadows. I could hear Cassandra talking as I borrowed Cole's penlight to peek into the covered trays and dishes the owner of Seven Seas Succulents had provided. As Cassandra told an audience member his daughter would get the scholarship she'd applied for, I whispered into Cole's ear, "Which one?"

He took my hand and pointed the light at a star-shaped glass plate loaded with escargots. He trained the light on one of them. It had been placed just at the tip of one of the points. "That's it," he murmured. "You can tell it's the right one because there's a little chip broken off the bottom of the tray just underneath." I felt along the base of the star and, sure enough, my finger found the indentation.

On the other side of the curtain, Cassandra said, "I am growing tired. Perhaps just one more item from the audience?"

I heard scraping and shuffling. Then Cassandra said, with barely concealed regret, "Sergeant Preston?"

*Uh-oh.* I peeked around the side of the curtain that divided our narrow space from the stage. Yup, SWAT man had volunteered his Seiko. He and his kid, a cute little dude about five or six with his dad's intelligent brown eyes, sat in the back row. Well, Preston sat. The kid stood on the bench, looking deeply enthralled. Suddenly Cassandra couldn't beat off her admirers with a rubber mallet.

"What is it you want to know?" she asked stiffly as her hands worried over the watch.

"There's a woman I'm interested in," he said, giving her a slow wink. "Will I see her again?"

She hesitated, but couldn't, even in this moment, bring herself to lie. You had to admire that kind of resolve. "Yes."

"You are allowed two more questions," said Vayl. I couldn't see him, but I could feel him, standing on the opposite end of the stage. He and Cassandra had agreed audience members could ask three questions of her, hoping it would whet Lung's appetite for a more in-depth reading for himself.

"Will I ever remarry?"

"I do not see that in your future."

He looked surprised, then shrugged. "And your last question?" put in Vayl.

"Okay, uh, there's no school tomorrow, so my boy and I are going fishing in the morning. Will we catch anything?"

Cassandra's hands, holding tightly to the watch, jerked. Her voice, when she answered, wound so tight I could almost hear her vocal chords twang. "Nothing you want him to take off the hook."

The whole audience held its breath. "Then I'll definitely be taking him to the zoo," said Preston. Everyone laughed, except him, Cassandra, and Vayl. Looking at Preston, I got the feeling he knew she was holding back the most important truths she could tell him.

Vayl stepped to the center of the stage. He held a gleaming black bowl in his hand. As planned, Bergman had piled the torn halves of our audience's tickets inside. "Now it is time to announce tonight's winner of a free private reading from Cassandra, preceded by a belly dance from the fabulous Lucille and accompanied by free refreshments. This will take place as soon as the tent has cleared. We are drawing by ticket number, so please look to your ticket stubs now."

He jumbled the papers as he said, "And the winner is . . . 103." He looked around the room. "Just bring your stub to me, if you would—"

Lung's male companion, who held their ticket stubs, began to whisper in his ear as he bounced in his seat. He looked as excited as an old fart who's just gotten a BINGO. When Lung nodded he jumped up and handed Vayl the ticket, which he pretended to study.

"This is the one!" said Vayl. He held his hands out to the audience. "Please give our lucky winner and all of our performers tonight a round of applause." The audience obeyed. As they shuffled out, Vayl said, "Thank you for your attendance and please drive home safely!"

I kept my eyes on Lung, who was getting it from both sides. His lady friend hissed in one ear, making fierce gestures that said she was not pleased with this turn of events. The new vamp chattered into the other, encouraging him to stay, relax, have fun.

Lung listened to them both, but his eyes followed the Xias as they exited the tent, lingering hungrily on Lai as he snoozed on Dad's shoulder. *Don't worry, you freak*, I thought. *We've got just the snack you need.*

Finally Lung focused on Vayl. "I am indeed fortunate," he said in a perfect British accent. "Would you mind if I stand, however? I find these benches somewhat taxing."

"Certainly. If you would just wait here, I shall escort Cassandra backstage to rest and Lucille will arrive to entertain you momentarily."

Gulp. I clutched at the curtain, as if only it could support me under a sudden spurt of nausea. Now I'd only be dancing for three, but the very intimacy of such a setting made me want to zip into an ankle-length parka. I closed my eyes and took a deep breath. *Quit being a wimp. You can do this. You* have *to do this.* I stroked the .38 riding my thigh as I might a beloved dog. It calmed me enough that I was able to meet Vayl and Cassandra with a pleasant smile.

"Ready?" I asked brightly, as if we were about to trot off to the church picnic alongside Tom Sawyer and Becky Thatcher.

Vayl nodded, releasing Cassandra and offering me his arm. We cruised back onstage. Lung now crouched on the bench, as we'd seen him do on the yacht. His companions continued to flank him. Vayl led me down the stage steps to meet them.

"May I introduce Miss Lucille Robinson?" Vayl asked.

Lung bowed his head. "You are grace and beauty personified. My name is Chien-Lung," he said. Nice words, yeah. But the eyes *so* did not back them up. They reminded me of Dave and his buddies that summer they grew about six inches apiece. Every time they trooped into the kitchen and opened the stove it was like some amazing new discovery. "Whoa! Sticky buns! *All right!*"

The girl in me wanted to slap Lung across his face and yell, "Get your eyes off my sticky buns, ya creep!" No, I don't usually mind. I get that straight guys are going to look at boobs and butts. But generally they're überdiscreet, and I appreciate that. This guy—*not*.

*Jasmine, don't tell me you're surprised this guy's a weaselly little perve,* I lectured myself. *Now cut the personal reactions and act like a pro already!*

The new vamp, who'd also enjoyed the show, displayed much better manners. He did, however, seem fascinated with the fake ruby I'd placed in my navel. He jumped up to greet me, his hand out and ready to grab mine.

"This is my assistant, Li Ruolan," Lung said as I slipped my hand into the new vamp's and murmured, "How nice to meet you." He'd come dressed in Western clothes: nice brown slacks and a short-sleeved blue shirt with a blue and gray striped tie.

Lung continued. "And this is my adopted daughter, Pengfei Yan."

*Yeah, right.* "Pleased to make your acquaintance," I said, working hard to keep it civil. She looked normal enough with her long black hair braided straight down her back. Some artist of a seamstress had embroidered exquisite white flowers all over her sleeveless blue silk blouse. Her black silk pants matched her flats. I even liked her dangly black pearl earrings. Nope, her physical appearance didn't offend me one bit.

But I'd seen her kill maybe six men the night before. Probably just a drop in the bucket for somebody who associated with a monster like Lung. And none of it showed on that smooth, pale face. In those clear obsidian eyes. Plus something about her psychic odor, the scent that signaled to me, as a Sensitive, that I was dealing with a vampire, turned my stomach. Pengfei emitted a burnt-offering sort of aroma that triggered mental images of mass graves.

Bergman still sat at the back of the tent, so I signaled to him that I was ready. Vayl took a seat across the aisle from Lung, where the Xia family had perched minutes before. As the music started, I moved back onto the stage and began dancing. The painkillers Dr. Darryl had prescribed wore off about halfway through the song, and by the time I finished my hands were throbbing like all the bones had sheered off midway and now scraped against each other like cheese on a grater. I managed to keep my poise, but *damn* it hurt. Though I hid it well, Pengfei Yan seemed to suspect. And the sick little bitch got off on it.

"Lovely," she said after I'd finished. She and Li Ruolan clapped enthusiastically. "Could you do another one?"

Jaz would've pulled the .38 and shot that smirk right off her lips. But Lucille Robinson had taken charge, smiled widely at her, and said, "Of course," before violence could be done. I looked at Bergman expectantly. He fiddled with some knobs and dials for a second, then said, "Sorry, my equipment's down. Looks like I need to replace some parts, but it'll be fixed by tomorrow."

My smile widened for him, only now it was real. The self-centered tech-head had just saved my aching ass. *Will wonders never cease?*

Vayl stood. "Thank you, Lucille. Would you and Cole bring in the refreshments while Cassandra prepares?" I nodded and rushed offstage as Vayl turned to Lung and said, "This is actually about the time we usually dine, so we hope you will join us."

I pulled the curtain back to admit Cole, who stood ready with the table. I helped him carry it up the back stairs and to stage left. Now that light shone on it, I could see the ivory lace cloth covering it. Yetta had chosen both silver and glass serving dishes. She'd also provided white china rimmed with red roses for eating, along with heavy silver forks, knives, and spoons.

Vayl inclined his head toward Lung. "You are the lucky winner, sir, so we invite you to fill your plate first."

"How kind." Lung went up the stairs to the buffet, followed closely by his cohorts. Cole and I stood on one side of the table, forcing them to walk along the other side, so the stuffed snail would be closest to them. Unfortunately Lung's wrapped hands wouldn't allow him to hold a plate, though he didn't mention it to us. He just kept them tucked inside his sleeves and let Li Ruolan fill one for him. Li took his time, arranging the food so neatly it could've posed for a still life. Luckily that painting would've been called "assassination," because the deadly snail definitely took a starring role.

We all sat on the benches to eat, as if we were at some bizarre family reunion. If Romeo and Juliet had lived to bear offspring, I imagined this was how the Capulets and Montagues would've behaved at the kid's first birthday party. Nobody even tried to converse. Our side watched theirs from the corners of our eyes, feeling slightly grossed out that Li Ruolan fed Lung every single bite he ate, and worried that Li seemed to taste everything first.

Li had the snail on his fork.

I picked up a tiny biscuit I'd doused with butter and honey and popped the whole thing in my mouth. *Like that, you kiss up,* I thought. *Shove that mollusk in your boss's mouth and let's get it on!*

Cassandra walked in and Li's fork hit the plate.

*Arrghh!*

Lung had been eyeing the escargot eagerly. Now he looked at Cassandra. A new hunger lit his eyes, one that had nothing to do with snails. And I instantly understood why the obsession with psychics. He wanted her blood. Sometimes vamps get fixated like that. They crave a particular type. Teenaged girls. Druids. Canadians. Feeding on one specific class gives them such a spectacular rush it becomes an addiction. When that happens they tend to be real hard to stop.

Li started to get up, maybe to introduce himself, but Lung forced him back down. The fact that he'd pulled his hand from its cocoon made me realize just how little he cared about witnesses at this moment.

I began to get a little cross-eyed, watching Li retrieve the escargot fork while Lung stalked Cassandra with unblinking eyes. She went to the far side of the buffet table, so that she faced us as she spooned a few goodies onto her plate.

Li's fork moved toward Lung's mouth.

Lung stood up.

Pengfei put a hand to his robes and murmured something in Chinese. She looked more annoyed than nervous.

Vayl and I tensed, ready to spring. Behind us, Cole and Bergman put their plates down. Behind them, the tent flap flew open and Preston strode inside.

"Cassandra!" he called. "I hoped you'd still be here." His expression, which had been open and friendly, began to lock down as he took in his surroundings. After a swift recon his gaze returned to her, his right hand moving slowly to his back. "Is everything okay?"

I could see the slow dawn of horror rounding out her eyes, nailing her feet to the floor. She tried to nod, but her head jerked to the side instead. Movement from our guests pulled my attention away from her.

Li had put the snail in his own mouth. I watched him swallow with a strange sense of distance, as if I were three hundred miles away, looking through the lens of a telescope. And in my mind, one word began to rotate around and around . . .

*Un-frigging-believable.*

Pengfei pulled harder on Lung's robes, trying to break his concentration, make him look at her. But the dragon was intent on his prey.

He leaped onstage without warning, closing the distance between them so fast Cassandra didn't even have time to scream. He'd just reached the table when Preston called out sternly, "Stop, or I'll shoot!"

I spared him a quick glance. He'd pulled his Kimber .45, all right, and if we good guys didn't stay low we might catch some of his lead.

"Preston!" Cassandra screamed.

Lung had turned on the SWAT man, his mouth just finishing its transformation into a muzzle. Knowing what came next, I ran at Preston and tackled him, driving us both to the ground just as Lung let loose with a massive jet of flame. Heat poured over the top of us, singeing but not searing.

I yanked up my skirt and grabbed my .38. I'd have to be damn close for a lethal shot, but it was better than nothing. I craned my neck, trying to see if Lung had another dose coming, but he'd turned back to Cassandra. Only she'd disappeared.

As he stood, momentarily baffled, both Vayl and Pengfei reached the stage. At the same time Bergman and Cole had each grabbed one of the fire extinguishers sitting in the back corners of the tent and headed toward the middle, where several benches were burning.

Smoke began to drift through the tent, making my eyes water. I looked for Li and saw him diving out the back way. Apparently he had no interest in fire or blood-hungry dragons.

On the stage, Vayl reached Lung just as he tipped the table over backward with a spectacular crash, revealing Cassandra crouching underneath. But she'd gone into hiding armed with a knife, which she drove toward Lung's groin with desperate speed.

As I reached the stage stairs Vayl's power rushed through the room, dropping the temperature by forty degrees. Frost coated every surface. Though being Sensitive gave me something of a resistance to vampiric powers, I still felt like I'd been ice fishing for an hour without a coat.

The back of Lung's robe ripped open, giving me an excellent view of those launchable spines. I feared Vayl would get a chest full, standing right behind Lung as he was, but ice had formed around the base of the spines, preventing their release.

Cassandra's knife didn't penetrate, but the blunt force caused Lung to roar in pain as it struck. At the same time, Vayl wrapped his arm around Lung's neck and pulled him backward. I didn't think he had a plan beyond getting him away from Cassandra.

A spurt of flame from Lung's muzzle caught the top of the tent. Fire erupted on the canvas and licked its way in every direction.

I heard Preston on the phone as he came closer, moving as if every one of his joints had frozen, calling for fire trucks, police, ambulance, the works. He climbed up on the stage beside me, helped me pull Cassandra to her feet and hustle her toward the back of the tent.

I stopped, trained my .38 on Pengfei. She was yelling at Lung in Chinese as she pulled two throwing stars from her pockets. I shot her as she wound up and she lurched sideways. She still managed to throw one, hitting Vayl in the thigh. It staggered him enough to weaken his hold on Lung, who tore away and grabbed Pengfei.

By now flames engulfed the entire tent roof. At any moment it would fall and then we'd be some crispy critters. Cole and Bergman backed toward the front exit yelling, "Get out! Get out!" I couldn't see Preston and Cassandra, which probably meant they'd already left.

I ran to Vayl, who had jerked the throwing star out of his leg. Blood spurted from the wound in steady bursts, soaking his pants and leaving a solid trail as I pulled him backstage and out of the tent. Cole and Bergman waited for us there, Bergman holding the RV keys in his hand.

"Help me with him," I told Cole as I led Vayl toward the seawall. Without a word, Cole put a shoulder under Vayl's arm. My concern deepened when Vayl allowed him to help.

"Okay if I move the RV?" Bergman asked.

"As soon as you bring us the first-aid kit."

That job done, Bergman drove our temporary headquarters out of the fire's reach, as Cole and I worked to get the bleeding under control. When the first step is yanking a belt around your patient's thigh, the project is not going well.

"In all your long life, didn't anyone ever once tell you not to pull out something after it had been stuck into you?" I hissed as Cole tugged the belt tight and I laid on the gauze.

Vayl didn't reply, though I could feel his leg stiffen under my hand. I thought it was a reaction to physical pain until Cole said, "Jaz, maybe you shouldn't yell at the bleeding guy who just pulled crazy dragon dude off our psychic friend."

"Oh my God." I looked from Vayl to Cole and back again. "I've become my mother. Quick, look, have I developed bitchy naggy lines beside my mouth?" I turned my head from side to side so they could see better.

"I have lived long enough to be able to tell the difference between genuine concern and petty complaints," Vayl said. He leaned his forehead against mine. "Now, calm down. This bleeding is simply a result of refusing to hunt. There is a quality in the blood of living donors that seems to go missing once it is packaged. Jasmine, I will recover, much sooner than any human could." His eyes crinkled at the corners. "And it was worth the wound to see the worry on your face."

When the belt finally came off and the gauze stayed white, the three of us sat side by side on the walk, our backs to the wall, watching the firemen pour the last of their water on the smoking remains of our tent. What a disaster. But it could've been much worse.

Cassandra came to join us. Between the smoke and the frost, her outfit had wilted into rags. I glanced down at my own costume. Yup, I resembled one of those poor souls who've been dug out of earthquake rubble. But while I felt like part of me still remained pinned under a refrigerator, Cassandra looked like her fairy godmother had just told her she was about to score a new ball gown and some glass slippers.

"The tent is a complete loss," she announced cheerfully. "Nothing standing nearby was damaged though. I couldn't believe how fast the firemen got there. Jericho said they are some of the best in the state."

"Who is Jericho?" asked Vayl wearily.

"The SWAT man," Cassandra said. "Jericho Preston."

I held up my hand so Cassandra and I could exchange hi fives.

"What are we celebrating?" Cole asked.

"Cassandra's vision went up with those flames tonight," I told him. "Which means she and Preston may be an item after all."

He immediately went to his knees in front of her. With both hands over his heart he said, "Please, my beauty, say it isn't so. Have you given your heart to another?"

"You are so full of it," she said, but she laughed as he got to his feet.

"I don't know about you guys," he said, "but surviving arson gives me the munchies. What do you say we hit the fridge? You look like you could use a pick-me-up, Vayl."

Vayl nodded. "But first, a shower," he said.

"Not if I beat you to it," said Cole, sizing him up. "And tonight, I think I can."

I said, "We all need to get cleaned up, and I'm betting the RV's water heater won't be able to handle the traffic." I thought of the hotel key, hidden in my weapons case, and suddenly my crazy move showed a bright side. "I'm getting a hotel room. That way I can have a long, hot shower while you guys are doing your three-minute shifts."

"That sounds wonderful," said Cassandra. "Can I come?"

I hesitated. Now I would either have to reveal my strange actions to her or pull some elaborate scam to make her think I was booking a room I'd already rented. You know what? Screw it. All the woman had to do was touch me and she'd know the whole story. "Absolutely. Let's go get our things."

Cassandra helped me to my feet. "Oh." I looked down at Vayl. "Will you be okay for an hour or so?"

He nodded, looking strangely stunned. As Cassandra and I walked away I heard Cole say, "What just happened?"

And Vayl replied, "We have been outsmarted. Just be glad they are on our side."

# Chapter Nineteen

Cassandra insisted that I shower first since it was my idea, my room, and my weird daydream that had led to the whole setup in the first place.

"You do understand this whole issue centers around your relationship with Matt, don't you?" she'd asked when I explained how I'd ended up with a key card.

I nodded.

"I just wish Gregory hadn't left when he did. I'm sure he could've helped. Maybe we should call him."

"I've thought of somebody else I can talk to," I said and we left it at that.

I don't much mind grime because of that squeaky-clean feeling you get from the shower afterward. I sat on the bed, flipping through the channels, feeling like I could star in an Ivory soap commercial when I heard a knock on the door.

*Probably Cole with that have-mercy look on his face, here to beg some hot water time.* I opened the door.

David stood in the doorway, dressed to kill in his navy blue body armor. "Jasmine, they're coming!"

"How did they find us?" I whispered as a little guy galloped through my mind on a sweat-soaked horse screaming, "The vampires are coming! The vampires are coming!"

"Maybe Matt told them."

I punched him in the arm. Hard. "Matt would never betray us."

Dave's look said he thought otherwise, but he was smart enough to keep his mouth shut.

I threw on my shoulder holster and strapped it tight while he monitored the hall.

*Clear*, he signaled.

I inched into the hall beside him. Light yellow walls. Burgundy carpet with a large floral print. Gold fixtures. Sweet, middle-class feel that somehow tripled the horror. All we needed was the *Psycho* soundtrack and we could just skip straight to the funny farm.

Dave jabbed my shoulder. "Pull yourself together!" he hissed. Leave it to a twin to know just when you're about to flip out.

You couldn't see the elevator from our vantage point, but the stairs were just two doors to our left. We were only on the second floor. It wouldn't take long for us to get to the lobby. To reach the sleek, black motorcycles waiting for us outside. That was, if we were lucky. We weren't.

The stair doorway flew open and at least a dozen human guardians streamed through. Dave sprayed the crowd with his M4. Maybe six dropped. The rest pulled back, giving us space to turn and run.

We raced down the hallway, trading looks of alarm as the elevator rang that it had reached our floor. Out of the alcove in which it sat strolled Jesse and Matt, looking unnaturally beautiful, uncharacteristically cruel. Blood streamed down their necks, but they hardly seemed to notice as they advanced on us.

"You bitch!" David screamed at me. "You let them die!"

The words tore into me with the force of a grenade. "No!" I

cried. "They could've lived. They could've been here with us!"

"Now, why would we want to do that?" asked Matt, smiling widely, his new fangs tipped with the blood of his own lips.

Rage rose in me, sudden and all-consuming. It burned in my mouth and at my fingertips. Part of me thought it amazing my hair didn't burst into flames. "You stupid FUCK!" I screamed at him. "You *turned*, you stupid, cowardly FUCK!" I ran at him, a juggernaut of wrath with only one goal: mow that son of a bitch over and get the hell out of Dodge.

I hit him so hard I thought my heart would burst. He fell flat, carrying Jesse down with him. David was still screaming behind me, garbled, angry words I heard but couldn't translate. I yelled back at him, "Come on! Come on! *Come On!*"

A large window marked the end of the hall. I raced toward it like a dragster, hit it feet first and flew through, covering my face so the shards only cut my legs, arms, and shoulders. A small price to pay for freedom. I hit the ground with soft knees, rolling like that poor downhiller who missed his gate in the last Olympics and damn near fell off the mountain. Quickly regaining my feet, I reached the edge of the parking lot before he caught me.

I turned, snarling like a cornered badger. It was Vayl. He let go of me, holding both hands up, as if I needed to know he went unarmed.

"You went to the hotel," he said, "to shower. I should not have let you go unguarded. I should have known you might fall asleep. Cirilai warned me of your danger." His eyes filled with tears as he took in the damage I'd done. I barely heard him say the next words, and maybe they only registered because I was so shocked to hear him swear. "Bloody fucking hell, look what I have allowed you to do."

I began to hurt, all over. A wave of weakness washed over me. "Vayl? I don't feel so good." I looked down at myself. Blood and glass covered me in fairly equal doses. A particularly large shard of window stuck out of my right thigh. "That's definitely going to need stitches," I murmured. Then I passed out.

# CHAPTER TWENTY

The next two hours drifted past like a slow boat through zombieland. Mostly I just stared. I did assure a concerned and quite humorless Dr. Darryl that I wasn't suicidal and he wouldn't be seeing me again this week. I agreed to see a sleep disorder specialist, and wasn't even surprised such a thing existed. But when Vayl and I walked out of the emergency room, I threw the appointment card in the trash can.

"Why did you do that?" he demanded.

"This is for three weeks from now. No way am I going to survive these nightmares that long."

We took a cab back to the hotel. I sat outside while Vayl dealt with the desk clerk. It was all very civil. They even shook hands at the end, though I wished there had been yelling. If she'd been pissed that I'd broken her window I wouldn't have felt so mental.

After assuring him I could handle the walk back to the RV, I found myself wishing I'd let Vayl carry me. It might've lessened his guilt, which currently could've powered Vatican City for a week. It didn't make a whole lot of sense to me. I mean, he hadn't even been there. But he felt like he should've. It was that *sverhamin* thing. I knew it without even asking. And guilt, well, it never plays fair.

"Are you hungry?" he asked. "We could get sandwiches."

"No, I'm fine."

"Cold?"

"Not really."

"Tired?"

"A little."

"You should sleep," he said. He banged his cane against the ground. "Never mind." His eyes raked my bandaged arms. Moved down to my leg.

"It doesn't hurt," I told him.

"But it will." Yup, soon the meds would wear off and I'd be one huge *ouch*.

*What to say?* "I forgive you." *That sounds arrogant.* "It could've happened to anyone." *Obviously.* "It's my problem." *Not unless I want to be alone forever.* Some words must exist, though, to thaw that frozen expression on Vayl's face, the one hiding that massive feeling of *I failed to protect you*.

"You definitely owe me one," I said.

"What?"

I touched his arm, stopped him so I could give him a long, frank look. "I'm gonna want some payback is all." I grinned. "And with me, you know payback will be a bitch."

He threw back his head and barked out a laugh that sounded ferocious and relieved at the same time. "I have no doubt about that. So, do you have any first requests?"

"Actually, yeah, I do. Could you clear something up for me?"

"I can try."

"Just how many gold mines did you win playing poker?"

Minor lift of the eyebrow. "Have you been gossiping with the office staff again?"

"Just answer the question, mister."

"One. I bought the other two about ten years later."

"Oh." I thought a minute. "You're definitely the only person I've ever known who owns three gold mines."

"Would you like to visit them with me someday?"

*I think my toes are actually curling at the possibilities that question raises.* "Yeah, I guess I would."

His eyes lit. "Did you just agree to go on a vacation with me?"

*Yipes! Why do I keep speaking before engaging my brain?* "Um, well, technically, I believe I may have. But at a date to be named much later. And when you wear me down to the point where I do finally contact my travel agent, we'll probably have to combine it with business so I don't totally freak on you like I'm about to do now, so let's change the subject, okay?"

The dimple made an appearance as he nodded. But all he said was "So what do you want to do with the rest of the night?"

"Work."

"Are you certain?"

*Are you kidding? I just stirred up every disturbing feeling I have for you and dumped it on your plate after jumping out of a second-story window! If I don't work I'll go bonkers!* "Oh yeah."

Bergman met us at the RV door. He didn't ask how I was feeling. It wasn't his way, but it still kind of ticked me off. I would've checked on him. "Would you guys get in here? I've got stuff to show you!" As we followed him inside he said, "I recorded all this earlier.

"Jasmine!" Cassandra jumped off Mary-Kate and came running to me. "Are you all right? I'm so sorry. I had no idea you would fall asleep. I've been beside myself!"

Cole wandered in from the kitchen. "She actually has been beside herself. Literally, she's been pacing back and forth so much I think she's met herself coming and going."

"Jaz is fine," said Bergman. "Look at her. It's obvious they took good care of her and she'll be okay or they wouldn't have released her. Now can we all take a look at this?"

"Oh my God," I said as my eyes tracked to the living area where dirty footprints led from where the carpet began at the kitchen to where it stopped at the cab. "Look at all those stains! Does anybody know how to get that out? I don't." I reached inside my jacket, wrapped my fingers around the deck of cards I'd tucked there. Just touching them made me feel a little better. But when I thought of Pete's reaction to those footprints I badly needed to shuffle. Could you get fired for losing your security deposit?

"I will call a carpet cleaner in the morning," said Cassandra. "That should come out easily."

"Really?"

"Sure."

*Okay . . . go ahead and breathe, Jaz.* I pulled my hand out of my jacket and let it drop to my side.

Bergman lined us up behind the counter that edged the banquette, Cole next to the wall, then Vayl, me, and Cassandra with Bergman nearest the door. "Everybody take a look, would you?" he begged, pointing at the middle frame on the monitor. The picture he called our attention to showed Lung, Pengfei, and Li stepping onto the back of the yacht from a small blue and white speedboat. They looked like they'd been dragged through a garbage dump.

They mounted the ladders to the middle level, where they'd staged the party/massacre the night before. Since then several blue-cushioned deck chairs had been set out, forming four different conversation areas, one of which included the bar. They walked straight through this area into the lounge, each choosing a different couch to collapse on. Pengfei had been chattering away in Chinese the whole time, her voice getting louder and angrier as the minutes passed. Her bullet wound had already closed.

"What's she saying?" I asked Cole. He leaned both elbows on the counter, watching the screen with interest.

"She's obviously irate. She's calling Lung and Li all kinds of names, Lung for losing control, Li for running." He listened awhile longer. "She's telling them there's a huge difference between slaying a few Chinese rebels and killing random Americans. They were supposed to stick to the plan. She's mad the cops got involved because it jeopardizes everything she's been working for."

He looked at me in amazement. "*She's* in charge. She's just using Lung as a figurehead because the Chinese would never respect or fear a woman the way she needs them to."

I watched Pengfei with new interest as she rose from the couch and began to pace around the room, first reading Li the riot act, then moving on to Lung. When he talked back to her she gave him a slap that rocked his head back hard enough to make it hit the wall.

"I had to kill the Seer!" Cole translated for Lung, who was rubbing his head. "I could see it in her eyes. She had already had a vision of me, and I could not allow her to repeat the prophecy."

"What prophecy?" demanded Pengfei.

Lung's face squeezed tight. "The one about the white dragon," he whispered.

"Ach, white dragon, white dragon. You are sick, obsessed, crazed with being defeated by this ridiculous white dragon! Why do you let one simple monk's prophecy haunt you after five hundred years, tell me? Did I not kill him thoroughly enough for you?" Pengfei asked harshly.

Lung looked down at his knees and nodded.

"Did I not save you from the boiling pot and nurse you back to health?"

Another bob of the head.

"Then remember to whom you owe fealty and keep your claws sheathed until I order you otherwise!" she screeched.

He didn't speak to her again.

"So Lung is superstitious enough to jeopardize their entire setup over a five-hundred-year-old prophecy, and Pengfei is our real target," I said. "Does that about sum it up?"

"Not quite," said Vayl. "Samos still remains part of the picture. We cannot discount his influence even if we cannot see him."

"We still need to get my armor back," Bergman said fearfully, as if we would consider leaving his baby behind.

"Yes, of course," said Vayl. "Unfortunately it will not be coming off Lung tonight." He gave Bergman a tired smile. "Li ate the snail."

"I saw." Bergman's shoulders slumped. "I never thought about Lung having a food taster. Who does that anymore?"

"People who've been around a lot longer than you and me," I told him.

"There is a silver lining," said Cassandra. "I recognized Li. He sleeps in one of the rooms with a camera, so you'll still be able to see if the pill works as you designed it to."

We all looked at her.

"Cassandra?" I asked. "Is this you? Looking on the bright side?"

"Go Jericho," Cole murmured.

"Uh-oh." Bergman's comment brought our eyes back to the TV. Pengfei had worked herself into a real tizzy by now. She leaned into Li's face, screaming, spraying spit, her fangs in clear view as her lips drew back in a furious snarl. Suddenly she pounced. Being more of a runner than a fighter, Li put up only token resistance as she buried her teeth in his throat. At the same time her claws sank into his chest and within moments he began to seize. Her strength alone kept him sitting upright as she bled him, her nails stabbing into him repeatedly, piercing every organ she could reach.

He lived a long time. And we stood, horrified spectators as she tortured him while Lung looked on, quietly waiting for her to finish. Finally she tore his chest open and pulled his heart out, reducing the gore to a dusting of ash and a puff of smoke. It reminded me so much of the reaver's grisly work that I wondered if there was some connection. Could she have been one? Known one?

"Sorry, Bergman." Cole clapped him on the back. "Guess you don't get to see the pill work after all." He was trying for that I'm-a-normal-guy tone, but the undertone said, *I didn't want to see that, and now that I have, I'll never forget it. This sucks!*

I watched him, pressing my lips together so I wouldn't yell at him for signing onto this insanity in the first place. Idiot. Now he'd never be the same.

# CHAPTER TWENTY-ONE

As the violence on the TV screen dissipated we all moved away from the counter, each looking for a way to insert some sense of normality into our atmosphere. Cole and Bergman set up a game of chess at the table. Cassandra spent some time digging in her purse, an olive-green, bead-covered monstrosity, before emerging with a book of crossword puzzles. I opened the refrigerator. What did I expect to see? Eggs? Bacon? There they stood in a line, just as the five of us had at the counter. Clear plastic bags full of blood. I leaned in. Did Vayl prefer a certain brand? O Positive? Plasma Lite?

"Looking for something?" asked Vayl quietly.

I jumped, banging my head against the rim of the door. *OW!* I straightened up, rubbing my sore skull. "Sometimes a girl just wants some milk and cookies," I said. And not because she's been stitched shut for the second time by a doctor who's too honest about how it hurts him to see scars on beautiful women.

"Is your head all right?" he asked.

*What kind of question is that? It's attached, isn't it? Otherwise — too damn personal, if you ask me. Which you just did!* "It's fine."

"Let me see."

"No."

Slanting of the eyebrows. Translation—*now you're just being stupid stubborn.* "Come, let me take a look."

"Go on, Jaz," said Cole as he took Bergman's rook with his bishop. "You could have a concussion or something."

Vayl reached for my head. "I'm fine!" I snapped as I jerked back, banging it into the freezer door.

"Okay, now I'm not," I said, rubbing both sore spots. But suddenly I was. I began to grin. "Vayl, I've got it."

Concern poured from his eyes. "What is it, a migraine?"

"Would you stop worrying? It's going to make you crazy!" I skirted him and went to the guys at the table. "Bergman, I need to watch the footage of Pengfei lecturing Lung and Li again."

"Can it wait a sec? It's my move."

I grabbed his queen, slid her eight spaces forward, and told Cole, "Checkmate."

He frowned at the board as Bergman pulled his laptop off the seat beside him. "Looks like my schedule just opened up," he said with a smirk. As he powered up the computer he told me, "If you want to see it on the TV it'll take some time to find the spot on the DVD. But if you want to watch it straight from here, I can have it up in less than a minute."

"The sooner the better," I said.

We all crowded into the banquette to watch the recording of Pengfei's hissy fit. When it had played out I said, "Did anybody see it?"

Vayl began to nod, the look of dawning comprehension making him seem younger. Less burdened. He said, "When she slaps him his armor does not react."

"Exactly!" I said. "Look! Scales don't run up his face like they did when he was threatened last night."

"That's interesting," said Cassandra. "But how does it help us?"

"That's how we get past his defenses. By making him think I'm Pengfei. We'll have to take her out first, but"—I shrugged—"that was going to happen anyway."

I could tell the idea intrigued Vayl, but the risk to me took him so far out of his comfort zone that he had to think it over. He slid out of the banquette and went to retrieve his cane from the bedroom. I could hear him muttering all the way there and back, though he stopped talking before I could do any actual eavesdropping. I would've told him only crazy people talk to themselves, but I was in no position to judge.

Cole also got up. He went to the fridge. And as he poured himself a mug of orange soda he said, "I don't see how we can pull that off, Jaz. You're about two inches too tall, for one thing."

"Plus you can't speak Chinese," added Bergman. "And even if you stuck with English, you couldn't manage an accent without sounding like some idiot redneck making fun of all Asians everywhere."

"He's right about the accents," I told Cassandra regretfully. "I can't even do that nasal Chicago twang, and my dad lives there."

"Well, I can't help you with sounding Chinese, but looking the part could be easier than you think. What about some sort of disguise spell?" she asked.

I felt Bergman shiver, as if he'd brushed up against a low-voltage electric fence. Keeping my face turned well away from him I said, "Generally I stick with the old-school method, but I'm willing to try it. Can you do something like that?"

"Maybe. But—"

"What? No! You're a psychic," Bergman told her, as if she'd suddenly developed Alzheimer's. He spoke so loudly I wanted to stick my fingers in my ears. "You have visions," he insisted. "You don't do spells. That's for witches. And wizards. And, and"—he noticed we were all looking at him funny—"those other oogly boogly types." He wiggled his fingers to emphasize his point.

I shook my head. "Bergman, I kid you not, if you don't get your head into the twenty-first century I am going to take you out behind the woodshed and tan your hide."

"What?"

Cassandra reached over me and flicked Bergman on the shoulder to get his attention. "A bomb is a powerful weapon, yes?"

"Of course."

"So not just anybody can build one."

"Well . . ."

"I could not get on the Internet, find a good plan, and by the end of the day construct myself an explosive device, could I?"

"Yeah . . . but it's not a fair comparison."

"Why not?"

"They're two entirely different things."

Cassandra leaned forward. "They're both tools used as a means to an end."

"The philosophy behind them is light-years apart."

They were nearly nose to nose now, not a comfortable position for me, since I sat between them. "Bergman," said Cassandra, "I could build a bomb if I wanted to, although it would help if I had an interest in science. And if you had a bent toward magic, which by the way you *do*, you could cast a spell."

He recoiled so fast you'd have thought she spat in his face. I held up my hand. "Stop," I told him. "I know you're about to say something I'll regret, so don't even go there."

"But—"

"Bergman, I love you like a brother and I respect your right to believe whatever you want to believe. But you can't be on this team if you offend somebody every time you open your mouth."

He opened his mouth. Then he shut it again. "Excellent choice," I said. I stared at him for a second longer, trying to see how deeply this magic thing disturbed him, but he'd barred the gate. So I said, "Now, Cassandra, about this spell . . ."

"I'm not sure it would work, after all," she told me. "It would only affect your looks. Your voice would remain the same."

"Well, crap."

We sat in silence for a while, all of us staring at one monitor or another, hoping for inspiration to come give us a big kiss on the forehead. Instead something cracked against the side of the RV.

Bergman ducked, as if some two-hundred-pound jock had just thrown a Frisbee at his head. "What was that?"

Cassandra swept aside the curtains. "It's too dark outside to tell."

"Close the curtains!" we all yelled. Her hand jerked back like the cloth had grown teeth and snapped at her.

The cracking sound came again, two, three, four more times. By now Bergman was practically under the table. He motioned for Cassandra to join him. "Get down!" he ordered Cole. "That reaver might be back for Jaz!"

"I'm checking out the bedroom monitor," said Cole. Bergman and Cassandra, thinking that was a bright idea, followed him to the back of the RV to see what the security cameras had picked up. Vayl and I preferred the direct approach.

He'd already stepped out the door. I shadowed him, drawing Grief, activating my night vision, snapping the band on my watch to shield the sounds of my movements. Vayl motioned for me to skirt the back of the RV since he'd chosen the frontal approach. Another round of cracking sounds accompanied me, along with hurried whispering.

Though my instincts told me our attacker wasn't a reaver, I still rounded the corner carefully. I sighted my quarry almost immediately. Just as quickly I pointed Grief at the sky and thumbed the safety. "Kids," I muttered with disgust.

They stood about twenty feet away in the pool of light provided by the barbecue cook-off competitors. They wore jeans, plaid button-down shirts, and tennis shoes. They'd combed their short hair neatly to one side. Not the types I would expect to catch heaving eggs from the white eighteen-pack they'd set on the green picnic table between them. However, I did recognize them. They were the boys I'd picked to go AWOL from the *other*-hating picketers. But to ride the Tilt-A-Whirl till they puked. Not to plaster our pullouts with cooking essentials.

I holstered Grief and strode forward, preparing to grab them by their collars and shake them until they pleaded for mercy. Vayl had other ideas.

The bottom half of his cane shot through the air and impaled the carton. Eggs flew everywhere. I almost laughed when the boys jumped, yelped, and darted off into the night. Well, they tried.

"Stop," Vayl ordered. So, of course, they did. "Be seated." They parked it on the benches. "Tell me your names and ages."

The kid on the left, who'd apparently chosen to fight his acne battles with a steady diet of donuts and Doritos said, "James Velestor. Fifteen."

The one on the right, a brown-haired twig whose glasses kept slipping toward his braces, muttered something. "I cannot hear you!" Vayl barked.

"Aaron Spizter, fourteen."

"Who brought you here?"

The boys looked at each other and smirked. I stepped forward. "Come on, Vayl, this would be a lot more fun if you'd let me bang their heads together a few times."

That sobered them up. James looked up at me, both chins shaking slightly as he demanded, "Why do you hang with *others* like that psychic? She's an abomination in the eyes of God, you know."

Aaron piped up, speaking more to his buddy than to me. "What about *this* freak?" he said, jerking a thumb toward Vayl. "I mean, look how it's working its mind control on us right now!"

"You sound like a couple of brainwashed little ruffians to me," I told them in my let's-read-a-nursery-rhyme voice. "I'm guessing Mommy and Daddy have made it clear to you that the human race is by far superior to any *other*, and therefore you should feel free to damage their property and treat them like dirt every chance you get. I'm guessing they went so far as to buy you the eggs and give you directions to our place. Am I right?" I leaned over and looked hard into the brats' faces. They couldn't believe how I'd figured them out on such short acquaintance.

"Where are they?" Vayl asked grimly. When he didn't get an immediate reply he bellowed, "Where?"

James and Aaron both pointed shaking fingers over their shoulders. Eventually we deduced that their fathers were parked in the hate-crimes van near the marina. Vayl put his dripping sheath back where it belonged and we escorted the boys, along with their eggs, to the real scene of the crime.

Generally Vayl's power feels like a calm arctic ocean, mystic blue with countless tiny waves on top and an icy cold current running beneath. But as we followed the boys, I decided any decent sailor with my increased Sensitivity would agree the bottom had just dropped out of the barometer and we were in for a helluva blow.

"Um, Vayl? Are you sensing how I'm feeling right now?" I murmured. Usually I want him to stay clear of my emotions. Like continents away. But at the moment . . .

"No."

"Well, pay attention."

I allowed myself a small sigh of relief to see not a spark of red in his eyes when they met mine. After a moment he asked, "Why are you concerned for me?"

"Because I know what I do when *I'm* too pissed off to think straight. And the aftermath is never pretty. So I'm thinking maybe you should not follow your first instincts when we speak to these boys' fathers, because tearing their arms off and beating them over the heads with them is not going to solve the ultimate problem."

"Huh."

Oh God, he was even beginning to sound like me.

However, he did not pull a typical Jaz move when we arrived at the van. He walked over to the driver's side as the boys took refuge within and stood patiently until the man rolled down his window. I took my place by the passenger — a guy with the pasty, sagging features of the perennial couch squatter.

"What do you want?" demanded the driver. Maybe he felt safe because of his size. He certainly filled out his powder-blue blazer, and if he had a neck, it was squatting behind his thin black tie.

"I want to know why you felt it appropriate to send your son to damage my property," Vayl said in his I'm-about-to-lose-it voice. It can be deceiving to those who don't know him because it's so soft. Almost unassuming. But when people get next to it, and ignore it, generally they can count the remainder of their lives in breaths.

Since the driver was a stranger to Vayl's more dangerous moods, I expected him to make up some bullshit story about how one of the boys had lost his wallet and they'd just driven them back to the festival so they could try to find it. At nearly three a.m. On a Monday morning. Maybe he knew how lame that was going to sound, though, because he said, "Our boys are doing God's work and we are proud of them. Psychics are no more than witches, and they are an affront against God."

"An affront," my fella agreed.

"What's your name, fella?" I asked him.

"George Velestor," he said.

"You ever formed an original thought in your life, George?"

He looked at the driver.

"Apparently not." I kept talking because Vayl's power had spiked, and I figured if I didn't do something quick, we'd soon be dealing with a van full of Popsicle people. "What's your name, driver?"

His glance took in my hair, boobs, eyes, boobs, and then eyes again. I wondered how many people would miss him if he quietly disappeared. "My name's Dale Spizter, ma'am."

"You married, Dale?"

"Sure am."

"Then keep your damn eyes off my chest."

His head jerked away and I thought I heard the boys snicker. Vayl opened the door. "What are you doing?" demanded Dale.

"Get out."

"I will not."

Vayl's voice rang with cold, hard power. "The four of you will exit this vehicle and precede us back to the RV." His face might've resembled a mask to our guests, but I could see the muscles in his jaws working, the vein in his forehead throbbing. Not happy signs.

Like good little puppets, they jumped to it. The men, however, looked like they expected to be struck down from above at any moment. They drooped even farther when we reached our destination and mustered up a couple of bowls full of soapy water and some paper towels. Vayl set up the lawn chairs, invited Cassandra outside, and the three of us watched them clean up the mess they'd made. He'd also brought out a flashlight, so she got to point out the spots they'd missed. She found quite a few.

I thought Vayl had taken enough satisfaction from this revenge until he stood and started pacing. I couldn't take my eyes off that cane, digging deeper and deeper gouges into the ground with every other step.

"We're done," said Dale. He dropped his wad of paper towels in the water and rolled the sleeves of his suit coat down.

I stood up. "Fine. Get out."

"No. I have a few words to say," he announced.

*They always do.*

"Dale, maybe we should go," said George. I liked him better when he was echoing my opinions.

"God has brought us here for a reason, George," Dale said in that singsong TV-preacher voice that makes my molars ache. "We must uphold our responsibility to hiyum—"

I felt the power winding up in Vayl and suddenly understood where blizzards begin. I also knew clearly why my guy needed an *avhar*. If he killed these men in front of their sons, beyond the obvious tragic consequences, he'd be doing irreparable damage to his own soul. Both my instinct and a sudden heat from Cirilai told me so.

I strode forward, planting myself firmly between Dale and my *sverhamin*. "Dale, you are so far out of line that if this was a NAS-CAR race you'd be in the grass. I'm not going to argue philosophy or religion with you. Think what you think. I really don't give a crap. But here's the deal: Standing behind me is a vampire who's quite capable of icing you like an Alpine ski slope. He is deeply pissed that you've insulted his Seer. But she's a grown-up and he'll eventually get past that."

I closed the distance between us because Dale had puffed out his chest and begun rocking from foot to foot, starting his little I-am-the-man dance before I'd even finished. I slammed him hard in the diaphragm with the heel of my hand, backing him up, taking the strut right out of him.

"Listen up, asshole," I hissed. "Because what I'm about to say may just save your life. My boss here is trying very hard not to rip a great big hole in your throat, but more and more he's thinking, 'Why the hell not? Here's a guy who thinks nothing of sending his son, who should be more precious to him than his own soul, into mortal danger. Aaron will probably be safer if I just kill his father now.'"

I looked at George. "Same goes for you and James, Xerox."

Aaron came up to me and grabbed my arm. "Please"—his desperate glance went to Vayl—"please don't kill my dad."

I told him, "Once a farmer murdered two boys just about your age. Why? Because he was ignorant. Too stupid to ask questions. Too narrow-minded to wonder if maybe things had changed while he was looking the other way. If I'd known the man before that instant, I would've killed him. And by killing him, I would've saved those boys' lives." I stared into Aaron's eyes. I spent some time on James as well. "Vayl is wondering if he needs to save your lives now, the same way I would've saved his sons. Or if you have the brains and the courage to do that for yourselves."

Aaron and James looked at each other. It was the first time I've ever seen a boy grow up. I just wish both of them had.

# CHAPTER TWENTY-TWO

As soon as the eggers left our sight I slumped back into my chair, my arms dangling over the side, my feet stretched out in front of me with the toes of my boots pointing straight up at the sky. "So tired," I muttered.

Vayl brought his chair close to mine and sat down.

"Can I get you something?" Cassandra asked.

"Caffeine," I said.

She hurried inside.

Cirilai had quieted back down and, for that matter, so had Vayl. "You did well," he said. "I . . . Sometimes it is harder than others. This year is shaping up to be a bad one. I lost my boys in April and already . . ."

"I know." He nodded. Though it sucks to have such tragedy in common, it's nice not to have to talk about how torturous the anniversaries can be. He just knew I'd be there to get him through. And come next November, I had a feeling I might not be the complete wreck I'd been last year.

Cassandra returned, carrying a carafe of Diet Coke. "Original and uplifting," I told her with a smile. She also brought Bergman.

"I've been thinking," he said.

*That's half your problem!* My mouth was fizzy full, so I just nodded and let him continue. "I might be able to come up with something that would make you sound like Pengfei," he said. "I've been working on some instant translator software for a while and if I could . . . Well, let me see what I can do, okay?"

I gulped my drink, thanking my lucky stars it went down the right tube. "Really? I mean, really, really? Bergman, that's awesome!"

"Well, it's not a sure thing yet—"

"Dude, if anybody can do it, you can."

I didn't realize how much he'd slumped until he straightened up. "Thanks. I guess I'll get started then."

"Excellent."

As soon as Bergman left earshot Vayl said, "I am going to buy you some pom-poms and a short pleated skirt—"

"Hey, if Bergman needs a cheerleader, that's what he's getting."

Vayl tipped his head to one side and smiled wickedly. "I was just thinking perhaps I need a cheerleader as well."

Cassandra got up. "If that's where this conversation is headed, I'm leaving."

"She wants some pom-poms too," I told Vayl.

"I do not!" Moments later we heard the RV door close behind her too.

"Oh man." I dropped my head back as far as it would go. "I am so wasted. And you know what's sad about that?"

"What?"

"I'm the only person I know my age who can say that and not mean too many Fuzzy Navels."

"Do you need to sleep?"

*Hell yeah!* "Nope."

"Do you want to visit David?"

*Definitely not.* I looked at the wide Texas sky and thought about the golden cord I'd see stretching across it if I gazed up through different eyes. It connected me and my twin, and I could use it as a path to visit him anytime I wanted to have an out-of-body experience. It's more dangerous than it sounds. But that wasn't what was stopping me.

I turned my head, let my vision fill with the vampire who'd brought me back from the brink more times than I cared to mention, the last being less than two months before, when the year was new and I feared my grip might have finally slipped for good. I was afraid this trip might take me right back there. I opened my mouth, my lips already burning with the difficulty of the words I knew I had to say. "I feel like I'm finally beginning to heal from what happened back then. It doesn't seem wise to dredge it all up again. It's like picking at old wounds. How smart is that?" I asked him.

He did a quick visual inventory of my recent injuries, which were all aching despite the painkillers Dr. Darryl had prescribed. "Perhaps that is the only way they can truly heal," he suggested. His eyes lifted to mine. I'd never seen such naked honesty in them before. "I would wish that for you." His eyebrows shot up, as if he'd found something surprising behind some inner door. "Even if it came at my own expense, I would like for you to be whole again. Maybe David can help you find the way."

I sighed, feeling slightly better, but not nearly enough to make this trip okay with my churning gut or my pounding heart. "I'd better go."

Vayl sat forward, his presence wrapping around me like a blanket. "I will be right here beside you."

I nodded my thanks, unable to translate my gratitude for his presence into speech. I wanted to pull into myself like a turtle, as if that could provide some extra protection for the trek ahead. But my stitched leg wouldn't cooperate. Neither would my chair. In the end I simply closed my eyes and bowed my head.

I still remembered the words Raoul had given me the last time I'd traveled outside my body, when the fate of my country had been at stake. Frankly I preferred those circumstances to these. I murmured them now, concentrating on Dave's face, his high forehead, stern green eyes, unsmiling lips, and dark brown hair touched with just a hint of red.

I shot from my body like a rocket. I'd forgotten how fast I could move outside physical being, or what a rush flying across time and space with so little to slow me down could be. I followed that yellow streak of lightning right to Dave's shoulder. And if I'd been a little more corporeal when he turned his head to pull a breath before leaning back down to continue CPR, he'd have literally seen right through me.

The woman who needed his air was one of his, a sun-bitten veteran whose blond ponytail splayed across the dirty floor of the deserted house like a lotus floating on a pond full of scum. A tourniquet had been wound around her mangled thigh and a bloody bandage encased her head. She lay on the ground floor in the corner farthest from a bank of windows. Five guys and a woman wearing desert gear and armed with M4s kept up a steady barrage from those openings. A couple of them had taken damage as well.

I heard more assault weapons, including a SAW, ripping off rounds from upstairs. It looked to me like they'd planned a raid and had either been ambushed or outgunned. Either way, they'd had to pull back to this position. The firing slowed as, one by one, Dave's unit picked off their targets. He evidently trusted them to do their jobs without direct oversight, because his mind was so elsewhere.

"Come on, Sergeant," Dave said desperately as he compressed her chest with the heels of his hands. "Come on, Susan. Stay here. Stay with us."

I had said the same words to Matt, begged him as I wept over his body the night Aidyn Strait had stabbed him to death.

My brain seemed to split. I wanted to scream from the pain of it. At once I hunched in the past, my heart exploding as I called for Matt to return to me. And I stood beside Dave, wishing I had eyes to weep when I saw Susan's exquisite crystalline soul lift from her body. Like Matt, she had somewhere else she needed to be. And, as my love had left a part of him behind, so did she. The azure jewel that comprised her being spun and split. Nine gems separated from the whole, sought out and found each of her brothers and sisters in arms. Those who shared the room with her paused to gaze at her one last time. And then the main part of her flew up, up into the sun. A-mazing.

"She's gone, Dave," I said.

He looked up at me, his green eyes startling against his taut brown skin. I took it as a sign of his utter distress that he wasn't even surprised to see me. "Son of a bitch! She was our fucking medic!" He wasn't mad they'd lost their doc. Just that she could've maybe saved any of the rest of them if they'd suffered the same injuries. I crouched beside him. The gunfire had almost ceased. The sound of approaching helicopters signaled imminent rescue. In a few minutes they'd land, Dave's unit would clear out, and life would move on. For now we sat beside Susan's body, mourning her, yeah, but grieving for the rest of our dead as well. We'd racked up way too many in our lives. Mom and Granny May. Matt and Jesse. The Helsingers.

"Did I tell you I was one of the casualties at the Helsinger massacre?" I asked him. "Aidyn Strait broke my neck."

"Yeah."

"I did?"

"Yeah. When I called."

"When was that?"

"The day Dad told me you were in the hospital."

"I'm sorry. I don't remember that."

"You were pretty far out of it. They had you on about as much morphine as you could handle."

*Huh. I wonder what else happened then that I've forgotten. Must remember to ask someone I trust. Definitely not Albert.* "So you know about Raoul?"

"We've met," he said dryly. He pulled Susan's jacket closed. Smoothed her hair. "About a month after I joined up I was shot and killed during a live-fire training session," he told me quietly enough that his men couldn't hear. "As they tried to resuscitate me, I went to some sort of middle place, though it sure looked like a hotel room outside of Vegas to me."

*Damn.* Though he knelt right beside me, my heart still squeezed at the thought of my brother. Dead. No matter how temporary, that state still messed with my mind when it came to family. I realized I'd always expected to go first. Before him. Long before Evie. Even before Albert. And I suppose I had. I'd just returned unexpectedly.

"So Raoul gave you a choice?" I asked, trying to clarify Dave's experience in my boggled brain.

"Yeah."

"And you chose to come back. To fight."

"I'm here."

"I . . ." Geez this was hard to say. "I've been having some problems sleeping. Actually, sleeping's okay. It's what I do while I'm asleep that's not so cool."

"Like?"

"Jumping out of second-story windows."

His eyes shot to mine. He looked me over hard this time and, by the way his brows dropped, didn't appreciate what he saw. He shook his head. "We are damaged goods, Jazzy."

"I can't go on like this much longer. But coming here, seeing you lose Susan, at least I've figured out my main problem."

He waited.

I shrugged miserably. "I believe after Matt died, he talked to Raoul just like you and I did. Only he decided not to come back. He didn't love me enough to stay. Subconsciously I've known this for a while and, well, it's killing me."

I felt this horrendous wave of grief and anger claw its way up from a pit of agony I hadn't even acknowledged, like a rich snob who walks past the same starving homeless dude every day, clicking her high heels on the dirty sidewalk in time to the music in her head. I began to sob, my non-stomach feeling as if it had just been kicked with a steel-toed boot. For a while I couldn't speak. I just stood and cried, while Dave looked on helplessly.

"He stayed while he was alive, Jasmine. You gotta give him that. Even the Bible doesn't require relationships to last after death. If you're going to be pissed, aim it at the son of a bitch who murdered him."

"But Matt's there and I'm here. What does that say about what we had?" More sobbing. I was like the ghost in the Hogwarts bathroom. Sad, pathetic girl.

"He loved you. You know that. I know that. He just needed to move on."

"What about what *I* needed?"

He shook his head. "I don't guess you and I were meant for marriage and kids and cable TV. That's more Evie's thing."

"Of course not. But—"

"Jasmine. Honest to God, you could have gone anywhere to cry. Why did you come here?"

That dried me up, as I was sure it was meant to. "You're the only one I know who's survived this kind of loss. I thought I could learn from you. You know, before I sleep again."

Dave regarded me thoughtfully. "You're a survivor too, Jaz. You just have to accept it."

# Chapter Twenty-three

Like hair waxing, the best way to reenter one's physical form is quickly and without warning. I greeted myself with a full-body cramp that yanked me to my feet and extracted such a shout I'm sure the Mexicans thought Texas had finally gone and seceded from the Union.

"Jasmine!" Vayl had both arms out, as if he expected me to collapse at any moment.

"I'm okay," I gasped, leaning over for a second until I was sure I wouldn't be leaving supper all over the grass.

"You should sit down," Vayl suggested, pulling my chair right up behind me so all I needed to do was bend my knees. It suddenly seemed like a fine idea. Vayl sat in front of me so our legs were nearly touching.

An eerie calm settled over me. I wasn't sure what it meant. I might be perched in the eye of a gigantic storm, in which case Vayl should probably run. Or it could be that the waters around me had utterly stilled because no energy existed anywhere in me to move them.

"Did you find what you needed with David?" Vayl asked.

"Kind of. It's — the dreams — they're about Matt."

Vayl's hands convulsed around his cane, which he'd laid across his lap. It bugged me that he hadn't cleaned it off yet, that little bits of goo still hung on to tiger heads and backs and tails here and there and dirt soiled the tip. My hands itched to grab it from him and scrub it shiny. "What about Matt?"

"He died."

It was such an obvious, simple thing to say, I was kind of surprised Vayl didn't smack my forehead with the palm of his hand. Instead he said carefully, "Matt died terribly."

"He wasn't supposed to," I added.

"No."

"I thought I'd gotten over it."

Vayl leaned forward, rolling his cane back so he could rest elbows on his thighs. He clasped his long fingers together. "That would signify an end. You meant to marry the man. You felt a love for him that should have lasted a lifetime. That feeling will not necessarily change just because he is gone. I still love my sons as much today as I did the day they were born. Perhaps the best either of us can hope for is not to get over our pain, but to move past it."

Yeah, *move*, I'd figured out that word was key early on.

When I'd lost Matt and my crew, my life as I knew it ended. And time stood still. But I'd discovered ways to force the minute hand to tick the seconds off. The trick, I'd thought, was to keep moving. And yet the nightmares had still caught up to me. Had done everything but slam my head into a brick wall.

In the end, simply moving isn't enough. Not when all you're doing is circling the source of your grief. The thing is, when you let that go, what's left to hold on to?

# CHAPTER TWENTY-FOUR

Occasionally just before waking I realize exactly how I look, and I'm generally glad nobody can see me. This morning I knew my mouth gaped like an empty mailbox. Drool dripped down the side of my chin. I'd just finished a prodigious snore and a green cloud of halitosis orbited my head.

I snapped my mouth shut, rubbed my chin on my sleeve, wincing as I opened a barely healed cut on my arm, and opened my eyes. Cassandra was frying bacon, drat her, which explained the drool. Bergman tinkered with both computers on the table. Cole sat with his legs up on Mary-Kate, his eyes drifting from Cassandra to me, apparently deeply entertained by having Jekyll and Hyde in the same general vicinity.

I sat up. Slowly. Between the belly dancing, the fire, the visit to Dave and its aftermath, the night had taken its toll.

"You look like crap!" Cole said merrily. "I like the hair though." He made a camera frame with his thumbs and forefingers and in the genie voice from *Aladdin* said, "Now, what does this say to me? Homeless woman? Tornado victim? Britney Spears? I've got it! Preschooler who's misplaced her gum!"

I regarded him balefully. "You're a morning person, aren't you?"

"You make that sound like a bad thing."

"Not if you stop talking." In a sweeping, dramatic gesture he covered his closed lips with the back of his hand. "Better." I swung my legs off Ashley and looked at Cassandra.

"How come the breakfast foods?" I asked as I noted eggs scrambling beside a freshly baked tin of cinnamon rolls.

She smiled with anticipation. "Jericho is coming." I should've known. She looked date primed with her hair wound around her head like a crown. She'd chosen her best jewelry and a sheath of a white dress covered with red peppers.

"Does he know this?" I asked.

"He will after you call him."

Oh, right, I'd told Shao I would talk to him this morning. Of course that was when I had high hopes of eliminating Lung and heading back to E.J.-land.

"Do I have his number?"

Cassandra pushed a business card across the counter toward me along with my phone. I dialed him up.

"This is Preston."

"Sergeant Preston, this is Jaz Parks. How are you feeling this morning?"

"Well, I'm not extracrispy, thanks to you."

"I can tell you we're all pretty relieved to have gotten out of that mess alive, and it was great to have your help. Which is sort of why I'm calling. We were wondering if, uh, before you and your son take off for the zoo, maybe you could come to breakfast. We had some things we'd like to discuss with you."

"Sure, I'll be right there." *Click.*

I held the phone up and looked at Cassandra. "He hung up. Is that rude, or am I just—?" A knock at the door interrupted me. Bergman closed the laptops, leaped out of his seat, snagged the sheet I'd been sleeping under, and covered the table with it. Then he raced to the bedroom to check whose face would be filling its monitor as Cassandra went to answer. I gave her a wait-a-minute gesture as Cole and I powered down the living room TV and all its related equipment.

"How we doing, Bergman?" I called.

"We're good to go," he said as he strolled back into the kitchen.

I nodded for her to open the door. Preston stood on our welcome mat, hands on his hips, only slightly out of breath.

"Where were you?" Cassandra asked.

"Fishing."

"I don't see a rod and reel."

"For evidence," he explained. "That freaky dude who attacked you last night disappeared. I figure I can put him away for a long time with you all as my witnesses, so I was looking around, trying to figure out where he went off to."

"Well, isn't that sweet?" Cassandra said, looking at me with a forced smile. "Jaz, isn't that sweet?"

"It certainly is." *How many strings did this guy pull to be in this place at this time?* "Do you like eggs, Sergeant Preston?"

"Please, call me Jericho."

So we called him Jericho and he met Cole and Bergman formally, after which we ate. I excused myself for a quick cleanup since I couldn't stand myself any longer. When I came back Cole raised his eyebrows at my outfit.

I wore my newest purchase, a cobalt-blue blouse with three-quarter-length sleeves and a high, Victorian-style collar that would hide the bite marks if there were any to conceal. There weren't. But you never knew. I'd been forced to bare my neck to Vayl on our last mission when his blood supply had been tainted. I also wore gray pinstriped dress pants and my black leather jacket, which hid Grief.

I carried my usual assortment of backup weaponry, including the bolo in my right pocket. I slipped my hand into my left pocket, touched the ring that rested there. For the first time I thought, *Maybe it doesn't have to remind me of Matt's death, and how horribly I still miss him sometimes. Maybe it can help me remember our lives together before that. God we had some great times.*

Jericho and Cassandra had settled on Mary-Kate directly opposite Cole, who'd decided, once again, to put his feet up. He looked geared for a beach party in jean shorts and a green Hawaiian shirt covered with palm leaves. Bergman, wearing brown work pants and a T-shirt that said METEORS RULE on it, had spun the passenger seat around for himself, so I took the driver's seat, which also turned to join the crowd.

Vayl and I had not discussed this situation at all, so I really didn't know how much of our mission he'd be comfortable revealing to Jericho. Therefore I thought it might be a good idea to do a little fishing myself before I revealed all our nifty secrets.

"So what exactly is your role on the SWAT team?" I asked.

"It depends on the situation," Jericho said. "For instance, if we're busting in a place to take down a known drug dealer or a black magic marketer, I'm usually the guy swinging the ram. If it's a standoff, or a hostage situation, I'm one of the snipers."

That gave me such a phenomenal idea I nearly jumped on Bergman and throttled him with it. But Jericho's presence forced me to sit very still and wish somebody in the immediate vicinity would rob a bank. Wouldn't they call SWAT for that?

Jericho's phone chose that moment to ring, which I thought might be a sign from God. If so, I would gladly attend church at least once this year. At almost the same moment a knock came at our door. Cole went to answer it. He spoke to our visitor, who I couldn't see from my vantage point, then looked at me with puzzlement. "This guy says where do we want them to put our new tent?"

The question tore me, because Jericho had started barking into his phone, which meant I could bend Bergman's ear with my new plan. But not only was I beginning to feel sorry for whoever had invited SWAT guy's anger, I badly wanted to know what he was saying. Luckily Cassandra and Bergman were shamelessly eavesdropping, so I shelved my brilliant idea and joined Cole at the door.

A short, round man wearing a white jumpsuit and a Stetson nodded at me. He spoke around a wad of chewing tobacco that threatened to leap out of his mouth with every other word.

"Good mornin', little lady," he said to me. "No need to trouble yourself with this mess. Your man here's about to take care of it."

Cole put his arm around me, an outwardly friendly gesture, but actually a warning. *Jaz, do not strangle the Elvis wannabe.* I looked at the man's scuffed white cowboy boots. They rested squarely in the middle of Bergman's zapper mat. The *pfffzzzt* button practically blinked at me from its control box, which stood not five feet away. It would be so easy . . .

*Come on, Lucille, handle this. Jaz is practically frothing at the mouth.* "I'm sorry, I didn't catch your name or the name of your company," I said pleasantly.

"Name's Tom Teller of Tom Teller Tents and Awnings." Oops, a thin line of tobacco juice dribbled down his chin. He swiped it off with the cuff of his sleeve, leaned sideways, and spat. Problem was, he didn't lean far enough. A huge, semisolid mass of material hit the zapper mat, which, being a Bergman prototype, turned out to be a tad more sensitive to liquids than originally intended.

After consulting a work order on the clipboard he held, Tom Teller told Cole, "We been hired by Chin Lang Acrobatics to clean up the mess from last night's fire and erect a new performance tent with *aaaAAAhhhh*!"

Tom Teller lifted up on both toes, raised his hands in the air, and proceeded to do a remarkable imitation of the ballerina that had once danced in a circle every time I opened my jewelry box the year I was eight. Showing remarkable restraint in that he didn't burst into laughter, Cole held out a hand while making sure not to touch our visitor. "Dude, are you okay?"

"What the hell was that?" Tom Teller demanded.

"I believe you've just been shocked by electric ants," I told him, jabbing Cole with an elbow when I thought I heard a giggle.

"Are you kidding me? That felt like a damn 'lectric *chair*!"

"Well, they tell me everything's bigger in Texas," I replied, giving him Lucille's sweetest, fakest smile.

He wiped a bead of sweat off his brow. "I guess I've heard that myself. Uh, I just wanted to know if you'd like the new tent in the same place as the old one. Some people got superstitchuns. They don't want new stuff in the same *aaaAAAhhhh*!"

Again with the zappy dance. "Wow," I said. "No doubt about it, we're going to have to call an exterminator." I looked up into a sky so blue it seemed to confirm every story I'd ever heard about heaven. *Okay, you win. After the phone call to Jericho and now this, I'm definitely at your service.*

Behind me SWAT man blew up. "What the hell do you mean the case is closed? The case has barely started! A woman was assaulted last night! Some lizard face tried to kill a cop!" A moment's pause. "I don't give a crap what the governor—" I recognized the sound that followed because I had, in fact, made it myself a couple of times. It was the crack of a cell phone exploding against the wall.

Once again, Lucille Robinson came to the rescue. She smiled

graciously at Tom Teller and said, "You know, that spot really worked well traffic-wise, so I think we'll just keep it. Do you know when the work will be finished?"

He pranced from foot to fried foot, bobbing his head back and forth in an effort to see our furious guest. Cole pressed his mouth to my ear and whispered, "He looks like a constipated turkey."

My smile went into rictus mode as Tom Teller spat another wad of chew onto the faulty mat. *Holy crap, the guy's going to tase himself into a coma!* But again he wouldn't address me directly.

"We should have it all done by five," he told Cole.

"Did you hear that, boss?" he asked me brightly. "The tent will be up by five!"

I just wanted the idiot off the mat and to hell with my wounded pride. "Wonderful. Thank you so much." I slammed the door in his face, and Cole and I helped each other back to the empty couch, where we traded stunned stares with Cassandra. On the one hand we wanted to laugh until we cried. On the other, we wondered just who Jericho meant to annihilate first.

Bergman had rescued the parts of his phone and taken them to the covered table, where he was trying to put them back together again. Jericho badly wanted to tear out the door and cave in somebody's face, but he kept looking at Cassandra and she kept shaking her head. Uh-huh. No fractured skulls this morning, SWAT man.

"Cole," I asked, "have we got any pop in the fridge?"

"Yeah, I just bought a case of orange soda yesterday."

"Perfect." I stood up. "Jericho, come with me."

Twenty minutes later Cole returned the sledge to the ring-the-bell-if-you're-man-enough-game guy, I put the last crushed can in the trash, and Jericho dropped into the chair beside Cassandra, looking nearly as calm as he had when he'd walked through our door. Only Bergman had stayed inside to work and watch the monitors.

Cole came back with fried ice cream for everyone, which we inhaled along with the orange-scented air.

Jericho wagged his finger at me. "That was genius. Where did you come up with the idea?"

"I had to be nice to a sick baby and two sleep-deprived, panicky new parents for three weeks. It was either this"— I waved at the trampled, soda-soaked grass beneath our feet—"or a killing spree through an upscale Indianapolis neighborhood."

He nodded. "Sound choice."

"Thanks."

I took a bathroom break. A necessity, but also an excuse to grab our safe phone from the bedroom. I ignored the way my heart skipped when I opened the door. What I couldn't avoid was the sudden realization that I'd slept right through my last trip to z-land. No trying to shoot myself in the head. No stepping into traffic or jumping out windows. No dreams at all. Just sweet, deep silence, like the kind Vayl enjoyed every single day.

As I took the phone off the dresser, I considered the black tent that hung over the bed like a huge, bloated bat. I really cared about Vayl. More than I should. Way more than I wanted to. But did I want to be like him? Still pining for what I'd lost two hundred and more years down the line? Somehow that seemed stunted and wrong.

But wasn't I doing exactly what he was doing? Wasn't I holding on to Matt as if I thought I'd find him in the fresh-food section at Aldi's one day, feeling up the grapefruits with that wicked look on his face that always made me laugh? My anger at him made more sense seen that way. Like I felt he'd cheated on me by moving on.

And, as a logical progression of that thought, I was being faithful by standing in place.

The buzz started low in my head and grew so loud I banged the palm of my hand against my temple. *Not now. I've got things to do!* But Raoul had his own schedule, and I'd finally learned that when he wanted to talk I'd better listen. I closed my eyes before he grabbed my vision to get my full attention and said, "You rang?"

That enormous voice boomed in my head. *TURN IT ONE MORE TIME TOO.*

For some reason I twisted the phone in my hand, so if I held it to my ear the receiver would be on top. No, it wouldn't work that way. *Turn it one more time too.*

Matt had left me.

*TURN IT.*

And I had left him.

At the height of our love, we'd let death separate us. Some part of me had never believed it would happen. In fact, at some level I'd despised us both for allowing it. I'd been furious at him for leaving. And I'd hated myself for staying.

*NOW THINK.*

"What?"

*THINK!*

*Holy crap, Raoul, that's all I've been doing!* Thinking about Matt. More than I wanted to. So few people knew him. But they all liked him. Especially Albert. I put the phone to my ear, only mildly surprised I'd already dialed his number.

"Yeah?"

"Albert?"

"What's up? Everything going okay?"

"I was thinking about Matt today."

"Me too."

"Really?"

"What a poker face. Did I ever tell you he bluffed me out of a twenty-dollar pot with a king high? That's it! And I was sitting there with a pair of tens!"

"No kidding."

"You know why I liked him though?"

"Not really." *You don't like anybody hardly.*

"Because the day you two got engaged we had a little talk. And he said to me, 'Colonel Parks, I just want Jaz to be happy. That's it. It won't matter where we are, or what we're doing. If we're a million miles apart or stuck like glue. As long as she's happy, I'll be fine."

*Don't. Cry.* "Why are you telling me this now?"

"Your brother called. He was worried about you." My dad is a lot like a baseball pitcher. He has a windup that he goes through before he throws his curve. I should've recognized the tone in his voice as the windup. But it had been a while, and I was distracted.

"What did he say?"

"He said you were a goddamn mess! Now you listen to me!" he barked. "Shit like this buries you, if you let it! You're up to your neck in shit, Jasmine. Is that how you want to go down?" He'd pitched it into a full-out roar now, just like he had when I'd walked into the house covered with mud at the tender age of six. Then I'd wanted to cry. Now I wanted to kick him in his battered old knees. Maybe he'd raised me right after all. I'd finally learned to hit that curve.

"No sir."

"Then get off your ass and do something about it!"

"Yes sir."

"You nailed that boss of yours yet?"

"What?"

"You obviously need to get laid, Jaz."

"Oh my God, tell me we are not having this conversation. Albert, we are not having this conversation!" I hung up, horrified, yet laughing. The man belonged in a cage. In a zoo. On Mars.

But in his disgusting, direct way, Albert had given me the answer. Matt and I had loved each other to the end of our lives. To the dawning of our eternity. I sure hoped he was delirious with joy wherever he'd ended up. Did he feel the same about me?

*REMEMBER*, said Raoul, keying in my mind the one scene I never wanted to replay. But my psyche pictured us anyway, dead on the kitchen floor of a patently unsafe safe house, my body draped across Matt's, our souls rising in our last act together. Then his soul, this amazing work of art with so many multicolored facets I could stare for days and never get bored, split. And part of it came into mine. Melded with mine. He'd left a part of himself with me. So I would know. So I could rest.

# Chapter Twenty-five

Before I found true peace, however, I had to finish this job. And now that I knew how to do that, I needed to put the plan in motion. I dialed the home office.

"Demlock Pharmaceuticals," answered Martha in her rough and ready voice.

"Marketing department, please."

Three clicks and a buzz later Martha felt safe to say, "Go ahead."

"It's Jaz. Is Pete around?"

"Where else would he be?"

"Tap class?"

"Ha! Hang on, hon."

Pete's greeting was typical. "Tell me you haven't wrecked a car."

"How could I?" I replied bitterly. "All you sent was a moped."

"Have you taken a look at that palace Vayl leased? It's costing me an arm, a leg, and a couple of vital organs!"

"Well, I'd better tell Bergman to get that supercharged V8 off the floor then, huh? Do you think Palmolive gets out Pennzoil?"

Pete makes this unique sound when he's about to have an

I've-reached-the-bottom-of-my-wallet fit. It used to scare me, but I've begun to enjoy it. I know, sick.

"I'm kidding; the place is in mint condition." Well, it would be as soon as the carpet cleaners showed. "However, the performance tent burned down last night."

Again with the sound, a subtle blend of choking-on-rib-eye, suffering a megawedgie, and walking barefoot over broken glass. I quickly added, "The people who burned it are replacing it as we speak. Which leads to my problem." I explained last night's scenario, Jericho's involvement, and how Pengfei—through Lung—had begun to cover their tracks. "They've already pocketed the governor of Texas. Has anybody been on you to shut us down?"

"No," he said thoughtfully. "But I have been asked to brief the president tomorrow morning on an unrelated matter. Now I'm wondering . . ."

"Yeah, me too. Is there any way you can make yourself scarce until then? Just in case?"

"You can get this done tonight?"

*I have no idea.* "Absolutely."

"Then I'm feeling queasy. Must've been that cream cheese on my morning bagel. I'm going home now, Jaz. Twenty-four hours. That's all I can promise you. And you know what? Thanks for the excuse. I hate this suit I'm wearing today. It hits me right in the pits. Can't wait to shuck this coat and—"

"Oh my God, Pete, I think I have a lead."

"What?"

"You mentioning your suit just brought it together in my head. Samos's *avhar* told me he'd gotten this obnoxious purple three-piece at a men's store called Frierman's. Then, later, the reaver Samos hired said he'd bought some cowboy boots at the same place."

"We'll check it out."

"Hang on. Let me think. Let me try to remember the conversations . . ." I took my mind back to the talks I'd had with Shunyuan Fa and Yale. "The store's in Reno."

"Excellent."

# Chapter Twenty-six

Since Pete had given me his blessing to bring Jericho in as far as I thought necessary, I was set to spill the beans when I went back outside. But the old desire to protect those frail lives surrounding mine started banging cymbals in my head when I saw him talking earnestly with Cassandra.

*This guy's a dad, and not an Albert type either. Right now he's safe. Even his department wants him off this case. So let him off.*

Which was when Xia Ge showed up. Like Cassandra, she'd taken some extra time in front of the mirror this morning. She wore her sleek black hair down, which complemented her red V-neck sweater. Her black slacks looked immaculate, one of the advantages of having a kid who doesn't regurgitate his meals on a regular basis. Baby Lai, dressed in a blue one-piecer dotted with monkeys, cruised in the stroller in front of Mom, looking so cheerful he might've been smashing miniature baby bottles all morning.

Cole had already risen to greet them. The light in Ge's eyes when she smiled at him disturbed me. I didn't think she'd ever act on her crush, but the fact that she felt it at all made me hurt for Shao. *There should never be another man. Not in your fantasies.* I looked at Ge. *Not in your dreams.*

I crouched by the stroller and spent some time talking to Lai, suggesting maybe someday he could give E.J. lessons on how to bounce without spitting up. Within a couple of minutes Ge squatted beside me. Though she smiled at the baby she spoke to me.

"Shao gone to airport to pick up his brother, Xia Wu. He asks have you spoken to police yet?"

I nodded to Jericho. "That's him."

Ge looked so relieved I nearly patted her shoulder. But she clearly thought we were being watched, so I played along.

"What he say?" she asked.

"Something bad has happened and powerful people are trying to cover it up," I told her. Her hands tightened on the sides of the stroller, but otherwise her expression remained serene. "The regular police have been ordered away from here."

I lowered my voice. "I am not regular police, but I do work for the U.S. government." I tickled Lai under the chin, making him giggle madly. "I can't tell you why I'm here, only that your family will be safer when my job is done. If I give you a phone number, will you remember it?"

"Yes."

I gave her the numbers in sets for ease of recall. I said them three times and made her repeat them back three times. "Tell Wu to call when it's safe for me to come aboard the *Constance Malloy*. Tell him under no circumstance is he to try anything on his own. He will fail. We have the only means known to defeat Lung."

She hesitated for so long I finally looked at her. She was digging in the diaper bag, hiding her face from view.

"What is it?"

Tears slurred her voice. "That our countries should cooperate is so unlikely. I fear the worst. Wu will die. Shao will be struck with grief. Perhaps Lung will kill him too. Maybe his rage will turn to Lai and me."

Since we seemed to be going through diapering motions I un-strapped Lai and lifted him from the stroller. Good grief, the kid packed a lot of weight in a little package! "I see we've eaten our Wheaties for breakfast," I told him. He grinned and, as a token of goodwill, deposited a long loud stinky in his Huggies that I was only too glad to let Ge address.

I tried not to sound harsh, though it leaked through as I said, "You tell your brother-in-law to hell with China and the United States. This is for your family. Got that?"

She nodded. So did Lai. Then he farted and we both laughed. Meeting adjourned.

# Chapter Twenty-seven

After Ge and Lai left, I went back into the RV. Bergman sort of lunged on top of the table, realized it was me, and sank back into his original position, hunched over his toys, a magnifying glass clamped over the left lens of his regular glasses, looking like a jeweler evaluating diamonds.

"Bergman, I have an idea."

"What."

"Quit snapping; you'll love it."

He sat back. "Jasmine, I have about ten hours to make a translator that currently sounds like this"—he hit one of the laptop's keys and a robotic voice started speaking stilted Chinese—"sound like this"—he hit another key and the computer began to replay Pengfei's last tirade.

"Hmm, that's quite a difference."

"You think?"

"Bergman, this is where you shine. You'll nail this easy. Which is why I'm sure you'll have time for my other idea."

He slumped so far in his seat I thought he might actually slide under the table. But his knees hit the other side and he stopped. So I went on. "The pill we wanted to feed Lung last night? Can we put it in a bullet and speed it up? You know, so the reaction is nearly instantaneous?"

As if someone had hauled him up by the armpits, Bergman rose in his seat. "What caliber?"

"Well, the bullet has to stay embedded, but I'd like to use Grief. That way the crossbow would be backup. I'd just go with that from the start, but I have to be so accurate with it, you know? This way I could hit Pengfei virtually anywhere and *bam*!"

He sat up straighter. "More like *sizzle, wap*!"

I nodded. "Cool."

Bergman smiled. "I'm on it."


I went back outside. Cassandra and Jericho were still talking. Cole had joined in, so laughter interspersed the conversation fairly often. I pulled up a chair and they all looked at me expectantly.

"How do you know I have something to say?" I asked.

"Cassandra told us you would."

I made a face at her. "Remind me never to try to throw you a surprise party. Okay," I went on. "She's right. Here's the deal." I caught Jericho's gaze. "We're after lizard face. We're pretty sure we have to get him tonight because by tomorrow whoever crawled up your governor's ass may slither on into the president's liver. Now, I know you can't do anything official. But something is going down tonight. Hopefully it will happen on that yacht"—I pointed to the *Constance Malloy* — "far away from here. But if we can't contain the violence, the people who are here at the festival will not be amply protected. I've seen the security in this place and it sucks."

*Now why is that?* asked a part of my brain that really should've said something earlier. *We have the potential for large crowds, so you need cops just to cope with those problems. We've already had a mini protest from other-hating fanatics, which, while pitiful in itself, could certainly breed bigger, scarier rioting if not dealt with correctly.*

"Why is Lung here?" I asked.

"I take it you're not looking for the obvious answer," said Cole.

"He's stolen an invaluable item that, if he can duplicate it, will make his army damn near invincible. So why isn't he riding a rocket to China?"

Cassandra said, "Don't you mean why hasn't Pengfei made herself scarce?"

"Yeah, I guess I do."

"I'm lost," said Jericho.

I sat forward in my chair. "Look, tonight Lung will have a full Chinese crew aboard that yacht of his. He's been biding his time, waiting for them to arrive. What's that say to you?"

They looked at me, their faces a study in blank.

"It's his getaway car — er, boat," I explained. "That's why he's still here. He couldn't do anything because his crew was still traveling here from China."

"So is he leaving tonight?"

"I think so, but something else is happening first." I turned to Jericho. "Logistically speaking, this place is primed to blow. It's going to be packed with people. Security bites, and what people the organizers have hired are largely untrained."

A thought hit me. "That little drama last night with the burning of our tent might even have been a test run to see how much chaos they could cause and for how long." Then I remembered Pengfei ripping out Li's heart. "Or not. At any rate, I would feel a whole helluva lot better if you could have this joint swarming with off-duties tonight. Just make sure if something goes down they all know you're in charge."

He'd begun nodding about halfway through my speech. As

soon as I finished, he was off his seat and on the phone Bergman had repaired, walking away from us, strolling down the winding path toward the Acrobats' Arena.

Cassandra watched him go, slumping a little as the distance between them grew. "He was so nice."

"Yeah."

"And look at that butt."

I considered said item. "Definitely superior. But not for Cassandra hands?"

She shook her head sadly. "Another woman stands between us now. He'll meet her within the month."

"Is she prettier than you?"

Cassandra started to smile.

"Well?"

"No."

"Ha!"

"Jaz!"

"Honey, we've got to take our victories where we can find them."

# Chapter Twenty-eight

Jericho returned, but not for long. Duty called. So after making plans to meet up again later in the evening, we said our goodbyes.

"What now?" asked Cole.

The three of us stood in front of the RV under the awning. I was beginning to feel guilty about leaving Bergman so much on his own, but he liked it so much better that way. I'd have to make honing his people skills a priority on our next mission together even if he didn't think it was necessary. I said, "That's really up to you, Cassandra. What kinds of things will we need for this disguise spell?"

She held up a finger. "I was studying that last night. Let me get the book."

She went inside. I waited for the growly, snarly sounds that would signal the snapping off of her head by our resident neurotic, but she emerged unscathed carrying a smelly old tome bound in something that sure looked like—

"Tell me that's not people skin," said Cole.

"Not," she agreed. "I think it might be lamb."

"Lamb isn't much better," I told her. "You know, where I grew up between 1988 and 1990, you couldn't even buy lamb in the grocery store."

Cassandra shook her head sadly. "That certainly explains a great deal about you," she said.

Cole laughed softly until I kicked him in the foot. "So," he said, "what does the book with the creepy cover say?"

She opened it up to a place she'd marked with — I kid you not — a square of toilet paper. It creaked. Cole and I traded glances. He did a haunted house shudder and I rolled my eyes.

"Would you two stop fooling around?"

"Sorry," said Cole.

"You're a disruptive influence," I informed him.

"You'd be surprised how many of my teachers said the very same thing."

"I doubt it."

"We need to make a shopping list," said Cassandra. She'd brought her purse out with her. After rooting around inside for half a minute, she emerged with a small pad of paper and a pen, which she handed to Cole.

He waved the pen around appreciatively. It was wrapped with soft red material, and a spray of fine red feathers had been hot glued to the top. "Cassandra," he said, "I hope you know that poaching Muppets is illegal in this country."

"Just be quiet and write." Cassandra read off the list, which included some common herbs like catmint and basil and some items I'd never heard of before like derrentia and triptity. "Where are we supposed to find that stuff?" I asked.

"Corpus Christi's a big city," Cassandra replied. "There's bound to be at least one coven running a supply store here, and most likely it will be near the bay." She came to the end of the list and stopped, though I knew she wasn't done.

"What?"

"We need an item of her clothing."

"Of course. Can't we save that till the end though? You know, until I'm physically on the yacht?"

She read over the spell. "Yes," she said slowly. "But we need something of hers —"

"What, like a lock of hair?"

Cole threw up his hands. "How the hell are we supposed to get that? We can be pretty sure they don't spend the day on that boat. They'd be too vulnerable."

"Actually, I had another idea. Bergman may need to help though."

I winced. "He's slogging through a blizzard of work as it is."

"Then let's leave it for now. It may even be something we can accomplish without him. First, the shopping."

"Can I go?" asked Cole. "Oh, stop looking at me like that. Bergman won't let me watch him, much less help. Vayl's down for the count, and all the beautiful babes are at work." He wiggled his eyebrows. "Or at the mall."


Four hours later, laden with bags and, okay, a cute green dress covered with silver stars that was on sale and in the same store as the triptity, so cut out the guilt, we returned to the RV.

Cassandra opened the door and stopped with her foot on the first step. I strained to see around her, especially when I heard Bergman humming to himself. *"Bum, bump-bump, tah-dah, toodle-loo."* I tucked my head under Cassandra's elbow.

Bergman was dancing.

Okay, it actually resembled an old man's attempt not to break his hip while proving he could still shake a leg at his great-granddaughter's wedding. But still.

"Bergman," I said, "is that your happy dance?"

He grinned at me.

"Cassandra, look," I said. "Bergman has teeth."

"They're very nice," she replied.

"Lemme in before my arms fall off!" Cole demanded. We piled inside and dropped the bags under the monitor, which revealed a lot more activity than it had in a while. I spared it another glance. The Chinese crew had arrived. But Xia Wu hadn't called. Well, I knew I might not be able to depend on him. If he didn't contact me by the time Vayl woke, we'd modify our plan accordingly.

I turned back to Bergman. "What'd you do?" I asked. For an answer he held up a long thin wire. It took a tremendous effort not to snatch it, but I kept my hands to myself as I asked, "Is that the translator?"

He nodded, showing those perfect white teeth again. He came toward me and draped the wire over my head. "The idea," he said, "is to weave this into your hair. If you have it kind of hanging down by your face like this," he demonstrated, pulling a handful of curls forward and winding them around the wire, "it should never show. Okay. Say something."

"How is it powered? I mean, it's so thin. Where's the battery?"

Nobody answered. They just stared. I watched slow amazement dawn on their faces.

"Oh my God," said Cole. "You sound just like that bitch!"

"Watch your mouth, young man," I snapped.

Cassandra nodded. "Exactly."

Bergman moved closer. "Now say something."

"This is so incredible, Bergman. You are a flipping genius!"

"That's what I thought." He wasn't responding to my comment. "When I stand this near I can hear the English before it's translated. So make sure you keep everybody at least three feet away from you. And figure out how to hide your lips. Use a fan maybe."

"How'd you do it?" asked Cole.

"Well, I couldn't have without already having Pengfei's voice on the computer. Other than that . . . none of your business." He sounded very offhand, but his shelter-beagle eyes begged, *Feed me, pet me, love me*. I wanted to be careful with what I said though. It would suck to jinx the whole deal with too much optimism. You saw that every day on Cinemax.

"This is stellar work, Miles. Probably your best ever, considering the deadline pressure. Why don't you take the rest of the day off? Forget that idea we talked about earlier. I can nail Pengfei with a bolt, no problem."

"Are you kidding? I'm on a roll, Jaz. I'll have that sucker ready for you by dusk!" Scary light in his eyes now. Kinda fanatical, like Dale Spitzer and the *Others* Suck crew. Scarier still that I could relate. The work did it, man. It seeped right into your marrow if you let it or, in our case, if you courted and sweet-talked and sometimes pleaded with it.

I hesitated. "Okay, but I'm warning you. We can't play outside anymore. Cassandra's got to do her half of the Pengfei disguise. *And I need to figure out how to get back onboard the* Constance Malloy. *Come on, Wu, grow a set and give me a call!*

A couple of hours later he did just that. Good thing too, because I'd just finished doing eenie meenie minie mo to decide which of my crew I should strangle first, and the future looked bleak for Bergman.

The biggest problem was that four grown adults weren't meant to hang together in such a small space with so much at stake. Playing euchre, fine. Making preparations to assassinate two vampires who could easily turn their rig into kindling — nuh-uh.

Nobody found Cole's antics amusing, which made him want

to grab his toys and go play somewhere else. He disappeared into the bathroom for a while. Nobody even wanted to guess what he was up to in there. Then he ended up in the driver's seat, flipping through radio stations so fast Cassandra finally yelled at him to either settle on one or put in a damn CD. Yes, she said "damn." She was really starting to sweat.

I blamed part of it on the steam rising from the big pot bubbling over the stove. I don't know why she felt she had to lean her entire face over it every time she stirred the contents, but there you go. I guess some spell casters are very hands-on that way.

Part of the problem was Bergman.

"These instruments are very sensitive to temperature," he'd announce to the room at large. Then he'd subside. Five minutes later, "The metal is perspiring. How am I supposed to do intricate work like this with a metal that's perspiring?"

Cassandra strode out of the kitchen and disappeared into the bathroom. Moments later she returned and slammed a stick of deodorant on Bergman's table. "Try that on your damn metal!" she snapped as she went back to her work.

He raised his eyebrows at me like, *What's gotten into her?* I pointed directly at him. Then I pressed my lips together, made a zipping motion across them, acted as if I was turning a lock at their center, and threw the imaginary key out the window.

I managed to keep them from open warfare, but Wu definitely heard the relief in my voice when I answered his call.

"I am sorry I have not phone before," he said, sounding genuinely apologetic. "There was much work to be done before I can break free."

"Don't worry about it," I said. "I'm impressed that you're willing to give us a chance."

"I am willing to talk," he hedged.

*Dammit, I don't have time for negotiations!* But one way or another I had to get hold of a Pengfei outfit. And a fan. And maybe some of her makeup and hair doodads. No sense in pushing this spell so hard it burst at the seams. Plus it would be nice to separate her from Lung to start with. Our plan would sail so much smoother if I could kill and become her before Lung even saw her this evening. If I could get into her room, maybe I could find a clue as to where to find her. *My job would be so much easier if I just knew where you two stiffs holed up during the day.*

"Miss Robinson?"

"Sorry, Xia Wu, my mind was wandering there for a second. Um, yes, talking would be great. Can I meet you onboard?"

"Certainly. As cover, please bring with you the dry-cleaning from J-Pards on Twenty-sixth and Elm. I neglected to retrieve it while in town as an excuse to have it brought to me."

"Very clever," I said. *Dry-cleaning! Argh!* Pengfei had left an outfit here on land, ripe for the picking, and I hadn't even considered the possibility.

"My brother, Shao, have the ticket. He makes sure you get it within the hour. Please to be here before five."

Okay, now I had two reasons not to like this guy, maybe three. One, he wasn't going to jump right in line from the start. Two, he didn't have a problem involving his brother. Though with a family to support, Shao could not afford to stand this close to the kind of danger Lung represented. And maybe three, isolated by the telephone, the timbre of Wu's voice led me to suspect the People's Liberation Army had been recruiting *others*. And I didn't think Wu's particular brand cared much for mine. In fact, I thought he just might be a reaver.

# Chapter Twenty-nine

My first instinct was to get the Xia clan the hell out of town. Stash them somewhere safe until Pengfei, Lung, and Wu were no longer threats. But then it might be obvious they had American allies and that could be even worse for them than what they faced now. Plus I could be wrong about Wu. So, though I would deeply regret it later, I decided the best course of action would be none at all.

However I had to get that dry-cleaning tag, and the Xias had been seen around our camp way too often. "Cole, you look bored."

He rotated his chair to face me where I stood between Mary-Kate and Ashley, still holding the phone. At the moment he was making faces. By that, I mean he'd pinched his eyebrows between the thumbs and forefingers of each hand and was rearranging his expression in time to the song on the radio, which happened to be that timeless classic "Help Me, Rhonda" by the Beach Boys.

I pocketed my phone. "Are you what happens to little boys when they grow up without ever having gotten to play with Mr. Potato Head?"

He pulled his eyebrows into a frowny face. "I'll have you know my lack of PlaySkool toys from ages seven to nine has scarred me for life. Did you know one Christmas I actually had to settle for a deluxe double upside-down loop racing set from Tyco?"

"I'm amazed you haven't blown up an entire chain of toy stores by now. Come on, let's get outta here."

"You're leaving?" Cassandra and Bergman chorused, their soprano (him) and tenor (her) combining to provide our listening ears with a lovely harmony of trepidation and outright alarm.

"Yes," I said, "although I prefer to think of it as escaping. If you two kill each other before we get back, make sure you leave written—and by that I mean printed, not cursive—directions on how to use your gadgets."

I didn't actually run out the door, but it was definitely one of my quicker exits. Caught by surprise, Cole couldn't keep up with me and was forced to dodge a barrage of demands and requests before finally rejoining me on the outside.

"I like those two," Cole offered, "but only when they're apart."

"I agree."

"Together they're like spilled oil and Alaskan sea creatures."

"Well, for our sakes I hope they find a way to mesh. Otherwise, I think, eventually, one of them will have to go."

Cole put his fingers to the corners of his lips and pulled them down.

"Would you cut that out!"

He shrugged, as if at a loss as to understand my lack of humor. "So where are *we* going?"

"To find the Xias." At this time of day we should have been able to catch them at home, since Shao was between shows and, I kinda thought, they were expecting us.

We wandered the area, smiling at the people we saw, hoping we'd find the Xias before we had to stop somebody and ask for them by name. Then I had an inspiration. I grabbed Cole by the hand and dragged him back toward the path, where a row of game booths had just opened up for business.

"You played baseball as a kid, right?" I asked him.

"Of course."

"And your dad coached the team?"

"Yeah," he said with a curious, how-on-earth-did-you-know tone. Did I really look that stupid?

"So you were the pitcher."

"I was the only kid who could get it across the plate without bouncing it first." Slight defensive tone now.

I pushed him up to the counter of a place designed to look like a dugout. At the back, bowling pins had been set up on four different tables. The more you knocked down, the cooler the prize. I directed Cole's attention to a little brown bear sitting on a shelf. Cost — ten pins. "That's the one I want."

The proprietor of the establishment, a fifty-something gentleman missing at least four teeth whose greasy brown hair framed his sad, skeletal face came forward to take my five bucks. I held on to my end, forcing him to meet my eyes.

"Tell you what," I said. "I'm a cop, but I'm here to have a good time. So I don't really want to check to make sure you're running a straight game. What do you say you take a stroll to the back there and do that for me before we begin?" I let my eyes tell him exactly what I'd do to him if I discovered he was trying to cheat me, and he released that bill like I'd coated it with ricin. He kept his back to us as he fiddled with the middle game table. I saw his hands go to the mini apron tied around his bony hips; then he turned and looked at Cole.

"Ready to play?"

Cole smirked. "Always."

Three throws later I had my bear and we were headed back to trailer city. We only had to stop a couple of people and explain that a baby whose parents were acrobats had left the bear in our tent during our show the night before. One guy couldn't speak English. The other pointed us straight to the Xias' trailer.

Shao answered the door. He wore a white T-shirt and loose black pants that tied at the waist. His hair stood on end, as if he'd been running his hands through it repeatedly. His eyes were puffy and red. *Oh God, Ge's left him.*

But she came to the door next, laying her hand on his shoulder. The cords in his neck and shoulders immediately relaxed. *Whew!* I didn't realize how badly I wanted their family to stay together. It was because of the little dude I could see in the background, sitting in his high chair, banging on his plate with a plastic spoon, future drummer for the Cheerios Crushers.

I held out the bear. "Your baby left this in our tent last night. We wanted to return it because we thought he might have a hard time sleeping without it." I smiled, hoping they'd catch on. They did. All too quickly.

Shao bowed deeply. "Thank you. Thank you. Please to come in?"

I glanced at Cole. "Sure, I guess we have a minute."

I'd describe the design scheme for the Xias' camper as Early Toddler. Otherwise a clean, dust-free environment, the place was artfully strewn with balls, rattles, Sesame Street puppets, and teething rings. Ge went to clean up the interior decorator while Shao showed us to a rust-colored love seat that sank nearly to the floor when we sat on it. As soon as I managed to remove my knees from my throat I said, "I spoke to your brother just now."

Shao's face puckered. He dropped into a chair next to us. "My brother is no more."

*Aha.* "What do you mean?"

He put his elbows on his knees and dropped his forehead into his hands. For a while he just sat that way; then he ran his fingers through his crazed hair and looked up. "He was fine when he got off the plane. Himself, yes?"

I nodded, as if I'd recognize Wu anywhere.

"We say hello. We hug. He must stop at the bathroom. So I wait for him. When he come out . . ." Shao shook his head.

You never expect to find the bogeyman in the bathroom. But it's a favorite hangout. He seems to lurk in the stall marked OUT OF ORDER, waiting until your pants have fallen around your ankles and the other patrons have left. "Did you see anyone go in or come out right after him? Anyone, you know, funny-looking?"

Shao shook his head.

"I know you were distracted by Wu's behavior and your suspicions, but think back to that moment. You're standing, where, by the men's room door?"

He nodded. "Leaning against the wall. Wu's bags are at my feet."

"Wait, go back a couple of steps. Wu puts his bags down. Does he do anything before he goes into the bathroom?"

Shao squeezed his eyes shut. "He pinching my cheeks. Saying I still cute as little bunny rabbit. Makes me want to put him in head-lock like when we kids. When he turn to open bathroom door he nearly run into old man."

I leaned forward. "Describe him," I demanded.

"White hair like this." Shao held his own hair straight up and down. "Eyes, ah . . ." He got up, went into the kitchen, and grabbed a pan. Pointing to its silver exterior, he said, "Like this color only a little bit blue. Also covered with hair." Shao made quick circular motions with his hands crisscrossing his face. "Just everywhere. And in his ear a sparkly ring."

I would bet a year's pay Xia Wu had encountered the reaver Desmond Yale.

Shao returned to his chair as he went on. "When Wu come out

of the bathroom, there is someone new behind his eyes." He shook his head. "This is no good way to describe it. Also there is a feeling." He touched his fingers to his chest several times, said something in Chinese, and looked at Ge for help.

Though Lai gabbed and gurgled as if he had important things to say, she kept her eyes glued to her husband as she carried their son into the room. "I think the word is 'evil,'" she whispered.

For once, baby Lai didn't want to play. He seemed to sense matters were not right in his world, not by a long shot. Though Ge put him down inside a ring of fascinating toys, he crawled right over the top of them straight to his father, who immediately picked him up. They both seemed grateful for the cuddle.

I couldn't think of a single thing to say that would be of comfort to these wonderful people, so I decided to do my business and get the hell out. The sooner I left, the quicker they could heal. "Wu said you had a dry-cleaning ticket for me."

Shao nodded. He dug out his wallet and handed the voucher to me. "What will you do?" he asked.

"I'm sorry, Shao. I can't tell you that."

He nodded, surreptitiously wiping away tears as he returned his wallet to his pocket. "My brother worse than dead now," he said, his eyes suddenly fierce on mine as his rage and his accent thickened. "He trapped. Never to be freed until by death. You end it, let his soul rise away so his family can honor him, as should be right!" He stood, holding Lai in one arm, as Ge wrapped her hands around the other. "Please to understand," he said earnestly, "Chinese people honor all their ancestor. Very ancient tradition. Wu must be honor!" What he couldn't tell me with words I saw in his face. This was as important to him as breathing.

Suddenly I couldn't speak. My throat simply closed on the terrible reality that a man should be forced to ask someone to kill his brother in order to free his soul. But Shao read the answer in my eyes and nodded grimly.

"We have to go," Cole said softly. He took my hand, pulled me off the love seat, led me out of the Xias' home.

He found us a cab, got us to the dry-cleaners, even paid the bill. We never said a word. Finally, when we got back to the festival, he said, "How do you suppose demons get into their host bodies in the first place?"

The question caught me by surprise. "I always just assumed the victims were in the wrong place at the wrong time."

"I don't know," Cole said. "I've been thinking about this ever since Shao told us about Wu. I mean, you have to choose to become a vampire. Maybe it's that way with possession too."

"Are you trying to make this kill easier on me?"

Cole pondered that question. "Actually, I think I'm trying to make it easier on me."

We were nearing the RV now. It was almost time to meet Wu, but we had a second to grab a black metal bench overlooking the bay. I took Cole's arm and led him there, draping the dry-cleaning between us.

"Okay, here's your chance. This may be your only one," I said, "so I suggest you take advantage of it. Ask me anything."

He looked out at the rippling blue water when he asked, "Does it get any easier?"

I thought of Vayl's ex. "Some are easier than others."

"Do you ever stop being afraid?"

*Huh, good question.* I thought back through my career. "Yes, there are times when you stop. Other times you just manage the fear. If you do a good job it works for you. If you suck, it hurts you and everybody around you."

He scratched at the faint stubble that had come in since he'd neglected to shave that morning. Still he refused to meet my eyes when he asked, "Do you think I'm going to be any good at this job?"

"If . . . Yeah, I think you'll do fine."

"What were you going to say to start with?"

*Sigh. I really need to learn how to lie to people I care for.* "I was going to say, if you survive long enough to get the experience. But then I decided I'd just make sure you did."

He looked at me then and grinned. "Excellent."

"So let's quit slacking and get to work, huh?"

We took the clothes inside. The atmosphere had cooled considerably, and not just because Cassandra had ditched the kitchen in favor of the living area. Bergman had left the RV altogether.

"His frustration just mushroomed," Cassandra told us. "He swore several times. Then he threw some parts. Then he yelled, 'I'm not set up to do this kind of work!' He finally decided he needed a special tool, and as soon as the Internet showed him a store in the city that carried it, he left."

I couldn't decide. Should I feel guilty for nearly driving my old friend nuts? Or should I continue to try to keep him busy so he wouldn't drive everyone else crazy with his infantile social graces? *Um, Alex, could I have Never Hire Your Former Roommates for $200 please?*

I threw Lung's clothes beside Cole on Mary-Kate and held up the two dresses Pengfei had taken to the cleaners. "Which one should I wear tonight?"

Cassandra considered them both. "I like the black with the green phoenixes. Or is it phoenixi?"

"No idea," I replied. "Black it is. I'm taking the rest to the yacht now. Cole, could you go to the marina and rent us a speedboat? And not one that's going to sink any minute like the Seven Seas Succulents' ferry, okay?"

"Will do." Cole took off. I went to the bedroom, taking the dry-cleaning with me. I hung my chosen dress in the closet and pulled out my weapons bag. If, indeed, Wu had turned reaver, he'd be a tough kill even as a newbie. So I wanted lots of options.

With Grief already snug in my shoulder holster, I slid Great-Great-Grandpa's bolo into its built-in pocket sheath. The .38 went between my belt and the small of my back. I strapped a sheath full of throwing knives to my right wrist, although they were for last-ditch attacks. My front-line weapon slid out of a ten-by-twelve envelope. A translucent sheet of robotic cells some think tank at the DOD had created, it adhered naturally to almost any surface. I pressed it against the plastic covering Lung's suit and stood back. Yup, it blended seamlessly. I ran my hand across the plastic. Easy to feel where the sheet left off and the real plastic began. Good.

With my offensive strategy in place, I felt prepared to deal with Wu, who, I reminded myself sternly, wasn't Wu at all. As I moved to leave, I brushed my fingers along the outside of Vayl's sleeping tent.

*Maybe I won't be back,* I thought. *These reavers are badass. I have a feeling one of them may actually get me one of these days.*

I realized with a sort of shock the thought wouldn't have bothered me at all a couple of months ago. But now I understood a lot better why my boss kept coming back to this life. It was so damned interesting. Especially when you shared part of your day with someone who could make your heart do gymnastics with the barest touch of his hand. Problem was, I knew firsthand what could happen when you fell off the balance beam.

I found Cole at the dock, manning a bright red speedboat that actually looked seaworthy. He'd found himself a captain's hat, which he wore backward.

"You know," I said as I handed him the plastic-wrapped clothing and scrambled aboard, "you're probably breaking some mariner's law with that headgear."

He blew a green bubble. "Does that make me a pirate?"

I rolled my eyes. It was becoming such a typical reaction to him that I feared they might stick that way and people would begin to confuse me with Rodney Dangerfield. "Okay, Johnny Depp, reel it in. I need you to be alert if things start to fall apart. On the face of it we're just delivering the dry-cleaning. That's all the rest of the crew knows. My guess is they're all Lung supporters, so they'll behave until given contrary orders. You stay in the boat. Be ready to move out fast."

"What if I hear loud noises?"

"Like what kind?"

"Like fighting noises? Do I come investigate?"

"Cole, I can barely kill reavers and I can see their shields. No offense, but you wouldn't have a chance. Stay in the boat until I come out or you're sure I'm dead. Then leave. Got it?"

His second bubble went limp when I said the word "dead." But he nodded. "It sucks being the rookie."

"Yes, it does. Look at it this way: I can't get off the yacht without you."

He brightened at that thought. Just call me the feel-good girl.

# Chapter Thirty

What I'd said to Cole about managing fear was about four parts BS and one part wishful thinking. Fear is like a pig at the 4-H Fair. You can follow it around the ring with your little pig prodder and most of the time it'll go where you tell it. But the sucker weighs over three hundred pounds, and if it decides it wants to jump the fence and run down the road, leaving a trail of green poop plops all the way back to the farm, by God it'll do just that.

Mine still trotted in obedient circles, but that fence was starting to look damn appealing. I had learned long ago that kindness and/or bribery do not work with my particular pig. *Just keep moving,* I told it bluntly. *I'm tired of wading in crap and you are not adding to the pile.*

As Cole pulled up to the *Constance Malloy,* I grabbed the dry-cleaning and hopped on deck. I let him take care of the tying off since Wu had appeared on the deck above and leaned over the rail, a toothy smile on his face. "You must be Miss Robinson from the dry-cleaners! Please to come up. I will show you where to hang the clothes."

Yeah, he just oozed nice-guy attitude, but he let me climb the ladder to his deck holding three hangers full of heavy brocade and silk clothing. Not an easy feat, especially when you're anticipating an attack.

He nodded at me as I made level ground and led me through the outdoor seating area where so many had died so recently. I tore my eyes from the spotless floor and trained them on his back.

Wu wore a dark blue uniform-tunic and pants with black cuffs on the hems of each. His boat shoes and hat were also black. He resembled Shao, but not enough to make his termination a nightmare moment for me. I squinted, trying to make out the dark outline of a reaver's shield. Nothing. But it was a bright, sunny day, the kind that seemed to hide these shields the best. Time for test number two.

"Aaah!" I pretended to stumble, grabbing at the rail with my right hand as I raised the clothes high with my left. I kept my eyes on Wu. As he spun to see what had happened, part of his face remained half a step behind. So did his hands as they reached out to help me. I stepped back so he couldn't touch me, though I smiled. "Thank you. I'm fine. I fell over the plastic." I pointed to the trailing bits of wrap as I watched the parts of Wu coalesce.

My head told the dread gnawing at my intestines to go chew on someone else for a while. I was pitting myself against a brand-new reaver here, not a seasoned vet like Desmond Yale. Wu's future demise should be no problem. The dread laughed, the way a couple of high-maintenance teenaged girls will after they've just made fun of your hair, your earrings, your shoes, your jeans, the way you walk, the way you talk, and the fact that you blink every thirty seconds or so . . . and went right back to supper. Because I now had to assume that Wu had set his sights on my soul. I wasn't sure how he'd been able to ID me. Maybe the reavers had a Seer working their side of the aisle. Maybe Desmond Yale had been carrying a passenger in his head when I'd fought him at Sustenance. One he'd passed to Wu's body in the airport bathroom. Either way, it looked as if the rules that governed reaver kills allowed for payback.

And Wu had suddenly discovered it was his turn. He was probably struggling not to gloat that I'd pretty much dropped in his lap. It's the worst kind of bad luck. But it happens.

I followed Wu through the big combo room, where three more uniformed men were dusting and scrubbing as if their lives depended on the sparkle they left behind. Who knows, maybe they did. A hall led from the dining section into the cabin area I'd found on my first trip. We ignored the closed doors to either side of us and went straight to the one at the end of the hall. Wu opened it with a key he took from his pocket.

I anticipated a problem if he wanted to act the gentleman, but he headed into the room first. He did close the door, and I heard him lock it, but that was cool with me. I didn't care for interruptions either.

"This is Pengfei Yan's room," said Wu.

Vayl would have loved it. And it bugged me that he and Pengfei shared similar tastes. What did it say about two people who enjoyed enormous beds lifted up on their own white marble pillars that are somehow lit from within? The bedding matched the carpet and drapes, all a creamy white with an overlay of intertwined buttery circles. White dressers with soft yellow knobs flanked the bed, over which hung another gauzy curtain of a startling scarlet red. The matching pillows had been thrown against the white upholstered wall that backed the bed like big globs of blood.

A white folding screen painted with red dragons stood in the corner opposite the door. This was where Wu told me to hang Pengfei's dress. I kept Lung's suits, holding them next to me as if to relieve some of the weight on my arm. "Tell me," I asked as I peeled back a corner of the plastic sheet, "what's your job on this boat?"

"I am just one of the crew," he said, clasping his hands behind his back as he went to stand at the corner of the bed nearest the door.

"But, I mean, do you help cook, or clean, or—"

"Oh, I understand," he said, smiling. "I serve the guests. We have several onboard, though most are sleeping, since they try to keep the same hours as Pengfei Yan and Chien-Lung."

I watched him carefully as he spoke. Inside, with the curtains drawn and the door shut, I could see his shield now, follow its outline as it moved with his body. As with the first reaver I'd met, it opened mainly when he moved his head.

I could shoot him, but if I managed to squeeze a bullet behind that shield it would splatter blood and brains all over the room, not to mention make a loud boom that the rest of the crew would find curiously out of place in the peace of the late afternoon. Not too thrilled with the whole stabbing scenario either, considering the amount of blood it would produce, and the fact that I'd be charading as Pengfei and might need these digs later on. Well, those were plans B and C anyway. Given the fact that his shield seemed to weaken at the head as I'd hoped it would, Plan A might actually work.

"So, about my assignment—" I began.

"I am afraid my government could not possibly cooperate with anything you have planned, despite the fact that Lung is our mutual enemy." Huh. Wu had completely lost the broken accent he'd used over the phone. Was he done pretending then?

I let my arm sag and winced, as if the robes were getting too heavy for me. I moved toward the bed, where I obviously intended to lay them down. "What?" I asked. "You think helping us out would make you look bad? Afraid maybe North Korea will call you a big weenie and go play with its nukes all on its own?"

Wu smiled, showing far too many teeth. I imagined if he unrolled his tongue the tip would hit his belly button. "I believe it has more to do with the fact that we think you Americans are assholes."

I had reached the bed by now. Laying the robes down just right became a big production. One that allowed me to get much closer to Wu. As I worked myself within range I clicked my tongue at him and gave him my you've-been-a-bad-little-boy look. "Only narrow-minded pricks cling to stereotypes like that, Wu. For instance, *I* might have thought that as a member of the People's Liberation Army you were a dyed-in-the-wool card-carrying Chinese Communist." I continued to lean over the dry-cleaning, making sure he thought I was off balance, and that he could see both of my hands touched the plastic covering the robes. I went on. "But because I'm willing to consider many different perspectives, I've come to realize you're actually just a soul-snatching reaver."

He lunged, just as I'd hoped he would. To have allowed myself a single thought in such a vulnerable position would have been the death of me. So instead I acted. I tore the clear film off of the plastic.

I spun sideways as Wu hit the bed and rammed the film, which I called my portable pillow, through the break in his shield.

It wiggled down his face like a living mask, covering his mouth, nose, and eyes so tightly I could see their outlines beneath the material.

He clawed at the material, falling off the bed in the process. I rolled him to his stomach, stuck a knee in his back, and held him there, grabbing his hand from his face and twisting it so hard he was forced to let me pull it behind him. I yanked the other back the same way, pushing them both high up his back and securing them with a plastic strap.

When his struggles finally ceased, I rolled him over and retrieved the portable pillow, folding it into eighths and stuffing it into my pocket. I jumped backward as the third eye opened on his

orehead. Unlike Wu's regular eyes, it was colored light green. I
vaited, but nothing wafted out of it. It stared at the ceiling, empty
ind sightless as the originals.

"Where are you, Wu?" I whispered. Then I realized I'd never
een the soul of the first reaver I'd killed either. Which
neant . . . "Reaver's can't kill anybody who's not marked. But when
hey enter a body, the soul leaves. So these people, these reaver-hosts,
nust agree to the whole idea up-front." Cole was right. Wu wanted
o be a reaver. Samos must have made the life seem awful damn ap-
ealing. Godlike, even. With power over life and death. No pesky
norals to hold you back. And the benefits package! "But at what
ost? Where's his soul now?" I had a pretty good idea, actually, but I
lecided right then and there never to breathe a word of it to Shao.

I hid the body behind the screen. Surveying the room again, I
hought how handy it would be to pull up a floorboard under some
andom closet and find Pengfei and/or Lung ripe for the staking.
Jut I didn't sense a single vampire aboard.

I yanked open the closet doors and stifled a yelp. A row of
vhite Styrofoam heads covered with wigs stared at me from the
helf. Just for a second I'd thought they were real.

I grabbed a medium-sized carpet bag with a gold clasp from
he closet and filled it with the long-braid wig, which had been
hoved behind the others and probably wouldn't be missed, along
vith a few of Pengfei's vanity supplies and a fan. With Lung's
lothes and the bag in hand I left the room. Though I badly wanted
o take the shortest route back to the speedboat, when I passed the
tairs that led up to the pilothouse I stopped, considered the huge
aps in my knowledge, and decided to take a detour.

As I'd expected, an actual captain inhabited the pilothouse
luring this, my second visit. *Amazing how effective that hat can be
vhen worn the right way around.*

"Excuse me, sir. I thought I saw Xia Wu come this way." I held up the dry-cleaning. "He told me to bring this to Chien-Lung's quarters, but I got lost. Your ship is so massive!" Ladies, for future reference, when speaking with nautical men, ship equals private parts. The captain melted like chocolate in my hands. "Anyway, I wanted to tell him I realized we didn't get the stain completely out of this robe, so I'd like to take it back and reclean it for free. I can have it done first thing in the morning."

"I am afraid that will not be possible," the captain said in British-accented English as he gave me a come-sit-on-my-lap smile. "We are leaving port this evening."

"Oh, no! Are you going right away? Because I can take it straight to the store to clean and have it back here in a couple of hours."

He rose from his chair and sauntered over to me, which was when I realized he resembled Sulu from the old Star Trek series. I'd always thought Sulu was kind of hot, so it was easier to make the flirty face when he said, "Actually, we're not scheduled to weigh anchor until midnight. In fact, my employers said not to expect them aboard until after ten. So why don't you bring the dry-cleaning back around seven, and you and I can have a late supper?"

Well, it looked like I could cross the yacht off my list of potential Pengfei hideouts. At least I wouldn't have to worry about her returning and missing the goodies I'd stolen. If I'd given it a second's thought, I'd have realized she and Chien-Lung, having already cleaned up after the tent fire, would feel no need to return to the yacht when they rose to repeat the process. Wherever they were, their evening's adventures would begin as soon as their eyes opened. Which meant I needed to get the hell back to shore.

I looked around the pilothouse, not having to act impressed at the blue-lit instrument panel. "Wow, supper on a real yacht? That would be amazing!"

He leaned in. "And bring your bikini. Maybe we'll just have dessert in the hot tub."

Which was when he went too far. I wouldn't even take a dip with Sulu, and he was genuinely cute. "Thanks, that would be great!" I looked out the window. "Oh, there's my ride!" I pointed to Cole and waved, as if he could see me. Then I waved at Captain Sulu and ran down the steps that would lead me to the lower deck and the speedboat home.

# Chapter Thirty-one

Even if I get Alzheimer's I will never forget the sight of Bergman huddled over his work. It's one of my first memories of him. I'd made friends with a girl in English Lit named Lindy Melson. She and her roommate, a grad student named Miles, needed some help with the rent. When she showed me the place, the first thing I saw when she opened the apartment door was Bergman hunched over the white Formica counter, fixing the toaster so it would sound an alarm when the waffles were done.

"Miles," I said as I walked into the RV and saw him bent over the table, "what's up?"

"Not your bullet, that's for sure." He sat back and rubbed his eyes with the knuckles of both hands, a sure sign of high-end stress.

"Where's Cassandra?"

"Bathroom, running water over the *magical item*." He said the last two words as if they had personally shoved him against the lockers and tried to steal his lunch money.

I sat down across from him.

"Don't—"

I held up my hands.

"—touch the stuff."

I scooted over until I was right next to him.

He looked down at me suspiciously. I put my head on his shoulder, breathed him in, and felt myself begin to unfold. After a kill, it's always hard for me to get back to real. In the six months I'd worked solo . . . Well, let's just say this was the safest way I'd found to reground. "What's wrong?" I asked.

"You mean besides the fact that I need my entire lab to build something this intricate?"

"Yeah, besides that."

He moved, forcing me to look at him. "Jaz, you want a bullet hard enough to penetrate but soft enough to break apart once it's impacted so that it doesn't exit the victim. Hard enough to protect the inner casing but soft enough, again, to break up and allow that inner casing to light up a vampire from the inside. Do you understand how tall that order is with the equipment I have available to me?"

I stretched my hands toward the ceiling.

"Taller," he drawled.

Cole had been leaning against the kitchen counter, absently watching the cleaning frenzy on the monitor as we talked. Now he looked at us and said, "You know what this situation calls for?"

Bergman and I shook our heads.

He reached into his pocket, pulled out his fist, sat at the table, and offered us his open hand. "Bubble gum."

We dug in and sat in relative silence except, of course, for the blowing and the popping. Suddenly it came to me. "What if it's not a bullet?" I asked.

Bergman sat up, a sure sign of interest. Cole blew another bubble, so who knew. I went on. "What if it's a dart?"

"Nah," said Bergman. "The needle's too thin. We need something round enough to contain the pill."

"Crossbow bolt?" suggested Cole. His eyes went from my face

to Bergman's and back again. "Hey, quit looking so shocked. Just because I have beautiful tresses doesn't mean there isn't a working brain underneath. Look at Cassandra."

We tried. She'd just emerged from the bathroom, so we craned our necks, bending nearly backward to see not only her lovely long locks but also the shining silver medallion she carried on a chain between her outstretched fingers.

"Is it ready?" I asked.

"Quit bouncing, Jaz," Bergman growled. "You're going to knock something off the table."

"Lemme out!" I ordered. Bergman stood up, allowing me to exit stage left. I went to Cassandra and took the medallion in my hands. When she'd put it into the pot along with all the other ingredients, it had just been a plain silver disc. Now she'd imbued it with the powers of the herbs. And magical writings, the words she'd whispered over the pot, had carved themselves into its face.

"Cool," I whispered. She grinned with pride.

"Do you remember me telling you we needed something that belonged to Pengfei to make the spell work?" she asked.

"Yeah?"

She tapped the side of her head with a newly manicured fingernail. "I think I figured it out. While you were gone, Bergman raised Pengfei's image on his computer."

"Under protest," Bergman cut in.

Cassandra ignored him. "That helped me make a detailed transfer to the *Enkyklios*. Then I dangled the medallion in the image replay while I spoke the words of permeation. Go on, see if it changes you," she suggested.

"Okay, but I want to put on the dress first." I ran into the bedroom, shimmied out of my clothes and into Pengfei's. They were loose in the bust and tight in the butt, which made me hate her all the more. I hurried back to the living room.

Bergman and Cole had moved to the driver and passenger seats, which they'd turned to face me. Cassandra stood waiting beside Ashley.

"Okay," I said. "Lay it on me."

She draped the medallion over my neck.

I looked from her to Cole to Bergman. When all the color left Miles's face I knew the spell had worked. "Take it off," he whispered, "before it curses you!"

Ignoring him, I looked at Cassandra expectantly. "Well?"

For an answer she clapped her hands one time, hard, and smiled so big you'd have thought she'd just won the lottery.

Cole popped a bubble. "Hey, Cassandra," he said. "Can you make me one where I look like Keith Urban?" He glanced at Bergman. "Isn't he still married to Nicole Kidman? God, what a babe."

But Bergman seemed to have developed blinders. Cole could've been broadcasting from the Space Station for all the attention Miles paid him. His hands jerked, and I realized he'd dug his fingernails into his chair's armrests up to the first knuckle. He leaned forward, and for a second I thought he was going to lunge out of his seat, rip the medallion off my neck, throw it down, and stomp on it like some enraged second grader. Instead he fell back in the seat, closed his eyes, and took off his glasses. As if that still wasn't enough to keep the scene before him from playing out behind his eyelids, he turned his seat around.

*Okay, be that way,* I thought, ignoring the fact that my inner voice sounded awfully middle school. Why did I keep letting Bergman bring out the gnarly teen in me?

"Cassandra, you did great!" I said, twirling around so she could get one last look before I dove back into my comfy clothes.

"She'll probably turn into a pumpkin at midnight," Bergman muttered.

"All right, that is it!" I strode to Bergman's chair and spun it around. His eyes opened, startled and a little scared. *Good.* "I don't care if your brain's the size of a watermelon and your gadgets make my mouth water. I'm tired of your snippy little comments about Cassandra and everything related to her. She is a member of this crew and deserving of as much respect as you!"

His eyes narrowed and I could see him start to make mental excuses. *My inventions are much more important and effective than her stupid little toys. I sell my goods to government agencies. She owns an organic grocery store whose top floor she's turned into a haven for loonies and fringe dwellers. I make people better at their jobs. She just scares them. Who's the true pro here, really?*

I zoomed in on him, practically pressing my nose to his. "Your prejudice against the supernatural is affecting my mission. I can't have that. You want to be a bigot? Go do it on your own time."

Silence. I backed up, trying to gauge the effect of my words. I'd pissed him off, naturally. But had I blasted my way through that bank vault of a science guy door? I didn't think so. For the sake of our relationship, I tried one last time. "I'm telling you, Bergman, if I don't see a shitload of tolerance pouring out of you, and I mean soon, this is it for us. We'll never work together again."

*Okay, smooth exit.* I spun and walked down the hallway to the bedroom. No trippies. Not once. Yahoo!

Once I'd changed, I called Albert. Generally talking to him upset me. But since I was already there, no big deal. I figured I'd given him plenty of time to dig up some extra added info on the reavers. And even if he didn't have anything more than we'd already unearthed, maybe he could help me figure out why Pengfei and Chien-Lung, two bad guys who'd so far accomplished everything they'd set out to do, were not planning to fly the coop as soon as they woke this evening. I'd decided it must have something to do with Samos. But what?

Half an hour later I had the glimmering of an idea. "Reavers need a sponsor," Albert had told me after I'd been forced to leave a message on his machine. He'd said he was screening his calls because he'd had so many hang-ups. Weird, but far from my problem.

"You mean, like in AA?" I'd asked.

"It's a little more diabolical than that," he said. "Reavers burn through bodies pretty quick. So the sponsor has to agree to provide the reaver with at least one new body for every week he spends on earth."

During which time, as we already knew, the reaver could be gathering souls. As long as he followed the rules.

"I don't completely understand," I said. "I know, for instance, that one reaver went into a bathroom and two came out. How does that work?"

"Apparently more than one can travel in a single body for brief periods of time until all of them are dispersed."

*Huh. That gives a whole new perspective to hearing voices in your head.*

I didn't ask Albert where he got his information. It was none of my business, for one thing. Plus, I imagined the story would be just as heartrending as the one we'd seen on the *Enkyklios* and frankly, at this point, I wasn't sure my ticker could take it. But I did want to know what any demonic creature could bring to the table that would be worth so much risk.

"This reaver you mentioned," Albert said. "Desmond Yale?"

"Yeah?"

"My sources believe his sponsor is Edward Samos."

Wow. So the Raptor had obtained the services of a majorly badass reaver. "Go on."

"Whatever Samos is planning, it's probably going to be big. As in, international-incident sized."

"How do you figure that?"

"Because reavers are very specialized creatures. They only deal in one arena."

"What's that?"

"Triggering world wars."

# Chapter Thirty-two

The bedroom felt too much like a tomb. It made me antsy. I sat down on the floor, took out my cards, and started to shuffle.

Albert and I had never parted on such a grim note and yet on such good terms. "So Samos is trying to start a Chinese/American war," I told myself. "Are you really that surprised? You saw Lung consorting with Chinese generals not thirty-six hours ago. That's kinda what they do."

The cards whooshed from bridge to pile. Cirilai warmed my hand, warning me of Vayl's imminent return. As I returned the cards to my pocket, I listened to him catch his first breath. When he came out of the tent I smiled. The last time I'd barged in on him right after he'd risen he'd been oooh-baby naked. Sometimes, late at night, I still brought out that picture and admired it. *Woof*, what a bod.

However, I had requested that he wear something when he slept so, on future missions, I wouldn't even be temporarily distracted should I be called to save his not-so-bare ass. He'd obliged. At the moment he wore a pair of black silk pajama bottoms, tied at the waist. That was it. He raised his eyebrows to find me waiting.

"Is something wrong?" he asked.

Maybe we should discuss the virtue of pajama shirts. Although it seemed almost sinful to cover that broad, muscular chest and that luscious flat belly.

"Jasmine?"

"Huh?"

"Not that I mind, terribly, but why are you sitting in my bedroom?"

I sighed. Ogling my boss's pecs, while deeply pleasurable, did nothing for my inner morale. Not only was it just plain unprofessional, it wasn't even wholehearted. Big sections of me still wanted nothing to do with any man. So why did my sex drive keep revving the engine? Stupid mindless radiator full of idiot hormones.

"RVs are too small," I said in hurried response to Vayl's get-on-with-it jerk of the head. I explained about the medallion and my talk with Bergman. He nodded and began to collapse his sleeping tent. While I helped him, I filled him in on my recent conversation with Albert as well.

Vayl slid the tent into its carrying case, sat back on the bed, and laced his fingers behind his head. "So what do we know about Samos?"

"Not much," I said, leaning against the wall, fighting the frustration that would only mar my thinking. "He's an American-made vamp who came up through the ranks of a Vampere household. Though how we found that out I'll never know. The Trusts are traditionally impossible to penetrate."

A flickering in his eyes told me maybe I'd discovered our source. "Vayl? Were you ever Vampere?" After the words slipped out I wanted to cover my mouth. Apologize. It was the equivalent to asking a priest if he'd ever been a mule for the mob.

His hands dropped to his lap. "Yes."

I waited for excuses, but he made none. So I threw one in. "I imagine you were very different back then."

"You would not have known me. You would not have wanted to."

"What . . . why did you get out? *How* did you get out? You and Samos are the only two vamps I've ever heard of who've managed that."

"As your *sverhamin* I am bound to answer those questions, but I must ask you to take them back. It would be too dangerous for you to know."

*Dangerous for you, or for me?* I wondered. However, I simply nodded and went on with my Raptor review. "Samos seems to spend most of his time recruiting allies from the supernatural community. Though vampires usually shun all *others*, seeing themselves as far superior even to vamps from other nests, Samos is known to have partnered with weres and witches, not to mention humans."

"So is he building is own army?" Vayl wondered.

"It sure looks that way. With Pengfei and Lung as his allies, and this reaver in his pocket, he goes from America's problem to a worldwide threat. Which makes it all the more imperative that we get that armor."

"Yes," Vayl agreed. "And I believe we must find a way to eliminate the reaver, Desmond Yale."

# Chapter Thirty-three

A s we entered the living room area, Vayl took the crossbow he
would use off its perch on Mary-Kate. A sleek black model
made from mahogany and stainless-steel, heavy, but accurate, it
had been Matt's weapon of choice. And I'd carried it with me
faithfully since his death. Now it held the bolt Bergman had modi
fied to make sure it dropped its internal load once it penetrated
Pengfei's skin. I thought I'd be okay with Vayl pulling the trigger
to Matt's weapon as long as we got our outcome.

Cassandra, Cole, and Bergman, still finishing supper at the ta
ble Bergman had finally been able to clear now that he'd finished
his projects, kept snatching glances at the bow. I watched them
trying to fathom their thoughts. If I had to guess, I'd say Cassan
dra wondered if she could bear the visions that would arise in her
mind if she touched it. Cole tried to see himself pulling the trig
ger. Bergman prayed the mechanism he'd designed to release the
inner light would work before Pengfei had a chance to rip our
guts out.

Vayl cleared his throat, calling their attention to him. "I would
like you three to move about the new tent they erected for us as if
you were preparing for another show. We do not want anyone who
might be watching to become concerned with our behavior."

Cole looked up, wanting badly to say something, but we both
stared him down. "It sucks being the rookie," he said.

"I'm going to get changed," I said.

I went to the bedroom, pulled Pengfei's dress off its hanger and ranked it down over my butt. With slits up both legs clear to the upper thigh, it left no hiding place for a leg holster. That was the downside. The upside — though it looked quite formal, it had been designed for ease of movement.

The matching low-heeled slippers I'd found in Pengfei's closet didn't fit. Her feet were too narrow, making me feel like Cinderella's stepsister. Cassandra owned a flashy pair that would work, as long as I didn't mind nursing blisters on my heels for the next week. I did. So I went with my boots. Let people laugh. Next time Pete could just give me fair warning that I'd be costumed like a geisha at some point in my upcoming assignment.

Vayl came in and sat quietly on the bed while I worked on my makeup. I could tell he had something on his mind. And the acid-laced squeegee in my stomach said it would be one of those hard-to-face issues. So I concentrated on the makeup and hoped he'd let me pretend we had nothing to discuss.

The eyes were the tricky part. Pengfei laid it on thick and yet somehow made it out the door without resembling a prostitute. I managed a pretty good likeness and moved on to the accessories. Long black earrings. Braided wig over my tightly bound hair. The translator wires wound happily among the fake tresses. I took the necklace Cassandra had made off the dresser where I'd laid it when we'd come in.

Vayl stirred, making the springs in the bed squeak in protest. I agreed with them. "I was waiting for you to mention it before, but you seem to be following your usual tactics of dodge and ignore so I will say it straight out. Last night, you slept," he said. "I guarded you until dawn and you did not move a muscle."

I turned to look at him. Moved close enough for him to hear me speaking English. "No, I didn't."

"I take it those troubles that spurred you to sleepwalk have settled themselves."

I nodded carefully. "I'm never sure with me," I said. "But I think it's done with." I wanted to stop there. I tried. But a guy who sits with you for hours to make sure that your snoring doesn't turn to shooting deserves something for his efforts. So I struggled to put what I'd learned about the dreams into words. "I've needed, wanted to move forward. But I haven't been able to, knowing that meant I had to let Matt go. I think that's why I kept dreaming of him as a vampire. Because he didn't want to live on in that form any more than Jesse did. It would've been easier, in a way, to say goodbye to him if he had turned in the end."

Vayl nodded soberly. "It matters so much the way in which people leave us. Perhaps it should not. Dead is dead. But the why and how make such a difference to the survivors."

*And I am one. David told me that.* Evie's words came back to me now too. "You can only cry so long before it doesn't do you any more good." I was done crying. The time to grieve had passed. Because I knew Matt would want me to be happy now. But I needed to make something clear to Vayl. "I'll always love Matt. Things will sometimes remind me of him. And sometimes I'll miss him. When I'm ready to commit to another guy, it won't mean I love him any less because of that."

Vayl nodded. "I understand."

"But . . ." I cleared my throat, lowered my eyelashes, trying not to seem too eighteenth-century miss and blushing like a schoolgirl anyway. "I don't, I still feel kinda"—I made a gagging sound that raised both of Vayl's eyebrows as I continued—"when I think of relationships."

Again with the dimple. *I have got to find a suitable sound effect to herald its arrival, it's that rare. Do they make portable foghorns?*

Vayl said, "I am happy you have found a sense of peace. And perhaps, someday soon, you will meet a man who does not make you want to vomit?"

I shrugged, trying for nonchalant and utterly failing. "You never know."

"In the meantime, would you care to fill me in on the rest of your day's agenda?"

"Actually, it sucked. I had to kill Shao's brother because he was possessed by a reaver. And now that I know what reavers are about, I'm almost certain Yale and Pengfei mean to disrupt the festival somehow." I told him Jericho and his buds would be providing undercover security, for which I heaved an audible sigh of relief.

Vayl said, "It sounds to me as if you need some fresh air. Shall we find ourselves a Chinese Dragon Lady?"

"Yeah, but how? And if she's with Lung—"

"Which is likely—"

"How do we separate them?"

"If we are masters at anything, besides assassination, it is thinking on our feet. We will work it out when we have a situation to actually—how do you say—scope out."

"Okay. So. Finding her. That's going to be a challenge. It's a big city, Vayl."

"I think you have the ability to track her, Jasmine," he said earnestly. "Remember how you found me in the parking lot of our hotel in Miami?"

"Yeah, but you were within a few yards of me."

"That is true. But we must begin somewhere. And perhaps wearing Pengfei's dress will help direct your Sensitivity even further. These are not just random ideas, you know. In the past, Sensitives have been documented as having the ability to hunt vampires."

"Do we have any idea where to start looking though?"

"We can make an educated guess. We know Pengfei and Lung do not spend their daylight hours aboard the *Constance Malloy*. Which means someone must ferry them to shore. I suggest we find the boat that brought them to land last night and try to follow their trail from that point."

"Okay." If I sounded less than enthusiastic it might've been because I thought it was a really far-fetched idea. Unfortunately I couldn't come up with a better one, so we were stuck.

Fully dressed, with the medallion tucked under my collar and the translator wire woven in and around my wig hair, I minced down the RV's hallway. I'd spent what moments I could spare that afternoon watching Pengfei reruns on Bergman's laptop, trying to master her mannerisms. I was doing my best, but something felt wrong. *Probably just my underwear inching up my crack because the damn dress fits too tight.*

Cole had a great view from his perch in the driver's seat. He whistled when he saw me. "Freaky!"

"I agree," said Cassandra. She had donned a new Psychics-R-Us costume and was helping Bergman pack the last bits of his modular lab away in plastic bins. That he had allowed anyone, much less her, to touch his sacred bits said that he'd taken my last lecture pretty seriously. I hoped this was a solid sign he didn't want to grow up to be a big, skinny creep.

He noticed me watching him and said, "Our benefactors sent over a sound system about an hour ago. As soon as we get done here we'll go over there and set it up." He left what he was doing to hand out mouth-mints and hearing aids. "We'll be using the same communications system as when we set up video surveillance on the yacht. Transmitting wasn't a big deal there because we were all so close. In this case it'll be more of a challenge."

He gave Vayl and me the fake tattoos we'd used on our last mission. Mine was a dragon. Ironic, huh? Vayl's was a line of barbed wire. They would allow us to transmit from much greater distances. Once Bergman had outfitted and tested us, Cole nudged Vayl to get his attention. "Are you sure you don't need some help? I could carry your crossbow." He glanced at the weapon, which Vayl lifted from its resting place as if it weighed nothing.

"This is a job for two," he said.

"Okay" — sigh of disappointment — "call if you need me."

"I will need you," I reminded him. "Don't assume Pengfei's going to speak to me in English. I'm gonna need a fast translation of whatever she says and it can't be from some guy lurking in the bushes. You know what I mean? This has got to be done right."

Cole nodded, sitting a little straighter now that he understood the crucial nature of his role. "Gotcha."

"Do we still have Jericho's card?" I asked Cassandra.

"Yes."

"If something goes down, call him." Cassandra dove into her purse. After unearthing three pairs of sunglasses, a tile sample, and a box of tampons that made Bergman literally leap for the door, she found it.

"Good job," said Cole as he took it from her and keyed the number into his phone. "Remind me to bring you on my next mining expedition."

"I need this stuff," she said as she returned the items to their rightful places.

I shook my head. I didn't even own a purse. "We have to go."

They nodded. Cole held up his phone to indicate he'd be ready if it all went to crap.

"Good luck," said Cassandra.

Outside we caught Bergman halfway to the tent. He glanced at the crossbow in Vayl's hands, nodded at the bolt nesting in its position, ready to fire as soon as Vayl switched off the safety. "I hope it works."

"Don't worry," I said, patting the gun holstered under my armpit. "We have a backup plan." Actually I could've patted other areas of my body as well, but then I'd have either looked like I was hunting for matches or feeling myself up. Either way, a lame way to communicate that I'd added some blades to the mix as well. Bergman nodded and moved on.

Oddly enough, a Chinese woman wearing black boots and a large Rumanian man carrying a crossbow don't draw a whole lot of attention at a large entertainment venue. We stayed off the path as much as possible, but in some places were forced to join the growing crowd as we made our way to the marina. The office was open and it only took two crisp twenties to discover the docking point for our vamps' water taxi.

They'd tied it close to the path. Vayl helped me climb in and my doubts mounted. We were wasting valuable time in this spotless vessel. Not one shred of Pengfei remained for me to detect.

"Take your time," suggested Vayl. "Try a few different seats. Maybe she has left a bit of herself behind."

She wouldn't have driven, so I sat in the rear. Nope, nothing. But, hey, we were talking about Pengfei here. She wasn't interested in backseats.

I moved to the front.

Nothing.

With a mounting sense of unease I let my eyes roam the vessel, the dock, paths she might have taken from there. Hundreds, if not thousands, of lives could depend on me figuring out Pengfei's location tonight and my Sensitivity hadn't stirred since—

"Hey, wait a minute." I pointed to Vayl as if he'd done something wrong. "You're not simmering."

"I . . ." He scanned down his body, as if debating whether he should check for BO or blisters. "Pardon me?"

"I can't feel your power. I can't sense you at all. You're like a big blank to me!" I got up, tight waves of fear rising and falling in my chest. I held out my right fist, shaking it at him. "I can't feel the ring, either. Usually it's warm on my finger, especially when you're around. What the hell is happening to me?"

Cassandra's voice boomed in my ear: "Jasmine, listen to me."

"What?"

"I think the magic of the medallion is squashing your Sensitivity. Take it off."

Easier said than done when it's tucked inside a tight dress underneath a long wig intertwined with a translator wire. What a pain in the ass. Yet as soon as I'd shucked it, relief washed over me. Yup, the underwear had definitely wriggled out of the crack. I felt Vayl's cold, controlled powers doing their usual slow roll. I could see better too, as if I'd been running around wearing sunglasses at night and just remembered to take them off.

I slumped back in the seat, the medallion bunched in one hand, the other braced against the cushion. I hoped to maintain my balance if the boat went rocky, rocky. Instead it whispered, "Pengfei." But not loud enough. I'd never be able to follow that murmur of sound all the way to its source.

I leaned over the side of the boat, stared into the water, knowing what I needed to do, wondering how to broach the subject. Vayl had resisted almost violently the first time, and he'd been in dire need then.

"I feel like we're running out of time," I said as I gazed, almost mesmerized, into the tiny waves the boat's movements made in the bay. I tore my eyes away from the water, thinking Vayl's weren't so different. Deep pools you could get lost in forever, if you wanted to.

"What are you saying?"

"I sense her, but it's not enough. I need to heighten this ability. And I only know one way to do that."

His focus sharpened, narrowed to me. "You mean, you want me to take your blood."

Multiple intakes of breath as our crew reacted. I'd almost forgotten they could hear us.

"Yes. And before we spend the next twenty minutes arguing the morality of the issue, why don't you just admit I'm right, it's a great idea, and we may save a lot of lives this way?"

His presence, a constant hum at the back of my head, began to expand. It was as if my request had released some huge inner padlock, opened a creaky old door, and allowed him to fill with the true blood of his personality. For an instant I felt the full brunt of his power. It spun out of him like a tornado, sparking visions like lightning strikes. I saw the labyrinth of rage, pain, and violence he'd mastered on his way from his own downfall to my side. His strength and sense of purpose impressed me. I recognized his devotion to the job, his passion for justice. And the hope that he would someday meet his boys again, which gave everything else shape and direction. Gawd Almighty, if you could capture his essence in clay or oils you'd have yourself a masterpiece. And then, just as suddenly, he pulled it back. "All right," he said, his voice husky with the bit he couldn't quite suppress.

"Wow," I whispered, struggling to keep my head on straight. He had such a way of turning me sideways. Hadn't that bothered me once? "That was faster than I figured."

Twitch of the lip. Glint in the eye that took me slightly aback. It was so . . . hungry. Which was when I realized he hadn't eaten yet.

Must've meant to take his fill from Pengfei and Lung. And the reaver, if we could find him. He'd told me once that he did it as a failsafe. His way of knowing for certain he wasn't taking out innocents. He was already sitting next to me. Now he slid closer. "Tell me you are certain."

"Well, I was."

"And then?"

"Then I remembered how much you like the taste of Jaz."

Out came the dimple again. Hell, if it was going to become this common I'd have to announce its arrival with a bicycle bell. "If it makes you feel better, I will let you bite me first."

"No!" The chorus of negatives boomed into my ears like a megaphone alarm.

"Um, team, I would function better if I could hear tonight," I said.

Cassandra's voice came, thankfully softer, but just as deep as the others. "We just wanted to let you know how much we enjoy the fact that you're human."

I assumed we were using the term loosely, considering both my history and foreseeable future. "Don't worry, kids. I'm not vampire bound. Just intent on enhancing some of my finer traits." I looked up at Vayl. "You're going to enjoy this, aren't you?"

His eyes glittered with an otherworldly light as he regarded me. "I am vampire, Jasmine. Would you have me pretend otherwise?"

"Ummm, no." I realized we were done with the foreplay. Vayl's arm, already across my shoulders, dropped behind my back and pulled me close. "These marks can't show," I murmured.

"I will take care to conceal them," Vayl assured me, his words muffled as his lips crossed the line of my jaw. My neck tingled as the tips of his fangs brushed my carotid. They moved lower as he pulled back my collar and thumbed open the top button of my dress. I think my eyes actually did a one eighty in their sockets as his teeth pierced the skin just below my collarbone.

The last time Vayl had taken my blood I'd blacked out partway through. This time I stayed up for the whole show. And it rocked. I tried to work out why, but that part of my brain hit the deck first. The rest of me, well it doesn't seem quite decent to describe the feelings Vayl woke in me. Knowing Cassandra and the boys could hear the whole shebang, I stayed silent, though I badly wanted to moan, encourage, and at the very end, shout in triumph, as if I'd summited Everest without oxygen, or a map, or even a Sherpa to guide me.

When Vayl straightened, he looked as astounded as I felt. "It was actually better this time. How can that be?"

"Age?" I hazarded. "You know, like fine wine?"

His laugh, which generally held not one iota of amusement, made me smile. "How do you feel?" he asked as he fished his handkerchief out of his pocket and laid it against the mark.

"Great, actually," I said. "Though it probably won't last. I crashed pretty hard the first time."

"Then we should move quickly."

"Agreed."

# Chapter Thirty-four

He checked his handkerchief. The bleeding had already stopped, so I buttoned up. "Vayl, it worked."

"Already?"

*Oh yeah.* I realized I could practically see in the dark, even without activating my special lenses. And I could see Pengfei as well, with that other, mental eye that sensed vampires the way bloodhounds scent rabbits. She had sat in this very spot. Still. Serene. Her head tipped toward the stars as if enjoying the ride but, in reality, leading the charge.

I closed my eyes, concentrating on her psychic trail. "I think we're going to be able to find her. My Sensitivity—it's definitely enhanced."

"Something is happening to me as well," Vayl said. "A change I cannot as yet pinpoint." I'd never heard that particular tone in his voice before. Then I realized. It was wonder. I opened my eyes. How long had it been since anything had made him marvel? We stared at each other. "I chose rightly in you, my *avhar*."

"Why, Vayl, that almost sounds like a compliment."

"Do not let it go to your head."

"Don't worry. If I do I'll probably just end up ramming it into another tent pole." I stood, sat back down as the dizzies hit me, and said, "Maybe you should go first."

Vayl disembarked, helped me out, and then waited patiently while I shut my eyes again. Yup, there it was. A definite Pengfei bouquet, kinda like skunk only lethal. I opened my eyes because, let's face it, this was going to be hard to do if I kept running into things like, oh, I don't know, the Gulf of Mexico. The trail faded somewhat, but I could still sense it. I squinted and it came clearer. Okay, so I guessed I'd have to do this looking as if I needed a good pair of bifocals. Why, oh why, couldn't I once receive a Gift that required a good tan and my own personal stylist?

Vayl made a noise that I translated as a badly disguised chuckle. "You just keep your smart-ass remarks to yourself," I said.

"I did not say a word."

"You didn't have to. Let's go." I headed toward the parking lot from which groups of Texans were still emerging, talking and laughing, gearing up for big fun. I wanted to run them off, one and all, and to hell with the consequences. Instead I followed Pengfei's trail east, to the open area Cole and I had driven past on our scouting expedition. An antiqued silver sign labeled it as Sanford Park. The bay with its seawall still ran to our right. Pengfei's trail led us on a straight course up a grassy slope to the band shell.

In the summer I supposed the hill would fill with families carrying blankets and picnic baskets, old couples with lawn chairs, maybe a few young lovers looking for a cheap date, listening to free concerts given by the local symphony. But judging by the fact that BRITNEY LUVS MARK was written in big red letters across the back wall, I supposed nobody had played a note here in months.

Built to withstand some nasty blows, the building looked sturdy as a post office. Excellent foundation. Solid floors. Expensive, recessed lighting. All the wiring snaked under the stage, so when Pengfei's scent took me to a trap door at the front I wasn't surprised. Vayl lifted the door and went down first. I followed.

We found their resting places almost immediately. Two shallowly buried coffins, open and empty.

"Dammit," I said.

"You guys okay?" It was Cole, sounding worried. I nearly snapped at him, but held it in check. It's always hardest to wait.

"We're fine," I said. "They've already risen, that's all." *Of course they have. You knew that. Vamps don't sleep in, you fool. They have places to go. People to eat.* I moved on, following Pengfei's trail back onto the stage. She had walked to the rear, taken the stairs off the east side, headed toward the gazebo. Even by night it beckoned. *Stop here. Look at the bay. Step out of yourself for one second and acknowledge that there's something more, something better out there.*

"Vayl," I whispered as we reached the building.

"I know."

Had he, like me, smelled it before he saw it?

*No. Not it. Her. That bitch, Pengfei, does not get to reduce anyone to an it.* But she'd tried. Her victim lay on the floor of the structure, what was left of her anyway. Pengfei had mangled her neck like a poodle's chew toy. Then she'd torn open the woman's chest. Or maybe something else had. Because most of the contents were missing, including her heart. *Reaver,* whispered my mind, and my churning gut agreed.

In fact, inspired by its proximity to real acrobats, my stomach proceeded to attempt a quadruple double-twisting backflip. Since it still hadn't sifted through all the grease from its last meal, the results were not pretty. I left them in the bay.

"Pengfei and Desmond Yale." I spat out their names along with the taste of vomit. Weren't they just the pretty pair? Which took my mind back to Samos, the Matchmaker from Hell. He should have his own Web site — psychodates.com. I could just see him making the morning talk show circuit. "Honest, Regis, it works every time! Our clients fill out a thirty-page personality profile. Yes, there's a nominal charge, but we make a *killing* from the revenues! Haw, haw, haw!" How satisfying would it be to charge right out of the audience and shove my fist through his face? On a scale of one to ten? Ninety.

Vayl's hand on my arm brought my attention back to the present. "You cannot function if you let such feelings take hold," he said.

*Don't I know it.* I looked down at my hands, shaking with the rage I felt at this senseless death. And yeah, a little bit at being the one who had to find her body, feel her pain, take her revenge. These were the times I wished I'd been more like Evie. If I could've been satisfied with her kind of life I could've avoided a buttload of pain.

"What do we do?" I asked.

"Find Pengfei."

"But this woman's soul —"

"— may still be in the eye of the reaver, or may already be lost. Either way, there is nothing you can do right now, especially if Pengfei is planning a disaster, as you suspect."

"For a guy who wants to live forever, you sure have a callous way of looking at death," I snapped.

Vayl stared at me until I met his eyes. "I could ask you where you get off saying such a thing, considering your profession," he said, his tone so even I knew he was working to keep it that way. Which meant I'd better back down before he decided I needed a little hardening and I spent the next six weeks viewing corpses in all sorts of gruesome situations. "However, recognizing you have made the mistake of identifying with this woman, I will simply remind you to keep your mind on the job and save the souls you can."

I turned away. Vayl was right. I couldn't rescue them all. I looked over my shoulder, hating myself because I couldn't cry — because it would smear my makeup. Boy was I ever into my part now. All I had to do was steal some kid's cotton candy and I could easily pass for the biggest louse on earth.

"Jasmine, stop slouching," ordered Vayl, taking out the remnants of his ire on my posture. "Pengfei does not slouch."

"She should. Actually, she should slither. Then, the next time I see her, I can just stomp her head in." With that grimly satisfying picture in my head I followed Pengfei's steps back to the Winter Festival, down the same path Cole and I had taken only a couple of days before. What a contrast now. Crowded with bright-eyed, laughing families, lined with carefully painted booths and rides that looked like they'd been built by NASA and lit by the White House Christmas decorators, the Corpus Christi Winter Festival seemed like an idea plucked from the mind of Einstein.

We left the path just before we reached the Chinese Acrobats' Arena. Pengfei's route had taken her behind the multicolored building into the center of the acrobats' camp. The place practically echoed since the show was on. We could hear *oohs* and *aahs* and occasional bursts of applause from where we stood, staring at the back of a small Winnebago.

"Nice propane tanks," I said lamely.

"Yes," Vayl agreed.

"I don't get why her presence is heavier here. Nothing seems out of place to me. How about you?"

Vayl stooped and looked beneath the camper while I climbed to view the top of it. When we'd rejoined each other we both shook our heads. Nothing.

"Moving on?" I asked.

"I suppose so," he said.

I went back into squint mode and followed Pengfei's by now familiar trail. It led us directly to the arena. She'd bypassed the main entrance and followed one puffy red wall to the back of the building where a smaller purple structure attached to the main body. It allowed the acrobats quick access to the large open space within.

"She went in here," I whispered. The crowd applauded as something impressive just happened. We stepped inside the entryway for a better view, but a black curtain had been drawn to hide the area in which we stood along with about two feet of the back wall. The house band switched from tension-building music to a dance-in-your-seat tune. I grabbed Vayl's arm. "She's in here."

We peered through an opening in the curtain. "There," said Vayl. "She is in the front row, wearing the white short-sleeved top with the turquoise pants, sitting next to Lung in the gold robes." Vayl looked down at me. "How are you going to explain the change of clothes to Lung when you finally see him?"

"Won't have to. He'll already know somebody spilled a Cherry Coke on me."

"So that is how you are planning to separate them?"

"Yup. I've got twenty bucks in my pocket says I can get one of the upstanding young men in this audience to do me just that favor before this show is over. Look." I pointed to a set of stands to our right. "See that tall lanky college kid on the back row? The one drinking two beers at once? I'm thinking he's the one."

"Would you like me to do the talking?" he offered, perhaps thinking the two of them would bond immediately, being male and all. I thought he'd probably scare the hell out of the kid. Even with his powers banked, he still carried with him an I-could-easily-kick-your-ass air that kept most guys at a safe distance. But I didn't say any of that.

"Nope. Let's leave it to the money." We began to move, but stopped as the entire perimeter of the floor rotated counterclockwise, circling our frat boy, along with the rest of the audience, a quarter of a turn to the left. A stream of acrobats ran past us and onto the performance floor, which had remained in place. The audience cheered and stamped their approval of this innovation. We exchanged impressed glances.

"Wonder who thought that up?" I said.

"Do you think they have their own resident Bergman?"

"If they have to steal from ours?" After a couple of failed attempts I got college boy's attention, found out he adored pranks and money, and had myself a new partner.

I couldn't see Pengfei or Lung since the audience had rotated. I stood on my tiptoes and jumped up and down to no avail. "How's it going?" I demanded. "Is he there yet?"

"Jasmine, trust more than your eyes."

Vayl was so calm that I stood absolutely still, opened up all my senses, and simply sponged it all up. It took about three minutes, but at last I could say, "She's moving."

"Are you certain?"

I nodded. "She's leaving. There's an exit directly opposite ours. She's headed out that way."

"Go get her."

Turning, lunging out the door, I avoided another group of acrobats with an agility that, since the Sensitivity had risen in me, had become a rarity. As soon as I regained visual contact with Pengfei I put the medallion back over my head right along with the edgy feeling of discomfort.

The real Pengfei was pissed and practically trotting, but I still managed to catch up with her on the path headed back toward the marina and that pretty blue ferry to the *Constance Malloy*. I grabbed her arm and hustled her off the trail to an unlit clearing just west of the festival. That she allowed me to move her at all reflected the depth of shock she felt at seeing her own face mirrored back at her from what should have been a total stranger's countenance.

She recovered quickly, yanking her arm out of my grasp. "That is my dress!" she spat, enraged as any woman would be at the unmitigated gall. I kind of understood what she was saying just by her expression, but Cole translated almost as soon as she spoke.

I backed up, making space for my equipment to do its work as I spread her fan in front of my mouth. "Yes it is," I said, "and you know what? Your ass is flat!" I felt better already.

"Who are you?" she hissed.

I spoke in a slow, stately manner so any hesitation I might make while waiting for Cole's translation would be misinterpreted as an aged woman taking the time she so richly deserved. "Do you not recognize me, Pengfei Yan? I am your great-great-grandmother!"

Shao, with his talk of ancestors and honoring Wu, had given me the idea. I wasn't sure about contemporary Chinese, but the old ones like Pengfei had worshipped their ancestors. Given that Vayl still carried a ton of the 1700s around with him, I hoped Pengfei remembered where she came from just as clearly.

Mustering some matriarchal ire, I added, "I cannot believe you do not recognize your own ancestor. But perhaps it is no surprise when you have not venerated me lo these many centuries as you know you should have, you ungrateful whelp." When I saw I'd struck a superstitious chord I closed the gap between us just long enough to give her face a slap. Her hand went to her cheek as I backpedaled, pressing my lips together to keep my delighted chortle strictly mental. "Now tell me why I should not visit great plagues of the most foul luck upon you for the next three thousand years?"

"I have devised a wonderful plan, Honored Grandmother," Pengfei said eagerly. "It will transform China into the world's most powerful nation, as you and I know it should be." My gesture told her to quit pissing around and get to the details. She leaned toward me and whispered, "I am blowing up the Chinese acrobats."

I nearly slapped her again. Anything to strike the glee from her shining black eyes. But then people still might die, little people like Lai and E.J., and I couldn't have that. "What a marvelous plan," I drawled, "destroying your own people." I spun my finger next to my temple and rolled my eyes. "Brilliant."

"No, Grandmother, don't you see? I have mailed letters to the *Washington Post* and the *New York Times* taking responsibility for the explosion on behalf of the American fanatics who demonstrate outside the gates of this festival. My partner was able to transfer their fat leader's fingerprints to the envelopes and even to the bomb itself. No one will doubt the story, because it is widely known that the Chinese acrobats are managed by vampires."

"I do not understand. What American fanatics? Who are you framing?"

"The church people!" Pengfei cried. "Their hatred for the supernatural is well documented. They actually wrote a threatening letter to us when they heard we were bringing the acrobats to Corpus Christi. It was what gave us — well, our partner — the idea."

"And who is this partner?"

Pengfei's eyes practically glowed. "His name is Edward Samos. He sponsored a group of reavers to come and help us achieve our goals. What a ruthless beast their leader is!" She must be referring to Yale, who, I assumed, had carried both the security guard and Wu along inside him until Samos had found bodies for them. I wondered if there were any more out there that we should know about. But before I could frame a reaver question that wouldn't sound too suspicious, I thought of one that was much more important.

"And this Samos. Why should he care about China?"

"He cares about the entire world! Every creature born or made with something extra, something that makes them *other*, falls under his protection as far as he is concerned."

"And what is he protecting them from?"

She looked at me like my brains might be leaking out of my nose. "Humanity, of course."

So Samos had found himself a cause, huh? Or was he just masquerading behind a worthy issue as a way to net more allies, soup up the power until even his battery overflowed?

"So when this bomb explodes?" I prodded. "What happens then?"

"Our countrymen will be enraged when so many of our people are killed so horribly on foreign soil. Words will erupt into bullets and those into bombs. And in the midst of the carnage we will emerge with a new army." She clasped her hands in front of her chest as she imagined it, smiling madly at her vision of the bloody battlefield. "Men armored as dragons will lead the march across this land of self-absorbed, avaricious barbarians, leaving nothing but ash in their wake."

"And just how did a little girl like you learn how to blow people up?" I demanded, planting my free hand on my hip. I sensed that Vayl had reached his position. I could signal him anytime now.

As I'd hoped, my dig offended her. "Women can do anything they wish these days, Grandmother. Sometimes all they have to do is read the right books or hire the right engineers. It is no longer necessary to marry the right man."

I nodded as if I appreciated her point of view. "And so?"

"I wired the explosives to one of the campers. After the acrobats finish the show they will all return to their temporary homes to shower and change. And so, in"—she checked the diamond-studded watch on her right wrist—"fifteen minutes, all forty of our acrobats, including twelve children, will be dead!"

"You bitch!" yelled Cole so loud into my earpiece I thought for a second my hearing would be permanently impaired. I have rarely had to work so hard to keep the pain off my face. "Sorry, Jaz," he said immediately. "Sorry, sorry. Won't happen again."

"But what if someone sees the bomb?" I asked.

"Never." She said it with such utter confidence that my hopes of finding the device in time to disarm it died. "My *cantrantia*"—by that she meant her core power—"is that of concealment. Even if you stood directly on top of it you would never detect it." Her laugh, a light and pleasant tinkle, caressed the air. "Even I could not find it now."

*It sucks to be right.* If I hadn't been so worried about the acrobats and their kids, not to mention innocent passersby, I'd have been deeply depressed. But Pengfei obviously wanted some Granny praise for her dirty deeds, so I said, "How exciting! You have certainly done well for yourself, Granddaughter. Please, let me do you the honor." I bowed, deeply enough that the bolt from Vayl's crossbow flew six inches over my back and straight into Pengfei's stomach.

The sound she made was less of pain and more of shock and denial.

I stood up. "That's what you get for ignoring your Granny." Mocking words, but my mind was on the corpse lying in that gazebo. Not just dead. Soul raped. *This one's for you, victim lady. And when I get hold of that bastard Yale . . .*

Both of Pengfei's hands wrapped around the bolt, trying to pull it out, but Bergman had foreseen this possibility. As soon as it had penetrated her body, two long spikes had emerged from the tip, anchoring the bolt securely in her abdomen long enough for the wax covering the pill to melt. Theoretically, at least. She screamed as she pulled and things inside her body gave that should never have moved.

"Come on," I murmured. "Come on, come on." It was like standing in a cavern waiting for the tour guide to turn on his flashlight. But instead of brightening the night with an inner sunburst, Pengfei yanked the bolt free. *"Shit!"*

*I should've known. Dammit, didn't that welcome mat teach you anything, Jaz? Bergman's prototypes only work half the time, and then not always how they're supposed to.* Stupid! Never want something to succeed so bad you totally deny reality waiting for it to work.

My hand itched to pull Grief, but I hadn't been honest with Bergman when I'd said the gun served as our backup plan. It didn't. Because Pengfei was Vayl's kill. And I'd learned early in our partnership that you don't stand between him and his target unless you want to remind him gently and repeatedly that you're on his side while his eyes spit red fire and his cane sword waves dangerously close to your throat.

"Hey, what's that over there?"

"I dunno. Let's check it out!" Young, piping voices, headed our way.

I looked over my shoulder. Vayl had intercepted two wayward kids, and I saw several more looming right behind them. *Damn, now he's sidetracked by crowd control. What to do? What to do?*

Pengfei dropped what was left of the bolt, which was when I realized the business end had remained in her body. But its reaction continued to delay itself far beyond our scheme. Originally the ignition had been timed for two hours. I'd asked for instant.

"Bergman!" I hissed, covering my mouth so, hopefully, the

sound wouldn't reach the translator. "Where's the *sizzle, wap* you promised?"

"How long has the pill been active?"

"I don't know, a few seconds."

"Give it time," he pleaded. "I know it'll work."

"Do you have any idea what you're asking?"

"I know it's dangerous, but this could revolutionize the way we fight vampires. Please, Jaz. I put my heart and soul into this."

*Oh, for crying out loud.*

Pengfei began to back away.

"Where are you going?" I demanded.

"Yacht," she muttered. "Safe there. Heal better there." As she spoke, blood spilled from the side of her mouth.

I strode toward her. "I don't think so," I said, pulling a classic bully move—ankle behind the calf, hard shove that took her to the ground. Except I hung my arm out there a little too long. It gave her time to grab hold, pull me off balance, and flip me over onto my back. Remembering how lethal her hand-to-hand fighting skills had shown themselves to be during the yacht massacre, I quickly rolled to my feet. The wound had slowed her some. She'd only just made it to vertical herself.

I moved in fast, aiming multiple kicks at that bleeding midsection, hoping to weaken her more. She blocked every one.

Having seen her style, I expected a counterattack of such blinding speed that all thought would be suspended in the simple act of survival. But the wound had taken its toll on her aggression as well. She came at me with one arm down, guarding her stomach. The other snaked out, stabbing at my throat.

I dodged the blow, landing one of my own in the middle of her chest, which staggered her. Closing in, I tried to take her down again, but she backed me up with a series of low kicks, a couple of which landed square enough to leave my shins black-and-blue for days.

I faked a kick to her abdomen and she dropped her arm, leaving her head wide open. So I pulled the kick and powered it upward, landing it just above her right eye.

She dropped to her knees.

Vayl came to my side. "She's all yours," I said.

"Actually, I think Bergman has taken care of her," he replied.

I peered down at her. The skin had begun to peel off her hands, neck, and face in thin, curling strips. Heat built inside her quickly after that, so fast I could feel it blasting from her, as if I was standing too close to a bonfire.

We backed off as steam rose from her body. It soon became a torrent of smoke that bubbled and blackened along with her skin. Her hair and clothes finally caught fire, and I heard a couple of kids say, "Hey, check that out!"

Vayl caught them before they'd stepped more than a foot off the path. "Go home," he said grimly. They turned tail and went.

# CHAPTER THIRTY-FIVE

As we hurried away from Pengfei's smoking remains I said, "Cole?"

His voice boomed in my ear, loud, low, and excited. "Just got off the phone with Jericho. The evacuation has started. He said the bomb squad may be able to contain the blast some, but it'll still be big."

"Okay. Tell them we're going to put a great big mark on the camper that's wired. They won't be able to find the bomb. Tell them not to waste time trying; it's magically concealed. But at least they'll know its location." Who knew, maybe they'd be able to blanket the place with some sort of retardant. As I recalled, it wasn't that big. At least if it was the one we'd inspected earlier. And I knew it was. What a crock of crap. We'd looked all over the thing without once realizing we were staring straight at the bomb. A thought occurred to me. "Uh, would you move the RV again? If that sucker gets damaged Pete will be twitching well into the next decade."

"Sure."

Vayl touched my arm. Even now, with everything behind us and all we were about to go through, that light stroke of fingers on skin fired my attention. "Yes?" I said, working to keep my voice level.

"Our time is limited. I will go mark the camper. You find Lung."

Without even a "See ya later, alligator" he was gone. As I strode toward the main path I thought, *This is going to be harder now. Lung's in the crowd that's being herded toward the building exits. He knows they've been compromised. What am I supposed to tell him? What would he believe?*

I'd reached the Acrobats' Arena. Wide-eyed people came pouring out of the main entrance, clutching each other and their children, talking in high voices, many of them crying. But nobody was screaming. Nobody had broken into a run. Credit the off-duty SWAT guys who flanked the exit and the path and who I could hear inside the building, speaking in calm, authoritative voices.

I tried to sense Lung among that mass of humanity. He shouldn't be that hard to pick out. I recalled the scene in our tent, just before it burned. What was his scent like again? Wait, I was still wearing the medallion. Then I realized it didn't matter.

"This is bad," I muttered.

Vayl, hearing me through his earpiece, asked, "Is the crowd out of control?"

"They're okay. I'm not. It's Lung. Vayl, I never scented him. Not once. It was always Pengfei or the other vamps around him, but never him. The armor covers it up. I haven't seen him yet, and if I can't pick him out of this crowd, I have no way to find him. Wait a second. Something's happening around back."

I ran behind the building, led by the sound of a woman shouting and crying. I rushed forward when I recognized Xia Ge struggling in her husband's arms. "Ge!" I said. "What's wrong?"

She took one wide-eyed look at me, screamed, and passed out. That was when I remembered I still looked like Pengfei.

I leaned in close to Shao. "Dude, it's me, Lucille Robinson. What happened?"

Poor Shao looked half dead himself, but he managed to say, "Chien-Lung is kidnap Lai."

"How?"

"Lai strap in stroller. Ge sitting in front row, watching show. When evacuation begin she going out acrobats' exit. That where Chien-Lung strike her down and take Lai away."

"Where'd he go?"

Shao pointed back toward the marina.

I squeezed Shao's arm. "I'm going after him, Shao." I wished I could promise to bring his baby back. But both of us knew we didn't live in that kind of world.

I took off after Lung. "Cole, I want you out looking too," I said. "Not confronting, just looking."

"I'm on it!" he replied.

Vayl said, "I am inside the camper trying to find something to mark it with, but I will be with you shortly."

"Try mustard," I suggested.

"Ahh."

"It shouldn't be that hard to find the guy," I told them. "How many Chinese men wearing gold robes pushing baby strollers do you see on a daily basis?"

"None," Cole replied. "But people are starting to trickle into the parking lot where I'm standing. I've got a pretty good view down the path behind them too, and the thing is, I'm not seeing any now either."

*What the hell? He should be sticking out like Santa Claus on a nude beach!*

"Maybe he has the chameleon's ability to blend in," suggested Vayl.

Bergman's voice came tight and shaking over our earpieces. "Listen, when we put the armor on certain animals they *were* able to blend in with their surroundings. And these were mammals whose coats did not typically change colors with the seasons. It could be that he's ditched the robes and the armor itself has become his disguise."

*Shit.* Part of me just wanted to sit down on that dirty path along with the discarded candy wrappers, soda straws, bits of popcorn, and wads of tasteless gum and give the hell up. You think you're almost to the top of that bastard of a mountain. You've killed the Empress of Doom. Saved the innocents. Staved off world war. And then some psycho dragon wannabe makes off with the second most adorable infant on earth, *and* he might as well be invisible. What the hell is *with* that?

But I kept moving, kept studying faces, kept following the path. Then I heard it. Not clearly, but not distant either.

I couldn't run. Not unless I wanted to start a stampede. But I picked up the pace big-time. Took that path nearly to the marina and then stopped again to listen. Above the babble of scared voices, crying children, and stern cop voices shouting directions, a baby screamed.

I said, "Guys, I spent enough time with E.J. to know the kid I hear crying right now is not hungry, wet, or tired. That is a freaked-out baby who wants his mommy."

Vayl said, "I am on my way, but do not wait."

"Cole?"

"I can see you."

"Good. Keep me in sight. Be ready for anything."

I zeroed in on the source of that sound. Within thirty seconds I found Lai, bawling so hard his chubby little cheeks were beet red and soaked with tears. Pushing his stroller was a person with Lung's facial features. That was it. He had, indeed, shed his robes. His armor had crafted itself into a plain black suit, the long sleeves of which covered his hands. He even had matching shoes and a fedora. *Bergman would be so proud,* I thought bitterly.

Reminding myself to behave exactly as Pengfei would, I marched up to Lung and wrenched the stroller out of his hands. Maintaining translating distance was tough with people jostling us from every side, but I managed.

"Are you out of your mind?" I shrilled at him, remembering just in time to spread the fan in front of my mouth with my free hand.

Lung jerked the stroller back. "Samos betrayed us, as I warned you he would! You should never have trusted our grand plan to one who does not put China foremost! Now we are going to do this as *I* wished to! This child will be the start of an army trained from infancy to our way of thinking. With Chinese boys outnumbering girls five to one there is no limit to our supply. And now that we have the armor, we can ensure their invincibility on any field of battle on earth!"

Even in this horror-framed moment, when I understood if I so much as cocked my head in the wrong direction this lunatic would kill baby Lai, I couldn't quite understand how Lung managed to contain all that insanity inside his spare frame. It seemed to me something monstrous should erupt from the top of his head, maybe a gigantic pus-covered fist holding a twenty-foot billboard flashing a warning to all comers not to be taken in by the fact that this guy could fake normality for long periods of time.

The words came out so fast I suspected I might be channeling Pengfei. A pleasant thought, as long as she loathed every second of it. "We'll never get out of Texas with this baby, Chien-Lung. His parents have already sent the police after him. The FBI will join the search soon. Before we are out of American waters his face will be on millions of television sets. Additionally, think about this, we don't have the resources to take care of one baby, much less the thousands we would need for an army." I grabbed at the stroller. Lung yanked it to his right, out of my reach.

"Do not touch it!" he snarled.

I kept talking, which was stupid, I know. Lunatics don't follow logic. But we were still surrounded by people. Vayl hadn't arrived. There was Lai to consider. So . . . "Lung, please believe, the idea is strategic disaster. You must understand, Americans value children above all. They will be in no frame of mind to war with the Chinese when their hearts are breaking for Chinese parents who have lost their baby. At least let this one go. Wait until we get back home. Then you can take as many babies as you wish."

The stroller inched toward me. My palms itched to seize it. Instead I smiled. "I have arranged for our speedboat to meet us in a private place, away from the crowds. If a reporter recognizes us we may never reach the yacht."

What was that in his eyes? A moment of reluctant sanity? "All right." The stroller came into my hands. As I pushed it into the crowd I felt, more than saw, Cole take command of it.

"Come." I led him past the marina, across the auto-filled lot to Sanford Park. Why was it suddenly so dark? Oh yeah, the amulet squashing my enhanced vision again. Luckily I still had my night-vision contacts in, so I shut my eyes tight. When I opened them everything showed up much more plainly despite the fact that the whole area looked to have been pissed on by a drunken leprechaun.

I took Lung to the gazebo. The body lay where I'd found it. Lung crouched over it, wrinkling his nose at the smell. "I see you allowed Yale his share." He stood. "Well, now that Samos is no longer our ally, at least we are rid of the reavers."

"Yes. There is that." I set the fan on the railing. Surely it was dark enough here he wouldn't notice a lack of lip synching. Plus I needed both hands free now.

One cool thing about the dress I wore, the sleeves hid my wrist sheaths nicely. I'd loaded my syringe of holy water into the right one. The one on the left held my throwing knives. My bola had posed the biggest challenge. Cassandra had helped me solve it by braiding the wig hair around it and wrapping the bit of hilt that showed with red ribbon. It had never looked so pretty or given me such a headache.

"I don't see any boats yet, do you?" I asked. I used my left hand to point back toward the marina. My right pulled back, activating the sheath's automatic-feed system. Within a second I held the syringe.

As Lung turned to look, I lunged forward, jamming the syringe into his ear. But the armor saw me coming. It had moved at half-speed, as though confused by my disguise. But it had warded off my attack. By the time the needle hit, the scrape of metal on metal told me scales already covered the side of his head. However I knew better than to depend on a single attempt. I'd already begun reaching for my bola as I made my first move, and by the time I knew the syringe was useless the knife hilt filled my left hand.

Shocked that Pengfei would attempt to kill him, Lung's first reaction was defensive. He crouched. After a brief delay, maybe only two or three heartbeats, the armor raced to cover his head. Already he had horns and fangs.

But that short pause had given me the opening I needed.

Using both hands to power the move, I jammed the bola through his cheek and into his nose. He screamed and jerked away, launching one of the spines off his back, more out of instinct, I think, than any real attempt to hurt me with it. It landed halfway up the hill and exploded, sending grass and dirt flying.

I yelled, "Vayl! Gazebo! *Now!*" Trying to avoid getting blown to bits or crispy-curled, I stayed in close, and I mean tight, like a tick on a German shepherd in the middle of July. Lung did his expanding act while I slammed kicks into his growing torso, trying to keep one eye on his tail and the other on his fire-breathing apparatus.

But it looked like the knife had done a number on the mechanism. In fact, a quarter of his face from cheek to forehead still remained scale-free. Blood splattered across his shoulders, me, and the grass as he shook his head, trying to dislodge the knife, but it wouldn't budge.

When his claws ripped out of their wrappings I darted clear, remembering the damage they'd done his attackers on the yacht. But he seemed more intent on using them to knock the bola free. He roared as he somehow managed to wiggle it deeper, and a fresh gout of blood ran down his cheek and neck.

I popped the top button of Pengfei's dress and drew Grief. It felt like taking aim at an F-18 with a spit wad. I was so not packing the necessary heat to smoke this monster. Hell, that kind of firepower might not even exist. But Vayl's sudden presence along with his reassuring "I am here," made me hope otherwise.

He ran past me so quickly I barely saw the blur as he leaped at Chien-Lung, making my heart stop for a terrifying two seconds as he went straight for the face and I thought, "Oh my God, what if

the fire erupts now? What if he burns? He'll never come back!"
The possibility took the starch right out of my knees.

In movements so swift my eyes could barely follow, Vayl jerked
Lung's head around, using the hilt of the knife as a handle, and
sank his fangs into the exposed skin of his face.

Lung went nuts. He screamed as if all the demons in hell were
shredding his soul bit by tiny bit. He launched every single spike
from his back, blowing so many pits in Sanford Park's hillside it
looked like the land had developed a skin-eating infection. His tail
whipped wildly from side to side. He beat Vayl with his claws. He
raked at his back, which should've left deep furrows that should
have filled first with poison and then with blood. But they did
neither.

Vayl released Lung and jumped away from him. I scrambled to
my feet, keeping my eyes on those nongrievous wounds. I couldn't
believe what I saw.

"Vayl," I whispered. "What's happening?"

"The power you gave me tonight with your blood," he said, his
voice ringing with triumph. "Remember I said I could feel the
change?"

"Yeah."

"It is a second *cantrantia*. The ability to consume another
vampire's power and make it my own."

I came close to him, close enough to touch the torn edges of his
shirt, the gaping openings of which revealed — "Ice," I said. "You're
armored in ice."

Bergman's voice came tinny and distant in my ears. "Jaz, what's
happening? What did you say?"

"Bergman, I thought you said this armor was . . . was man-
made. How could it . . . How could this . . ." Speech failed me as I
watched scales cover the rest of Vayl's back, neck, head, and face.

Frosty-white scales that covered him with his own thick, hard armor. He didn't get the dragon face. Didn't grow to massive proportions or develop freaky claws. He simply looked as if he'd stood outside during a vicious ice storm.

I touched his back and yanked my fingers away, singed by the cold. His clothes weren't holding up too well either. Rips developed in the thighs of his pants and his shirt pretty much disintegrated. Beneath — beautiful white scales. Even though I knew Vayl had somehow commandeered the biological portion of the armor and rebuilt it according to his own powers, my brain said, *Bullshit,* as my head shook from side to side in absolute agreement.

Lung couldn't believe it either. "NO!" he screamed. "Not the white dragon!"

*That's right. He went after Cassandra so she wouldn't repeat some long-dead monk's prophecy to him. Something about* — I looked at Vayl, shocked into utter stillness by his alien beauty — *a white dragon.* Nope, I didn't see it. But then Lung wasn't operating even close to reality. If I had to place Vayl in some sort of prophecy I'd call him a white knight. And we all knew how those stories ended.

He zeroed in on Lung like a torpedo, and Lung, with flight no longer an option, lowered his head and took it.

They slammed into each other like a couple of bull elephants. Scales and blood flew. The ground beneath their feet churned. They clawed and grappled, lost their balance, and rolled down the slope to the edge of the water.

Chien-Lung's immediate disadvantage was grip. He couldn't find a purchase on Vayl's slick armor. His claws scraped harmlessly down Vayl's sides, off his head and back.

Vayl, having never battled within that hard shell, moved like a freshman football player, slow and awkward, unsure of angles or even his own strength. But as he fought and didn't lose, he gained confidence. Always aware of Lung's vulnerable spot, he attacked the face again and again until it was an unrecognizable pit of blood and gore.

But during the course of his attacks, he broke the blade free. Lung blew one fiery breath. The armor encasing Vayl's head and right arm cracked and blew apart, shards flying in every direction. I ducked, covering my head with my arms as deadly cold missiles landed all around me. When I looked up I discovered the clash had continued, but now Vayl fought to keep Lung from raking his vulnerable right side with claws, tail, and teeth. So far, so good, but he had no way to fight the flame.

"Bergman!" I yelled. "How long does it take to recharge the fire?"

"Thirty seconds!"

*Shit!* I couldn't just stand and spectate anymore. I looked at Grief waiting in my hand. *Nuh-uh. I need a big-ass, surefire weapon, and I need it now!*

There! On the ground where Vayl had dropped it, the crossbow that had killed Pengfei lay as if waiting for this moment. Waiting for me.

I holstered Grief as I went for the bow. I grabbed it and ran toward Lung and Vayl. They still battled, half in and half out of the muddy water.

Keeping in mind that I held a finely crafted weapon made to last, I ran like hell, putting all my might into my swing as I came upon Lung, heaved that bow around, and whacked him sideways with it like he was a gigantic red baseball. My arms buzzed in protest as the crossbow banged against his armor. The right half of the both snapped off and flew back, hitting me in the middle of the

forehead, opening a wound that bled straight down my nose. Soon
I spat and snorted blood like some half-dead horse. But I could still
see, and at this point that was all that mattered.

I spun the crossbow around and gave Lung another hard hit,
breaking the remainder of the lath free. Now I held a stake. The
pointy end was actually the stock of the crossbow, but the lath no
longer stretched both ways to impede its vertical movement.

"Fifteen seconds, Jaz!" said Bergman, urgency pushing his
voice a couple of notches higher.

"Vayl!" I screamed. I scrambled up Lung's heaving body, desperately trying to keep my balance as I moved toward his head.
"Gonna need your strength," I whispered, hoping Vayl heard, that
he understood.

He had, but so had Lung. The voice that thundered in my head
next was not Vayl's or Bergman's. Raoul yelled, *DUCK!*

I flattened myself on Lung's armored back as his tail swept
overhead, the whoosh of air at its passing nearly ripping the wig
from my head.

"Ten seconds!" howled Bergman.

I stood and ran up Lung's spine. Out of the corner of my eye I
could see his tail swinging back around. This time it would hit me,
throwing me so far up the hill I'd probably land on the hood of
someone's SUV. Unless . . .

"Vayl! Lock down on his jaw!"

"Five seconds!"

The angle had to be just right. Nearly vertical. Just like swinging on a pop can. I reared back with the stake and shoved it deep
into the wound Vayl had opened.

"Now, Vayl! Pound it home!"

"Time's up, Jaz!"

I jumped backward, landing in water so cold I thought my skin

was going to pull anchor and motor off the job there for a second.
waded out fast, keeping clear of Lung's thrashing body as Vayl
ammered at the stake with his fists, plunging it deeper and deeper
into Lung's body.

It happened suddenly.

One moment Lung was writhing and shrieking. The next moment he was gone. My ears ached in the silence as I watched the smoke of his remains rise into the night.

*Armor,* I thought dully. *We're supposed to get the armor.* I'd taken my boots off to dump the water out, so I left them on the grass as went back to the waterline. My toes sank in the cold mud as I ooked the only bit of visible armor. The rest had sunk quicker han lead-weighted bait. Keeping my eyes on Vayl, I pulled the armor out hand over hand, feeling like a fisherman after a long day's work.

"Bergman, come get your armor. Bring Cole with you for backup." His joyous whoop nearly deafened me. But it brought a smile to my face too. We'd saved his baby. Speaking of which: "Did Lai calm down after you handed him to his parents?" I asked Cole s Vayl pulled himself upright and struggled onto land. I retrieved his cane from where he'd dropped it near the crossbow and tried o hand it to him.

He stared at me from transformed eyes, vertical pupils, silver rises, alien territory that still managed to look irritated with me. I hought it was because his hands, still encased in ice, couldn't close ver his cane. As I let it fall awkwardly to my side, he said, "I cannot believe that is the first thing you have to say to me!"

I took off the medallion, the better to anticipate his next move. f he decided to go all frosty on me (oh, great pun, Jaz, hardy har) ve were going to have real problems. "I was actually speaking to ur interpreter," I informed him.

Cole said, "The baby was fine as soon as you took him from Lung. It was like he knew he was safe." I nodded, satisfied now I knew we'd truly saved the kid.

I wished I could just shove my nose right up against Vayl's and say, "As for you, what the hell crawled up your ass? We just won!" But I liked my job too well to piss off the guy who had the most influence on my continued employment. I could see his breath as he exhaled. He turned his head just before it could freeze my face.

Something about the way he held himself made me look over my shoulder. His shoulders, chest, legs were all still tensed, as if at any moment he'd have to leap back into combat. *But I'm the only one here. Why's he still playing defense?* Then I had one of those *aha* moments.

I took a deep breath. These were the times when I missed working solo. Just a little. Just the part where you don't have to worry about hurting anybody else's feelings. Ever. "Vayl, I'm a girl."

"I do not need to be reminded . . ." he began, pulling himself up to his full height.

"Yes, you do. Obviously you do. Because I'm a girl, a baby's safety will always come before how cool it is that you can encase yourself in ice and that you kicked Lung's ass."

"You . . . you think it is cool?" Did I detect a slight thaw in the ice-man?

"Are you kidding me? Look at this!" I touched a scale and pulled back quick, showing him my burned finger. "You are such a badass!"

He took a look at the evidence of his struggle with Chien-Lung. "Yes, I suppose I am."

"And yet, if I hadn't liked your new outfit? Would it really hav made that much difference to you in the long run?" I asked. I wanted him to say no. I didn't want to have that much influence. But I knew better.

"When you did not immediately speak, I thought you were going to say, 'How is it that you can summon from within yourself such coldness that you only find in the Arctic? Where nothing lives? Where nothing grows? Where there is only emptiness?'" His original accent had crept into his voice, a sure sign of inner distress.

"Dude, you're all about the chill. We humans even have a name for vamps with your abilities. Do you know how much clout having a Wraith on staff gives the CIA?"

He waved me off with a that's-not-the-point gesture. "Jasmine, you wear my ring. You guard all that is left in me that is good. With a second *cantrantia* such as this, I cannot be sure if the powers I gain will benefit me, or those I serve." His voice dropped. "Especially the ones that make me feel invincible. I am strong. I am powerful. But I am still limited by my perceptions, my experiences. If you find my powers are changing me, warping me, tell me. I will reject them." He ran his hands down his chest, which was currently better protected than if he'd been standing behind bulletproof glass. "Even if I cannot imagine being without them ever again."

I couldn't help the cynicism that laced my next question. "You'd dump the armor? Just like that?"

Twitch of the lip. "Perhaps not. But you are a persistent and creative woman. I feel you will find a way to convince me."

Cole and Bergman arrived then, Bergman to gather up his armor, Cole to envy Vayl's new form. "So is this a permanent thing?" Cole asked hopefully.

"Probably not," Bergman said, eyeing Vayl from a respectful

distance. "My guess is that it will recede as soon as you sleep, just like it did with Lung. You may even be able to call it up and make it go at will. But"—he shook his head—"I don't really know. This shouldn't have happened. I mean, yes, as a biological tool the armor would have changed Lung in very basic ways. And by taking his blood, I guess Vayl could have conscripted that change for himself. But . . . I never anticipated . . . any of this." His eye darted from Vayl's shining armor to the medallion dangling from my fingers.

"I have to go, Jaz," he said, hugging Lung's armor to him like some long-lost teddy bear. "I'm sorry. But I have a lot of work piling up at home." He started to back up. "I can't deal . . . I have to go."

"I understand," I said. "Really. It's okay."

He bobbed his head, turned, and walked away.

Beside me, the smell of grape gum accompanied by the pop of an exploding bubble distracted my attention from Bergman's receding back.

"Well, that sucks," said Cole. "He left before he could make me a cool gun. Like yours, only better."

I sighed and gave him a look that I had a feeling was going to be especially reserved for him from now on. "First of all, tell me your mouth-mint is not covered with Hubba Bubba."

"No, Bergman took it after you guys got Lung."

"Okay, then I'll tell you Bergman is not walking straight from here to the airport. He's going back to the RV to pack. He may even sleep there if he can't get a flight out tonight. So follow him back and ask him to make you a gun that you promise you will pay for. No. Wait." I grabbed his arm before he could move away. Something had moved between my shoulder blades, a feeling between a tingle and a pain. "I don't think you have that kind of time. Something's coming and it's not a vamp. It's just a feeling, one I've never had before, but Vayl said I should open myself up to these things."

"There is a bandstand just up the hill," Vayl told him. "Take cover there."

Cole nodded and quickly moved away.

"You too, Vayl," I suggested. "Whatever it is, I don't think we want news of a scaled vamp to get out, at least not until we know what we want the story to say."

"Very well," he said, gliding uphill with remarkable grace for one so new to the armor. He should've shone like starlight, but I could feel him using his power of camouflage to make himself seem to disappear.

I went to the gazebo, not inside, just to the doorway, and gazed down at somebody's daughter. Somebody's wife. Pitifully dead woman with her body ripped open. I wanted so bad just to cover her. But that wasn't what she needed now.

"Pengfei Yan, shouldn't you be on the yacht?" Desmond Yale asked as he emerged from the shadows.

*Holy crap, it's the reaver!* I slipped the medallion over my head as he closed the distance between us, praying he couldn't see in the dark as well as I could. At least he was speaking English. He came into the three-foot zone to get a good look at me. "You look roasted, toasted, beaten, and battered. What happened?"

I wanted to run to the nearest Renaissance Faire, grab a really nice breastplate, and strap it over my chest. Barring that option, I crossed my arms. "Chien-Lung began to have his own ideas about our revolution. I had to teach him a lesson. What are you doing here?"

He spread his hands out in front of himself, palms up, a big gold ring flashing on the first finger of his left hand. "Did you plant the charges as I instructed? And the evidence implicating the religious fanatics?"

Right on cue the air went *BOOM!* and the ground shook. Yale's icy-blue eyes hardened so sharply he could've sunk every boat in the marina just by looking at them. "Where are the dead, Pengfei Yan? I sense not a single casualty."

"The police found out somehow," I whispered. "They got all the people to safety." Time had strung way out this evening, like a ribbon of taffy that just keeps winding. I could've sworn the hit on Pengfei, the search for Lai and Lung, not to mention the battle and its aftermath had lasted a couple of lifetimes. Nope. Fifteen minutes, start to finish.

"What use are you, Vampire?" Yale demanded. "You brag of your awesome powers of concealment, and yet these myopic little godspawn outmaneuver you." He stepped toward me. Looming. Threatening. "I want my souls!"

"I guess I'm just going to have to owe you."

He stopped. Took a second to think. "Yes, and I have just the debt in mind."

"You do?"

"Her name is Lucille Robinson."

"Go on."

"I want you to kill her."

*He's waiting for you to say something. So say something! Wait, don't swear. Don't call him an asshole. Okay, go ahead.* "And tell me why I have to do your dirty work for you?"

He sighed with disgust. "Reavers cannot kill unless their victims have been Marked and paid for, or unless they can prove self-defense. Why do you keep making me say that?"

"Because I know it pisses you off?"

"I despise rules."

"You know I never do anything unless there is some advantage to me," I said.

Yale fixed me with that yellow glare. It was like looking into the eyes of a python. "The woman, Lucille's, Spirit Eye is beginning to open."

*Spirit Eye . . . what the hell is that? It just can't be good. Not even if it's bad for reavers. What if it's in the middle of my forehead, like theirs? Eeew!* My hand itched to travel up my face and feel the familiar lines that creased my brow whenever I frowned. Would there be a new one with an eyeball underneath? The thought made me want to gag. *Okay, get a grip. You're working. Freak out on your own time.*

I said, "How should that affect my plans?"

"It already has. She can see the weakness in the young ones' shields. She has killed two of them, including Wu, who I'd placed aboard your yacht just today." He jabbed a finger at me as if it was my fault. Which, of course, it was. Speaking of shields, I couldn't see his. Not at all. The medallion was working for, and against me, once again.

"Are you sure it was her? Perhaps—"

"I am sure. I do not know the source of her power, but she is beginning to See, Pengfei. And when her Eye fully opens, she will also begin to Know. After that none of us will find life as easy or as lengthy as before. Do you understand?"

Though I didn't understand, I nodded, because I figured I was supposed to. I said, "Tell me how to find her."

"Lure her to you. She will not be able to resist the chase once you have killed the woman she was with the day I met her."

"Do you know where to find this woman?"

"Her name is Cassandra. The cab company picked her up at this location. I believe she is one of the entertainers."

"Oh my God, was that cool or what?" The voice belonged to a young guy, coming this way by the sound of it.

"You have got to be the king of first dates!" Sweet-sounding girl. Cruising for a make-out spot? *Go away!*

Yale's eyes glowed as he nodded at me and licked his lips with the tip of that grisly pink tongue.

"There they are," he whispered to me. "The boy has been Marked by his ex-girlfriend. I was going to share him with Wu, but given the circumstances, why don't I treat you to dessert?"

*Aw, hell. Could this be worse timing?*

Yale pulled aside a flap on the right leg of his sleek leather pants that hid a long, slender sword. I used his momentary distraction to draw Grief. Taking a deep breath, I yelled, "Get lost, kids! There's a maniac with a sword over here!" Girly scream and sounds of running feet. Apparently they'd seen some horror flicks recently and knew better than to come exploring. Good for them.

Yale, having seen his share of battles, didn't stay surprised long. Still, I had time to nail him with every bit of ammunition Grief held. Bullets. Bolts. They backed him up, gave me room to kick in the only blade left on me worth using. Vayl's.

I twisted the blue jewel at the hilt, launching the carved sheath at the reaver. It hit him in the throat. *Dammit, he didn't even grunt!* Hoping to score some intimidation points, I came at him fast and figured out quick that I'd discovered his niche. Only my age and training prevented him from transforming me into a Jaz-kebob right then and there.

Clearly he'd been parrying and riposting since long before my Granny's gran was a baby. *My* techniques, all learned at the knees of my martial arts teachers, barely kept their feet under his concerted attacks. Even if I lucked out and squeaked in an offensive move here or there, I didn't know where to direct them because . . . *the medallion's still blocking my view of the shield. Take the damn thing off, Jaz!*

God, he could wield that blade. Was it actually coming faster or was I just getting worse?

I grabbed the chain around my neck and yanked. "Ow!" Chains always break easily in movies. This one may have caused minor whiplash. But that was fine and dandy, because suddenly I understood about the Spirit Eye.

As I parried a slash that saved a good part of my forearm I noted the heat in Cirilai. Even for those few minutes I had felt disturbingly incomplete without it. Its increased warmth assured me Vayl was on his way. I just needed to survive.

But maybe I could do more.

Yale's shield showed plainly against the backdrop of the shoreline, no longer a single color now, but deep velvety black with lighter areas of purple and blue where I'd hit him and, theoretically at least, weakened his resistance. It didn't waver the way the first two reavers' had, however. Not encouraging when sliding a weapon in those breaks was the only way I'd found to kill them.

He fought purely as a swordsman, and it took all my concentration to keep him from slicing and dicing me like a sack of Idaho russets. But I wasn't beneath throwing in a kick or a punch when I could manage them. It felt like connecting with an old freezer, but the shield lightened in those spots too.

I kept moving, trying not to let him back me into the water where I'd be trapped. But with all my attention on that swift, sharp sword of his, I had none left for footing. I stepped into one of the craters left by Lung's explosive spikes and went down, the breath bursting from my lungs so utterly I lay there gasping like an asthmatic.

Yale grinned, the tip of his tongue wagging free as he swung his sword in a long arc, meaning to split me wide open. I rolled clear, the blade slicing the point where my throat had been seconds earlier. Just as quickly I spun back, using the trick he'd pulled on me at Sustenance to catch him behind the knee. Already somewhat off balance, he fell easily.

*LOOK*, Raoul's voice boomed in my head, focusing that part of me that saw beyond color and form into the realm of *other*. What Yale had called my Spirit Eye. To keep myself from freaking further about the eyeball-in-the-forehead possibility, I imagined it as a lovely, azure blue, long-lashed orb floating above my head, slowly waking to a new, bigger reality.

Just now it saw ratty Jaz and stunned Yale lying on the ground mere yards from a gazebo containing a badly mutilated corpse. Yale moved better than Jaz, which did not bode well for her future health. Especially since his shield, while wearing the purples, blues, and even yellows of a bad bruise, still seemed wholly intact. However, a ridge in the middle of his forehead was rimmed in bright, glowing red like a big, circular target.

*Huh.*

Snapping back to myself, I bear crawled over to Yale, grabbed him by the shoulders, and head-butted him so hard that for a second my regular vision completely winked out. It returned just as Yale staggered to his feet and retrieved his sword. Spurt of fear as I realized I didn't know where my weapons had gone. In fact, the last thirty seconds were kinda hazy. I put my hand to my forehead and felt the bump.

*OH MY GOD, I AM GETTING A THIRD EYE!* The fear woke me right up. Nope, probably just a slight concussion from the skull tackle. What a relief.

That delay had allowed Yale to formulate his next plan of

attack. He came at me, swinging his sword in a circle as if to take my head off. But his pace, slow and unsteady, gave me the time to duck and scramble away.

I lost my balance and fell from trying to move too fast with a battered brain. But it worked out for the best. When I crawled across something hard and sharp I realized I'd found Vayl's sword. What luck! Maybe my knee wouldn't feel the same later on. But it's really all about perspective.

I meant to jump to my feet and wade into the battle, but the dizzies returned, so it became more of a wide-footed waddle. How I was going to defend my life, much less defeat the reaver, I wasn't sure. He walked toward me, his expression changing from caution to confidence with each step. He swung once, twice, three times, and each time I barely saved my neck. The fourth time a large, glittering arm intervened. Yale's sword went *clack* and stopped dead. We both stared at it in confusion. We looked up. I smiled. "Hi, Vayl."

"I am sorry it took me so long to get back down the hill," he said. "I believe your transmitter has fallen off, and Cirilai did not warn me of your danger until just now."

I looked at Yale. "My boss is here now. You are in such trouble." I looked back to Vayl. "That is so not something I would usually say. I think I have brain damage. That son of a bitch has a hard head."

Vayl nodded. "Shall I dispatch him for you?"

I smiled again. "Sometimes you are so eighteenth century."

Yale finally got tired of the patter. With a growl, he withdrew his sword. But he came back fast, his attacks a blur of motion that Vayl met with a backhanded blow that flipped him completely over and landed him flat on his back, where he lay, wheezing.

"Get up, Reaver," said Vayl. "My *avhar* wants vengeance for that woman you killed and I mean to get it for her, even if it take all night."

Yale struggled to his feet. Despite the fall, his shield hel firm. He could probably fight all night as well. And on into the morning.

Except he also had an enormous bump on the forehead. I looked about as painful as mine felt. Now, what was the deal with that, really? I'd shot the guy multiple times and it hadn't ever stained his pretty plaid shirt. But knock him in the noggin and he's gonna need an ice pack for the next twenty-four. Why wa that?

*Because it's not his eye,* my mind whispered. *Remember the En kyklios movie? When the reaver gave up that soul, he had to take som poor woman's eye to replace the one he'd lost. If it's not part of him maybe it's not protected as well. Maybe it's his weak spot.*

"Go for the forehead, Vayl!" I yelled. "That's his Achilles' heel!" I stopped. Okay, was that just the stupidest thing I'd ever said The jury didn't have time to weigh in because Desmond Yal chose that moment to make a run for it.

Vayl started after him, but he was slow in this form. Slowe even than me. "Dammit, he is going to get away!"

I said, "I think I can track him, just like Pengfei. But we nee some wheels!"

Vayl started listing possibilities. "RV. Mopeds. Taxi. Comman deer a vehicle."

"Cole!" I yelled.

"Yeah!" I could see him running toward us down the hill dodging craters like a ski-less moguls pro.

"Call Jericho! We need wheels at the RV, now!" I turned t Vayl. "Does that work for you?"

"As long as it happens quickly."

"Agreed." We ran to the RV. Vayl waited outside for our ride while I went in to change. A headache that promised to build to massive had replaced my dizziness, so I called for a couple of Advil on my way to the bedroom. Within five minutes I'd ripped off the dress, donned blue jeans, a burgundy sweater, and my black leather jacket, reloaded Grief, stuck a spare clip in my pocket, slipped my muddy feet into Cassandra's blister-builders, and promised to buy her a new pair.

"Jericho's here!" Cole yelled from the front of the RV. I ran forward, my feet already aching. I passed Bergman, who'd paused in his packing and stacking to get the lowdown from Cole as he stood in the open doorway.

"I know you're in a hurry to leave," I told Miles as I passed him, "and I don't blame you. In fact, I commend you. But Vayl is still stuck inside that armor. If you happen to think of anything he might try that will allow him to lose it before dawn, let us know, will ya?"

Bergman nodded. I took the pills and a glass of water from Cassandra, who gave me an I-wish-I-could-help look. "Stay inside," I told her. "The reaver has targeted you as a way to get to me." If I was lucky, by the time I returned she would have joined Bergman in the exodus.

I sped through the near empty streets of Corpus Christi on a hot, red Kawasaki Ninja 250. Jericho's personal ride. Vayl sat behind me, one arm wrapped tightly around my waist. I could no longer feel my back, and my teeth were starting to chatter. Otherwise, I felt fine. Beautiful motorcycles will do that to me.

"We're getting close," I told Vayl through the mike. When Cole had discovered we'd be on two wheels rather than four, he'd pulled our helmets from the trailer. They went much better with this bike than the mopeds. He followed us with Jericho and the three cops he could round up in a sleek black dual cab $4 \times 4$. I didn't think their presence was necessary or even smart. But I didn't have time to argue. And frankly, if I owned the bike I presently rode, I'd be keeping a close eye on it myself.

The reaver's scent pulled me past classic Southwestern buildings dressed in rich earth tones that abutted glass and steel highrises. Even complemented by row after row of stately palm trees, the mix bewildered me. There seemed to be no transition between present and past here, nothing to keep the city from somehow cracking as it tried to assume far too many personalities. Then I saw the *others*. Vampires mostly, the kind who want to blend. But my new senses told me they weren't alone. I wanted some confirmation though.

"Vayl, ask Cole what he's sensing."

Vayl obliged, and moments later he relayed the news. "Cole notes an abundance of witches, weres of some sort, though he is not sure exactly what. And he believes those two lovely women we just passed are nereids." I glanced into the rearview. Wow. When you knew what to look for, it made sense. Those two ultratall silver-haired girls obviously spent more time swimming the ocean than they did pounding the pavement.

The streets of Corpus Christi weren't all that different from those of Chicago or New York or L.A. after all. They seethed with magic. Power. Creatures who could remember when horses drew wagons full of settlers down their muddied lengths. Maybe that's what keeps any city from blowing sky high.

Two blocks later we saw the reaver, a single dark blur running down the center of a two-lane avenue. Traffic was so light he'd probably only freaked out a couple of drivers with his antics so far. Make that three.

The light turned red and Yale wrenched open the door of a silver Pontiac Grand Prix. Out flew the driver, a kid who couldn't have had his license over a week. In went Yale. The tires squealed, the kid shook his fists, and off we went, chasing the reaver deep into the heart of the city.

"Do you think he has any idea where he is going?" asked Vayl.

"I don't even think he knows what he's doing," I replied. Yale looked to be one of those old-school demons who lets somebody else do the driving while he sits in the back and does open-torso surgery on the innocents. The car fishtailed like the right rear was losing air and we hadn't even taken a turn yet.

But Yale did have a plan after all. Crashing the Pontiac into the concrete barrier that kept the steep hill to our left from falling down onto the roadway probably wasn't part of it, but it did stop the car. He jumped out of the vehicle and onto the barrier like a cross-country runner and began slogging up the hill.

I pulled up right behind him, Cole and his truck full of SWAT men hard on my tail. But as soon as my feet hit the pavement I knew we were outnumbered. Outgunned. Out of our minds to even think of climbing that mound. Underneath this road, that grass, a million fiends writhed in their unending tortuous dance. Like the women at a Little Italy festival, they bounced round and round an enormous vat, their hooves pounding relentlessly on the souls of their victims, turning them into Satan's wine.

"I would make a terrible merlot," I muttered.

"What did you say?" asked Vayl as he dismounted with a heartfelt groan. I didn't reply. Something was stuck in my throat. If I was a guy, I'd have sworn they were my testicles.

I looked up as I set the kickstand. On top of that slope stood an abandoned church. Its steeple still stood intact, though part of the roof had caved and all the windows had been boarded up. Though

I swung my leg over the bike, it moved slowly, because it was hard-wired to that part of my brain that insisted we'd found hell's front porch and we needed to RUN!

"Vayl," I gasped. "Do you feel it?"

"Yes," he murmured. "It seems as if the road is filled with flesh-eating beetles, although my eyes insist we are fine."

Behind us the guys were having even more trouble. Cole had made it out of the truck and was struggling toward us as if the as-phalt was sucking at his shoes. The SWAT men, bereft of any form of protective powers, shared the narrow-eyed, tight-lipped look of soldiers who would turn and run but for their love of and loyalty to one another.

Jericho had brought what looked like the cream of the crop. A wiry, gray-headed gentleman carrying a Remington SPS Varmint sniper rifle nodded and introduced himself as Sergeant Betts. Cor-poral Fentimore had apparently not been satisfied with his original collection of muscles and decided to build himself a complete extra set on top of them. He and his barrel-chested, broad-shouldered buddy, who said shortly, "Call me Rand," were both armed with SIG-551s. These men were cut from the same cloth as my brother, and my father in his prime. Just looking at them, you felt you couldn't shake them with a mortar. And yet they danced from foot to foot like sprinters at the start line.

Which was when I realized the place was spelled. I hadn't grasped it right away because the magic was so big. It had stunned my Sensitivity the same way your brain goes into over-load when you first walk into an art museum. Until you step back and convince it to take one thing at a time, you never see a single picture.

I dumped my helmet and helped Vayl off with his. Cole had joined us by then. "There's some kind of expellation spell on this hill," I told them all. "What you're feeling isn't real." And just know-ing that, all of us would be able to function a helluva lot better.

"What about them?" asked Jericho, nodding toward the hill.

I looked over my shoulder. A line of dark shapes was pouring out of the desecrated church. *Shit!* "Those are a different story."

# CHAPTER THIRTY-SIX

Half of Hell Hill stood between us and Desmond Yale. He'd made good time, but too, he'd already been running a while and the wear and tear on his earthly body had taken its toll. His knees kept buckling, forcing him to the ground every few steps. His tongue hung out like a hound dog's, and blood seeped from the weakened parts of his shield. That was the good news.

Evidently he'd found himself a little cult of well-armed humans to guard his exit. Well, I'd known he was a canny old demon. I should've figured he had an escape plan.

His acolytes had taken cover behind an abandoned minibus that had OUR LORD'S MISSION OF CORPUS CHRISTI painted on its side, and were firing down on us while Yale moved toward them. They didn't seem to be able to shoot worth a damn, but then they had an enormous advantage in terrain. All they really needed to do was keep up a steady barrage while Yale struggled the rest of the way up the hill and he'd be completely out of our hands.

As soon as Yale's gang had opened up on us, we'd taken cover behind the four-foot-high concrete barrier at the base of the hill to figure out our next move. Also to keep from getting our heads blown off. Even idiots get lucky once in a while.

"Jericho, you got anything available in the form of air support?" I asked.

"On its way," he told me, pocketing his phone, "but probably not in time for us to catch the old guy."

"Dammit!" I pressed my back to the barrier and traded glares with Vayl. I wasn't sure which of us was more pissed. To come this close and lose. Neither of us cared to do that. We had to get up that hill, and fast!

"The armor makes me nearly bulletproof," he reminded me. "But it slows me too much. I am afraid one of those nitwit gunmen would put a bullet through my brain before I could reach him." He motioned to the part of his head Chien-Lung's breath had cleared of ice. Though a gunshot wound wouldn't kill him, it would knock Vayl out of the game, and we couldn't afford that at this point.

*Come on, Jaz, look around you. What are your tools? What can speed you up that hill without dying before you have a chance to take out the monster?*

"Jericho, you guys got a ramp in the back of that truck?"

He nodded. "We need some way to get the ATV out to the sticks."

"That's what I wanted to hear. Vayl, how's your dexterity?" He flexed his hands. He could only close them halfway, but that should be more than enough.

Funny how just knowing somebody's got even the first part of a plan will galvanize everybody else on a team. While Fentimore and Rand used their SIGs to keep the reaver gang from totally controlling the field, the rest of us assembled the ramp. We had to do some adjusting, but when we were done it sat firmly against the concrete barrier. If the highway department were so inclined they could drive their tractors right up the thing, mow the hill, and then motor back down without a hitch. I had a slightly different plan.

"So," said Jericho as I climbed into an old suit of body armor someone had thrown behind the driver's seat of his truck, "you're going to turn Evel Knievel on us?"

From our current vantage point, crouched by the 4 × 4's front tire, we gazed first at the ramp, then at his precious cycle. "It's going to be a steep little jump," I told him. "But we'll give ourselves plenty of room to build up speed. And we've got to get wheels on that hill. Nothing else is going to catch our reaver. Unless you can think of a better, faster way?"

As Jericho pondered the possibilities, my armor began to press down on me. Hard. So of course that was the moment my motherboard decided to do a short internal scan, throw up its hands, and screech, "Dear Lawd, a VAMPIRE has taken mah blood!" and initiate a general shutdown. I took a seat on the nearest flat surface—the truck's running board.

"You all right?" asked Jericho. Cole, squatting by the back tire as he helped Vayl on with his helmet, gave me a worried look.

"I'm fine," I said, pulling on my own helmet before my pallor could betray me. This was the immediate price I paid for increased Sensitivity. I had a feeling there would be long-term implications as well, but now was no time to obsess.

Problem was, once that cushioned Kevlar dome encased my head, not even the pinging of badly aimed bullets could distract me from the bone-chilling realization that, this time, I just might have bitten off one that would choke me blue.

I leaned back, banging my head against the door. "Goddammit!"

"What is it?" Vayl asked.

Since I didn't want to discuss my current need to roll up in my blanky and snooze for a week, I risked a look through the window. "Yale has reached the top of the hill." He was leaning over, both hands on his knees, puffing like an overweight smoker. Sergeant Betts hit him and he went down.

"Yes!" Betts shook his head in disbelief as Yale got back up. "What the hell?"

"Middle of the forehead, boys!" I yelled. But they couldn't hear me. As if it would do any good. Yale would never turn toward us. Not willingly.

Vayl had mounted Jericho's Ninja and started it up. He drove it over to me and Cole helped me on. "Aren't we just a pair of lightweights?" I told Vayl as he gunned the engine, driving us across the street and into the lot of a rundown gas station.

"We would be if we were on the moon," he replied, which somehow struck me funny. I laughed, and hoped to God Jericho's tires were fully inflated.

I looked up the hill. As if on cue, Yale opened up another secret compartment in those dandy leather pants of his. I'd have made some smart-ass comment about setting up the reaver's tailor with Mistress Kiss My Ass, but then he pulled out a plastic bag. The dark red organ inside seemed to squirm, as if trying to escape its fate.

"Oh my God." I wanted so badly to look away. Save that little bit of myself that still thought it wasn't a complete waste to wish upon a star and that Santa Claus was a dandy old dude, even if parents had to do the heavy lifting for him. But part of my job required me to be a witness. You couldn't aim true if you kept closing your eyes.

Yale launched the heart, splattering it against the side of the defiled church, releasing a rain of blood that slowly built itself into a door. Just as it began to throb, Vayl hit the gas.

I clutched him around the middle, thankful for the sudden spurt of adrenaline that allowed me to hold on. We shot toward the ramp like a couple of stunt junkies, hit that puppy right in the sweet spot, and jumped the barrier so clean you could've driven a semi underneath us as we flew up the hill.

If my bladder hadn't been empty I might have peed myself as Vayl nearly lost the front wheel on our landing. We swerved so far to the right I smelled earthworms, then overcorrected so badly to the left my calf spent a long moment pinned between the grass and the muffler. The heat burned completely through my jeans and left a blistering souvenir on my skin. Only Vayl's vampire strength saved that bike — and us — from major wreckage.

Halfway up the hill a couple of bullets zinged off Vayl's armor, but they stopped when I pulled Grief and returned fire. It's tough to hit your target when you're accelerating up a bumpy incline, but I got close enough and my backup shooters were doing their jobs so well, the reaver gang decided maybe they should keep their heads down for a while.

We motored toward Yale, quickly regaining the ground we'd lost at the bottom of the hill.

"This is going to be close," Vayl said.

Yale had nearly reached the door. It had begun to open. Unearthly light, black and razor sharp, like the kind that shielded him, gaped through the crack.

I took aim at Yale, trying to steady my hand though it was like balancing a marble on a bowling ball. I squeezed off a shot. It pinged off Yale's temple. He staggered and fell to his knees. Without even trying to get up, he crawled toward the door, lunging for it when he finally came close enough. It opened farther and he wrapped his fingers around the edge, giving it a helpful tug.

Vayl drove the Ninja right over the top of Yale's legs, forcing a scream from him that made bats fly out the church's chimney. We both rolled off as Vayl ditched the bike. I struggled to rise, but something punched me in the back so hard I thought for a second my lung was going to come flying out of my chest. I keeled over onto my face, realizing instantly that I'd been shot. The body armor had done its job, but it still hurt like hell.

"You son of a bitch!" I looked up. *Is that Cole's voice? Oh, can I have a big amen!* He'd found a gully running up the west edge of the hill. I could see it from here, though it hadn't been visible from our original vantage point. He'd made good progress, though he was still positioned probably fifty yards below us. I saw a flash from the muzzle of his gun and heard the scream of a dying man. Cole had brought his own rifle with him.

"Jasmine! Some help, please!" called Vayl.

Another boom from Cole's gun and another scream let me know it was time to get a move on. I scrambled to Vayl's side. He seemed to have entered a tug-o-war match. Clawed, bony fingers the color of raw, sunburned skin had wrapped around Yale's wrists and were trying to pull him through a crack that had widened in the doorway. Yale himself had dug a small trench in the ground with his boots in his efforts to break free of Vayl's hold.

Vayl had him around the middle, but with a grip composed mainly of ice he found it nearly impossible to maintain his grasp. He kept having to reanchor himself, and every time he did, Yale gained ground. Before I had a chance to take aim, Yale's accomplice pulled hard enough to get his head behind the door.

"We have to pull him out!" said Vayl. "Grab on!"

I latched on to those old man legs and yanked, eliciting a scream from their owner that told me the cycle had done some damage. Good. I kept pulling, and with Vayl's help we got Yale's head back into target range. But as soon as I let go to take the shot, Vayl lost his grip.

"Goddammit! I am so freaking tired of this shit!" I yelled as I took hold of the calves above the cowboy boots I'd once admired and heaved to. "I've been shot and stabbed and burned on this mission! I'm so freaking worn out I could sleep through a nuclear explosion, and I have just realized I'm going to have to kill yet *more* of Samos's underlings before I finally work my way up to him. I am so pissed off!" I gave one last big jerk and fell on my back.

I'd just struggled to my knees when Vayl said, "I see the third eye!"

"Well, what the hell do you want *me* to do about it!" I bitched. "If I let go he's just going to slide back in!"

"Well, *somebody* has to shoot him!" Vayl growled.

The thunder of Cole's gun drowned out my reply.

The legs in my hands went limp. I turned to look. Cole's shot had been right on target. The reaver died where he laid, his fingers still curled around the edge of the door. And out of that blasted third eye emerged a lovely magenta soul that flew off into the night like a comet.

Vayl and I both moved back. I trained Grief on the spot where the reaver gang had holed up, but the ones who'd survived had scattered as soon as Yale passed.

The clawed hands continued to pull Yale's body through the doorway, and as his feet crossed the threshold the entire door disappeared with the boom of overhead thunder.

# CHAPTER THIRTY-SEVEN

·

Cassandra and Bergman met us at the RV door.

"You're back to yourself!" Bergman said the second Vayl pulled his helmet off.

Vayl nodded wanly. "Apparently I simply needed some quiet time in the aftermath of the battle."

"Also a towel would've been nice," I added. Although Vayl thought he'd reabsorbed a great deal of the armor, he'd still ended up wringing wet. And since I'd driven us home, that meant I now looked as if a football team had tried to douse me with the Gatorade cooler and only done half the job. The back half.

We'd said our thank-yous and goodbyes to Jericho and the guys at the site, with a promise to return a cleaner, shinier Ninja to Jericho in the morning. The SWAT guys had volunteered to supervise the cleanup since we'd sort of saved the day with the festival. An unusually quiet, introspective Cole had stayed with them.

As if reading my mind—and who knows, maybe she was— Cassandra said, "Where's Cole?"

"He'll be back soon," I said. "He's with Jericho right now."

"And?"

"I'm worried about him. He killed a couple of humans and the reaver today. He definitely wasn't acting like himself when we left."

"He will be fine," Vayl said irritably. He sounded almost . . . jealous. His next words confirmed my suspicions. "Why do you never concern yourself for me? The change I underwent has left me exhausted."

"Dude, you're immortal. It's not like you won't get a second to catch up on your sleep." Plus, I was feeling deeply drained myself, which left no room for commiseration in my book. Especially not with the vampire who'd sucked Cole into our business in the first place.

Even though I wanted to roll into the RV and hit the bedroom so bad my bones actually ached, I dismounted Jericho's Ninja with reluctance. I was in love with another man's bike. It felt like a sin.

Unfortunately Cassandra blocked my way inside. Which was when I finally registered the guilty look she shared with Bergman. He began. "We thought, you know, before you tear us a new one? We wanted to say we're sorry."

"Yes," Cassandra agreed. "It was our fault."

"Naturally," I said, though I was at least a chapter behind them.

Cassandra said, "I should have told you that spelled items can inhibit natural Sensitivities, like being able to see the weaknesses in the reaver's shield. I knew that. But I said nothing because I thought Bergman would make some snide remark about magic. And because of my omission you . . . you could have died." Tears sprang into her eyes.

"And I should never have let my fears turn me into such an asshole. I . . . don't want to cut our ties completely. You're so damn interesting." Plus, I was one of the only friends he had left. But being a guy, he wasn't going to go there. "I just, it got so intense. But I'm sorry I let you down." He looked at Cassandra and she nodded. "We both are."

It's so true that the people most likely to kill you are those closest to you.

I crossed my arms over my chest so I wouldn't be tempted to shake them or maybe bang their heads together. I nearly told them if they wanted to hang out with me they'd better start acting like grown-ups instead of a couple of two-year-olds fighting over the good toys at the day care center. But then my arms started to ache. So did my hands and legs for that matter. I remembered Cassandra's face when she took me to the hospital, and Bergman's expression when they found me standing in the bay with the gun he'd built for me pressed against my temple.

I took a deep breath. "I know this mission wasn't easy for either one of you. You're both so great at what you do. I mean, you have that passion that is really integral to being exceptional, and so of course you're going to clash. And yet here you are, doing the hardest part of the work and making a damn good team." I shrugged. "I forgive you."

Cassandra clapped her hands once, hard, the way she does when she's delighted. And Bergman's eyes shone so bright he had to take off his glasses to keep from blinding himself. They gave each other high fives, which Bergman found painful from the way he rubbed his hand down his thigh afterward, and trooped back into the RV. Within seconds Bergman came back outside with our safe phone. "It's for you," he said, handing the cell to Vayl.

"Yes?" Vayl listened for maybe twenty seconds, his eyes darkening as the news filtered through his emotions. "Of course we want this. We will be there in twenty minutes." He snapped the phone shut. "You had better get changed."

"Yeah?"

"That was Pete. He said they found the men's clothing shop you mentioned. The one that had served both Shunyuan Fa and Desmond Yale?"

"Frierman's? In Reno?"

He nodded. "After about an hour of rather intense interrogation the tailor admitted that Edward Samos has many of his meetings in his shop and that one is scheduled for tonight. Pete has chartered us a plane. We have"—he checked his watch—"eighteen minutes to make it to the airport."

I went for the door.

"Jasmine?"

I turned back.

"Remember to load your gun."

# CHAPTER THIRTY-EIGHT

I slept on the plane. The best kind. The healing kind. Deep. Without dreams. Definitely without sleepwalking. Where, when you wake up, you don't even care if you snored.

Pete had a car waiting for us, one driven by a bright-eyed young pup wearing a black knit hat and matching jogging suit. He offered us both coffee, opened the doors for us, and kept quiet while he sped us through the neon-lit streets of Reno. We parked on the street. Frierman's was small, but it still managed a luxurious feel. I attributed it mostly to the black tuxedos hanging in the windows, backed by red velvet curtains and lit by sparkling chandeliers.

"You're cleared to go in," the driver volunteered, holding up the paperwork so we could see.

I could've said, "Sweetie, my boss would never go to the expense of flying us anywhere if he wasn't sure we could make it through the door once we landed." Instead I nodded and followed Vayl out of the car.

The driver went around back, ostensibly to block the exit should anybody at the meeting decide to make a break for it. But as soon as we stepped into the alcove created by the recessed doorway I had a feeling running wouldn't be a problem.

"I don't sense any vampires in the vicinity besides you," I whispered to Vayl as I worked the lock. It didn't stop me long. I wore a

311

necklace, compliments of Bergman, whose shark-tooth centerpiece could mold itself into any key, given a couple of seconds. "In fact, I don't sense any *others* at all."

"And the only strong human emotion I am picking up on is our driver's," Vayl said. "He is quite excited about this whole event."

"Huh." I'd caught that too. Annoying. Mostly because he was about my age and yet he made me feel *old*.

We inched inside the store, skirted racks of trousers and dress shirts, made our way to the back of the retail area, where shelves of shoes guarded a door whose sign warned us we'd better be employees if we wanted to go any farther. We went anyway. But only to the other side.

The sight and smell that hit us when we entered the back room stopped us after only a couple of steps.

"I never would've believed such a tiny man could hold so much blood." I leaned into Vayl, trying not to puke, cry, pass out, or swear. It was easier than it should've been.

Morty Frierman had been hung from a ceiling joist with a noose made from his own measuring tape. Then someone — *Samos, you sick, twisted bastard, I cannot wait until the day I end your fiendish existence* — had ripped him open reaver style. It looked to me like all his parts were still intact, so I kinda thought Samos had just learned a new trick from that old dog Yale.

Our phone buzzed against my thigh. I went outside to answer it. "Yeah?"

"Jasmine? It's Cassandra."

"What's up?"

"Cole came back." Long silence while I decided things did not bode well back at the home place.

"What's he up to?"

"He's been very . . . professional." Okay, that in itself was just weird. "He didn't say anything about what happened while he was gone. But, of course, he had told Jericho about the massacre on the *Constance Malloy*. So he began talking about how Jericho's people had boarded the yacht and begun detaining generals and recovering bodies. Then, without even calling Pete, Cole decided he should be the CIA's liaison in that matter, so he ran off to watch. And just before he left he said, 'Oh, by the way Cassandra, Jericho said to tell you he probably wouldn't get a chance to see you again, so goodbye.' He was just so cold about it, Jasmine. As if I should grow up and get over it, you know, yesterday."

Oh boy. My first instinct was to order Cassandra and Bergman to drag Cole off that yacht and dunk his head into the bay until the pompous ass washed right out of him. But I knew this wouldn't work as a long-term solution to the problem. Which was, in fact, that he had become an assassin tonight. That he would be doing more killing as time went by. That he would have to find a way to eliminate his targets without breaking off little parts of himself every time he did so.

"Okay, Cassandra, thanks for letting me know. I'll, uh, I'll think of something."

Vayl came outside. "Problems back in Texas?"

"Yeah. I'll tell you on the way. We're done in there, right?"

"I believe we have found everything we could. We will let the specialists deal with the rest."

"Then let's get back. Cole is reacting badly to his first kill and the two people who should be walking him through the aftermath aren't there."

"What is it you think we can do for him?" Vayl demanded, his voice as hard as the cane at his side.

"Could you just drop the whole misplaced-jealousy gig? When I'm ready to jump into the sack with someone, I guarantee it's not going to be a guy who chews bubble gum and wears high-tops with his suits."

Vayl didn't exactly swoop in on me, but it suddenly felt like we'd just finished a dance, that's how close we stood. I forgot to breathe as he held my gaze. "What kind of man will it be?" he asked softly, his eyes the pure, blazing green I'd begun to equate with these supercharged moments.

For the first time I was certain of the answer. And that realization gave me the confidence to go up on tiptoe, bring my mouth to within an inch of his, and whisper, "One who doesn't piss me off with too many questions." I backed off a step and hid a grin as Vayl raised his head. A vamp that old, I don't suppose you get to see them speechless too often. So I enjoyed the moment. It ended when our driver came around the corner.

"Come on," I said to Vayl as he pulled up to the curb. "We've got one last mission to accomplish before dawn."

# Chapter Thirty-nine

Vayl and I spent most of our trip back to Corpus Christi on the phone, reporting to and getting reports from our Reno contacts, from Pete, and from Jericho Preston. By the time we reached the RV we'd tied up as many of our loose ends as we could. Which meant we could focus on Cole.

It wasn't tough to get him off the *Constance Malloy*. I just mentioned the problem to Jericho during our last call and he sent Cole back home. He was making coffee when Vayl and I walked in. When it began percolating I said, "Cole, we need to make a rather elaborate plan, which cannot even begin without the aid of some major bubble blowing. Gum, please."

Bergman and Cassandra had each commandeered a twin and were watching Cole with an air of tense frustration, like parents who can't seem to get their thick-skulled teen to listen to reason. Without quite knowing what I was about, they gave me their attention while Cole dipped into his stash. Accompanied by the scent of Dubble Bubble and the steadily increasing interest and input of the object of our concern, our plans were made and carried out like clockwork.

I admit we nearly got caught, because we were giggling like maniacs throughout the whole exercise. (Okay, Vayl wasn't even smiling at first. But once we convinced him we had the higher moral ground, even if it was only by an inch, he at least showed occasional signs of fang). But it was good for us, Cole especially, to imagine the faces of the *others*-are-not-our-brothers protesters when they discovered Lung's and Pengfei's coffins hooked to the bumper of their hate-crimes van in the morning with JUST BURIED spray painted in big white letters across the lids. We made it back to the RV with just enough time for Vayl to stagger to the bedroom, pop up his tent, and crawl inside. Such a silly exercise. But it had helped Cole shed his shell and rediscover his hilarious old soul.

Mission accomplished.

# Chapter Forty

Cole, Cassandra, Bergman, and I stood outside the RV, watching dawn break over the city.

Cole took a sip of his coffee. "I don't get why you're so relaxed, Jaz," he said. "I mean, you thought you had Samos nailed last night. But he slipped through your fingers again. I haven't known you long, but I'm thinking, typically, you'd be gnashing your teeth and pulling your hair out." He looked to Bergman for confirmation.

"Oh, yeah," Miles said. "One time, in college, she got so mad after our apartment was burglarized that she smashed her fist through the bathroom door."

"I did find that guy," I reminded Bergman.

He nodded. "She got all our stuff back and made him replace the door too."

"So what's the deal?" asked Cole.

"I'm curious as well," said Cassandra. "You told us the Reno crime scene investigators found no fingerprints. No sources of DNA. No scientific proof that Samos killed Morty Frierman. So why are you so tranquil?"

"Because I came away from Frierman's with the goods on that son of a bitch," I told them, feeling a grin spread across my face and not minding a bit if it looked slightly evil. "I discovered something that will allow me to pick Samos out of a crowd. Given the time, and opportunity, it'll lead me straight to him. And then Vayl and I will take him down."

"So what did you bring home from Reno?" Cole asked.

I wanted to chuckle and rub my hands together. But under the circumstances that seemed too maniacal, so I just took a sip from my mug and said, "The scent of a vampire."

# EXTRAS

www.orbitbooks.net

# About the Author

**Jennifer Rardin** began writing at the age of twelve, mostly poems to amuse her classmates and short stories featuring her best friends as the heroines. She lives in an old farmhouse in Illinois with her husband and two children. Learn more about Jennifer and her books at www.JenniferRardin.com

Find out more about Jennifer and other Orbit authors by registering for the free monthly newsletter at www.orbitbooks.net

Introducing

# BITING THE BULLET

the next Jaz Parks novel

by

# Jennifer Rardin

The reavers rolled into us, firing seemingly at random. But there was a method to their madness. Reavers operate by strict rules. I didn't know what the punishments entailed, but they must've been extreme, because even the old gnarly ones wouldn't break them. The main no-no revolved around killing. Reavers were only allowed to eliminate people who'd been marked for murder. In other words, me. Everybody else had to survive. So while the reavers had to take me out, they only wanted to take everybody else down.

What they didn't count on was the supreme skill and professionalism of their foes. Though they outnumbered us at least three to one at the start of the attack, within sixty seconds we'd whittled their numbers to fifteen.

Our guys had taken a couple of more hits. One second Otto had been standing beside me, a half-grin on his face, saying, "If I had a wheelbarrow full of dynamite I'd blow these fuckers to Mars." The next second he lay writhing on the ground, trying not to scream, his hip shattered. As I stood over him, nailing reavers when I had a clear shot, pulling up when I realized I'd just aimed at one of my own, I saw Ricardo drop beneath a mass of monsters. Grace had made little progress toward the truck, and was bleeding heavily from a facial wound. Still, I thought we had them.

Then two more groups appeared, coming from both our flanks. These didn't have firearms, but we already knew the power of their claws, and several swung swords. Terrence and Ashley fired into them, but they didn't have the right angle to get more than one or two head shots per burst.

"Everybody to me!" yelled David.

Our guys from the farmhouse joined us and we tried to move forward, but they swarmed us. Terrence went down under a reaver's claws. Vayl, seeing him fall, took the reaver's eye with his sword and pulled him to his feet. I holstered Grief and grabbed his machine gun. Switching it to three-round burst mode, I fired into the crowd of reavers coming at me, their tongues lolling in anticipation of tasting my soul.

"Jasmine!" called Vayl. "Keep moving!"

Easier said than done. I inched forward, almost tripped over a body, ducked quickly to avoid a neck-ripping swipe and nearly screamed as the body between my legs lurched to its feet. I managed to mute the scream into a squawk as I jumped back, banging into Cole in my rush to avoid the rising reaver.

"Son of a bitch!" he cried, "I missed!"

"Watch out! Watch out!" I yelled. "The dead are rising!"

All around us the reavers we'd defeated the first time around had rediscovered vertical. Multiple thoughts streaked through my mind simultaneously. Not all of them made sense, but a skilled translator might put them in the following light:

*Oh Jesus! Oh crap! Zombies! The Wizard's a necromancer. He could be around here somewhere, pulling their strings. So I should just run off into the night like some rabid raccoon and hope I luck into him? How stupid is that? Plus it's not him. It's probably an apprentice. You know that. It may even be the mole. Is anybody murmuring a spell? How the hell can I tell? We are so outnumbered! Did Ashley just go down? My God, I think the semi is farther away than ever. Is that possible? Oh Jesus, was that Terrence's leg? Don't turn your head. I said don't—never mind. Holy shit, that's the barrel of a Colt .45 aimed right at your face.*

The reaver, a live one, grinned wide enough to show the gap between his front teeth as his finger squeezed the trigger.

"Vayl," I whispered, my eyes somehow tracking straight to his in my final moment.

"Jasmine!" He lunged toward me, too late. The gun boomed and I went down almost at the same time. Only the horrifying pain I expected never split into my brain. A zombie had tackled me, its puppet-like efforts to take off my head such a welcome relief to point-blank assassination I actually giggled. I know. Inappropriate. That's pretty much how it always happens with me.

The zombie's weight left me as Vayl picked it up and threw it at least twenty feet. I took the hand Vayl offered and remembered to grab the SAW as he jerked me upright. Ahead of us Cole lifted Terrence onto his shoulder. Two reavers came at him, one living, one dead. Somehow the zombie missed our guys and clawed the living reaver instead, taking out most of his face. When he turned to us I took out his legs with my machine gun.

"What is it with these zombies?" I asked Vayl. "Not that I'm complaining. But you'd think they'd come from 2,000 year old corpses the way they're behaving."

"Maybe their master is new to the art."

"Huh."

"Aaaah!" I spun at the sound. The zombie behind me clutched at the gaping hole in his chest. A living reaver had circled back to the farmhouse door. Had taken a bead on me. Somehow the zombie had gotten between the two of us.

I took aim at the zombie. Hesitated. Moved my sites to the reaver. It yelled at the zombie. Clearly telling it to move out of the line of fire. Instead the zombie shambled straight toward the living reaver. *What the hell?* I glanced over my shoulder, hoping for some confirmation from Vayl that he'd witnessed this bizarre event as well. He was with Otto, lifting him off the ground. Grace and Ashley were already limping away ahead of them.

I looked back. The zombie had reached the living reaver. Grabbed the gun. Moved clear. I took the shot. The reaver fell dead. I waited for the zombie to make its next move. It hesitated. Appeared to study the gun as if it wasn't sure what to do with it and, in the process, managed to blow its own head off.